ALSO BY TINA FOLSOM

SAMSON'S LOVELY MORTAL (SCANGUARDS VAMPIRES, BOOK 1)
AMAURY'S HELLION (SCANGUARDS VAMPIRES, BOOK 2)
GABRIEL'S MATE (SCANGUARDS VAMPIRES, BOOK 3)
YVETTE'S HAVEN (SCANGUARDS VAMPIRES, BOOK 4)
ZANE'S REDEMPTION (SCANGUARDS VAMPIRES, BOOK 5)
QUINN'S UNDYING ROSE (SCANGUARDS VAMPIRES, BOOK 6)
OLIVER'S HUNGER (SCANGUARDS VAMPIRES, BOOK 7)
THOMAS'S CHOICE (SCANGUARDS VAMPIRES, BOOK 8)
SILENT BITE (SCANGUARDS VAMPIRES, BOOK 8 1/2)
CAIN'S IDENTITY (SCANGUARDS VAMPIRES, BOOK 9)
LUTHER'S RETURN (SCANGUARDS VAMPIRES – BOOK 10)
BLAKE'S PURSUIT (SCANGUARDS VAMPIRES – BOOK 11)

LOVER UNCLOAKED (STEALTH GUARDIANS, BOOK 1)

A TOUCH OF GREEK (OUT OF OLYMPUS, BOOK 1)
A SCENT OF GREEK (OUT OF OLYMPUS, BOOK 2)
A TASTE OF GREEK (OUT OF OLYMPUS, BOOK 3)

LAWFUL ESCORT
LAWFUL LOVER
LAWFUL WIFE
ONE FOOLISH NIGHT
ONE LONG EMBRACE
ONE SIZZLING TOUCH

VENICE VAMPYR – THE BEGINNING

GABRIEL'S MATE

SCANGUARDS VAMPIRES #3

TINA FOLSOM

Gabriel's Mate is a work of fiction. Names, characters, places, and incidents are the products of the author's imagination and are used fictitiously. Any resemblance to actual events, locales, or persons, living or dead, is entirely coincidental.

2010 Tina Folsom

Published in the United States

Cover design: Elaina Lee
Cover photo: Bigstockphoto.com
Author Photo: © Marti Corn Photography

Printed in the United States of America

PROLOGUE

Wearing only his breeches, Gabriel gazed at the woman who stood before him in her virginal night rail. The lace trim around her neck and sleeves only accentuated her innocence. Earlier in the day, the minister had declared them husband and wife before God, but now it was time to make Jane truly his.

This was his wedding night, a night he had anticipated with the eagerness of a young buck ready to start his own brood. Except for a few kisses, he hadn't been intimate with Jane. Her strict religious upbringing had demanded he wait to touch her until they were married. He'd waited because he truly loved her with all his heart, but also because he had his own inhibitions about making love.

Jane took a tentative step toward him. Gabriel met her halfway. His arms snaked around her back and pulled her to him. The fabric under his fingertips was soft and so thin it felt like he was touching her naked skin. As he lowered his lips toward hers, he inhaled her perfume, a mix of roses and jasmine which had been the flowers of her wedding bouquet. Underneath it was her own personal scent, the heady smell of Jane, a scent that had made him dizzy when he'd first taken it in. He'd been hard and ready ever since.

"My wife," Gabriel whispered. The words felt right when they rolled off his lips and collided with her sweet breath. On a soft moan, he kissed her with all the passion he'd been holding back, waiting for her to become his wife. Her body clung to him more eagerly than he had expected, yielding to his touch, imprinting him with the love he'd seen in her eyes long before he'd asked for her hand in marriage.

Without breaking the kiss, he untied the little ribbons on the front of her gown, then brushed the garment off her shoulders and let it fall to the floor. With a soft rustle, it pooled at her feet. She would never again need a nightgown: he would warm her every night from now on. The shiver he noticed going through her lithe body wasn't from being cold. No, she was nearly as aroused as he was.

Gabriel released her lips and looked at her. Small round breasts topped with dark hard nipples stood firm. Her hips were wide, her skin soft and yielding to his touch. When he lifted her into his arms and carried her to the bed they would share for the rest of their lives, his desire for her spiraled.

Already, his breeches were so tight he could barely breathe, but now his cock expanded even farther, impatient to impale her. He laid her onto the bed and watched her as he opened the buttons of his fly with trembling hands, his heart beating into his throat. Perspiration built on his brow. All the while his anxiety escalated. As he stripped, Jane's loving gaze drifted from his face lower down his body. Then her expression suddenly changed. It was what he'd secretly feared most.

"Oh, God, no!" She jerked up, her gaze transfixed on his groin, horror distorting her features. "*Get away from me!*" she screamed and jumped off the bed on the other side.

"Jane, please, let me explain," he begged and went after her as she ran out the door. He should have prepared her for this, but it was too late for that now. He'd hoped that if he was gentle and patient with her, she would accept him.

He caught up with her in the kitchen.

"You monster, get away from me!"

Gabriel snatched her arm and stopped her from running any farther. "Please, Jane, my love, listen to me." If only she would give him a chance, he would prove to her that inside he wasn't a monster, that inside he was the man who loved her.

Her eyes wild, Jane darted frantic looks around the kitchen, before she struggled free from his grip and turned.

"Don't ever touch me again!"

"Jane!" He had to get her to calm down and listen to him. Their future depended on it.

When she turned back to him, all he saw were her horrified eyes. Too late did he see the gleaming knife in her hand—too late to turn away and avoid its blade slashing his face. But what hurt more than the stinging blade cutting his flesh was seeing his wife recoil from him in horror.

"Now women will shy away from you like they should—you're a monster, Gabriel, you're the devil's creature!"

The scar that would form on his previously-handsome face reached from his chin to the top of his right ear, and it would be a constant reminder of what he was: a monster, a freak at best—not worthy to be loved by any woman.

1

San Francisco, Today

The *click-clack* of her heels echoed against the buildings. Maya could barely see the pavement through the fog which hung like a thick mist in the night air, amplifying every sound.

A rustle coming from somewhere behind her made her accelerate her already hasty steps. A chill so severe it felt as if an icy hand had touched her skin went through her. She hated the dark, and it was on nights like these that she cursed her on-call duty. Darkness had always scared her, and lately even more so.

She opened her purse as she approached the three-story apartment building she'd been living in for the last two years. With shaking fingers, she fished for her house keys. The moment she felt the cold metal in her damp palm, she felt better. In a few seconds, she would be back in bed and get a few hours of sleep before her next shift started. But more importantly, she would soon be back in the safety of her own four walls.

As she turned to the stairs leading up to the heavy entrance door, she noticed the darkness in the foyer. She glanced up. The light bulb over the door must have burned out. A couple of hours ago it had been burning brightly. She put it on her mental list of things to tell her landlord.

Maya felt for the railing and gripped it, counting the steps as she walked up.

She never reached the door.

"Maya."

Her breath caught as she spun on her heels. Engulfed in the dark and the fog, she couldn't make out his face. She didn't need to—she knew his voice. She knew who he was. It almost paralyzed her. Her heart hammered in her throat as fear inside her gut spiraled.

"No!" she screamed and scrambled back toward the door, hoping against all odds she could escape.

He'd come back like he'd vowed.

His hand dug into her shoulder and pulled her back to face him. But instead of his face, all she could focus on was the white of his pointed teeth.

"You will be mine."

The threat was the last thing she heard before she felt his sharp fangs break through her skin and sink into her neck. As the blood drained from her, so did the memories of the last few weeks.

***

"And you've tried surgery already?" Dr. Drake inquired without looking up from his notepad.

Gabriel released a frustrated huff and brushed an imaginary dust particle off his jeans. "Didn't work."

"I see." He cleared his throat. "Mr. Giles, have you had this . . . " The doctor winced and made a nondescript hand movement. ". . . uh . . . all your life? Even when you were human?"

Gabriel squeezed his eyes shut for a second. After puberty, there wasn't a day in his living memory that he'd not had this problem. Everything had been normal when he'd been a little boy, but the moment his hormones had started raging, his life had changed. Even as a human, he'd been an outcast.

He felt the scar on his face throb, remembering the moment he'd received it and jerked himself away from the memory. The physical pain had long since passed, but the emotional pain was as vivid as ever. "I had it long before I became a vampire. Back then, nobody thought of surgery. Hell, an infection would probably have killed me." If he'd known how his life would turn out, he would have taken a knife to himself, but hindsight was always twenty-twenty. "Anyway, as you probably know better than I do, my body regenerates while I sleep and heals what it perceives to be a wound. So, no, surgery hasn't worked."

"I assume this has caused problems with your sex life?"

Gabriel pressed himself deeper into the chair opposite Dr. Drake's, having ignored the coffin-couch with an internal shiver upon entering the office. His friend Amaury had warned him about the doctor's choice of furniture. Nevertheless, the coffin that had been fashioned into a chaise longue by removing a side panel gave him the creeps. No self-respecting vampire would want to be caught dead in it. Pun intended.

"What sex life?" he mumbled under his breath. But of course, the doctor's superior vampire hearing assured the words weren't lost to him.

Drake's shocked stare confirmed it. "You mean . . . ?"

Gabriel knew exactly what the man was asking. "Other than with an occasional desperate prostitute who I have to pay outrageous sums of money to service me, I have no sex life."

He dropped his gaze to the floor, not wanting to see the pity in the doctor's eyes. He was here to get help, not to be pitied. Still, he needed to impress on the man how important this was for him. "I haven't met a woman yet who hasn't recoiled from my naked body. They call me a monster, a freak—and those are the kind ones." He paused, shuddering as the memories of all the names he'd been called came rushing back. "Doc, I've never had a woman in my arms who wanted to be with me." Yes, he'd fucked women—whores—but he'd never made love to a woman. Never felt a woman's love or tenderness, or the intimacy of waking in her arms.

"How do you expect me to help you? As you said yourself, surgery hasn't helped, and I'm only a psychiatrist. I work with people's minds." Drake's voice was infused with rejection, every single syllable of it. "Why don't you use mind control on human women? They won't know any better."

He should have expected as much. Gabriel leveled a glare at him. "I'm not a complete jerk, Doctor. I won't use women like that." He paused before he went on, bringing his anger at the dishonorable suggestion under control. "You helped my friends."

"Both Mr. Woodford's and Mr. LeSang's problems were different, not . . . " He searched for the right word. " . . . physical like yours."

Gabriel's chest tightened. Yes, physical. And a vampire couldn't alter his physical form. It was set in stone. It was the exact reason why his face was marred by a scar reaching from his chin to the top of his right ear. He'd received the wound when he was human. Had he been injured as a vampire, there would have never been a scar, and his face would be untouched.

Two strikes against him—already the hideous scar scared plenty of women away, and once he dropped his pants . . . . He shuddered and looked back at the doctor who patiently sat in his chair.

"They both claimed you used unorthodox methods," Gabriel baited him.

Dr. Drake gave a noncommittal shrug. "What one might call unorthodox, another might deem natural."

That was a non-answer if there ever was one. Subtle hints wouldn't get Gabriel the information he sought. He cleared his throat and nudged forward on his chair.

"Amaury mentioned you had certain connections." He emphasized the word *connections* in such a way the doctor couldn't mistake what Gabriel was referring to.

The almost unperceivable straightening of the doctor's body would have escaped most others, but not Gabriel. Drake had understood only too well what he was after.

The doctor's lips tightened. "Maybe I can refer you to another physician among my connections who might be able to help you more than I can. Nobody here in San Francisco, of course, since I'm still the only medically trained vampire here," he confided.

Gabriel wasn't surprised at the revelation: since vampires weren't susceptible to human illnesses, very few became doctors. Given that San Francisco had a vampire population of under a thousand, it was lucky to have even one medical professional within its city limits.

"I see we both agree that we're not a good match," the doctor went on.

Gabriel knew he had to act now before the doctor dismissed him completely. When Drake moved to the Rolodex on his desk, Gabriel rose from his chair.

"I don't think that'll be necessary—"

"Well, then, it was a pleasure meeting you." The doctor stretched his hand out, his relaxed face now showing relief.

With a light shake of his head, Gabriel dismissed the gesture. "I doubt the Rolodex contains the name of the person I'm looking for anyway. Am I right?" He kept all malice out of his voice, having no intention of alienating the man. Instead, he let a half-smile curve his lips.

A flash in Drake's blue eyes confirmed he knew exactly who Gabriel was talking about. It was time to bring in the big guns. "I'm a very rich man. I can pay whatever you wish," Gabriel offered. In his nearly one hundred fifty years as a vampire, he'd amassed a fortune.

The doc's cocked eyebrow indicated interest. There was a hesitation in Drake's movement, but seconds later he pointed to the chairs. They both sat back down.

"What makes you think I'm interested in your offer?"

"If you weren't, we wouldn't be sitting."

The doctor nodded. "Your friend Amaury speaks very highly of you. I trust he's well now."

If Drake wanted to chit-chat, Gabriel would indulge him, but not for long. "Yes, the curse is broken. I understand that one of your acquaintances was instrumental in figuring out how the curse could be reversed."

"Maybe. But understanding how to fix something and fixing it are two different things. And as I see it, Amaury and Nina reversed his curse all by themselves. No outside help was needed."

"Unlike in my case?"

The doctor shrugged, a gesture Gabriel was getting increasingly tired of. "I don't know. There might be a perfectly plausible explanation for your ailment."

Gabriel shook his head. "Let's cut to the chase, Drake. It's not an ailment. What plausible explanation am I going to give a woman who sees me naked?"

"Mr. Giles—"

"At least call me Gabriel. I think we're past the Mr. Giles stage."

"Gabriel, I understand your predicament."

Gabriel felt heat rise inside his chest as anger churned up, something that was becoming more common as he dealt with his *predicament*. "Do you? Do you really understand what it feels like to see the disgust and fear in the eyes of a woman you want to make love to?" Gabriel swallowed hard. He'd never made love to a woman, never truly made love. Sex with prostitutes wasn't love. Sure, he could use mind control like the doctor had suggested and lure some unsuspecting woman into his bed and do with her whatever he wanted, but he'd vowed never to sink that low. And he'd never broken that vow.

"You mentioned payment," he heard Drake say.

Finally, there was light at the end of the tunnel. "Name your price and I'll wire the money into your account within hours."

Drake shook his head. "I'm not interested in money. I understand you have a gift."

Gabriel straightened in his chair. How much did the doctor know about him? He knew Amaury would have never revealed any of his secrets. "I'm not sure I understand—"

"Gabriel, don't take me for a fool. Just as you must have made your inquires about me, I have looked into your background. I understand you're able to unlock memories. Would you care to explain your gift to me?"

Not particularly. But it appeared he had no choice. "I see into people's minds and can delve into their memories. I see what they've seen."

"Does this mean you can look into my memories and find the person you're looking for?" Drake asked.

"I only see events and pictures. So unless I find a memory that shows her at her house or other such criteria, I wouldn't be able to find her. I don't read minds, only memories."

"I see." The doctor paused. "I'm willing to give you the whereabouts of the person you're looking for in exchange for the one-time use of your gift."

"You want me to delve into your memories and find something you've forgotten?" Sure, he could do that.

Drake chuckled. "Of course not. I have perfect recall. I want you to unlock another person's memories for me."

Hope deflated. His skill was only to be used in emergencies or when someone's life was at stake. He wouldn't rape someone's memories for his own gain, no matter how important this was for him. "I can't do that."

"Of course you can. You just told me—"

"What I meant to say is I won't do it. Memories are private. I won't access a person's memories without their permission." And he was sure the person whose memories the doctor wanted revealed to him wasn't going to give their consent.

"A man with high ethics. What a pity."

Gabriel glanced around the room. "With the money I'm willing to pay you, you could redecorate quite lavishly." And get rid of the coffin couch.

"I like the way my practice looks. Don't you?" Drake gave the offensive couch a pointed look.

Gabriel knew then that the negotiations were at an end. The doctor wouldn't budge, and neither would he.

2

The moment Gabriel arrived at Samson's Victorian home in Nob Hill, he took a deep breath. He needed to leave for New York now, the sooner the better. Maybe if he was back in his usual environment, he would be more content and not hope for the impossible. Why he'd suddenly started feeling like he could do something about his problem here in San Francisco, when he'd given up on it years ago, he didn't know.

Having to clear his departure with his boss, Samson, he was glad that he'd been called to the house the moment he'd stepped out of Drake's office.

With a determined gait, Gabriel entered the foyer, leaving the mist and fog behind him. The house was brightly lit despite the late hour, just like the house of a fellow vampire would be. It came alive at sunset and would quiet down once the sun rose. Gabriel let his eyes wander around the entry hall with its dark wood paneling, its elegant rugs, and antique ornaments. He liked Samson's home—it had retained all the charm of the Victorian era it was built in while shucking the claustrophobic feeling of its small rooms. Samson had opened up the space to give it an airy feeling. Yet the charm remained.

Gabriel lifted his head toward the ceiling. There was a commotion upstairs. Footsteps belonging to several men came from the upstairs corridor. A moment later, Samson made his way downstairs.

First Samson's long legs came into sight as he dashed down the pristine mahogany stairs. Then his entire body came into view. His raven black hair was in stark contrast to his hazel eyes. Being well over six feet tall and well built, he was an impressive figure. His sharp intelligence and strength had earned him admiration and respect from both his colleagues and his friends. His decisiveness and determination set him apart: Samson was the boss. And Gabriel was proud to be his second-in-command.

As Samson noticed Gabriel, he raised his hand in greeting. "Thanks for coming so quickly."

Behind him, two men came down the stairs. Gabriel recognized one of them as Eddie, Amaury's now brother-in-law who worked as a bodyguard for Samson's security company, Scanguards. But there would be no reason for him to be at Samson's private residence unless there was a social event planned.

Samson turned to the two men. "You have your orders, and not a word to anybody for now."

The two grunted their agreement and, with a nod of their heads to Gabriel, strode out the door.

"What are they—?" Gabriel started.

"We have a situation." The look on Samson's face was serious. "Come, we need to talk."

Samson waved him into the living room with its authentic Victorian-era furniture. Gabriel followed, a strange sense of foreboding settling in his gut. His boss and friend of many years always had a calm demeanor, but tonight he was different. His black hair was ruffled, his eyes worried, and the lines on his face spoke volumes.

Samson stopped in front of the fireplace and turned back to Gabriel. Even in June the fireplace was lit to provide warmth against the foggy night. "I know you're anxious to return to New York—"

"I was planning on taking the jet to—" Gabriel interrupted.

"I'm sorry, Gabriel, but I'll have to pull rank on you. I need you here. You can't leave." Samson's announcement came as an utter surprise.

"What?"

"I know you want to go home, but I need you to run point on this for me. Ricky is useless right now. Ever since Holly broke up with him last month, he's just not the same."

Samson ran his hand through his hair. Ricky was Gabriel's counterpart in San Francisco—the Operations Director. Gabriel didn't say a word. Something was wrong, seriously wrong if Samson found it more important for him to stay in San Francisco than to get back to work in New York.

"This is too important. Believe me, I would have Amaury take care of it, but he and Nina need some time together. He's practically on his honeymoon, holed up at his place. I can't do that to him right now."

Gabriel nodded. "What's going on?"

"Sit down."

Gabriel sat and waited until Samson did the same. "I've never seen you like this."

Samson gave a mirthless laugh. "I guess my responsibilities as a husband and expectant father don't go well with having a newly turned vampire in the house."

"A newly turned vampire?" This was indeed a shock. A newly turned vampire was a danger, unable to control his urges, liable to attack anybody. That Samson was uneasy made perfect sense. His wife Delilah was human and pregnant with their first child. She would be a prime target for any new vampire.

"She was attacked tonight."

Gabriel felt adrenaline shoot through his veins. "Delilah? Delilah was attacked?"

"No, no. Thank God. Delilah is fine. No. This woman—a human— she was attacked and turned. The two bodyguards who just left—Eddie and James—scared off her attacker and went to help her. Her eyes had already turned black, so they knew the process had started."

A human's eyes turning entirely black with not a speck of white remaining was a sure sign of the turning. Only once the turning was complete would the eyes turn back to normal.

"They brought her here about half an hour ago," Samson continued. "She must have been attacked on her way home. We have to find her attacker and take him out."

Gabriel understood. "A rogue. As long as he's out there, he's a danger to everybody and particularly to her if he realizes we're sheltering her."

Gabriel and his colleagues despised vampires turning unsuspecting humans against their will. It was a major infraction in their society—a crime in fact—punishable by death. A vampire's life wasn't easy— Gabriel of all people knew this for a fact. He therefore believed in protecting a human's right to choose and wouldn't force this life on anyone. He'd punish anyone who violated this right.

"Yes. That's why I need you. I need somebody I can rely on."

"What do we have?" Gabriel was all business now. This was his job. This was what he did best. A case to sink his teeth into and turn his thoughts away from his personal problem was what he needed. "Do we know who the woman is?"

"She's a doctor. She works at UCSF Medical Center. We found her ID. Her name is Maya Johnson, age thirty-two, lives in Noe Valley. We haven't been able to ask her anything yet. When Eddie and James brought her in, she was unconscious. I hope she can give us a description of the vampire who attacked her when she wakes. In the meantime, I'm keeping radio silence on this. It could be anybody. Until we know who might be behind this, I don't want anybody to know she's here."

"That's smart," Gabriel agreed. Until they could talk to her, they had to play it safe. Of course, that was assuming she could tell them anything. "You know she'll be in a panic when she comes to." Not only would she be traumatized by the attack, but once she realized what she had turned into, she would *truly* panic.

Samson closed his eyes and nodded. "I can imagine only too well."

"Should we bring somebody else in to help her through this?" Gabriel knew he wasn't the right person to guide a woman through a life-altering transition like turning into a vampire. He wasn't good with women.

"I've already sent for Drake. He'll know what to do. Maybe he'll be able to calm her down when she starts to become hysterical."

Considering his own interactions with Drake, Gabriel doubted the man would do any better than he. But he wasn't going to contradict Samson, who clearly held the doctor in high regard.

"Yeah, let's hope he can. Should we have a woman here when she wakes up? Having a bunch of six-foot-something vampires gawking at her when she comes 'round might be a little intimidating." Gabriel glanced into Samson's eyes. He sure had no interest in being the one to tell her the bad news. He also wasn't reluctant to delegate things he had no business doing. It was better if a woman, someone with a little more sensitivity, did the job.

"Not Delilah. I want her nowhere near the woman. You know as well as I do what a newly turned vampire is capable of. She won't be able to control her strength even if she doesn't mean to hurt anyone."

Gabriel held up his hand. "I wasn't thinking of Delilah. Yvette hasn't left for New York yet. I gave her a couple of days off to do some sightseeing." Yvette was a good bodyguard and, despite the fact that she could act a little prissy, she was solid and had a strong sense of right and wrong. He was sure the two women would bond instantly. Didn't most women?

Samson let out a breath. "Sure. Yvette. That's a good idea."

Heavy steps sounded on the stairs. A moment later Carl, Samson's trusted butler, rushed into the room. He was a stout man, heavy around the midsection and somewhere in his fifties. As always, he wore a formal dark suit. In fact, Gabriel had never seen him in anything else, and he was sure the man didn't own a single pair of jeans.

"Mr. Woodford, the woman is doing worse."

"Dr. Drake is already on his way. There's nothing I can do until he gets here. You shouldn't leave her alone," Samson said.

"Miss Delilah is with her," Carl responded.

Samson and Gabriel jumped up.

"I told her you wouldn't like it, but she insisted," Carl added quickly.

"Damn it, Carl!" Panic struck Samson's face as he bolted up the stairs. Gabriel ran after him and stormed into the guest room.

"Delilah!" Samson's voice was full of alarm.

Samson's petite wife sat on the edge of the bed and wiped the woman's face with a wet cloth. "Samson, please, I'm trying everything to make her comfortable. You storming in here screaming doesn't help." Delilah's scold was soft. Her long dark hair fell into her face as she bent over the woman. Despite the fact that she was pregnant, her body showed no bump yet. According to Samson, she was only three months along—which meant she'd gotten pregnant almost instantly after the couple had blood-bonded right after Chinese New Year.

"You shouldn't be here at all. We don't know how she'll react. It's too dangerous for you." Samson put his hands on her shoulders and pulled her up and away from the bed. "Please, sweetness, you're taking decades off my life by doing this." He looked over his shoulder at Gabriel and gestured toward the bed. "Gabriel, would you?"

Samson wanted him to play nurse? That was not part of the deal. He would investigate who'd done this to her, even protect her if she was still in danger, but under no circumstances would he sit by the woman's bed and play nurse.

It was best to tell his boss right now. Babysitting a newly turned vampire female was not what he needed right now, especially not when he was expected to actually interact with her on such an intimate level. A few interrogations, sure, he would be more than willing to do that, but not this, not sitting by her bed, taking care of her.

Hell, he would have no idea what to do. His knowledge of a woman's body was limited to some hurried sexual interactions and many not-so-hurried porn movies. Surely nobody could expect him to take care of a vampire female? Where the hell was Drake? Shouldn't he be here by now?

Gabriel turned toward Samson, who was leading Delilah out the door, ready to decline the job expected of him. But a low moan from the woman in the bed made him glance in her direction.

His breath caught in his chest as he saw her for the first time.

Gabriel heard the door close and knew he was alone with her.

The woman lay on top of the blankets, her clothes bloodstained. She wore pants and a T-shirt, a loose, white doctor's coat over it. In red letters her name was stitched over her breast pocket: Maya Johnson MD, Urology.

Maya's face was pale, and it looked even paler framed by her shoulder-length dark hair. It wasn't perfectly straight, but had large waves which seemed to caress her face. Her eyes were closed, thick dark lashes standing guard. He wondered what color her eyes would be once they returned to their normal state. Her skin had an olive tint to it, hinting at Latin, Mediterranean, or even Middle Eastern ancestry.

She had bruises and cuts on her face, mostly around her lips which were full and perfectly curved. She had fought her attacker, he knew instantly. Within hours her injuries would be gone, her vampire body healing itself while it slept.

He could only imagine the pain she'd gone through and the horror when she'd realized what was happening to her. She had died tonight at the hands of a rogue, and then he'd brought her back from the brink. She'd had to experience death to gain a new life. How painful had her death been?

Gabriel knew that every vampire's transformation was different. Many had horrifying memories of the event, things nobody spoke of. And this woman's memories would be terrifying—being turned against one's will would have been traumatic. Her wounds attested to it.

Gabriel looked past the injuries and the ugliness of the bite wound on her neck. It was clear the rogue had been interrupted since he hadn't had a chance to close the wound with his saliva. It would take longer to heal without it. Had he licked the bite wound, it wouldn't even be visible anymore.

Gabriel only saw the woman underneath the injuries: the sensual curve of her nose, the strong lines of her cheekbones, and the gracefulness of her neck. Her slender figure might as well have been bare, for he could almost imagine what her nude form looked like.

Elegant long fingers extended from slim hands, hands whose caress he wanted to feel on his own skin. Long legs he wanted her to wrap around his waist as he made love to her. Full breasts he could suckle from as he kissed every inch of her body. Red lips he would taste with his.

There was something so enthralling about her scent, something so foreign, yet so familiar at the same time. No other scent compared to hers. Rich and dark, it engulfed him, cocooned him in an aura of warmth and softness. Every cell in his body responded to her call.

She was perfect.

3

All Gabriel could do was look at Maya. Of their own volition, his legs carried him to her side where he sat down on the edge of the bed.

He bent over her and listened for her heartbeat. It was slow—too slow. A vampire's heartbeat was almost double the rate of a human's, yet this woman's heart was beating barely as fast as a normal human's. Concern spread within him as he noticed the shallowness of her breaths. He didn't need to be a doctor to know something was wrong.

Gabriel touched his palm to her forehead and felt the clammy coldness of her skin. He sucked in a quick breath. Her symptoms reminded him of his own turning and how he'd almost died a second time. His sire had been baffled by the events, but had never been able to explain it. It had been as if his body had rejected the notion of becoming a vampire, just as hers was doing, seeking death instead.

He wouldn't allow it.

"No," Gabriel whispered to her. "I won't let you die. Do you hear me? You will live."

He stroked her cold face with the back of his hand. There was no response from her. He reached for her hand and clasped the delicate fingers in his large palm. They were like ice. No blood was circulating in her extremities.

Shocked, Gabriel realized that her body had already started shutting down. Frantically, he rubbed her fingers between his hands, trying to generate heat.

"Carl!" he called out. Heavy footsteps came up the stairs. A moment later, the door opened, and Carl stepped in.

"You called, Gabriel?"

"Where's that damn doctor?" Gabriel didn't take his eyes off Maya.

"On his way."

"Help me. Take her feet and rub them."

"Uh—"

Gabriel shot Carl an annoyed look. "Now!"

Carl jumped into action. While he went to work on her feet, Gabriel continued massaging her hands, rubbing her long, elegant fingers between his large palms.

"What are we doing?" Carl asked.

"Trying to get her blood flowing."

"The turning isn't taking, is it?"

The butler had articulated what Gabriel didn't want to acknowledge. He squeezed his eyes shut and pushed all negative thoughts out of his mind. "It will. It has to." He touched her face again, but it was still as cold as it had been minutes earlier. "We have to help her body do the work."

Gabriel shifted and looked at Carl and the clumsy way he rubbed her feet. If there was anybody even more inept with women than himself, it had to be Carl. He was barely touching her toes. "Let me do that. Take her hands instead."

He shoved Carl aside and took Maya's feet into his hands. He needed to get her blood circulating so it could reach every cell in her body and complete the transformation. The turning was a complicated chemical process, but normally the body knew what to do. It appeared Maya's cells either didn't understand the instructions they were receiving, or refused to comply.

The skin of her feet was soft and smooth, her toenails beautifully shaped and pedicured. Ruby-red nail polish adorned them. He had never seen more kissable feet. Gabriel noticed how his own skin color virtually matched hers, though the texture couldn't be more different. His callused hands bore no resemblance to her softness. No, he couldn't let a woman as perfect as she die.

With renewed determination, he massaged her feet with his hands, rubbing up and down her soles, kneading them, then stroking up her ankles, then back down again. He wasn't sure how long he'd been doing it before he finally heard voices from below.

Drake had arrived. He heard fragments of the explanations Samson gave him as they rushed up the stairs. A moment later, they burst into the bedroom.

"About time," Gabriel growled.

Carl released Maya's hands instantly and stepped back from the bed, clearly relieved to be released from his duty. "I trust you don't need me anymore now that the doctor is here."

Without waiting for a reply, he bolted from the room.

"I'm not sure how much help I can be. I'm a psychiatrist, not a critical care physician," Drake stated, not that the explanation was needed. Both Samson and Gabriel were fully aware of the man's credentials, or lack thereof.

"That's the best we can do," Samson insisted. "The nearest vampire physician is in Los Angeles. We don't have time to get him up here."

"Fine, but I can't be held responsible if—"

Gabriel seized Drake by the throat and cut him off in mid sentence. "If you don't stop babbling, you won't have to worry about who's responsible, because you won't be around. Are we clear on that?"

"Gabriel!" Samson's reprimand cut through the tension in the room.

Gabriel released the doctor, who cut him a sour glance.

"Fine." With a jerky movement, Drake approached the bed and looked at the woman. Gabriel watched his every movement, for some inexplicable reason feeling protective toward her. And why shouldn't he, since Samson had assigned him this case? It was just like in the old days when he'd started working for Samson's company as a bodyguard, long before he'd worked his way up to his current powerful position as Scanguards' number two. He was merely acting as her bodyguard. Only, he'd never guarded a body as perfect as hers.

Drake lifted one eyelid then the other to look at Maya's pupils before he pried her lips apart and examined her teeth. He slid his finger along her upper teeth and probed.

"Hmm."

"What's wrong?" Gabriel asked, impatient to hear the doctor's assessment.

Drake turned to him and Samson. "Her fangs aren't growing, and the white in her eyes is not returning. Samson, you said your men found her and think they interrupted the vampire who did this?"

Samson nodded. "Yes, they saw somebody run away, but weren't fast enough to catch him. They were more concerned with getting her to safety first."

"Makes sense. I think he wasn't finished. The turning is only halfway done. She probably barely received any vampire blood. Her human body is fighting it. And her vampire side isn't strong enough. It's not sufficient to turn her, but it's sufficient to make her remaining human impossible. You have to make a choice."

"A choice?" Gabriel heard himself ask, then felt both the doctor's and Samson's stares on him. Did they realize that he had more than a passing interest in her?

"Either turn her fully or let her die."

Gabriel gasped. He took a step toward the doctor, ready to throttle him. "Let her die?" Before he could lay hands on Drake, Samson put a hand on Gabriel's shoulder.

"Gabriel. Stop."

He spun around to face Samson. "You can't let her die." Even as he said it, he knew what he was planning to do was against his own beliefs: to give a human a choice. But he wasn't planning on giving her that choice. Hell, she wasn't conscious to make this choice for herself.

Samson gave him a sad smile. "Then she has to be turned fully. Do you really want that responsibility?"

Gabriel swallowed. "You would prefer dealing with the guilt of letting her die?" He'd rather deal with the guilt of knowing he kept her alive as a vampire.

"Turning her means imposing your will on her." As if Gabriel didn't know that himself.

Samson continued, "The rogue has already taken her choices away. Are you gonna do the same? Are you prepared to make that choice for her? What if she'd rather die?"

"What if she'd rather live?" Gabriel countered.

What if I want her to live?

"Do you really want to play God?"

While he knew Samson to be a man who believed in God, Gabriel had lost his faith a long time ago. But he'd never lost his sense of right and wrong, good and bad. Letting her die now was wrong. "I'm prepared to play the Devil if it means she'll live." Gabriel's decision was clear: under no circumstances would he let her die. Consequences be damned! If she hated him for it later, so be it, but while she couldn't make a decision, he would make it for her. And he hoped she would agree with him in the end.

A resigned nod was Samson's answer. "Drake, what do you suggest?"

Drake cleared his throat. "She'll need to be fed more vampire blood."

"How much?" Gabriel asked, even though it didn't matter. He'd give her as much as she needed. However many pints of his blood she wanted, he would happily supply it.

"I don't know yet. I'm afraid we'll have to wing it." The doctor gave a shrug.

Gabriel unbuttoned his left sleeve and shoved the fabric back to his elbow. "I'm ready."

"When did you last feed?" the doctor asked, concern etched in his face. Suddenly he was all focused, his flippant attitude gone.

"A few hours ago."

"Good." He waved Gabriel to the other side of the bed. "Get onto the bed and sit next to her. I need you to open your vein. I'll hold her mouth open, and you'll have to start dripping the blood into her."

Gabriel nodded and did as the doctor asked. He sat next to her on the bed. Willing his fangs to extend, he pierced his own wrist with them. Droplets of blood instantly appeared.

In the background, he heard the door open and close. Samson had obviously decided not to watch. Gabriel didn't care—he didn't need his boss's approval. This was his decision to make. His case. But Gabriel knew full well that this was not merely a case for him—this woman meant more. He didn't know why, but he trusted his instinct enough to know what he had to do. And his instinct had never failed him.

Keeping her alive was his mission now.

***

Maya was cold. A shiver racked her frame. She tried to curl into a ball to preserve her body's heat, but all her muscles felt stiff and unresponsive to her brain's demand. She felt paralyzed. When she sensed a movement next to her, she realized she lay on a bed. As the mattress depressed next to her, heat reached her. Whoever—or whatever—was next to her provided warmth, and she craved it.

Trying to move the millstone holding down her chest, she fought against the heaviness of her body and shifted herself ever so slightly to her left. As if the heat source knew what she wanted, it came closer, and a moment later it pressed against her side. Suddenly warmth flooded into her, and she let out a contented sigh.

But the moment she tried to take a deep breath, her lungs stung from the effort, and a bolt of pain shot through her body. Pressure built in her lungs as they were unable to expel the carbon dioxide. It felt like drowning.

She opened her mouth to force herself to cough, to push out the used air, but before she could do so, she felt a hand at her mouth holding it open. Then drops of warm liquid hit her tongue. She wanted to scream. But all she could do was to swallow before the liquid would drown her.

The more she swallowed, the more liquid entered her mouth. She couldn't taste anything, but she knew it wasn't water. It was thicker, almost creamy. And to her surprise it eased the pressure in her chest. It had to be medicine. Somebody was giving her medicine. So she opened wider and arched toward the source of the liquid.

"Slowly, slowly," a deep voice cautioned.

Softness touched her lips. Warm skin—and from it came the liquid that eased her body's pain. She didn't care what it was, didn't even want to speculate. All she knew was it was helping. Greedily, she sucked, wanting more and more before somebody would deny her and stop the flow. She had to get enough before there was no more.

The more she drank, the more aware she became of her own body and the source of heat next to her, the way it cradled her, protected her. Now that the burning pain in her body started to subside, she recognized the heat source as a man's body, a *very large* man's body. Who was he?

Her eyelids felt as heavy as an iron door; nevertheless, she tried to lift them. She succeeded just enough to see the shape of the man beside her—the man whose wrist she was still drinking from.

Shock coursed through her. He hadn't given her medicine—he'd fed her his blood!

Maya tried to pull away from him, but her body wouldn't obey. It stayed close to his broad chest that warmed her and his wrist that fed her. She forced herself to lift her lids farther to look at his face and wished she hadn't.

With horror, she stared at his disfigured profile with an ugly scar from his chin to his ear. At this close a distance, it throbbed menacingly.

His long brown hair was swept back in a ponytail. Some strands had struggled free of it and framed his square face.

She squeezed her eyes shut. No—she was *not* lying in bed being fed blood by a monster. It had to be a bizarre dream—there was no other explanation. More than eighty hours of work a week could do that to anybody. Long shifts, then nights of call after call, would bring anybody to the point of complete and utter exhaustion. It wouldn't be the first time it happened to her.

During her three-year residency, she'd broken down a couple of times and had needed twenty-four hours of sleep to recover. She would call in sick tomorrow. Yes, her body was definitely telling her she needed rest.

If she was making up bloodsucking monsters, then it was time for a little downtime.

She sighed deeply. Now that she'd made the decision to take a day off, she suddenly felt better—it certainly couldn't be because she still felt the warm body of the scarred man pressed against her. No monster would have this kind of calming effect on her. And for that matter, maybe it was time to change her movie rentals to romantic comedies rather than horror flicks, since clearly she couldn't handle the latter.

Had she watched a romantic comedy on the weekend rather than the latest B-movie in the horror genre, surely the man in her dream would have been handsome and not so horribly disfigured. Maya shuddered at the memory of the man's face.

4

"How is she?" Samson's voice came from the door.

Gabriel looked up from Maya's sleeping body and gestured for Samson to come in. He'd let her keep her clothes, too worried that once she woke and found herself undressed, her panic would be even greater. She would have enough to deal with—thinking a stranger had seen her naked wouldn't help the situation. "She has a chance now."

"You look tired. Here, I brought you some blood. You need to replenish." Samson handed him two bottles of red liquid.

Gabriel looked at the labels—*O-negative*—and made an appreciative grunt. "The good stuff."

"Only the best for my people. Listen, I wanted to apologize for what happened earlier. But you know what I think about creating new vampires against their will, and I thought you felt the same."

Gabriel looked at him and saw the concern in his boss's eyes. "I do. But there are times when we have no choice about what to do. It's a life—either way. What she'll do with it is going to be her choice. But at least she'll have a choice."

Gabriel popped open the bottle and took a big gulp. The thick liquid coated his throat. Damn it felt good. He'd felt drained. Maya had taken a good two pints out of him, but he hadn't had the heart to stop her. The doc had warned him, but he knew that her instinct would tell her how much she needed. When she'd finally stopped, she'd fallen back into a deep sleep. Her breathing was better now, and her heartbeat had sped up. The signs were good.

"You're right," his boss agreed. "Gabriel, I want you to do something for me."

Gabriel looked straight at him. "What's that?"

"I've decided to take Delilah on a short vacation until Maya is more stable. Call me overly cautious, but I could never forgive myself if she were attacked just because Maya can't control her urges yet. After all,

Delilah is the only human in the house, and Maya will be drawn to her blood."

There was a small pause, and Gabriel noticed how a soft smile crept around Samson's lips. With a twinkle in his eyes, Samson continued, "And I of all people know how tempting her blood is."

"You're one lucky son of a bitch, Samson." Gabriel grinned and for a moment forgot all his troubles. It was good to see his friend so happy.

"Don't I know it. I want you to stay here—Carl is making up the master bedroom for you. We're taking Oliver with us."

"You're taking a human bodyguard?" Oliver, a human, was Samson's personal assistant and took care of all his daytime needs.

"For Delilah. I'm sure she'll want to see some sights during the day while I have to stay indoors. I don't want to deprive her of the occasion. Oliver will keep her safe."

"I understand."

Samson looked back at the bed. "Maya needs to be watched twenty-four-seven. Thomas, Zane, and Yvette will be around to assist you. I'm sending Quinn back to New York. He can run headquarters during your absence."

Gabriel had no reservations about Quinn taking over New York; another name, however, tripped his alarm. "You sure about Zane?"

"He's your best man. You know how to keep him in line."

Samson was right, but having Zane around Maya made Gabriel feel uneasy. He couldn't pinpoint why. Zane was the meanest fighting machine he'd ever met, and having him on his side meant having the best protection available.

"I've also alerted Amaury, and he's offered to help, even though I'm sure he'd rather do something else."

Gabriel smirked. "I'll avoid calling him in on this—I'd rather not be at the receiving end of Nina's wrath. That woman sure has a mouth on her."

Samson laughed. "And she needs it to tame Amaury. But honestly, if you need him, call him. I'm sure he's got his ways of calming Nina down when she gets a little too wild."

Gabriel didn't want to think of it, since Amaury's ways would certainly involve sweaty marathon sex—it wasn't an image he needed right now. Not with the most perfect woman lying only feet away from him—helpless and vulnerable. His groin tightened at the memory of how her body had felt pressed to his when he'd fed her.

"You okay?" Samson asked.

Gabriel shifted in his chair to hide his growing erection. "Sure. I'll take care of things. Once she's awake and has accepted the change, I'll find out what happened. Maybe she can give us a description of the guy. She has to have seen something."

"Good. Carl will be here when you need him, and Drake is supposed to stop by every night to check on her. He called a few minutes ago."

Gabriel raised his eyebrows in inquiry. He felt no guilt for having been so harsh with the doctor earlier. "What did he want?"

"He forgot to tell you what to do when she comes round. She needs to get human blood within six hours of waking or her thirst will get too much for her and she'll turn crazy. I doubt it will be a problem feeding her—she'll be famished, and her instincts in the first few hours will be so sharp that you won't be able to keep her away from the blood. I suggest giving her the bottled stuff. It worked well for Carl."

Gabriel nodded. "Is the pantry stocked?"

"I've sent Carl out for more supplies, but there's plenty for you and her."

A sound from downstairs made them both look toward the door.

"And another thing," Samson added, "keep Ricky out of it. I think the breakup with Holly is really hitting him hard. Frankly, I was a little surprised when he told me that she broke it off with him. I always thought she was the one who was really into the relationship."

"Goes to show, you never know what goes on inside a person," Gabriel agreed.

"Anyway, I've instructed everybody to give him some space. The guys will only take orders from you."

"Understood."

Voices drifted upstairs. With a move of his head, Samson pointed downstairs. "Looks like we've got company. Let's fill them in."

***

The voices in her dream didn't completely disappear. While they seemed to have left her immediate area, Maya could still hear them farther away. She chuckled in her sleep, feeling like the bionic woman who could hear people talking from two hundred yards away. How funny would that be? She would be able to hear what her patients said before she even entered the exam room.

She couldn't remember when she'd called in sick to let her colleagues know to cover for her, but she was sure she had. She must have—she was the responsible type and would never let her colleagues down.

Voices came and went, doors opened and closed. She heard car engines start and garage doors open and close. Footsteps everywhere on this floor and below, like an army was trampling through her apartment building. She'd have to complain to the landlord about her noisy neighbors. Couldn't they just quiet down and let her sleep?

She let herself fall deeper into her dream. A warm hand caressed her cheek and brushed her hair out of her face. She felt safe. Encouraging words she forgot as soon as she heard them echoed in her head. Somebody spoke to her softly, whispering, almost breathing words into her ear. The words soothed her.

One dream led into the next and the next. And with each dream came more awareness.

Maya's body felt rested and strangely rejuvenated, almost as if she'd spent twenty-four hours at a luxury spa. Her bed felt more comfortable than it ever had before. The mattress felt softer, the linen fresher. And larger—somehow her bed seemed larger to her, too large for her small bedroom, where a full-size bed was all she'd been able to fit in while leaving space for her dresser.

Maya reached her arms out to her sides and still didn't meet the edge of the bed. Was she still dreaming? Maybe she wasn't even awake yet.

With more effort than she expected, she opened her eyes.

A scream pierced the silence, and with horror she realized it was her own.

5

Her ear-piercing scream made the man leaning over her jolt backwards.

The six-and-a-half-foot-tall stranger's head was shorn bald, and his face could only be described as cold and evil. And if that didn't ensure Maya knew he was a bad guy, then it was the fact that he was in her apartment hovering over her bed.

Frantic, she reached out toward her right to feel for the baseball bat she kept next to her bed and encountered—nothing. She spun her head away from the intruder.

And her heart stopped.

This wasn't her bedroom! This wasn't even her apartment!

She'd been kidnapped!

With her next breath, she found her voice again and yelled as loud as she could. "*Help! Somebody help me!*"

She scrambled off the bed, putting it between the bald guy and herself as a barrier. "Get away from me! Leave me alone, you sick bastard!"

Her eyes scanned the room. It was richly furnished, which surprised her. Didn't they keep kidnap victims in dark and dingy basements with just a bed and a chair? This room was anything but.

Perfect! She'd been kidnapped by some sick, rich bastard. At least somebody else would only want money—which she didn't have—but this guy, who knew what *he* wanted?

She stared at him. He hadn't moved since her initial scream, clearly enjoying her fear. Maya wiped her sweaty palms on her pants and realized to her relief that she still wore her clothes. In fact, she was dressed as if she'd just come from the hospital. Given the bloodstains on her clothes, she figured she'd been called into the emergency room on a consult. Had she never gotten home?

Before she could think any further, the door to the room burst open and three people stormed in. Great, now she was outnumbered.

"Zane, what the fuck are you doing in here?" a strangely familiar voice said. Her gaze zeroed in on the man who'd spoken. She almost choked on her next breath.

While he lunged at the man he'd called Zane, Maya could clearly see the large scar on the right side of his face.

He was the monster from her dream. He was real. And he was here.

He attacked the bald guy, pulling him away from the bed.

"Leave me alone, Gabriel. I just wanted to see what she looks like," Zane defended himself and shrugged off the other man's hands. "Don't be such a spoilsport."

"Get out!" the man with the scar thundered. The authority in his voice was undeniable.

With another shrug, the bald man left the room as ordered. Only now, the man he'd called Gabriel turned back to her.

"I'm sorry. Zane shouldn't have been in here. We weren't sure when you would wake up," he said, his voice an octave deeper yet softer than before.

Soft voice or not, he took a few steps toward her—which was something Maya couldn't allow. She scanned her vicinity for a weapon. "Stop right there, buddy," she warned him and reached for the wrought-iron candlestick on the bedside table, ready to throw it at him if he came any closer. She was relieved to see that he yielded. It gave her a moment to assess what kind of danger he represented.

He was almost as tall at the bald guy, but not as slim. His shoulders were broader, his frame heavier. The long, dark hair, which was gathered in a ponytail softened his square face somewhat, but the scar that marred one side of his face took all that softness away. Yes, he was dangerous, she was sure. She stared at his strong arms, his large hands, and knew those hands could choke the life out of her if he really wanted to do her harm. She wouldn't have a snowball's chance in hell. All she had was bravado. And she was skilled at bluffing.

"Where am I, and who are you? Talk fast—I'm not very patient."

Maya glanced past Scarface at the two other people who'd entered behind him. One woman, one man. The man was equally tall and looked like he worked out. What made his stature really impressive and intimidating was the fact he wore black-leather gear. Clearly a biker, possibly a member of a gang. The woman was as beautiful as they came. Short, black hair, porcelain skin, plump lips, a Barbie doll figure . . . She looked like a model—perfect body, and a perfect face, despite the fact that a frown curled around her mouth.

"I'm Gabriel. My colleagues here—" Gabriel gestured toward the man and the woman. "—are Yvette and Thomas."

As he turned his face to the side, Maya saw his unblemished half for a few seconds and realized there was nothing ugly about it. His left side was perfectly sculpted: high cheekbones, strong square chin, a long straight nose, and then those *eyes* . . . Framed by long dark lashes, they seemed to be as dark as chocolate, yet flecks of light sparkled in them. When she dropped her gaze lower, she focused on his lips. Full and slightly parted, they looked sensual. Before she could tear her gaze away, he turned his head back to her.

Now that she saw both sides together again, the scarred one and the perfect one, she had to admit that he didn't look like the monster she'd made up in her mind. Clearly, the large scar had destroyed his handsome face, but it had given him something else: a face with character.

Gabriel suddenly moved and looked as if he wanted to walk toward her. She instantly raised the candlestick above her head.

He lifted his hands in defeat. "I'm not coming any closer. I don't mean you any harm."

"How did I get here?" Maya asked, ignoring his comment.

"You remember nothing?"

She searched her memory, but couldn't figure out what he was talking about. So she took the bull by the horns. "You guys kidnapped me, didn't you? What is it that you want? Money?" They could have the few hundred bucks in her savings account. If they wanted more, they'd have to wait for next month's payday. Paying off her student loans had eaten up all her savings.

The woman, Yvette, shook her head and chuckled. "This'll take a while, Gabriel. Why don't I leave you to it?"

"Yvette," Gabriel snapped. "You're not getting out of this one. Samson assigned you to help, so you'll help."

Yvette's mouth twisted into a thin line. It appeared whoever this Samson was held power over her. Maya tucked the knowledge away—

maybe she could use it to her advantage later. The more she found out about her kidnappers the better.

Maya looked back and forth between Gabriel and Yvette, contemplating what he'd meant by his words. What was she supposed to help him with? Holding her down? Tying her up? No, probably not—they'd had that chance while she was unconscious. What the hell were they trying to do to her?

"You were attacked," Gabriel finally started.

"I figured that one out all by myself. So, what do you want?" Maya shot back. She knew she was outnumbered, so only calm thinking could get her out of this situation.

"We aren't the ones who attacked you," Gabriel claimed.

Maya gave a little snort. As if she was that gullible. Maybe she was lucky and these three criminals were too thick to have come up with a decent plan. She could probably outsmart them. For sure the woman, having gotten it all in the looks department, had been shortchanged on brain cells. And the biker: he might know about his ride, but did he have any other skills? She wasn't too sure how to evaluate Gabriel—he seemed to be in charge, but—

"He's telling the truth," Thomas continued in Gabriel's stead. "Two of our bodyguards found you after you were attacked. They brought you here to be taken care of."

Maya took a step back. Bodyguards? These guys had bodyguards? That could only mean they were Mafia, probably Russian. *To be taken care of*—yes, that sounded just like the Mafia. This changed everything. She wasn't dealing with a few hapless criminals out to make a few bucks. She was dealing with the Mafia, the Cosa Nostra, or whatever they called themselves these days.

Maya's stomach sank to her knees. If she'd seen something they didn't want her to see, if she'd been a witness to something, she was as good as dead. Maybe one of her patients had said something to her that implicated these guys in a crime, and they thought it was best to take her out. She read the papers. She knew what guys like these were capable of.

"I don't recall being attacked. What did you do, drug me?"

Gabriel shook his head. "We didn't drug you. But if you don't remember any of it. I wonder whether your attacker could have wiped your memory. Even though, it would be unusual . . . "

"Wiped my memory? Please, don't try to feed me this ludicrous crap. I'm not stupid." She lifted her chin in a show of bravery she didn't possess. But she wanted answers, no matter whether she liked what she heard or not. "Just tell me what you want and let's get this over with." If she hated one thing, it was uncertainty. Once she knew what was going on here, at least she could formulate a plan. She was good at making plans.

Yvette stepped forward and planted herself next to Gabriel. "You were attacked by a vampire."

For a second, Maya's heart stopped. Then she let out a breath. This was one big joke. It had to be. Nobody in their right mind, not even some criminal, could come up with such an implausible explanation and expect to be believed. She looked around the room. "Okay, where's the camera? This'll be on YouTube, right? Who put you up to this? Was it Paulette?" Her colleague could be a total prankster. She'd have to get back at her for this practical joke.

Unfortunately, nobody was laughing. Instead, Gabriel took a step toward her. "The vampire who attacked you—he started the turning process to make you one of us. We are all vampires, but we're here to help you."

None of his words made any sense. The whole lot of them must have escaped from the psych ward. She wished she'd listened more to her psychiatry professor on how to deal with lunatics. Unfortunately, her medical interests had driven her more toward how the body worked than the mind.

"Vampires don't exist, you creeps. You've been watching too many bad movies."

"I can prove it to you," Gabriel claimed.

"Oh, yeah? What, you're gonna put on some fake fangs?"

He shook his head and took another step closer, too close for her liking.

Maya hurled the candlestick at him and was astonished by her own forceful move. In a move that was faster than her eye could follow, Gabriel caught it and placed it onto the chair next to him. Startled, Maya looked at him. Okay, so he was fast. That didn't have to mean anything. It only meant she didn't have a chance at defeating him.

"Please don't do that," he asked in a calm voice. "I'm not the enemy."

Maya gave a mirthless laugh.

"Maybe you should give her a demonstration," Thomas suggested.

"No. I don't want to frighten her anymore than she already is," Gabriel replied.

"No, no, please, do give me a demonstration," Maya mocked. "I've got to see what you *vampires* do."

When none of the three so-called vampires moved or did anything to prove that they were really vampires, she knew she'd called their bluff.

Now she was convinced this was all a big setup. Her colleagues from the hospital had probably all chipped in and hired a few actors to play a prank on her. Hadn't they said only weeks ago that she was working too hard and needed to relax?

"Thought so. Now, tell me how I get out of here. Or do you expect to be tipped?"

"Tipped?" Gabriel gave her a dubious look.

"For your performance. Honestly, at first I thought you guys were Mafia. You should have stuck with that angle. Bodyguards, taking care of things—those were good lines. It would have been more believable. But vampires. Really? Nothing against your acting skills, but that's a tough role to pull off."

All three looked at her like she was some lunatic on leave from the asylum. She felt almost guilty for having spoiled their fun.

"Truly, you were good. But the vampire thing is just too much of a stretch. Sorry. Hey, what time is it? I hope you guys didn't make me late for my next shift."

Maya looked around trying to find her shoes.

"It's denial," she heard Yvette say.

"Clearly," Thomas agreed.

"I don't know how to explain this to you without frightening you, but I swear, I'm trying," Gabriel said.

Maya's breath hitched when she caught a movement next to him.

Yvette had grabbed the candlestick from the chair. "Catch!" Faster than her eye could process, Yvette flung it at her.

"No!" Gabriel yelled, but a moment later, Maya found herself seizing the candlestick effortlessly. She stared at the item in her hand and couldn't explain how she'd caught it when she'd barely seen it coming toward her.

She'd never even been a ballplayer—her hand-eye coordination sucked way too bad for that. And now she'd caught a candlestick flying at her at the speed of a car? How had that happened? And how had the woman *thrown* it at the speed of a car, for that matter?

Gabriel turned to the woman. "You could have hurt her!" His voice was harsh, scolding.

"Her reflexes are much sharper than those of a human." Yvette merely shrugged, then looked straight at Maya. "All your senses are enhanced. And you're stronger too. I knew you'd catch it—it's a reflex."

"Next time, you clear things like that with me. Do we understand each other?" Gabriel hissed at Yvette, who crossed her arms over her chest and ignored the reprimand.

Maya shook her head. "It's all a trick." She had no idea how she'd done it, but there was no way she could have caught the candlestick by herself. Something was wrong with her. She could feel it. With effort, she pushed back her rising doubts. She wouldn't let herself be tricked by them.

She set the candlestick onto the small antique sideboard. The fragile wooden piece splintered under the force with which she'd dropped the item. Startled, she stared at it. Had she misjudged her own strength?

"Do you believe us now?" Gabriel asked.

"No!" This didn't prove anything. Maybe the sideboard was some cheap prop designed to crumble under the slightest impact.

"Then go into the bathroom." He pointed toward a door near the fireplace. "There's a mirror over the sink. Look into it and tell me what you see."

Maya hesitated. Doubts had started bubbling up in her. She had nothing to lose by looking into a mirror, did she? Without letting Gabriel or the other two out of her sight, she cautiously walked to the bathroom door. She pushed it open and glanced inside. An elegant white marble bathroom greeted her. It was much more luxurious than what she was used to.

"I'll be waiting here," Gabriel said.

Maya stepped into the bathroom, but kept an eye on the door. As she approached the sink, she looked in the mirror over it. She stopped right in front of it, but there was no reflection of herself. She did a double take, then leaned forward to inspect the mirror more closely. Nothing.

"Another one of your tricks, I see," she commented. She'd heard of movie props like this: mirrors that weren't really mirrors so the light on a movie set wouldn't reflect back into the camera.

"It's not a trick. Vampires don't have a reflection. Our auras transmit on a frequency that the mirror can't process. So it reflects nothing back."

"I guess that means you don't show up in photos either," she mocked.

"We do if you use a digital camera," his response came from the bedroom.

"Bull," she answered. "I don't know where you're going with this, but whatever you're trying to do, it's not working."

"Take anything in the bathroom, a towel, soap—whatever you can find, and wave it in front of the mirror."

She snorted. She had no intention of following his stupid suggestion. What would it prove?

"Do it," Gabriel ordered in a voice that brooked no refusal.

Fine, she'd do it, and then she'd walk out of here and tell him to try his idiotic tricks on somebody else. She was done with this. It wasn't funny anymore. In fact, it hadn't been funny from the start.

With an impatient gesture, Maya grabbed the hairbrush from the white marble counter and held it in front of the mirror. As if held by an invisible hand, it appeared. She moved it, and it moved in the mirror. The mirror was working. Now that she looked more closely, she noticed that it reflected everything behind her, the shower, the toilet, the towels on the towel rack. Everything—except her.

With a loud clank, the hairbrush landed in the sink.

Maya opened her mouth, but no sound came out. No scream, no words.

Her lungs fought for air as her brain processed the news. She lifted her hands and stared at them. They were visible to her, she could see them, touch them, but the mirror showed nothing. As if she didn't exist.

What was she?

At the sound of her scream, Gabriel knew that the truth had finally sunk in. Her sobs started only a moment later.

He turned back to face his colleagues. "Leave us. I'll take care of this."

Thomas appeared relieved. "I'll be downstairs if you need me."

Yvette only raised a questioning eyebrow. But within seconds, the two left the room.

Now he was alone with Maya's sobs and his own pain. He could only too well imagine what she was going through, but this was more than empathy. He'd never felt another person's pain so intensely. Only kindred spirits felt each other's pain like this. So why did his heart ache for her when he barely knew her?

Determined to help her, he walked into the bathroom. Like a little bundle, she crouched against the bathtub, her arms hugging her legs, her head buried between her knees. With two long strides, he was at her side and picked her up in his arms.

She gave no resistance. All the fight had gone out of her. The woman, who had so bravely faced them thinking they were God-knows-what-kind-of-criminals, had crumbled.

Gabriel cradled her against his chest and carried her back into the bedroom, where he lowered himself into the armchair in front of the fireplace. He kept her in his lap and stroked his hand over her back in long and gentle motions.

"You're not alone. We'll take care of you." *He* would take care of her. He alone wanted that responsibility. He would make sure she would never have to cry again. He'd made the decision to keep her alive, so the responsibility fell to him. But this was more than a responsibility to him. He *wanted* to take care of her.

With every breath she took, new sobs left her chest. Her tears soaked his white shirt as she clung to him like a drowning woman.

Gabriel had no experience with women's tears, but he didn't shy away from hers. She had every right to cry. Her whole life had been uprooted. Nothing would be the same again. Choices had been taken away from her, and she didn't even know the half of it yet. Not only would she have to drink human blood and stay out of daylight, her life as a woman had changed irrevocably with that one fatal bite. The least he could do was comfort her and give her whatever she needed.

"Why?" she sobbed, taking a big gulp of air into her lungs.

Gabriel stroked his hand over her silky-soft hair and brushed a light kiss on top of her head. "I don't know, baby. But I promise you, we'll punish whoever did this to you."

He wasn't sure that she'd heard him since her sobbing continued uninterrupted. But he hoped his voice would soothe her, so he continued to talk to her, whisper meaningless words to her, if only to reassure her that he was here, that somebody cared. Word after word spilled from his mouth, soft words full of emotion. He didn't understand where they came from. He'd never been a man of many words, and he'd never had the occasion to utter sweet things to a woman.

His hands roamed freely over her back, her hair, even her legs, and she didn't push him away. All he did was soothe her, show tenderness and caring, because he knew she needed it at this moment when her whole world had shattered into a thousand pieces. He wouldn't let her bear the pain on her shoulders by herself. He would carry the burden with her as much as she allowed him to.

"I won't rest until justice is done," Gabriel promised, not just to her, but to himself. A rogue vampire had hurt her, and he would have to pay for it. No one should be allowed to hurt a woman like Maya, a creature so perfect, he shouldn't dare desire her.

But he did.

Holding her in his arms, feeling her sweet behind in his lap and her head buried against his chest was the most divine feeling he'd ever experienced. She felt small against his body, so vulnerable, even though now, as a vampire, she was physically stronger than she'd ever been as a human. There was little that could hurt her physically now: her heart was another matter.

"What am I gonna do?" she suddenly wailed.

He rubbed her back softly, trying to reassure her that everything would turn out all right. "We'll figure it out together. I'll be with you all the way."

Gabriel wanted her to trust him. Him, the stranger she'd stared at with horror when she'd awoken. Her look hadn't escaped him. Her eyes had widened with fear and shock when she'd seen his scar. She'd been unable to tear herself away from the sight, and he'd seen that look before many times. But to be scrutinized by her in that fashion had hurt somewhere deep down. Had he really expected she would look at him differently? Had he really thought she would be able to look past the physical disfiguration and see the man underneath?

Gabriel knew it was dangerous to dream. If he allowed himself to hope, he risked an injury more severe than any knife could inflict. It was better to forget about the feelings this woman stirred up in him, the desire she invoked, the lust she unleashed. He would help her get through this—no matter what. Whether she would see more in him than just a mentor was doubtful, and it shouldn't matter. She needed him, and he wanted to be there for her—in whatever capacity she desired.

Maya shifted in his lap and instantly made him aware of the tightness in his pants. Merely by holding her in his arms, he'd gotten hard. He cursed himself for his inappropriate response. The last thing this woman needed right now was a horny vampire. And damn, was he horny.

He took a deep breath and tried to concentrate on getting his erection down, but with the air he sucked in her sweet scent. It nearly undid him. Her essence was pure and tempting. With a sigh, he buried his hand in her hair and gave himself over to his body's wants. Just for a moment, he would allow himself to feel before he had to bury his desires in the deep recesses of his heart.

Whether he tilted her head up to him, or whether she did it herself, he didn't know. But when her face was opposite his and her big tear-soaked eyes looked at him, time stood still. He saw a flicker of red in them and knew that her vampire side had taken hold. And then he saw the passion within her, the wonder in her eyes. The moment her lips parted, he was lost.

Without haste, Gabriel brushed his lips against hers, expecting her to pull back at the last moment. Instead, she accepted his lips, even nibbled on them. He did nothing to force her, only held still to savor the softness of her mouth. When he felt her tongue slide over his upper lip, he slanted his mouth and took charge.

He knew he wasn't the best kisser in the world. He sure hadn't had much experience—prostitutes in general didn't kiss much, and most other women had shied away from him, repulsed by his face. But with this kiss he watched carefully for her body's cues, hoping she would guide him to do what she liked.

Maya's lips parted wider, and he took it as an invitation to explore her with his tongue. Slowly he slid it into her mouth, tested and stroked. A soft sigh told him she approved, and he did it again, stroked his tongue against hers. Her taste was even sweeter than her scent.

Wanting more of her, he pulled her closer and deepened his kiss. When he felt her hands on his neck and in his hair, he knew she wanted more too. He'd never had a woman respond to him with such passion. His heart beat faster, and he felt the rush of blood pump through his veins.

Maya kissed him with such enthusiasm, he wondered whether he'd read her initial reaction to him correctly. Had she really looked at him with horror in her eyes? Was this kiss merely her way of dealing with the news she'd been dealt? And even if that was true, why shouldn't he allow himself to savor these few moments of joy—relish them even as he accepted that more was never going to happen, that this was all she'd ever give him?

Realizing that this could be the only time he would taste her, he ravished her mouth with the fervor of an invading barbarian. If he'd expected her to pull back, he would have been disappointed, because she matched his ferociousness with her own. Her tongue dueled with his, alternately stroking against him, then withdrawing so he would come after her. By God, the woman could kiss. Only now did he truly realize what he'd missed out on all his life.

She was like fire in his arms, sizzling, burning, consuming. Nothing else compared. He'd never imagined he'd meet a woman with so much passion inside her. A passion she seemed more than willing to share with him.

He wanted this, wanted her more than he'd ever wanted anything else in his life. Even more than he'd wanted Jane so many years ago—and that shocked him. He pressed her closer to him, and had she been human, he could have easily crushed her the way he held her tight. Too late he noticed a change in her. Gabriel pulled away just as she pushed against him to free herself.

Then he tasted his own blood on his lips.

Maya had bitten him.

6

Maya stared at the blood on Gabriel's lip, and all she could think of was to lick it off him and swallow it. The scent of his blood assaulted her senses, and she recognized undeniably that she was thirsty—thirsty for blood. While she'd never been squeamish when it came to blood— as a doctor she certainly couldn't afford that luxury—she'd never liked the smell of it, let alone felt the kind of inexplicable craving she felt for Gabriel's blood.

Confused, Maya scrambled off his lap.

She couldn't explain why she'd kissed him, kissed the very man who'd scared her when she'd first seen him, whose disfiguration had repulsed her. When she looked at him now, however, she felt no disgust. Only a deep attraction to him.

Gabriel stood and looked at her with an unreadable expression on his face. "Maya, I'm . . . " There was regret in his voice, or was it shame?

She stepped back and turned away from him before she could jump him and take his blood. She wanted to ask him so many questions, but in her present state she couldn't guarantee she could keep her hands off him. And all her fragile ego needed right now was another embarrassing situation like the one that had just happened. "It was my fault. It won't happen again." All he'd done was comfort her, and she'd bitten him in the process. How ungrateful was that?

She looked at the bathroom door, searching for an escape to be alone with her thoughts and to get away from his tempting scent. If she stayed in his presence any longer, she would succumb to it and maul him like a hungry tiger. "I need to take a shower."

Gabriel cleared his throat. "I'll send Yvette in to bring you fresh clothes." She heard his footsteps as he crossed the room, and seconds later the door closed behind him. She was alone—more alone than she'd been in her entire life.

When she stood in the shower, rivulets of warm water ran down her body as if they could cleanse her of the shocking news she'd been handed. She hoped against all hope that she was still in a dream—a completely wacko, makes-no-sense-at-all dream—and her life was still the same: she was a doctor, a pretty decent one, with aspirations to advance her career in medical research and the desire to make a difference.

Her research in the field of human sexuality, or more precisely, sexual dysfunctions in both males and females, was going well. She was on her way to breaking new ground, and her chances of winning a major federal grant to support her work were high. She couldn't just flunk out now. This was her life's work.

Maya touched her arms and legs and could feel no difference in them. They felt just as human as before. And her skin color was still the same. Weren't vampires supposed to be all pale and pasty because they couldn't stand the rays of the sun? Or would her color fade with time?

Maya stared at the glass enclosure of the shower and watched tiny streams of water descend along it onto the white marble beneath. There was no reflection of her in the glass. Was it enough to prove her a vampire? Couldn't there be another explanation? As a research scientist, she knew better than to jump to conclusions or take other people's statements at face value. She would have to tackle this whole situation the same way she approached her research: with logic, not emotion.

Her stomach rumbled, reminding her of how hungry she was. But instead of salivating for a nice big steak, she visualized the blood on Gabriel's lip. She'd seen the shock in his eyes when he'd realized that she'd bitten him. Gabriel had stared at her as if she'd gone crazy. And maybe she had, but she'd craved his blood. The memory of its smell made her drool even now.

She opened her mouth and let her finger slip over her upper teeth. They were still the same, only . . . there, one of the incisors felt pointier. She rubbed against it trying to see if someone had stuck some plastic onto it to make it pointy, but she couldn't detect anything wrong—the tooth was intact. Did she really have fangs? Maybe the tooth had always been that way and she'd never really noticed.

She touched her finger to the teeth on the other side of her mouth, and the same structure greeted her there. But the sharp edge wasn't enough to qualify as a fang. She remembered that she'd seen no fangs on either Gabriel or his friends. Could it be that fangs didn't always show, that they only came out when you needed them?

Maya closed her eyes and thought of her hunger, visualizing Gabriel's blood again. To her surprise, she sensed a tensing in her jaw. Something was happening. Slowly, the two incisors lengthened and drew into sharp tips. Her eyes flew open. This couldn't be happening! No, there had to be another explanation.

Was she really a vampire?

She had fangs, fangs to bite people, fangs she'd already used to bite Gabriel. Wasn't that proof enough? She'd bitten him, tasted his blood and liked it—no, loved it. What kind of creature would do such a thing if not a vampire?

Maya tried not to think about what had led to the bite, but it was hard not to remember the kiss they'd shared. Well, maybe shared wasn't the right word—she'd basically thrown herself at him like some starved-for-attention teenager.

She'd always been aggressive when it came to dating and sex, but the way she'd acted with Gabriel had been purely wanton. His arms had been gentle enough to comfort and soothe a child, yet she'd reacted with lust and passion. She remembered how hesitant his kiss had been, how reluctantly he'd given into her advances. But the more he'd held back, the more she'd gone after him, pressing herself against his muscled body like a bitch in heat.

The tears she'd shed in his arms had taught her one thing: she was not dead. Whatever she was now—vampire or not—her heart hurt as much as a human's, and her emotions were as deep as always, if not deeper.

What her new life would bring, she didn't know, didn't even want to guess at this point. What would she tell her family? She thought of her parents. She was an only child. How long would she be able to hide from them what had happened to her? She wondered whether she would be a danger to them, if she would attack them when she was hungry like she'd practically attacked Gabriel.

Would she have to stay away from her parents to keep them safe? Never see them again? She couldn't do that. She loved her parents.

They'd given her every opportunity in life, supported all her endeavors. She couldn't divorce herself from them. The thought hurt too much.

And her work? If she was truly a vampire, she could kiss her job goodbye—she couldn't remain a doctor if the sight of blood made her think of dinner. Just remembering the few drops of blood on Gabriel's lips made her salivate. She'd never smelled anything so delicious. Her stomach growled at the thought. Oh God, how she wanted blood. This was more severe than any of her chocolate cravings had ever been.

Besides, who wanted a doctor who could only work when it was dark? She wouldn't be able to serve her patients when they needed her. She would have to hide what she was. For sure, nobody would want to come close to her once they knew she was a vampire. Hell, she herself wouldn't want to get close. She couldn't really blame anybody else.

They would see her as a monster that hurt people. And wasn't that what she would have to do? Instead of helping people, she would have to hunt them and feed off them. An ice-cold shiver went down her spine at the disturbing thought. It was probably what Gabriel had meant when he'd whispered to her that he'd take care of her and teach her everything she needed to know. Teach her to bite humans?

Frustrated, Maya slammed her fist into the tile wall. It instantly cracked. Stunned, she pulled her fist back. With horror, she stared at the tile, then back at her fist. She felt no pain when clearly the impact should have hurt a little. She was too strong. She could easily hurt somebody without even wanting to, without knowing what she was doing. No, she could never see her parents again—what if she crushed her mother just by hugging her?

She pushed the tears back, not wanting to fall apart again. Somehow she had to deal with this, come to terms with her new life. Gabriel and his friends seemed to have themselves under control. So, somehow they must have managed to deal with their lot. There was no reason why she couldn't. She expected full well that it would hurt, that her transition wouldn't be easy, but she was a strong woman. Somehow she had to try.

Maya swallowed hard. She had to forget what her old life was like. The more she cried over it, the harder it would be to settle into this new one. She tried to cheer herself up by reminding herself that the attack— of which she had no recollection—could have killed her.

As hard as she tried, however, she couldn't remember what had happened. All she recalled was the sound of her heels on the pavement, the thick fog that night, the darkness. Even thinking back now, a cold shiver ran down her spine despite the hot water of the shower. Why couldn't she remember? Had she been so traumatized by the attack that her mind blocked out all recollection of it?

She'd heard of patients who'd temporarily lost their memory of a traumatic event. Was that what had happened to her? She closed her eyes and forced her mind back to that night. She'd parked the car, then she'd walked to her apartment building. And then, nothing. Only fog, darkness—a burned out light. Maya concentrated and tried again until her shoulder tensed and she spun around and opened her eyes. The white of the tiles was all she saw.

She reached for the faucet and turned the water off. It was useless to try too hard. Things would come back to her when she was ready, she was certain. She would take it one day at a time. Or maybe that was one *night* at a time: days were probably off-limits to her from now on.

She had questions, hundreds of them, and somebody better be answering them very soon.

As she dried off, she heard the bedroom door open and light footsteps echo in the room. A scent drifted into her nostrils: it wasn't Gabriel. She would have recognized his scent anywhere. It was strange and fascinating how her sense of smell, as well as her sense of hearing, was so much stronger now.

Maya wrapped the towel around her torso and walked into the bedroom.

Yvette stood next to the bed and laid a few pieces of clothing onto it. Without turning, she spoke. "You're about the same size as Delilah. I'm sure she won't mind if you wear some of her stuff."

"Thanks. Yvette?"

The woman turned and Maya had another chance to admire her beauty. Her model looks were only diminished by the slightly sour look on her face. "Yes?"

Maya shifted from one foot to another. "I'm thirsty." She felt as if she'd just confessed that she needed a shot of heroine. And in her own eyes it was just that: forbidden and dark.

Instead of giving her a disgusted look, Yvette actually smiled. Maya could easily imagine how men flocked to her when she turned on the charm. "That's to be expected. I brought you a couple of bottles."

Bottles of what? "I mean, at least I think . . . I want some blood."

"I know. Over there." Yvette pointed at the bedside table. On it stood two bottles with unrecognizable contents.

Maya approached. As she inched forward, she read the labels. The only thing printed on them was *O-positive*. Was this what she thought it was? "Is that—"

Yvette responded before she had a chance to finalize her thoughts. "Human blood. Not all of us actually go out and bite humans. We have evolved."

They drank blood out of bottles? No biting? For the first time since she'd awoken, a sense of relief spread inside her. She wouldn't turn into an animal that attacked humans.

"You don't bite people?"

"No, not for food anyway."

Maya decided not to have Yvette explain her comment. Thinking back to her kiss with Gabriel, her instinct told her that biting wasn't reserved for the purpose of food intake. And right now she didn't want to think any further about what had happened with Gabriel.

She picked up one of the bottles and unscrewed the top. She sniffed and inhaled the metallic scent. Her stomach recoiled. It smelled nothing like Gabriel's blood. This wasn't what her body wanted.

"It smells awful," she commented.

"Awful?" Yvette's incredulous tone gave her pause. "I thought you were thirsty."

Maya nodded. "I'm famished. But this is not what I want." Gabriel's blood had smelled delicious, and the enticing package it had come in— well, she didn't even want to think of it or she would charge downstairs and try to find him to get what she wanted.

Yvette shook her head. "We all drink this. It's first-quality; Samson only buys the best. Drink."

Maya set the bottle to her lips. The moment the blood touched her tongue, she virtually gagged. She tried to swallow, but couldn't get the repulsive liquid down her throat. She spat.

"It's God-awful."

A shocked look passed over Yvette's features. "But you *have* to drink human blood: without it, you can't survive. We all feed once a day, sometimes more often if we're injured or expend more energy."

Maya still had the vile taste of the blood in her mouth. All she could think of was to get rid of it. She didn't care what the others did—she wasn't going to drink that disgusting liquid. "I'm going to puke."

She ran into the bathroom and scooped water from the faucet into her mouth to wash out the taste. When she turned, she saw Yvette standing at the door.

"Maybe you've got it all wrong. Maybe I didn't turn."

Yvette shook her head. "The signs were all there. And besides, I can sense your aura."

Maya didn't understand. What kind of new-age junkie was she? "What aura?"

"Every vampire has a certain unmistakable aura. Only other vampires or preternatural creatures can see it. It's how we recognize each other."

"I don't understand." She couldn't see any aura.

"You will. You're weak right now because you haven't fed yet. Once you've recovered, you'll slowly find your new senses. So feed or I'm calling the doc and tell him there's something wrong with you," Yvette said.

That was all Maya needed: not only was she a vampire, now something was wrong with her. She couldn't accept it. "Let me try again."

When Yvette handed her the open bottle, Maya held her breath. Maybe if she didn't breathe the scent in, she would be able to swallow. Again, she put the bottle to her lips and took a swig. A second later, she spewed the red liquid over the white-marble counter and the pristine mirror. The droplets on the mirror created little rivers and ran down toward the counter, creating an eerie pattern of long strings meant to trap her and tie her up. Like a net in which she felt captured.

"I'm calling the doc," was Yvette's only comment.

Maya braced herself on the counter. "Maybe I need real human blood."

"This *is* real human blood. It's fresh, it's bottled. There's nothing wrong with it." As if to prove it, Yvette took a sip and swallowed. "See?"

There was no denying it. Yvette drank the blood without problems.

"Maybe I'm allergic. Are there any other brands?" Even as a human she'd had a few minor food allergies, so maybe this was all it was: an allergy to one type of blood.

"Allergic? Impossible. I've never heard of a vampire who was allergic to blood." Yvette's dismissal came without any hesitation.

"Is that the only blood you have?" Maya asked in desperation. She was starving, and her body told her she needed to eat, or drink, or whatever vampires called it.

"Samson keeps some O-neg somewhere. Let me check with Carl." She started toward the door. "Get dressed in the meantime."

The moment Yvette left the room, Maya slipped into the clothes she'd left. Whoever Delilah was, Yvette had been right. Delilah's size was almost the same as Maya's. The faded jeans fit her almost perfectly, and the soft, red T-shirt was only marginally too tight around her toned biceps.

By the time she was dressed, Yvette was back with another bottle. Maya read the label when she took it: *O-negative.* She prayed that this tasted better than the previous bottle and unscrewed the top. The whiff that hit her was even more vile than what she'd spit out only minutes earlier. They expected her to drink *that*? Nobody in their right mind would touch that awful stuff!

She pushed the bottle back into Yvette's hand. "I can't. This is even worse than the other stuff."

Yvette gave her another skeptical look. "This is the best blood out there. Do you have any idea how expensive it is to get O-neg? It's like a bottle of the best champagne."

"I don't care what it costs. I don't like it," Maya snapped. "Why don't *you* drink it?"

Yvette raised an eyebrow. "I think I will. The bottle's already open. No use in wasting good stuff."

Maya's stomach growled again, and she hugged herself trying to counteract the hunger. "Maybe I'm not a vampire."

Yvette *tsk*ed. "I know it's a hard thing to come to terms with, but denial isn't going to get you anywhere. You're a vampire, just like the rest of us. Get used to it."

"But then why wouldn't—or couldn't—I drink human blood? That can't be right. Have you ever heard of a vampire who won't drink human blood?"

Yvette pursed her lips. "I haven't, but maybe the doc has. Let's go downstairs and wait for him."

"What's his specialty, vampirism?"

Yvette shrugged. "I'm afraid all they've got here is a psychiatrist. This is a bit of a quiet backwater. In New York, we could get you a real doctor, but in San Francisco he's the only one."

"There are plenty of doctors in San Francisco."

Yvette gave her a meaningful look. "Sure there are, but not one who's a vampire."

Of course Yvette was right. Maya couldn't go to a real doctor. How on earth would she explain her hunger for blood on the one hand, but her body's refusal to drink it on the other? She needed to see a vampire doctor. How a psychiatrist could help her was beyond her, unless he could hypnotize her into drinking the awful stuff. Maybe that was what Yvette was getting at.

For sure, he must have heard of cases like hers. If not, then her own theory made much more sense: she couldn't be a real vampire if she didn't want to drink human blood. They had gotten it all wrong—she hadn't turned. She was still human. Maybe her freakish strength and lack of reflection was just temporary. There was still hope that this nightmare she'd awoken into would end.

7

Gabriel kicked the gas pedal down and crossed the Golden Gate Bridge in Samson's Audi R8 with a speed of close to eighty miles per hour. Traffic was light, and an occasion like this didn't present itself very often. Besides, racing Samson's sports car was the perfect outlet for his frustration.

The kiss with Maya had turned him inside out. If she hadn't accidentally bitten him—and he was certain it was an accident since she was still unaware of her true strength—he wasn't sure where things would have stopped. Well, he was lying to himself. He knew exactly where it would have stopped: with him fucking her until she'd used her new strength to fight him. Until she would have looked at his naked body and called him a monster.

Gabriel turned off the freeway and headed down the steep road into Sausalito, the once sleepy artist's enclave where these days no struggling artist could afford the rents or the high home prices. It had become a playground for the rich. No wonder: the views into the city were stunning.

He looked out to his right at the sparkling lights. He didn't miss daylight. In fact, he welcomed the absence of sun in his life. Nights could be beautiful. They concealed the ugliness of the world and only showed those things that sparkled and gleamed. In the shadows of the night, he could hide the ugly side of his face and be respected for the man he was, not the monster some perceived him to be. At night, he could pretend to be an ordinary man with ordinary desires and dreams: a loving wife, a family, a welcoming home. He knew he would be a good husband, gentle and loving, if only he were given a chance.

But in all the years since his transformation he'd never met a woman who hadn't looked at him with horror. He'd never even tried to make advances on any of them for fear of rejection. As a human he'd dealt with enough rejection, and one side of his face had paid the price.

Despite what Jane had done to him, deep down he knew he couldn't even blame her. He should have prepared her for what she would see.

Gabriel blinked the gruesome memory of his wedding night away and looked at the street signs. He was at the other end of Sausalito and had left the quaint little downtown behind him. To his right was the Bay and a small colony of houseboats. He slowed down, looking for the correct turnoff. At the last pier, he brought the Audi to a stop and killed the engine.

The witch's houseboat was the last on the mooring.

He'd crawled back to Drake after the kiss with Maya, and he'd made a deal with the Devil, giving the doctor what he wanted: the use of his gift. He hated himself for it, for giving into his baser urges, because that's what it was. Because he desired Maya against all reason. Because he hoped against all hope that there was a chance she could accept him if only he dealt with his predicament. Because her kiss had awakened that hope.

Gabriel wasn't sure what to think of Drake's connection to a witch, and he didn't really want to speculate. But it was odd, to say the least. Vampires and witches were sworn enemies. To have a witch among one's acquaintances or—God forbid—friends was dangerous for a vampire. If other vampires found out about the connection, one could be called a traitor to one's race. Repercussions would be severe. But at this point Gabriel didn't care anymore.

When he'd heard from his old friend Amaury that a witch had done some research on his problem, hope had risen in Gabriel. Now it was time to see if she could help him too.

Admitting one's vulnerability to a witch was dangerous because their spells could be powerful, and a vampire had little protection against spells. But Gabriel didn't think he had much of a choice.

He'd tried everything already, and still his problem hadn't disappeared. No, it prevented him from taking a willing woman into his arms and making love to her. He didn't want that to happen with Maya. He didn't want her to run from him in horror. He wanted her to kiss him again, to roam her hands freely over his naked body, to caress him. If he was made whole, maybe she could look past his external scar and accept him. Or why had she kissed him in the first place?

"Get off my property, vampire," a female voice came out of the dark.

Gabriel raised his head and saw the witch standing on the upper-level balcony, leveling a crossbow with a wooden stake at him. Her thin figure was silhouetted against the moonlight, keeping her face in the dark. But Gabriel's vampire night vision compensated for it. It was sufficient for him to determine that she was an attractive woman in her thirties.

Gabriel understood her hostility only too well. If she showed up at a vampire's house, she wouldn't be made any more welcome. He didn't take it personally. "Miss LeBlanc, you were recommended by Dr. Drake."

A little snort indicated that she didn't give a damn about the recommendation. "To do what?"

"I need a problem taken care of," Gabriel confessed.

"You should know better than to come to one of my kind for help. None of you can be trusted."

Gabriel went out on a limb. "If that were the case, you wouldn't have told Drake where to find you. After all, he's one of us."

"Is that so?"

He saw her face and her frown. What was she trying to tell him? Was Drake not to be trusted, or was he not one of them? Gabriel knew for sure that Drake was a vampire—his whole aura radiated with a certain frequency and that was the way vampires recognized other vampires. Clearly the witch wanted to throw him off his game.

"I want nothing for free."

"And I'm not doing any favors," she countered.

"I ask none. I have means to pay you."

"Money is cold," she answered.

"So is loneliness." If he could get her to take his case, he would have to hook her in first.

"If you didn't suck people's blood, you wouldn't be lonely. Ever thought of that?"

"I don't bite people."

She raised an eyebrow. "Ah, you're one of those who think of themselves as more civilized because you drink it from a bottle. Doesn't make a hell lot of difference to me. It's still human blood."

"It's donated. Nobody gets hurt."

"Somebody always gets hurt," the witch claimed.

Gabriel shook his head. "We pay for what we take. It's not any different than you purchasing crow's feet for your potions."

She shrugged. "Unless you have something valuable to trade, I'm not interested in helping you."

"Don't you even want to know what it is I need help with?"

"Couldn't care less, vampire. Whatever ails you, I bet you deserve it."

"That's harsh, even coming from a witch," Gabriel responded, not giving up yet.

"Isn't the sun coming up soon? Maybe you should leave?"

"I always get what I want." He gave her an intense look. He'd never tried mind control on a witch, but it was worth a try. If she didn't want to play ball, maybe he could manipulate her. The ultimate goal was worth it.

"Stay out of my head, vampire. I'm stronger than you. Go back to your own kind. There's nothing here for you."

Realizing that tempting her with money wouldn't work, he tried to appeal to her humanity. "Have you never felt so lonely you thought the whole world had shut you out?"

There was a short pause. Had he gotten through to her? "You chose this life, vampire."

Gabriel had, but he was an exception: he'd chosen vampirism. Many of the older vampires like himself were turned against their will. These days, their society punished those who turned humans against their will—back in the old days, nobody had stood up for the innocents and their rights.

Only a handful of his kind were born into this life, and those were the hybrids, the lucky ones who could live in both worlds, the human and the vampire one, walk both in the light and the shadows. "Nobody really chooses this. We all get thrown in one way or another. Did you choose to be a witch?" he countered.

"None of your fucking business, vampire." She waved the crossbow. "Now go back to your own kind, and leave me be. I don't need any trouble. Not the kind you'll bring with you anyway. People like you are bad for business."

Gabriel squared his stance. He wasn't leaving. "I need your help." And he wasn't beyond begging either.

"Can't take no for an answer. Fine. Then try this."

He heard the release of the crossbow's string a split-second before the wooden stake whizzed through the air. Pure reflex made him jump. He landed in the murky water up to his waist, mud and silt working themselves into his boots and pants.

"Don't come back, vampire."

Gabriel watched her stomp off the balcony into the houseboat, slamming the door behind her. It appeared he had to come up with another way to convince the witch to help him.

8

"No!"

Gabriel heard the high-pitched scream the moment he stepped out of the car he'd just parked outside of Samson's house.

Maya! Somebody was hurting her.

He sprinted to the entrance, jammed his key into the lock and pushed the door open a split-second before he charged into the house without even bothering to close the door behind him. His muddy boots left a mess on the pristine floor, and his clothes were still damp from his unexpected bath. Carl would probably stake him if he saw the mess he was leaving in his wake.

Another scream came from the kitchen. "Let go of me!"

A moment later, Gabriel burst into the room. The scene he met with wasn't at all what he'd expected. Instead of an unknown intruder, his own colleagues Thomas and Zane were holding the struggling Maya against the wall, while Yvette was trying to pour a bottle of blood down her throat. Maya kicked viciously, her face furious, her lips pressed together now, refusing the bottle Yvette held against her lips.

"What the fuck is going on?" Gabriel shouted and rushed to jerk Yvette away from Maya. "Let go of her, now. All of you."

Neither Thomas nor Zane complied.

"She won't drink," Yvette explained as she let her gaze run over his form, a question mark clearly written on her face as she saw his muddy pants and boots.

"I said, let go of her, now." Maybe it was the fury in his voice or the fact that his fangs had pushed through and were showing, but Thomas and Zane instantly dropped their hold on Maya. She immediately moved toward him. Gabriel cupped her shoulders with his hands.

"What happened to you?" Thomas asked.

Gabriel gave him an impatient look. "Don't ask." There was no way he could explain his visit to a witch. Besides, he was the boss and didn't owe anybody an explanation. Gabriel's eyes scanned Maya's body for any injuries. "Are you okay?"

She nodded, but said nothing. Instead, she sought shelter in his chest as if she hadn't noticed his damp and messy clothes. Gabriel welcomed her trust in him, yet wondered why she felt comfortable with him. He was just as much a stranger to her as the others—a rather wet stranger at that.

As he put his arm around her back, he looked back at his colleagues. "Explain yourselves." He caught Yvette's look which focused on his arm around Maya. The flash in her eyes could only be interpreted as jealousy. The realization caught him by surprise. He'd never given Yvette any reason to believe that he was even remotely interested in her other than as a valued colleague. Or had he leaned on her too much for companionship and she'd interpreted him wrongly?

"She spit out the blood," Thomas explained. "We called the doc, and he said to get her to drink."

"Where's Drake?"

"On his way," Thomas replied.

Gabriel pulled away slightly from Maya to look at her face. "Is that true, that you didn't want to drink the blood?"

"It's disgusting! It tastes vile. It makes me puke," she spat.

"We weren't lying," Zane snapped.

Gabriel shot him a furious look. "And I guess it was your idea to restrain her and force her to feed." He didn't need to wait for Zane's answer to know he was right. "May I remind you that this is not World War II, and you're not running a torture chamber."

Zane's eyes narrowed. Gabriel watched as the cords in his second-in-command's neck bulged. At the same time, he felt Maya's body tense. Her instincts were sharp, he realized instantly. Zane had a short temper and a vicious streak. Violence was a way of life for him, and she was right to fear him.

"Whatever works." Zane's voice was cold and devoid of any emotion. If he weren't such a great fighter, Gabriel would have fired him years ago. But it was smarter to have Zane fighting on their side rather than an enemy's. And once Zane chose a side, he stuck with it. Where his fierce loyalty stemmed from, Gabriel could only guess, but knew he'd never know the true reason.

"You ever touch her again, I'll kill you," Gabriel warned, then swept his gaze over the other two. "That goes for all of you. Maya is under my personal protection. You harm her, you get to deal with me."

The shocked looks on his colleagues' faces told him that they took his threat seriously—as they should. He never made empty treats, and he never bluffed. He was the worst poker player ever for that very reason.

"Good." Gabriel turned his attention back to Maya. He was all too aware that he still held her in his arms, and maybe at this moment she felt the same awkwardness that he experienced, because she suddenly stepped out of his hold.

"Yvette was trying to force the blood down my throat when I'd already told her that it was making me gag," Maya said.

Yvette took a step forward. "I gave her the best-quality stuff. She's making it sound like I fed her animal blood."

"That's not what I said. The taste and smell of it makes me sick. I can't drink it. Don't you get that?" Maya fisted her hands at her hips and stared at Yvette.

Not wanting a cat fight on his watch, Gabriel raised his hand. "Okay, let's just go over this in detail. Yvette, what did you give her?"

"Nothing I wouldn't drink myself." When Gabriel raised his eyebrow, she continued, "First the O-positive bottle, then even the O-neg. You know Samson always has the best supplies. But she wouldn't even drink O-neg. I've never heard of such a thing."

"Maybe I'm allergic," Maya interrupted.

"Impossible," Thomas answered.

"Unheard of," Zane agreed with his colleague. "Vampires aren't allergic to blood."

Gabriel nodded. He had to agree with them. Never in his long life had he heard of a vampire who would be repulsed by human blood. "Maya, a newly turned vampire's overwhelming thirst makes sure you drink whatever human blood is available. It's instinct, pure and simple."

Maya's other instincts seemed to be working just fine—her instant response to Zane's aggression had shown Gabriel that she was fully attuned to her natural sense of self-preservation, but why she wouldn't feed, he couldn't explain.

"Maybe I'm not a vampire then," she replied.

Gabriel swept a long look over her form. He could clearly sense her aura, and if that wasn't enough to prove to him what she was, he remembered the moment she'd bitten him. He'd felt her fangs graze him. No, she was a vampire. "Something is wrong."

Maya swallowed hard at Gabriel's words. Wrong? There were a hell of a lot of things that were wrong. For starters, she was a vampire—even if she couldn't yet accept this fact—when she should right now be at the hospital diagnosing and healing patients. In addition, she was pretty much locked up in a strange house with four strangers—no, make that five with the butler—when she should be at her own little apartment. She wore the clothes of a woman she'd never met. Wasn't that enough?

Apparently not. So she hadn't turned into a normal vampire then—that was just her hard luck. Instead of craving human blood, like they told her every newly turned vampire did, she found it disgusting and gagged on it.

But what they didn't know and what she wouldn't—couldn't—tell them was that what she really wanted was to take a bite out of Gabriel. Literally. The moment he'd stepped into the kitchen to rescue her from his obnoxious friends, she'd fought against her urge to sink her fangs into his arm and feed from him. Yes, feed. That's what they called it.

When he'd held her to his chest, she'd inhaled his scent deeply. Her senses were so sharp that she could virtually smell the warm blood underneath his skin, so close for the taking. If only his friends would leave the room, maybe she could somehow overwhelm him and take what she needed. And what she needed wasn't only his blood. She wanted his arms around her and his naked body on top of her or underneath her—whichever way she could get him.

Maya shook the thought from her mind. She wasn't an animal that attacked without regard for its victims, but by God, she wanted Gabriel's blood. And she wanted his body just as much. What had she become? A creature driven by her needs alone? Had she lost all her humanity?

She didn't want to believe it. Her sense of right and wrong was still in place. Her fears still the same as ever, her passion unbridled and ready to be unleashed on the unsuspecting man who'd done nothing but help and comfort her.

She looked up at Gabriel. Strange. Only hours ago she'd been scared out of her wits at the sight of him. The ugly scar had looked menacing. But all the things he'd said and done since had started overriding his outside appearance. When she looked at him now, there was no ugliness, only a man who was trying to protect her.

And how did she want to repay him for his kindness? By biting him.

She couldn't allow herself to do that. She had to get out of this place. Without a word, she turned on her heels and rushed out of the kitchen.

"Where're you going?" she heard Gabriel's voice behind her. "Maya!"

But she didn't want to listen to him.

In the corridor, she turned toward the stairs. She needed her handbag with her keys so she could go home. Before she could set even one foot on the first step, Gabriel was already behind her and turned her around to face him.

"What's wrong?" he asked, his face a mask of concern and confusion.

She tried to find the right words, but nothing came out. How could she tell him what she really wanted? To sink her fangs into his neck while she explored his naked body with her hands, when all he wanted was to protect her.

"I promise they won't hurt you anymore. They fear me too much. I'm their boss. Nobody will touch you or force you to do anything you don't want to do," he promised.

Maya shook her head. She believed him, but it wasn't enough. "I don't belong here. I'm going home."

Gabriel's mouth dropped open. "You can't go home. That rogue is still out there. It's too dangerous."

"I need to go home. I can't stay here with you. This is not my life. This is not me." Tears started welling up in her eyes again, but she pushed them back. "I have a job, a life. My parents—what will I tell my parents? And my friends? Paulette and Barbara will be so worried if I don't tell them where I am."

"We'll help you figure things out. I will help you," Gabriel insisted.

"And what, make up lies to hide what I am? Or will I be dead to everybody else?"

His hand stroked over her arm in a gesture so comforting, she wanted to lean into him.

"We all have to make up new lives for ourselves. We stay young while everyone around us ages and dies. I'll help you figure out what to do about your parents and your friends. But for now, you can't tell anybody, not while we're trying to take out the rogue."

"And then what? What will I do with my life? I can't be a doctor anymore. That's all I know how to do—and now, I'm a freak, don't you understand? I'm not normal. And I won't drink human blood. I just won't."

"You'll die if you don't," a voice came from the entrance door before it slammed shut.

Maya's gaze snapped to the man who now stood in the foyer. Tall and skinny, he looked at her.

"That's Dr. Drake, and as much as I'd like to disagree with him, he's right," Gabriel added.

"Looks like I came just in time." Drake stepped farther into the house and stretched out his hand toward Maya. "We've met before, but I'm afraid at our last encounter you were unconscious." Then he turned to Gabriel and looked him up and down. "I see your visit wasn't welcome."

Maya had no idea what the doctor was referring to, but apparently Gabriel did, because his next word sounded more like a warning than a greeting. "Doc."

With a smile Drake perused her. "The turning completed well, thanks to Gabriel."

Maya looked at the doctor. What did Gabriel have to do with her turning? They'd told her a rogue had attacked her and turned her. When she gave Gabriel a questioning look, he dropped his lids slightly as if he wanted to hide from her scrutiny.

"What do you mean?" she asked the doctor, staring right into his blue eyes.

"Well, surely, they told you what happened."

Maya's hackles went up. They were keeping something from her. They hadn't told her the truth. "No. Why don't you?"

Drake looked from her to Gabriel and then back. He appeared flustered.

"You were in pretty bad shape when they found you. The turning had started, but it didn't take. We only had two choices: let you die or turn you fully."

Memories of the previous night flashed in Maya's mind. "You didn't let me die." She remembered the pain and the cold. And the strange dream she'd had.

"No, Gabriel turned you fully. He gave you enough of his blood for the turning to take. For all intents and purposes, he's your sire."

Maya's mouth gaped open as she looked back at Gabriel, who stood a mere three feet away from her. Now it all made sense. Her dream hadn't been a dream at all. That night she'd fed from Gabriel's wrist, she'd felt his body warm her, comfort her. Now it was no surprise that he was so protective of her. To him, she must feel like his daughter. No wonder he'd been so reluctant to kiss her and had looked so ashamed and guilt-ridden when the kiss had ended.

Was it regret she saw in his eyes now?

"There was no time to waste. I had to act," Gabriel said, and it sounded like an apology.

Had he acted rash and made a decision he now regretted? She didn't want to know, couldn't ask him, but his eyes said it all: so much regret, so much pain. He'd taken on a responsibility she wasn't sure he wanted. That's what she was to him: somebody he had to take care of because he'd turned her. He'd made her into what she was.

"You owe me nothing. You saved my life, and I thank you for it," she pressed out, trying not to cry. But she wouldn't take anything else from him. Not even his offer of protection, which clearly came from a misplaced sense of responsibility, knowing that it was his blood that had eventually turned her into a vampire. His blood that ran through her veins. Was that why she lusted after his blood? And was that the reason she felt this attraction for him?

"Dr. Drake, I'd like you to examine me."

"Certainly. Let's use Samson's study," he answered and pointed toward a door at the end of the corridor.

When Gabriel made a move to follow them, she added, "In private."

Maya caught his look from the corner of her eye. What she saw stunned her. He was hurt? Shouldn't he be relieved that she had released him from his obligation to take care of her? Yet he looked anything but.

Maya shut the door of the study behind her and let herself fall against it. The room was wood-paneled with dark wood and a collection of overstuffed bookcases. The large antique desk held two computer screens and other assorted gadgets. It appeared the owner of the house—Samson, she assumed—liked his electronic toys.

"How are you feeling?" the doctor asked.

She gave an impatient wave with her hand. "Let's cut to the chase and talk doctor-to-doctor."

He nodded. "Fine."

"Even though I hear you're a psychiatrist, I guess you're the closest they have to a real doctor in San Francisco."

Drake frowned. "Psychiatry is a *real* medical discipline."

"Anyway. Let's just hope you can clear up a few things for me—at this point I wouldn't care if you were a veterinarian."

"What is it I can help you with?" The doctor didn't seem to mind the reference she'd made, and silently she thanked him for his good-natured behavior. She needed his cooperation.

"You said that Gabriel sired me. Does this make me his daughter?" God help her if she was lusting after her father's blood—and body.

"Not at all. Of course, there's always a certain affinity between a sire and the vampire he creates, but mostly it's because when a vampire is created, he generally sticks with the sire and his family. Take Carl, for example. Samson sired him when he found him dying after a vicious attack. It was entirely natural that Carl would stay with Samson, since he was the only vampire he knew and could teach him all he needed to know. So, while friendships often develop, it isn't a matter of whose blood you carry. There have been plenty of incidents where a vampire killed his sire."

While Maya was relieved to hear that she wasn't considered Gabriel's daughter it didn't explain why she would want to drink his blood.

"Have you ever heard of a vampire who wouldn't drink human blood?"

Drake pursed his lips. "Well, it's very unusual. I admit I've heard rumors of vampires drinking synthetic blood somewhere on the East Coast, and even of some vampires who drink animal blood because they don't like the idea of hurting humans. But I've never actually heard of one who won't drink it at all. Tell me why it is that you don't want to drink it," he prompted.

"It tastes disgusting. I gag as soon as it touches my taste buds."

"Fascinating."

Maya gave him an exasperated look.

"Sorry," he apologized. "But you must admit that from a medical standpoint, this is quite intriguing."

She had to agree with him. Whether she wanted to or not. During her research while a fellow, she would have loved to be presented with a case like hers—something to really sink her teeth into—so to speak. But now that she *was* the case, the fascination wasn't quite as huge.

"How are your research skills?" she asked Drake.

He shrugged. "Reasonable, why?"

"Listen, I need you to do something for me. I need you to research what could cause this aversion to human blood. Anything you can find. Allergies, genes, preexisting conditions."

She would research it herself, but she knew nothing about vampires—where would she even start? No, Drake had a better chance of connecting the dots, and besides, she needed all her energy just to fight her desire for Gabriel's blood. Maya grabbed a pen and piece of paper from the desk and scribbled on it. "Here, this is my logon and password to my medical files. It will give you anything I've ever suffered from. I want you to find out what's wrong with me."

He took the paper from her. "You want me to access the Medical Center's electronic medical records?"

"You do know how to read a medical file, don't you?" She paused only long enough to acknowledge his frown. "How long do I have until my body starves?" When she spoke the words, a chill went down her spine. She pushed it away. If she wanted to succeed, she had to think logically. She couldn't let her emotions interfere.

"I'm not entirely sure, but the thirst will grow and it will become painful. Your body will be able to sustain itself for a few days, but you'll slowly start to go crazy from the thirst. Are you sure you can't drink it?" He gave her a pitying look.

She nodded. "I'm sure."

Drake turned toward the door, but she stopped him before he opened it.

"Another question. Have there ever been cases where a vampire thirsted for the blood of his sire?"

Drake's eyes went wide. "Once the turning was complete?"

Maya nodded.

"Dr. Johnson, if that's what your body needs, you have to tell him."

And be even more indebted to Gabriel, who clearly only saw her as an obligation? No—it wasn't an option. She shook her head. "Good night, Dr. Drake."

9

"What do you mean by 'nothing'?" Gabriel asked and stood.

"Exactly what I said. I don't remember a single thing about the attack." Maya looked past him at the other three vampires—Thomas, Zane and Yvette—who sat and stood around the living room listening to their boss.

After Drake had left the house, Gabriel had changed into clean clothes and assembled everybody. One hundred percent professional, he'd informed everybody that it was time to find the rogue. Maya's sharp sense of hearing had picked up the short conversation he'd had with Drake. True to his professional oath, the doctor hadn't revealed Maya's confession, other than telling Gabriel that he was looking into the problem of her not drinking any human blood and would come back with a solution soon.

If Gabriel was still concerned about Maya, he didn't show it. His face was a stony mask, showing no emotions. His scar seemed menacing again. Maya wondered whether she had imagined the handsomeness she'd seen in him only hours earlier. Maybe even the kiss she'd stolen from him had been imagined, because the hard man who looked at her now couldn't possibly have been so gentle and whispered all those sweet encouragements to her.

"What's the last thing you remember about that night?" Gabriel probed.

Maya sat back and let the sofa cushions support her. "I was on my way home from the hospital. It was late, well after midnight. I'd gotten called around eleven, and by the time my patient was stable, it was after twelve."

"Were you walking home?"

Maya shook her head. "No, I had my car, but I couldn't find parking that late at night, so I circled around the block a few times. In the end I had to walk two blocks."

"Did somebody follow you from where you parked the car?" Gabriel's questions came at her like bullets. If she didn't know any better, she would have thought he was a police officer, not a vampire.

"No. I didn't hear any footsteps. Just, uh . . . "

Gabriel gave her questioning look. "Just what?"

Maya made a dismissive gesture with her hand. "Nothing, really. Only, I had a strange feeling." She forced her mind back to that moment, and a cold whiff of air seemed to blow past her neck, raising the tiny hairs on her nape. But no memory of the fateful night was forthcoming.

"What happened then?"

"I don't know. I don't remember anything after that."

"You don't remember being attacked and being bitten?"

Instinctively Maya's hand went to her neck and rubbed the spot where the skin was still tender. "No."

Gabriel's gaze traveled to her neck. "That's where he bit you. He drained you until your blood pressure dropped so low your heart was about to stop. At that very moment, he fed you his own blood."

Maya swallowed back the bile that rose from her stomach. She was glad she didn't remember anything about the attack. "I'd rather not know what happened." It made forgetting easier.

"I know." Gabriel gave her a sad smile, and at that moment she could have hugged him for his show of compassion. Then he looked at his colleagues. "Maybe the shock made Maya forget? A way of her mind protecting itself?" he asked them.

Thomas shook his head. "Not so sure. Many of us were turned in the most horrible fashion, and most of us remember our turning. More like somebody messed with her memories."

Gabriel nodded. "I was afraid you'd say that. I've been wondering about the same thing."

"Don't mind me—I'm going out to have a snack while you demonstrate your gift," Zane announced and walked toward the foyer.

"There's blood in the pantry," Gabriel offered.

Zane gave a half-smile, if it could be called that. The man didn't seem to be capable of a true smile; instead, his lips merely twisted slightly. "Thanks, but no thanks. I prefer my food fresh." He gave Maya a salacious look and seemed to revel in her shock. "Back in an hour."

As Maya's mouth gaped open, Zane sauntered out of the house. Was he really going out to bite somebody? Hadn't Yvette told her that they were all civilized vampires who drank blood out of a bottle?

"Don't mind him. He's got his own rules," Yvette explained. "Not all of us can be as civilized as Gabriel. Isn't that right?"

Maya followed the look Gabriel and Yvette exchanged. Suddenly there was a tension in the room she couldn't explain. Was something going on between the two?

Thomas brought the conversation back on topic. "Well, Gabriel. Pry into her memories then and get us something we can work with. It's kind of hard to find a rogue when we've got nothing to go by. Even a bloodhound needs a little bit of a scent to spur him on."

There was something about the words Thomas used that seized Maya's attention. A scent. That was it. She could clearly distinguish the different vampires by their scents now, and Gabriel even more so because she'd had his blood. She leaned forward on the couch.

"All you need is a scent?"

"It would help," Thomas admitted.

Maya looked up at Gabriel. "You just said that the rogue already fed me some of his blood before he was interrupted."

"That's right," Gabriel answered.

"Then can't you take that scent that's in me and find the rogue with that?"

Thomas inhaled deeply, then shook his head. "All I can smell is your own scent and the faint underlying scent of Gabriel. Whatever was there from the rogue is long gone."

"Damn." Maya let herself fall back into the couch.

"It's not a bad idea though," Gabriel admitted. "Thomas, Eddie was one of the guys who found her. Why don't you talk to him and ask him if he noticed anything?"

"Sure. But you know Eddie is still young. Even if he smelled that rogue on her, there's no guarantee he'll remember the scent and would be able to find out who the guy was."

"Try it anyway. Talk to James, too. It's worth a try."

"No problem, I'll talk to Eddie when I get home. He should be done with work soon."

"You guys work?" Maya asked, totally confused. What kind of jobs would vampires have?

"Of course we do," Thomas answered. "Some need the money, other's the diversion. When you're immortal, you need a hobby or a job, otherwise you'll just get bored out of your skull."

Maya could only imagine too well. After a week on the beach she was generally ready to climb up the walls and try to find something useful to do. Not that lying on the beach would be an option these days. "What do you do?"

"We're bodyguards," Gabriel cut in. "We run a company called Scanguards. Samson started it, and one by one we all joined."

"Who does the company protect?"

"Politician, entertainers—anybody really who can afford our services."

"But you're vampires. I thought you can't go out in daytime." Something didn't make sense.

"That's right. But not all our employees are vampires. We have lots of human employees who work the dayshift."

"And your clients know?"

Gabriel raised an eyebrow. "About us being vampires? No. We're careful. Only some of our most trusted human employees know. And our non-human clients."

Maya could barely get her head around the news. Vampires who protected people. "You're a bodyguard too?" Maya let her gaze sweep over Gabriel's muscular form. She could fully imagine him protecting somebody—he could guard her body any day or night.

Looking at Thomas and then at Yvette, she could definitely picture them as bodyguards too. And Zane? Well, Zane was just pure evil and anybody who was willing to have Zane protect him had to be completely loony if anybody asked her.

"That's how I started out, but these days I don't do any fieldwork anymore. I now run the operations in New York," Gabriel corrected.

For some reason his statement made her feel disappointed. Why should it matter to her where he lived? Wasn't it better that he lived in New York and would soon be physically removed from her as a temptation? At least then she could come to terms with the hunger she was fighting. Even now, she could barely stop herself from attacking him to drink his blood. And the closer she was to him, the worse it got. Maybe if he were back in New York she could find a way to deal with this.

"Maya." Gabriel's voice jolted her.

"What?"

"I asked whether I can have permission to delve into your memories."

All three vampires looked at her expectantly.

"How do you do that?" The idea that he wanted to somehow probe around in her head didn't sit well with her. What if he saw things she didn't want him to see? Would he see that she lusted after his blood? And if he found out, what would he do about it? Lock her up so she couldn't attack him?

"It's a psychic gift I have," Gabriel explained calmly, "I can reach inside a person's mind and see their memories. It won't hurt."

Maya wrapped her arms around her waist. "Does that mean you can read my thoughts?"

He shook his head. "No. I can't read minds. I can only see memories of events the way the person saw them with their eyes. I can't see what a person was feeling or thinking."

Relief washed through her. At least this sounded less like a violation than she had first suspected. "Fine. Go ahead. But I'm telling you, I don't remember anything else."

"We'll see."

Gabriel sat down next to her on the couch. It only intensified the scent of his blood. "I can do it remotely without touching you, but it works more effectively if I can put my hands on you."

His statement made her flush. She felt blood pumping through her veins at warp speed. If he touched her, would she drag him toward her and sink her fangs into him? Maya swallowed hard and willed her voice to sound disinterested when she answered him. "Sure, you can touch me if that helps."

"Thank you."

Maya moistened her dry lips. She felt the heat in the room more intensely now, but it was nothing compared to what hit her when Gabriel took hold of her hands. A searing bolt of electricity shot through her body, and she jerked involuntarily.

"Relax, Maya. It won't hurt. I promise." His voice was soothing, but it did nothing to ease the uproar in her body.

She clenched her jaw shut, and for the first time she was truly aware of her fangs. They itched to descend and lengthen. She closed her eyes and inhaled to try and make herself relax. But it had the opposite effect. All she could smell was Gabriel's masculine scent and the richness of his blood, a mixture of expensive wood and the distinctive scent of bergamot.

The glands in her mouth salivated for a taste of him. Even just a little trickle of blood from his lip would ease her thirst. Maybe that combined with the soft press of his lips against hers, or a stroking of tongues against each other. And maybe by accident, her fangs would graze his lip and draw blood that she would lick from him as he lay panting underneath her.

"I'm not sure I can do this," Maya said, her skin feeling flushed and hot.

"Shh, I'll only go back to the night when it happened. I won't probe into anything else."

She hoped it would be quick. How many more minutes would she have to endure the soft touch of his warm hands that created a delicious tingling sensation on her skin? A woman could go crazy like that, or was it the lack of blood? Was it the insanity Drake had warned her about? Had it already started? If it was getting worse, she'd have to lock herself into a room and throw away the key; otherwise, Gabriel wouldn't be safe from her.

Gabriel held Maya's hands in his and realized that he had trouble concentrating. Normally, touching the subject made it easier to get access to the memories. In this case it was a complete distraction. But it was too late. He couldn't pull back now. It would only show everybody how she affected him. And he didn't want anybody to know, not his colleagues, and least of all her.

The fact that she'd dismissed him in front of the doctor like a naughty schoolboy had hurt and made him wonder about what had really happened between them. Had her kiss been spawned out of a temporary insanity brought on by the shock she'd experienced? Had she kissed him because she felt the same attraction he felt for her, or had it meant nothing to her?

A woman like her could have her pick of handsome men. He wasn't much to look at. Any of his colleagues were more attractive than he was. Sure, he was tall, muscular, and strong, but this wasn't the dark ages. Women these days didn't merely look at a man to provide for them. They wanted a handsome lover too. He wasn't handsome, nor was he a lover a woman would wish for.

Gabriel pushed away the unpleasant thoughts and concentrated on the woman he faced on the sofa. He pressed his thumbs into her palm and stroked gently, making little circles. Her scent drifted into his nostrils and engulfed him. He concentrated on her aura, a misty white fog that surrounded her. He could see it more clearly now, because he'd attuned his own mind to her frequency.

He closed his eyes. His heart beat at the same speed as hers, and he breathed when she did. Their bodies were in synch. He imagined himself in her mind, and a moment later he felt himself transported. When he opened his eyes, he didn't see a scene in Samson's living room in front of him. Instead, he saw a dark street.

He heard Maya's footsteps like she would have heard them herself, felt the chill of the night fog. She searched for her keys in her bag, pulled them out. There was no light in the doorway as she reached it.

Then a voice, calling her name. The rogue had waited for her.

Then nothing. Darkness, except for a faint veil over the picture, as if the movie had gone grainy. He knew what it was.

Gabriel forced himself deeper into her mind and went back farther in time. He saw her going about her work, shopping in town, eating at restaurants with friends, but everywhere he saw the veil. He went back in time for six weeks and found where it started. Before that, all memories were clear—after that they'd been altered.

Gabriel blinked and released Maya's hands. He'd broken the connection.

Maya looked at him, her expression curious. "Nothing, right? Just like I told you."

He shook his head. "You knew him."

She jumped up from the couch. "That can't be."

Gabriel rose. "I'm afraid it's true. He called you by your name. He was waiting for you."

"Did you recognize his voice?" Thomas interrupted.

Gabriel turned to him. "No. Maya feared him. That fear distorted her memory of his voice. I don't know who he is."

"But I would remember if I knew him. I would."

Gabriel looked straight into her worried eyes. "There's a reason you don't remember. He wiped your memory. A couple of times in fact."

"But I remember things before the attack, I remember fragments. I remember being at the hospital that night."

Gabriel nodded. "That's because he only needed to wipe out those memories that included him. When I looked into your memories, I went back about six weeks. I think you might have rejected him, so he wiped your memory and tried again. I saw the traces of where he altered your memories so there wouldn't be any gaps. It's like a veil. I think he stalked you."

He noticed the tremor travel through her body and wanted to pull her into his arms to comfort her, but he restrained himself. What if she didn't want his touch? When he'd taken her hands to delve into her memories, she'd practically recoiled from him. Did he suddenly repulse her? Did she regret their kiss?

"I suppose when I rejected him a second time, he decided to kill me," Maya mused.

"Not kill you," Yvette interrupted, "make you like him. Like us."

"But why?"

"Maybe he figured once your old life was gone, you'd accept him." There was a sad tone in Yvette's voice that Gabriel had never heard before. Was it the same loneliness he often felt?

"Makes sense," Thomas added. "Take away your options and you'll be more likely to accept what's being offered. Sick bastard."

Gabriel felt a much harsher curse on his lips, but stopped himself. It didn't help to curse the things he couldn't change. What was done was done. Now it was time to act.

They had to catch him. If this crime remained unpunished, it would result in lawlessness among their kind. But more importantly, he felt the urgent need to punish the man who had hurt Maya.

10

Maya was apprehensive about running into a neighbor as she, Yvette, and Gabriel approached her apartment. It was close to midnight, but with this being a Friday night, chances were high that somebody would come home late and see them. Gabriel didn't seem to be worried about it.

"We'll just use mind control on them, and they'll never know they saw you," he suggested.

"Excuse me?" Had she heard right? Was mind control what she thought it was?

Yvette smirked and answered before Gabriel could do so. "It's a very handy trick, and it's helped us stay under the radar all these centuries. I suggest you learn it quickly."

"One thing at a time," Gabriel cautioned and gave Maya a soft smile. Did the man have any idea how devastating his smile was when he unleashed it on her? "I want Maya to ease herself into her new life. And besides, in the beginning some of these skills can be tricky. If used wrongly, you could hurt yourself."

"Or one of us," Yvette said dryly. "You'd better not be trying out mind control on another vampire. It's meant for humans only."

Yvette's look told her there was more to the story. "What'll happen if I accidentally use it on another vampire—that is once I figure out how it works?"

Gabriel frowned. "The other vampire will automatically oppose your power and use his against you—it's an ugly fight, and generally only one comes out alive."

"Even if it's just by accident?"

"Doesn't matter," Gabriel explained. "When a vampire feels attacked by mind control, he defends himself out of instinct. Only the stronger of the two can break off the fight before the other's death." He put his hand on her elbow. "It's a dangerous skill. Thomas is the best teacher for it. I'll ask him to teach you when things are more settled."

"Why won't you teach me?"

"He's the better teacher, and you should always be taught by the best. I'll teach you other things, things that I'm better at than Thomas. I want you to learn everything you need to know from the best. Only then can I be sure you can defend yourself and be safe." The soft press of his hand on her elbow was reassuring, and so was the knowledge that he would teach her other things and wasn't passing her off to somebody else.

When they entered her one-bedroom apartment, Maya's hackles rose; it looked like somebody had been there. While the door had been locked, too many things weren't in their usual place. Even though she wasn't tidy by nature, living in a small place had taught her to keep the place in order.

"Somebody's been here."

Gabriel nodded. "I was counting on it."

"Why?"

"Because that means we have a chance of finding a trace of him. He might have left something."

Maya was surprised—she hadn't expected Gabriel to go all CSI on her. He surprised her at every turn. His skill of unlocking her memories had blown her mind, and he'd been right: she hadn't felt a single thing when he'd done it. Did this mean he could do this anytime, anywhere, and nobody would be the wiser? She cast him a sideways glance.

Gabriel looked imposing as he surveyed her living room with purpose, letting his eyes run over her bookshelves which were bursting with medical textbooks. His long fingers trailed along the spines of the books. When he shifted his stance to stretch for the upper shelves, she noticed his buttocks flex under his faded blue jeans. That man filled out a pair of pants like no other. Maya wondered what it would feel like to sink her fangs into the firm flesh of his ass and suck his blood.

She'd taken a step toward him when he suddenly turned. Startled, she gasped, hoping he couldn't read her mind as he'd assured her earlier. Before she could turn away, he put his palm on her forearm.

"Something wrong? Do you sense something?"

Maya shook her head and lied, "Other than the fact that I'm sneaking around my own apartment like a thief in the middle of the night? Not really."

"Daytime is unfortunately out of the question," Gabriel answered with a shrug.

"I figured that much. Don't mind me, I'm just cranky." More than that, she was hungry, and if she didn't put some distance between them, Gabriel would turn into dinner. "I'd better check my messages."

She walked to the phone and looked at the blinking answering machine. Three messages. She pressed the button.

"This is a recorded message from the Association of—" She pressed the delete button.

"Maya, honey, I just wanted to remind you to call Aunt Suzie next week. It's her sixtieth birthday, and you know how she likes to hear from you. And call me. I haven't spoken to you in a week. You're working too much."

She caught Gabriel's curious look. "My mother," she explained before the next message started.

"Where the hell are you? The chief is raving mad because you didn't show up today. Call me."

The machine went quiet. Maya put her hands against her temples. "Oh shit, that was Barbara. I completely forgot about work. They're gonna fire me."

She felt a small hand on her back. "Maya, I hate to break it to you, but you won't be able to continue as a doctor." She turned to look at Yvette and was surprised to see that there was compassion in her eyes. Yvette had said as much earlier. Maya didn't see it that way anymore.

"Actually, I don't see why I can't remain a doctor. It's not like I'm craving human blood. I should have no problems being around humans and treating their ailments. I'm not attracted to their blood." No, not to theirs, just Gabriel's.

"We don't know that yet for sure," Gabriel cut in. "For all we know, this is just a temporary problem. I guarantee you, once you're thirsty enough, you'll drink any blood that's available. Only once we know how you react to humans around you, can you even start thinking about whether remaining a doctor is an option."

She hoped he was right about the condition being temporary, but couldn't muster up the same certainty he displayed. And besides, there were other issues to be considered. "I'll have to live off something. Even if my food bill will go down that doesn't mean I won't need money to live. And that bottled blood can't be cheap either. Where do I even get that from? Mail order?"

Gabriel put a reassuring hand on her arm. "You shouldn't concern yourself with things like that right now. We have more important things to think of. And whatever you need, I'll take care of it."

Maya wasn't the only one who gave him an incredulous look. She noticed Yvette raising her eyebrows and twisting her mouth into a thin line. Had Gabriel just offered to pay for her living expenses? "Thanks, but I don't want to be a kept woman."

He grunted and turned away. Maybe her choice of words had been inappropriate, but the gist of what she'd wanted to say was there. She would not become dependent on a man. There had to be jobs that were tailor-made for a vampire. Working the nightshift at the blood bank? Guarding the cemetery at night?

Maya looked back at the answering machine. She should return her mother's call; she would be worried, and so would Barbara, the colleague she'd worked with for the last four years.

She lifted the receiver and punched in the numbers. Before the call connected, Gabriel's hand pressed the off button on the phone. "What the hell?" she yelled, already on the edge.

"Who are you calling?"

She would have told him, but the controlling tone in his voice pissed her off and spread uneasiness in her stomach. "None of your damn business. What am I, your prisoner?"

With a shocked look, he released his grip on the phone. "No. Of course not. Go ahead." He paused. "But be careful what you tell your friends and your family."

Maya let her shoulders drop. He was right. She had no idea what she was going to tell her mother; she'd just dialed without thinking what to say. Her gaze trailed to the photo of her parents on the sideboard. There was her father, his arm draped over his wife's shoulders, the two of them laughing at each other. She remembered when she'd taken the picture of them. It had been on the day of her graduation from medical school. Mom had put her golden hair up in an attractive bun, and Dad's short, light-brown hair was wet, as were his clothes.

"He told me he would jump into the pool with all his clothes on if I passed with a four-point-O," she said to nobody in particular. "I couldn't pass up the chance." When she looked up and away from the photo, she caught Gabriel looking at her, a soft smile around his lips.

"Call your parents. Tell them you're fine, but you're working extra shifts because a doctor is sick and you have to cover for him," he advised. "We'll figure out a more detailed and believable story later."

She nodded and swallowed back her tears. "It's too late. They'll be asleep. I'll call her tomorrow."

"Fine," Gabriel agreed. And then, as if he knew what she was thinking, he added, "You will see your parents again. I promise you. I'll arrange it for you."

She gave him a grateful smile. "Thanks."

"And now, can you look around and let us know if anything is missing or if there's anything that's not yours and might belong to him?"

Maya shuddered at the thought that the person who'd attacked her had been in her apartment. How close had she been to him? Had she kissed him, let him touch her? Or even slept with him? It wouldn't surprise her—unfortunately. She'd always had a varied sex life and most of her relationships hadn't lasted long.

She'd never been satisfied, not emotionally and never sexually. No man had ever been able to give her what she needed. Maybe it would have been easier if she'd been able to tell a man what she actually wanted and needed. But she'd never been able to voice her desires. All she knew was that they were dark, too dark for her own mind to put words to them. Whenever she'd had sex with somebody, she'd always wanted to feel more. Yet she didn't know what this *more* entailed.

Maya pushed the thoughts aside and went through her belongings, painstakingly going through drawer after drawer, shelf after shelf. Nothing seemed to be missing.

"Are you picking up anything?" she heard Yvette ask Gabriel.

"Nothing. He was careful." Gabriel's voice was even.

"Yes, odd. Do you think he knew we'd come here?"

"Definitely. It looks like he cleaned up after himself."

Maya stared out the window into the dark and shivered. She didn't want to stay here. The knowledge that he could enter whenever it pleased him, made her feel unsafe. "I'll pack a few of my things," she announced.

"Yvette, help her," Gabriel ordered. "We're done here."

In the bedroom, Maya threw a few clothes into a bag, then went into the bathroom. She opened the medicine cabinet over the sink and reached for her contraceptive pills.

"You won't need those," Yvette said behind her.

She hadn't noticed that Yvette had followed her, and the mirror didn't reflect either of them.

"How would you know? I'm not giving up sex just because I'm a vampire."

"Nobody is expecting you to. But you won't need those pills. Vampire females are sterile."

Sterile. The word hung in the air.

Maya gripped the sink for support. All these years she'd taken precautions against getting pregnant. All these years she'd been afraid of her contraceptives failing, a condom breaking, or any other stupid accident. And now, when she was told she no longer had to worry about that, she had to realize that she wanted to be a mother one day? How cruel could life be?

She felt Yvette's warm hand on her back and turned into it. "I'm sorry. I thought you knew. Only vampire males are fertile, and only when they're breeding with a blood-bonded mate. I know, it sucks."

Maya didn't understand what Yvette was trying to explain to her. "Breed? Blood-bonded?"

"Yes, in the end vampire males are just like their human counterparts. All they want is a woman who'll bear them a child. Only a blood-bonded human woman can take a vampire's seed. All we vampire females are good for is sex. So you'd do well not to lose your heart to a vampire—it'll only end in disappointment. I've seen it before."

Maya stared at Yvette with disbelief. This couldn't be true. Not only would she not have any children, children she hadn't known until now that she wanted, but no vampire male would want her as a long-term partner because she was sterile? Was this payback for how she'd treated so many men? For the fact that she'd broken if off as soon as she'd realized that the man couldn't satisfy her needs? For barely giving anyone a chance?

A sob tore from her throat.

A second later, Gabriel burst into the room. "What did you do to her?" he yelled at Yvette and squeezed between the two women, pulling Maya to his chest. She instinctively allowed herself to be cradled by him.

"I didn't do a thing to her!" Yvette shouted back and stormed out of the tiny bathroom.

Maya let out another sob. It didn't matter to her what Yvette's motivation for the blunt revelation was. In fact, she was glad for it, glad that she'd found out now.

Maya's sob went right through Gabriel's bones. He'd failed again. He'd promised himself earlier that she wouldn't have to cry anymore, and here she was, tears running down her face. He shouldn't have asked her to come to her apartment with them. She was still too fragile, still too sensitive to everything.

She pushed against him and pulled free. Did she not want his concern? "I'm fine," she claimed. He knew she wasn't.

"Why are you crying?" he probed.

"I'm not crying." She sniffed. "I think I'm coming down with something."

He tilted his head to the side. "What do you mean?"

"Just a cold or something."

Gabriel shook his head. Maya was avoiding him, and he didn't like it. "Vampires don't come down with anything. We don't get sick." Before he could get Maya to tell him what was really wrong, he heard a sound.

His head snapped to the small window over the bathtub. He hadn't noticed until now that it was open.

"Somebody's watching," he whispered to Maya and took her arm. He quickly led her back into the living room where Yvette sulked in an armchair.

"He's out there," he told Yvette, who instantly jumped up. "I'm going after him. You take Maya home."

"We have a better chance if we both go after him," Yvette protested.

Gabriel cut her off with a movement of his hand. "That's an order."

Without waiting for an acknowledgment, he stormed out of the apartment and out the front door.

The rogue had been watching them. That meant he now knew Maya had survived, but also that she was under Gabriel's protection. He might figure out where she was hiding. It was paramount that Gabriel found him before he could mount another attack.

The fact that he'd been watching her apartment—clearly in the hope that she would come back—made it clear to Gabriel that the rogue was obsessed with her. A stalker, just like he'd suspected. A jilted lover.

He hadn't seen the vampire who'd stood outside in the alley and had watched them, but he'd noticed that the alley was a dead end. This meant he had to have come back to the main street to escape. Therefore Gabriel didn't bother running down the alley and instead followed the faint scent of vampire the rogue left on his trail.

He zigzagged through Noe Valley. It was obvious to Gabriel that he was trying to get out of the quiet residential area and into a busier area so it would be harder for Gabriel to stay on his tail. Gabriel sped up, trying to gain ground on the rogue, but his relative unfamiliarity with the San Francisco neighborhood didn't help him. If this were New York, Gabriel would have cut the rogue off long ago, but chasing a man down on his own turf was much harder.

When he heard the sounds of music and partying, Gabriel knew he'd lost. A couple of blocks farther and he was in the center of the Castro. There seemed to be two dozen bars and clubs just on two blocks. And the sidewalks teamed with clubbers. Gabriel looked through the crowd and suddenly noticed the near-total absence of women.

Mostly men walked along the streets, some hugging, some holding hands, others kissing openly. Gabriel had been here before, many years ago. This was the gay center of the city, where the gay population had their special hangouts, where public exposure was the norm.

Gabriel stopped on a corner of a bar and pulled out his phone. A handsome young biker smiled at him and lifted his beer bottle toward him from the bar. Gabriel shook his head and turned away. Great, men were coming onto him—they obviously didn't mind his scar. Why couldn't a woman give him the come hither look? Not any woman— Maya specifically.

He dialed. His call was answered after the third ring. "What's up, Gabriel?" Zane breathed hard into the phone.

"Where are you?"

"Why?"

"Because I need you to do some work," Gabriel barked.

"I'm in the Mission, hot nightspot." Zane gave the address.

"I'll meet you there." Gabriel punched the address into the GPS on his phone. Zane's current location was only about six blocks away. For a moment, he froze. Could Zane have been the one he'd been chasing? Had he been able to run that far in the time since he'd lost his trail? Doubts coiling through him, he made his way to the address Zane had given him.

What Zane called a hot nightspot was more than just a nightclub. The bouncer at the door said nothing and let him pass inside the dingy establishment as soon as he was finished staring at Gabriel's scar. Occasionally, the darn thing did have its purpose. People seemed to be afraid of him and didn't give him any resistance.

It was dark, darker than in other clubs he'd been to, and the reason why became evident instantly. Along the outside walls were small booths, the entrances covered with transparent fabric, enough to distort the faces of the people behind them, but not sufficient to disguise what they were doing.

Gabriel wasn't surprised. His second-in-command's choice of entertainment always included sex, and if it was peppered with kink, even better. He followed his nose and found Zane in one of the booths. He stopped outside of it and looked through the gauzy fabric.

It was easy to make out Zane's distinct form. His bald head glistened. He was stretched out on a bench, his stiff cock sticking out of his leather pants. A woman was giving him a blow job while he had his fingers up the ass of a second one who was straddling his face.

The women were dressed, but on closer inspection Gabriel saw that the woman straddling Zane wasn't wearing any panties under her ultra-short skirt. By the looks of it, Zane had been here for a while.

Gabriel kept himself rigid as he watched how Zane sucked the woman's pussy and worked a third finger into her ass, ignoring the woman's attempt to pull away. With his free hand he slapped her ass cheek, and the woman squealed.

"Do as you're told," he heard Zane order her.

Gabriel contemplated interrupting him, but two things stopped him. Interrupting a vampire while he was having sex could turn ugly—Zane would turn his sexual energy into violence, and Gabriel didn't want to be on the receiving end of it.

The second reason was his own arousal. Gabriel liked watching—it often was all he got. And this time, it was more than just watching actors in a porn movie. This time, he could pretend that he was the man, and the woman above him was Maya.

The situation turned him on within seconds, awakening sexual desires darker than usual. Why he suddenly wanted unspeakable things—to indulge in sexual acts that seemed depraved and taboo—he couldn't explain. Was he getting so desperate that anything would arouse him these days? Gabriel shook his wicked thoughts off.

When Zane sank his teeth into the woman's thigh to draw blood, Gabriel knew the wait was over. A few moments later, he'd disentangled himself from the two women and sent them on their way. He didn't seem surprised that Gabriel was waiting at the entrance to the alcove.

Zane waved him in. "Been waiting long?"

"Long enough."

"You should have joined in; I'm not proprietary."

"No, thanks." Gabriel cleared his voice and sat down on the bench. He'd never gotten undressed in front of his friends or colleagues, and he wasn't starting now. Nobody knew what horror he was hiding. "I hope you wiped their memories."

"Standard procedure," Zane confirmed and stretched his long legs out in front of him. "You have a job for me?"

"The rogue was watching us at Maya's apartment tonight. He knows she's with us, so we'll have to step up our search. Have you found anything yet?"

Zane shrugged. "I'm working on it, as you can see."

Gabriel frowned—having sex with two women didn't look like working on finding a rogue.

"I have my methods."

"I'm aware of your methods. What could you possibly find out from two women you're fucking?"

"More than you think. Women talk. They notice things."

Gabriel gave a brief snort. "I want you to look into the alibis of all vampire males for the night of the attack. The editor of the *SF Vampire*

Chronicle will provide you with a complete list of vampire households. Supplement it with Scanguards' vampire staff list. Work your way through it. Only the males, only the straight ones. Exclude all blood-bonded males since they wouldn't physically have been able to drink her blood. I'm suspecting he's a jilted lover."

He hated the thought. Had Maya slept with him? Had she allowed him to touch her the way Gabriel wanted to touch her? At the thought his fangs itched.

11

Maya tossed in her bed. She'd told Yvette upon their return to the house that she was tired, and given that it was about an hour before sunrise, Yvette had shown no surprise at her request to rest.

Yvette had told her she was staying at the house on Gabriel's orders. She would be staying in one of the recently renovated rooms on the third floor.

At this point, Maya didn't care much about what anybody thought—the hunger pain was getting so bad that not even Yvette's open hostility could faze her. She could guess Yvette was annoyed—Gabriel's reprimand had probably stung.

But all Maya cared about was assuaging her hunger. She'd heard Gabriel come back shortly before sunrise, had heard him talk to Yvette before he'd come upstairs. She could have sworn he'd paused in front of her room, but then had walked to the master bedroom and gone inside.

Now everything was quiet.

Maya wrapped her arms around her stomach and curled into a ball. The cramps were getting worse. Not even her worst menstrual cramps could compare to the pain her empty stomach caused as it contracted in short waves. Having grown up in an affluent society, she'd never before experienced hunger. Was this what millions of people went through daily, or was it this painful because she was a vampire now, and all her sensations seemed to be magnified?

She couldn't let this hunger defeat her. She was stronger, she had to be. As the next wave of pain rolled over her and stole her breath, she knew she had to act. Maybe her hunger was great enough for her to overcome her aversion to the ghastly bottled blood. She would give it one more try—there was no way she could make it through the day. And there was no chance of Drake showing up until it was dark again even if he had good news.

Maya glanced at the clock on the bedside table. It was midmorning. No, she couldn't last till eight o'clock when sunset would occur.

Ignoring the pain, she swung her legs out of bed. She wore her short red nightgown but shivered in it, so she reached for her terrycloth robe and put it on.

Barefoot, she slipped out of the room and snuck downstairs. She didn't want to wake anybody, least of all Gabriel. He would make mincemeat out of her efforts to try human blood. Even now she could smell his blood. A shiver went through her, and she sped up and raced down the hall to the kitchen. The farther away she got from Gabriel, the better.

The kitchen was empty.

Maya opened the fridge and peered inside. As expected, it was filled with bottled blood. She grabbed one of the bottles and let the fridge door fall closed.

Trying not to give herself an opportunity to back out of it, she unscrewed the top. She held her breath like she'd done before and set the bottle to her lips. A moment later, she tilted her head back and took a gulp. The red liquid spread in her mouth. For all she knew, it could have been battery acid, so vile was the taste. She aimed at the kitchen sink and spat.

The drops that had reached her throat made her gag, and she coughed. There was no way she could drink this, not even if her life depended on it, which unfortunately, it did.

She held her mouth under the faucet and let the cold water wash out the taste in it, before she straightened. An instant later, her body cramped again and she doubled over. Trying to hold onto the counter, she accidentally knocked the bottle over, tossing it into the sink where it made a loud clank.

Unable to stand any longer, Maya tumbled to the floor. Black blotches appeared in front of her eyes. Before she could pull herself up from the cold floor, the kitchen door swung open. She first saw the long robe, then looked up and stared at Gabriel's face.

"Maya, oh God, what happened?" he asked, his voice frantic.

Without waiting for her answer, he crouched down and pulled her up. His scent instantly wrapped around her, making her hunger pangs even worse.

She pushed him away. "Nothing. Nothing happened."

He didn't let go. Instead, he clasped his hands tighter around her arms. "Let me help you. You're weak."

"Let me go," she demanded, knowing she couldn't resist much longer. She made a jerky movement and was surprised when she broke free of his hold. When he reached for her again, she lashed her hand at him, trying to stop him. Her hand swiped his forearm, but when her nails scraped over his skin, she realized her fingers had turned into sharp claws.

Blood trickled from the two short cuts she'd left on his skin. She stared at them. Blood. *His* blood. Right there. All she had to do was snatch his arm and pull it to her mouth, just lick it off him.

Her stomach lurched. Of its own volition, her hand reached out. She licked her lips in anticipation of the unexpected treat. Her nostrils flared, soaking in more of the delicious scent, and a deep growl dislodged from her chest. She felt like an animal, but she didn't care anymore. Her drive for survival was stronger.

Gabriel snatched her wrist before she could touch his arm and made her look at him. Realization flashed in his eyes. He dropped his gaze to the injury on his arm, then back to her.

She was prepared to fight for what she wanted.

"Oh God—it's my blood you want, isn't it?" he asked full of disbelief.

Maya only answered with a low growl.

"Come."

With an iron grip, he dragged her out of the kitchen and down the hall. Would he lock her up now to make sure she didn't attack him? She couldn't allow that. She had to fight him.

When he pulled her into the study, she wanted to protest, but her mouth was too dry to speak. She needed his blood, and she needed it now.

A second later she found herself on the couch, sitting in his lap.

"Why the hell didn't you tell me you wanted my blood?" His voice was furious.

She jerked at his hold, trying to get out of his arms, but he didn't allow it. "Damn you," she cursed.

"You stubborn woman. I could have fed you last night. Do you know how much I worried about you?"

Had he said *fed her*? Did this mean that he was prepared to let her drink from him?

"I need—" She broke off. She couldn't say it, feeling ashamed to express her need.

"I know what you need."

He pulled away the collar of his robe and swept back his hair. She hadn't noticed until now that it wasn't held back in its usual ponytail. As he exposed his neck to her, she watched him. Did he mean it? Did he want her to feed from him?

Gabriel caught Maya's confused look as he prepared his neck for her. He could let her feed off his wrist or forearm, but he wanted her closer, wanted to feel her body when she latched onto his vein and sucked the blood from him. Selfish, perhaps, but he wanted to experience the pleasure of having her pressed against him when she took his blood inside her.

"Sink your fangs into me," he ordered and pointed at the vein that he knew was clearly visible under his skin. "Here, I want you right here. And you won't stop until you're sated. If you even dare to stop before you've had enough, there'll be hell to pay."

"I don't want to hurt you," she mumbled.

He was astounded that, with the hunger he could clearly see in her eyes, she had any strength left to resist.

"You won't. Now drink or I'll make you." He recognized his own voice as gruff and knew it was because he was already aroused by the mere knowledge that a part of him would soon be inside her.

Maya nudged closer, and finally she dropped her head to his neck. Her plump lips brushed against his skin. He couldn't suppress the shiver that raced over his body, all the way from the spot where she touched him down to his big toes.

"Bite me, Maya, do it," he urged her. He'd never wanted anything more than her teeth in his neck.

Gabriel felt her fangs graze his skin and run slowly over his vein, which was ready to burst. Then her mouth opened wider and the sharp tips of her fangs pierced his skin, drove deeper and settled in his neck. When she sucked the first drops of blood from him, he shuddered.

Never in his long life had he experienced anything like it. Yes, she'd fed from him before, but she'd been unconscious and he'd given her blood from his wrist. Her fangs had never lodged within him. There had never been any occasion for anybody to bite his neck—no lover who might have done so in the heat of passion as he knew was common among vampire couples, not to feed, but to heighten their arousal.

He was completely unprepared for his body's reaction to her bite.

Paradise. It was the only way he could describe it. Like an electric current, a tingling warmth spread to every cell in his body, coiled around his spine and settled in his groin. His entire being buzzed with awareness.

Despite the bathrobe she wore, he could feel her body as if she were naked on his lap. Sparks seemed to jump from her body to his, like little electrical charges dancing between them. But there was still too much space between their bodies.

"Straddle me," he whispered into her ear. Without protest, she shifted, and he helped her move her legs to either side of his hips. For an instant, he wondered whether it was right to exploit the situation like he did, but it was too late: he wanted her as close as he could possibly get her. His body was craving hers.

With every ounce of blood she took from him, the euphoria in his mind increased. He'd never felt such freedom, such lightness, such bliss. Not a care in the world touched him. Loneliness was a word of the past. *Pain* might as well have been a Chinese word for he had no comprehension of the concept.

He buried his hand in her hair and held her to his neck, not wanting her to stop. His erection pressed against her, and she surely had to notice it, but she didn't pull away. He slid his other hand to the base of her spine and fanned his fingers. The light pressure he exerted was enough for her to respond: she moved to align her core with his hard length and rubbed against him.

Gabriel couldn't stop the loud moan from escaping his lips. He took a deep breath and inhaled her scent. Maya smelled of pure woman, ripe and aroused. He knew from his own feedings from humans—before he'd started on bottled blood—how sexually arousing it could be to drink directly from someone's vein. If he were a gentleman, he would ignore her arousal, stop pressing her against him and not take advantage. But the last thing on his mind right now was behaving like a gentleman.

Hell, he desired her, had from the moment he'd first seen her. Could anybody blame him for taking this little slice of heaven and enjoying it for as long as she wouldn't resist? For as long as she was too blood-drugged to care who was shamelessly rubbing his cock against her warm center?

The pressure in his balls built, and he knew he would have to stop holding her this tightly before he made a complete fool out of himself and came in his boxer shorts. But not yet. He needed to feel her a little while longer before he would go back to his bed, alone, only with her scent still clinging to him, and the ghost of her soft body pressed to his. Then he would touch himself and imagine it was her soft hand stroking him, and not his own rough calloused one that squeezed him tightly until he would release his seed, pretending he flooded her warm sheath with it.

Too soon, he felt her pull away and remove her fangs from his neck. He wanted to hold her back, tell her to continue, but he knew he couldn't. When he looked into her eyes as she faced him, he knew she was sated. Her face looked fuller, her skin glowed, and her eyes had a brilliant sheen to them. She'd never looked more beautiful to him.

"Thank you," she whispered and dropped her gaze as if she was ashamed of what she'd done.

"My pleasure," he answered and meant it. "You'll have to feed from me daily."

She raised her eyes to look straight at him. "But . . . I mean you can't—"

"Your body clearly needs it. We all feed daily," he insisted. It was the truth, but nevertheless, he felt like a thief—knowing he'd steal this pleasure from her every day.

"I can't just take from you without giving anything in return. It's not right," she claimed, proving to him that she had more integrity than he could ever muster.

"If it's the only thing you can drink, then that's what it's going to be. You'll feed from me. And you don't owe me anything." She'd already given him more than she could ever imagine. Just knowing that he would get to hold her every day when she fed from him was more than he could ever wish for.

"But I want to give you something in exchange; I can't just eat for free. It would just be like paying for dinner."

He smiled at her comparison. He had more money than he knew what to do with. There was nothing he wanted. Except maybe . . .

"A kiss," he blurted before he could stop himself. When he saw her reaction, he instantly wanted to take it back. Her eyes widened in surprise, and her lips parted as if she wanted to make a snide remark. Then her gaze zeroed in on the right side of his face where his scar marred his skin.

He swallowed hard and turned his disfigured face away from her. He'd screwed up the most perfect moment of his life because he'd let his desire rule him for an instant. It was stupid. Now, not only would she not kiss him, she would most likely fight the idea of having to feed from him again. "It's fine," he said, keeping his voice emotionless, "you don't have to. I, uh—"

He felt her hand grip his chin and tilt his face back to her until he was forced to look into her eyes.

"One kiss for each feeding?" she asked, then nodded slowly.

Each feeding? He'd only meant one kiss for all future feedings, but he couldn't bring himself to protest. He wasn't noble enough to admit that all he wanted was one single kiss. She'd misunderstood him, but he wouldn't correct her; instead, he just nodded.

"I think it's only fair. You want me to pay now?"

Suddenly he felt cocky. "How was dinner?"

"Delicious."

The knowledge that Maya liked his blood was more of a turn-on than he could have ever imagined. "Then I guess it's time to settle the bill."

Gabriel watched her as she slowly moved herself closer to him. Her position was perfect: she was still straddling him. He couldn't imagine a better position for a kiss, except maybe if she were stretched out beneath him. But he was getting ahead of himself.

Like a cat, she shifted closer until her mouth hovered above his. Her lips were slightly parted, and he could scent her breath. Her breathing was suddenly more uneven than before, and he wondered if she was afraid of what he would do. Would she regret her decision and pull back at the last minute?

"I can keep my hands on the couch, if you prefer," he offered and placed his hands palm down onto the cushions beside her thighs. He didn't want her to fear him and think he would take advantage of the situation, as much as he wanted to do just that. But knowing that this wouldn't be the last kiss she would grant him, he could tamp down his greed and only take what she was willing to give him, without crossing the boundaries of the kiss.

He could learn to savor this. Every day, he would have something to look forward to. But he had to play it cool, not overwhelm her with the passion he felt inside, not scare her away or she might cancel their deal. No, his response to her would have to be muted, so she wouldn't know the extent of his desire for her and be frightened by its magnitude. And every day he could allow himself to take a little more, make her more comfortable with him. Maybe she would start to feel the same attraction for him that he felt for her.

Maya's lips brushed against his, and Gabriel knew he would have a hell of a time keeping this kiss sweet and innocent.

His masculine scent was all around her. Maya couldn't believe her luck. After feeding on his blood she felt rejuvenated, stronger than she ever had, and hornier than she'd ever been as a human! And now what he wanted in exchange was a kiss? Could things be more perfect?

Kissing him was no sacrifice for her. When she touched his lips with hers, she enjoyed their perfect mixture of softness and firmness. She hadn't noticed until now how full his lips were. But now that she sucked his upper lip into her mouth and licked over it with her tongue, she was fully aware of their perfection.

Maya slanted her mouth over his, and under light pressure of her tongue, his lips parted. Greedily, she slipped inside and explored him. He tasted just as amazing as his blood. She knew that her reaction to him was purely chemical. The pheromones he was emitting ignited desire in her. Like an age-old instinct, her body recognized his as the perfect match. She'd read the clinical studies on the chemical process that produced lust and desire and knew this was happening to her. Surely this was all it was, pure lust. There couldn't be anything else involved. She barely knew anything about Gabriel. No emotions could have developed in such a short time.

She continued kissing him, stroking her tongue against his, but his reaction wasn't what she'd expected. Like any dominant man, she would have expected him to take charge, to make the kiss more demanding, but he didn't. He only responded with a stroke of his tongue against hers when she coaxed him long enough. When she tried to pull his tongue into her mouth, he resisted.

Frustrated, Maya broke away. She looked into his startled face. "Didn't you like it?"

His face turned from startled to confused. "Of course, I did," he claimed.

She dropped her gaze, not able to look at him when she asked him her next question. "Then why don't you kiss me back?"

His answer came as a surprise. "If I kiss you back, I won't be able to keep my hands to myself."

Defiantly, she looked into his eyes. "Nobody's asking you to."

All of a sudden she felt his arm come up and wrap around her body. "You don't know what you're doing to me."

No, she had no idea, but she knew what Gabriel was doing to her. He was driving her insane and would continue to do so if he didn't kiss her properly. "Kiss me, Gabriel. Kiss me now, or I swear I will—"

"Or what?" he bit out. "Deny me? I earned this kiss, and I'm damn well going to get it the way I want it."

Without giving her a chance to reply to him, he sank his lips onto hers and took her mouth in a fierce kiss. Maya melted into him. Now he was talking. Not wanting him to change his mind about the kiss, she sank her hands into his hair and stroked the sensitive area on the back of his neck. She felt him shiver under her touch.

As his mouth ravished her, his hands roamed over her back, stroking along her sides, pressing her ever so much closer to him. She could clearly feel his erection moving against her with every breath he took. She tried to get closer.

As if he knew what she wanted, he tugged at the belt of her robe and opened it. A moment later, his hand went inside it and touched her through the thin fabric of her gown. She moaned into his mouth the moment she felt his fingertips graze her breast. Warmth flooded her and ran from her breast down her belly to her core, setting her clit on fire.

She arched into his touch. At the same time, she pressed her pussy against his hard-on, dragging her sensitive flesh against his rock-hard rod. She was soaked through the nightgown where it clung between her pussy and his erection, which was hidden behind his silk robe. She'd never become this wet just from a kiss. Was this a side-effect of being a vampire, or had Gabriel done this to her?

Maya twined her tongue with his. With delight, she realized that he'd given up all restraints and kissed her with the reckless abandon of a starving man. When she pulled her tongue back slightly, he went after her, growling deeply. The sound went through her body, touching every cell, caressing her flesh.

With a swift movement, he flipped her over, and she suddenly found herself with her back on the cushions, trapped under his strong body. His mouth hadn't released hers for even a second, and now his hips ground against her, the erection behind his robe dragging against her center. With every move, the hard ridge of it rode over her clit. It was more than a mere tease, it was torture. Torture she was only too happy to undergo.

Her heart beat faster the longer he ground against her. Her nipples were hard points rubbing against his chest. Gabriel's mouth trailed down to her neck, and he dragged his teeth against her sensitive skin. She shuddered.

When he touched his hand to her breast and took the nipple between his thumb and forefinger, she let out a cry. "Oh, God, yes!" She wanted him, needed him now. Had to have him inside her, no matter what.

Maya slipped her hands inside his robe to caress his muscular shoulders. His skin was hot and soft, softer than she had expected. But she didn't get a chance to concentrate on him and his body, because he lavished her breasts with attention she couldn't ignore.

The sound of the door opening made her snap her eyes toward it, but she couldn't alert Gabriel in time.

As Yvette stepped into the room, staring at them in shock or disgust or both, Gabriel licked his tongue over her nipple, making the fabric transparent.

Only when Yvette let out a gasp did his head rear up and snap in her direction. He instantly jerked up from his compromising position.

"Shit!" Gabriel cursed.

12

Gabriel had barely listened to Yvette's apology or her excuses before he extricated himself from the embarrassing situation and stormed into the master bedroom.

He'd completely lost control and had been seconds away from fucking Maya.

And he'd sensed something else. Something was wrong with his body. Gabriel ripped his robe open and pulled down his boxers. His swollen cock was no surprise, but what had happened to the flesh above it was.

The deformity that stuck out about an inch above his cock was a mass of flesh and skin, normally three inches long and about one inch in diameter. It was what all women recoiled from in horror. He was a freak with an ugly and useless piece of flesh that got in the way when he wanted to fuck a woman.

Gabriel examined the protrusion. It was getting worse.

Instead of its normal length, it now stuck out almost five inches and its girth had increased by about half. The skin on its tip was shriveled as if it contained more layers of skin all stacked upon each other. He let go of the offending part.

Maya would have screamed with disgust if he'd tried to have sex with her just now. He was almost grateful to Yvette for having shown up at such an inconvenient moment. Her interruption had saved him from a most painful rejection.

And not only that: he'd shamefully exploited Maya's vulnerability by kissing and touching her when he knew that she was susceptible to quick arousal brought on by the feeding. She had no idea of this, but he, an experienced older vampire, knew all too well. It had nothing to do with whether she was attracted to him or not, it was a mere reaction to the bite. A euphoria she would experience. He was a cad for taking advantage like this. Somebody should beat him to a pulp for being such an ass.

He had no idea whether she was really attracted to him. He'd seen her look at his scar again, but then her arousal had taken over, not giving her a real choice of what she wanted. How could any woman look at him and find him attractive unless she was drugged? And drugged she'd been—by his blood. Why else would she have accepted his demand for a kiss? Or was it possible that she felt attracted to him? Was her blood-drugged state not to blame after all?

If only he knew what to say to her, how to explain his concerns. But he wasn't exactly adept at sweet-talking a woman. Hell, he had no idea how to interact with her. But he knew he had to come up with something, explain himself to her. Apologize for storming out of the study like that.

What was she thinking right now? Surely she must think him callous and uncaring, when he was anything but. But had he stayed, he would have made even more of a mess than the situation already was. No, he had to clear his head first and come up with an action plan.

After an uneasy few hours of sleep, Gabriel left the house as soon as the sun set, wanting to avoid both Yvette and Maya. He would face Maya after he got back. But first he had to take care of a few things.

As soon as he was outside walking the dark streets, he pulled out his cell phone and dialed the witch's number. It rang three times before it was answered.

"I told you to go away," the witch said without any greeting. Figured he wasn't the only one who used caller ID and could memorize a phone number.

"Please don't hang up. I'll give you anything you want if you help me." This time he meant it. The sight of his growing protrusion frightened him. He needed to get rid of it. Now. He couldn't face Maya like this. He wouldn't give her a reason to reject him. What had happened in the study between them had made him realize that he wanted her so much he was prepared to fight for her. Whatever it took.

"Anything?" The witch's voice was full of interest.

He knew it was dangerous to offer her whatever she wanted. "Anything."

There was a pause at the other end of the line. Had she hung up?

"I'll think about it. Give me a day or two."

A click and she was gone before he could say anything else. At least she would consider it and hadn't rejected him outright like the first time. It was a step in the right direction. He hoped she would help him. Maya's next feeding was less than twenty-four hours away, and if he couldn't control his urges then, the same thing would happen again.

He promised himself not to collect payment for her meal next time she fed from him. It was better not to tempt fate and to instead remove as much temptation as possible. Just having her feed from him again would cost him every ounce of control he had. An incident like the one that had happened in the study couldn't be repeated. Not while his body looked like it did.

Soon after his phone call to the witch, he reached Drake's clinic and was led into his office by his Barbie-doll receptionist.

"How is Dr. Johnson?" Drake asked the minute he entered the room, seemingly not at all surprised to see Gabriel.

It took him a fraction of a second to realize who Drake meant by Dr. Johnson. Gabriel didn't see her as a doctor. He just saw her as Maya. "She fed from me."

Drake only raised an eyebrow. "I figured that much."

Gabriel straightened. "Excuse me?"

The doctor shrugged. "She told me she was craving your blood. She was fighting it."

Gabriel glared at him. "And you didn't tell me?" He felt fury rise in his chest. Drake had let her suffer when Gabriel could have taken care of the problem had he only known? He took two steps toward Drake.

"Doctor-patient confidentiality."

"Fuck doctor-patient confidentiality!" Gabriel yelled and grabbed the doctor by his white coat. "You listen to me now: anything—and I mean *anything*—that concerns Maya, concerns me. Whatever you know about her, you'll tell me. Do you get that?"

Drake shrugged out of Gabriel's hold. "What is she to you?"

"That's none of your business."

"It is," the doctor disagreed. "Are you going to help her through this when things get tough? Are you?"

"I've helped her through this, haven't I?" Gabriel shot back.

"You've seen nothing yet!"

"The worst is over. She's gone through the change, and now that she's accepted her need to feed from me, I don't see what other problems there could be." Gabriel didn't like scaremongers. If the doctor thought he could raise his fee by making up some bogus ailments, he'd soon be at the receiving end of Gabriel's unrelenting fist.

"No, I don't know either *what* problems there'll be. But I know for sure there *will* be problems." He wiped sweat off his brow. "I have reason to believe that Maya is not entirely human."

Gabriel snorted. "Of course she's not human. She's a vampire."

Drake shook his head. "That's not what I meant. She wasn't entirely human before she was turned."

It took several seconds for the information to sink in. "Not human?"

Drake pointed to the chairs, and they both sat down. "I doubt she has any idea."

"You examined her?" The idea that the doctor might have touched her when he'd gone into the study with her made Gabriel's stomach twist.

"No. She gave me access to her medical records. I looked at all tests she's ever had in her entire life, and I'm telling you, something is off."

Good—the doctor hadn't touched her. It made him feel better. "Off—like how?"

"She's been having these attacks of fever ever since she turned thirteen. At least once a year, sometimes twice. The doctors can't explain it. They wrote it off to influenza or an infection. But the frequency, it disturbs me."

Gabriel shrugged. Humans were just more vulnerable to all kinds of things. There was nothing odd about it. "What else?"

"She had a genetic test done during her residency—a trial she took part in to make extra money," he explained. "The results are worrying."

"Spit it out," Gabriel ordered.

"The test showed two extra pairs of chromosomes: a total of twenty-five instead of twenty-three pairs."

"How could that happen?" Gabriel now was glad for the lonely days that had forced him to find things to occupy his time with. He'd long ago taken to watching programs on channels like Discovery and Science, and therefore had a rudimentary understanding of medical issues.

"The notes on the test say that they think the sample was contaminated and they excluded it from the clinical trial. But Dr. Johnson—Maya," he corrected himself, "she kept the test results in her medical record. She must have wondered if it caused her fevers."

"Isn't it possible that the lab who did the test was correct in saying there was contamination? It could happen so easily. You must know better than I how easily things get contaminated. Human error is always possible." Gabriel didn't want to accept that there was something wrong with Maya. She had enough to deal with already.

"That's what I thought too, but—"

"Do you think that the reason she doesn't want to drink human blood is connected to this chromosome issue?"

Drake nodded. "It's a distinct possibility. Frankly, I've never heard of a vampire who didn't drink human blood. It's true that some vampires drink each other's blood, but in general that's merely a part of their sex lives. Blood-bonded couples do it, but not at the exclusion of human blood." Suddenly the doctor looked straight at him. "I hope you're drinking enough blood while she's feeding from you. You have to keep your strength."

"Don't worry about me. I feed as much as my body tells me to."

Drake gave him a curious look. "How much is she taking from you?"

"As much as she needs." And for his liking, her feeding had been far too short. He would have liked to enjoy the sensation for much longer.

"Well, I suppose you know what you're doing. At least this will buy us some time until I can figure out what's wrong with her. As I said, I have a hunch that I need to look into. I have to get some information on her parents. Since whatever nonhuman component she has in her would be genetic, I need to get a medical history on her parents."

Gabriel nodded. "I'll get you their names and addresses. But you'll probably have to steal the medical info. Thomas can help you get access: he can hack into any electronic system. I'll talk to him."

"Good. It will help. Once I know what peculiar things her parents suffer from, I think I can confirm my suspicion."

Gabriel leaned forward in his chair. "So you have a suspicion? What is it?"

Drake simply shook his head. "I can't say anything so far. If I do without any proof, you'll most likely just call me crazy."

"Tell me. I promise, I won't call you crazy." *Not to your face anyway.*

"No. First we need to get information on her parents."

Gabriel didn't like it that the doctor kept his suspicions to himself. "Fine. But there's one thing I insist on."

Drake raised an eyebrow.

"Whatever you find, I will be the first you tell. You won't speak to Maya about it. I alone will decide if and when to tell her. I know better what she can take right now. And frankly, I don't want her to have to deal with anything else right now. She's too fragile as it is."

"Fragile?" Drake asked. "She's a vampire. There's nothing fragile about that."

"She isn't aware of her strength yet, or her urges. She can't control them. I don't want anything to upset her right now."

Drake rose. "As you wish. Who do I send the bill to?"

Gabriel grunted. "What do you want for it?"

"Don't worry. For this job, cash is perfectly fine."

Gabriel got up from his chair and walked to the door. "You have my address."

Before Gabriel opened the door, Drake asked, "Is there anything you wouldn't do for her?"

He threw a look over his shoulder and glared at the doctor. "Just do your job. My feelings don't matter to you." But they mattered to Gabriel.

***

Impatiently, Gabriel knocked at the entrance door of the modern home that hugged the hills just below Twin Peaks. The views from the home had to be stunning. Thomas sure had some nice digs. It didn't surprise him. As a vampire who'd lived close to a century, he, like many of their other colleagues, had accumulated a large amount of wealth.

The door swung open and Thomas appeared in the frame, clad only in a towel wrapped around his lower body, skin glistening from a recent shower.

"Sorry, Thomas. I should have called. We can talk later," Gabriel said.

Thomas waved him in. "Just come in. If you show up unannounced, I suppose it means it's important."

Gabriel stepped into the house and closed the door behind him. "Thanks. Appreciate it." His eyes roamed around the great room with its open-plan kitchen, trying to avoid looking at Thomas's half-naked body. He didn't know Thomas as well as Samson or Amaury did, particularly since Thomas had never lived in New York and Gabriel very rarely ventured out West. Seeing another man only partially dressed normally didn't bother Gabriel, but it was different with Thomas. He had no idea what the etiquette was when conversing with an almost-naked gay man. Did you look? Didn't you look?

"So, what's up?" Thomas asked, seeming entirely comfortable in his present state.

Gabriel cleared his throat. "I've just been to see Drake. Maya is still rejecting human blood."

Thomas shook his head. "We'll have to force-feed her if that continues, otherwise she'll starve."

"That won't be necessary. She started feeding from me this morning."

"From you? She's craving vampire blood?" Thomas ran his hand through his wet hair, the motion showing off his muscled torso.

The sound of the entrance door opening again made Gabriel turn his head toward it. He recognized Eddie trotting in. Eddie's gaze first fell on Thomas and lingered there for longer than Gabriel had expected.

"Hey," he greeted them.

Thomas wiped his hand on his towel as he looked back at Eddie. "Didn't know you hadn't slept here today."

Eddie shrugged. "Time got away from me. By the time I looked, it was too close to sunrise to make it back."

"Don't tell me you bothered Nina and Amaury to let you stay."

Eddie waved him off. "God, no. Those two are going at it day and night—I'd never get a wink of sleep." He grinned, his young face smirking, dimples and all. "Who knows what my sister sees in him. That guy is just totally overpowering."

"So is your sister," Gabriel retorted.

Thomas laughed. "That's right, buddy. She can keep up with the best of them."

Eddie made a dismissive gesture. "Whatever. Luckily, Holly let me crash at her place."

"Holly?" There was a sharp tone in Thomas's voice. "You're dating Holly?"

"Ricky's girlfriend Holly?" Gabriel asked and raised an eyebrow.

"Ex-girlfriend," Eddie corrected him. "And no, I'm not dating her. The woman is a total gossip."

Thomas seemed to relax and smiled back at Eddie. "What's she gossiping about now?"

"She was trying to convince me that Ricky was the one who broke up with her, not the other way 'round. As if I care even remotely. I tell you, I couldn't wait for sunset to get out of her place. She kept talking my ears full about how Ricky apparently set his sights on some other woman and dumped her unceremoniously. Next time, I swear I'd rather turn to dust in the sun than take shelter at her house."

Eddie walked toward the door leading to the sleeping quarters of the house. "I'm gonna get some shuteye for an hour. Is that cool with you?"

Thomas nodded. "Take all the time you need. And take a shower, will you? You smell like a girl."

Eddie sniffed at his T-shirt and frowned. "Damn Holly, she burns all that incense crap."

As Eddie sauntered out of the room, Thomas turned back to Gabriel.

"How's the mentoring going?" Gabriel asked.

"He's a good kid. And he's learning fast. In a few months, he'll be able to be on his own."

Gabriel recognized sadness in Thomas's words. "You like him?"

"As I said, he's a good kid." He paused. "And straight. End of story." Thomas inhaled. "So, you were saying you needed my help?"

Gabriel cleared his throat. Thomas's private life was none of his business. "About Maya. Drake can't explain why she rejects human blood and drinks mine instead."

"Lucky bastard," Thomas interjected and grinned. Gabriel knew exactly what he was referring to: the sexual arousal that came with letting another vampire feed off him.

An involuntary grin stole onto Gabriel's lips, but it died just as quickly. "The doc thinks something is wrong with her. And it might be genetic."

"What do you want me to do?"

"I need you to get her parents' medical records. We need to find out if they have any genetic defects. Can you do that?"

Thomas nodded. "Sure. Let me just have a quick word with Maya to get the names and address and we should—"

"Without letting Maya know," Gabriel interrupted.

"Oh. Okay. I'm sure you have your reasons."

"I do. Can you do it?"

"No problem. I'll call Drake when I have the info ready for him."

"Did you get a chance to talk to Eddie and James about the scent of Maya's attacker?"

Thomas made a regretful sigh. "I did. But neither of them could pinpoint anything. They said the scent was so faint that it could have been anybody. Besides, she was bleeding so profusely, both of them were just too overwhelmed by the scent of human blood that they paid little attention to the vampire's. Sorry, Gabriel; that one's a dead end."

"Thought as much. Let's try something else. I figured if she was dating him, he might have called her or she, him." The word *dating* hurt to even pronounce. Could she really have seen something in that man? "Can you hack into her phone records, both her landline and her cell, and get me a list of everyone she had contact with? Match the numbers up with names. Maybe we'll recognize someone."

"Let me see what I can find."

Gabriel stretched out his hand. "Thanks."

Thomas grasped it briefly.

"And one other thing: could you relieve Yvette at the house before sunrise? She needs some downtime." After the embarrassing encounter earlier in the day, Gabriel was the one who needed some distance from her. He wasn't keen on facing her right now.

"Let me guess. The women don't get on."

Gabriel shrugged. "Don't ask me. What the hell do I know about women?"

Thomas laughed and patted him on the shoulder. "A hell of a lot more than I do, that's for sure."

13

True to his word, Thomas showed up at the house two hours before sunrise and switched duties with Yvette, who seemed relieved at being able to get out of the house.

After his excursion to see the witch and then Drake, Gabriel had spoken to the editor of the *SF Vampire Chronicle* and made sure Zane would receive a list of all male vampires in San Francisco.

Now Gabriel stood in the kitchen, gulping down an extra bottle of blood. He would have to feed Maya soon. She hadn't said anything about being hungry; in fact, she'd practically avoided him ever since he'd returned.

He wondered whether she'd been mad at him when she'd realized he'd taken advantage of her. Unfortunately, he couldn't know for sure whether she liked him or not, or whether her arousal had been a mere byproduct of the feeding.

Damn, he could still taste her, even now after close to twenty-four hours.

"Hey, what's going on?" a familiar male voice came from the kitchen door.

Gabriel spun around. He should have heard Ricky come in, but obviously his thoughts were just too far away. Even though Ricky had probably used his key to open the front door, Gabriel should have at least heard the opening and closing of it, or Ricky's footsteps. What kind of bodyguard was he turning into?

"Didn't expect you here," Gabriel answered. Shouldn't Ricky be at some den of iniquity drowning his sorrows about the breakup of his last relationship?

Ricky shrugged. His red hair and freckles seemed to glow. "I just get too bored when I don't do anything. Heard you might need some help with protecting a new vampire. Thought I'd pitch in."

Gabriel nodded. He needed all the help he could get. With Thomas busy helping Drake look into Maya's medical history—a task he was currently performing in Samson's study—and Zane still out on the reconnaissance mission Gabriel had sent him on, nobody else was available to investigate other aspects of the attack.

"Actually, since Zane is digging through the underbelly of society to get any info on the rogue, I could do with an extra man."

Ricky grinned. "Guess Zane volunteered for his favorite job again: beating people up. Doesn't leave the rest of us any of the fun stuff, eh?"

Gabriel only frowned. "In this case, I don't mind who he beats up as long as he comes up with results."

"Knowing Zane, he will. So, do you need any help? Need an extra hand guarding the house?"

"No. I'd rather you investigate for me. She knew her attacker—"

"Well, then I guess you've got it under control." Ricky interrupted and leaned casually against the kitchen island. "Just a matter of finding where the guy is hiding then."

Gabriel rubbed his neck. "It's not quite that easy, I'm afraid. He wiped her memory."

"Bummer, but that's to be expected, right?" Ricky replied. "So, what now? How're you gonna find him? What do you want me to look into?"

Gabriel knew there was one avenue he hadn't had a chance to explore. While the rogue had wiped Maya's memory clear of him, he couldn't have wiped everybody else's, especially if he didn't know who else knew about him.

"Let's talk to Maya. I think she can help us with this." He opened the door to the hallway.

"But didn't you just say he wiped her memory?" Ricky asked.

"That's right. But I'm betting *only* hers." He stuck his head out into the hallway. "Maya, can you come down please?" He knew she would hear him—whether she complied was another matter.

When he heard her footsteps on the landing upstairs, he knew he'd have to face her, but he couldn't pretend that nothing had happened between them.

When Maya reached the foot of the stairs and turned toward him, Gabriel's breath caught in his chest. His heart pounded against his ribs as if it wanted to reach for her. God, was he in deep shit—there was no way he'd be able to stay away from her for long. She was like a magnet, and he a mere iron nail without any resistance.

He looked at her face and caught her lowering her eyelids as if to avoid his gaze.

"Maya," he said in a low voice, not wanting anybody to overhear him. What he had to say to her was private. "We need to talk about what happened earlier."

Maya took a deep breath. She wasn't ready to talk to him yet. When he'd hightailed it out of the study with a look of panic on his face, she'd felt more embarrassed than ever before in her life. She'd been ready to fuck him right there on the couch in the study. She'd been ready to devour him not giving a second thought to what he might think about her. But now, what he thought mattered to her. Did he think her easy?

"Gabriel, I don't know what to say," she stammered. Was she blushing? Could a vampire blush? She hoped not, because if she could, her cheeks would be a deep red, as red as Gabriel's blood.

There—it was all she could think of: his blood, his mouth, his hands on her, the way his erection had pressed against her. Another hot flush brought her to her senses. She could not turn into a quivering mess as if she were some virgin.

"I want to apologize," he said. "I shouldn't have run out like that."

She waved him off. She didn't want apologies. What she wanted to know was whether he'd felt something when he'd kissed her, or whether it had just been a typical male reaction. Did he like her? Did he want more from her? Suddenly Yvette's warning words rang in her ears: a vampire male wanted to bond with a human woman who could bear him children. All she was good for was sex. Was that how Gabriel saw her too?

She cast him a quick glance, but couldn't work up the courage to ask. "It's fine." Then she cleared her throat. "You called me?"

"Yes, will you join us in the kitchen please?"

Maya sensed the other vampire the moment she took a step toward the kitchen. She shook off an uneasy feeling, walked through the door that Gabriel held open for her and forced a smile. The man who was casually leaning against the kitchen counter was a quarter foot shorter than Gabriel. His red hair was slightly curly and his eyes were a dull brown, not the sparkling brown Gabriel's eyes were. Did she have to compare every man to Gabriel?

Straightening her spine, she glanced at Gabriel, who'd come back into the kitchen behind her and gave him a questioning look.

"This is Ricky O'Leary. He's the Operations Director of Scanguards, and he's offered to help us find the rogue."

Maya stretched out her hand and shook his. "Nice to meet you," she said automatically.

"Nice to meet you too," he said, giving her a friendly smile.

Gabriel cleared his throat. "I think we might have another way to get a lead on the rogue. But we'll need your help with this."

"Sure. But I thought you'd already looked at all my memories and found nothing." What else he needed from her, she didn't know. If she knew anything else, she would have already told him. She wanted that asshole found more than anybody else.

"Yes, your memories. But how about your friends'?" With a cryptic smile he continued, "We need to know which of your friends you might have told about him. See, he wiped your memory, but he can't know who you told about him. It might help us identify him."

"Great idea, Gabriel! I hadn't thought of that," Ricky praised.

Gabriel put his hand on her forearm. Why did he have to touch her like that? Didn't he realize that his touch burned her skin like a hot iron? Had he no idea that one touch by him made her want his hands on every part of her body?

"Maya, can you tell us who you might have told about him? If you were dating him, and then rejecting him, would you have discussed him with one of your girlfriends?"

"There are only two people I would discuss men with: Paulette and Barbara. Those are the only two I'm really close to. I'm pretty sure I would have mentioned a date to either one of them. And if I rejected him, and he was some jerk or something, you can be sure that we spent an entire evening over a bottle of wine bitching about him."

Gabriel gave her a surprised look, but Maya merely shrugged. It was what women did. Didn't he know that?

Ricky shifted his stance. "Well, that's great. Why don't I start with them? Let me have their full names and where I can find them, and I'll go see what they know. I'm sure it'll put us on the right track."

"Good plan," Gabriel agreed. "Make sure you're not too conspicuous. We don't want anybody suspecting anything. They don't know what happened to Maya, and we don't want them asking any questions."

"I'm not an amateur, as you well know. Trust me, I'll take care of it," Ricky assured him and looked at Maya. "So, where can I find your two friends?"

She reached for a notepad on the counter. "Here. I'll write it down for you. Paulette is easier to get a hold of. Her schedule is pretty regular, so at night you'll probably find her at home." She scribbled her friends' addresses on the pad. "Barbara has quite an irregular shift, so if she's not at home, you'll find her at the hospital." She looked up at Gabriel. "Shouldn't I maybe call them and talk to them?"

Gabriel shook his head. "And tell them what? They'll drag you into a conversation and you won't have answers for all their questions."

"But what makes you think they'll tell Ricky anything? No offense—" She turned to Ricky. "—but you're a stranger to them."

Ricky grinned. "Don't worry about that. I have a special gift."

Another vampire with a special gift?

Gabriel smiled at her. "He's right. Ricky can dispel doubts in people. That's why he's so good at his job. Whenever somebody raises doubts, Ricky uses his gift to make them disappear. It's a little like mind control, but it works on anybody, even vampires. And it's helped us many times to get difficult situations under control and avoid mass panics."

"But won't they notice when you're doing it?" Maya worried.

"That's the beauty of Ricky's gift," Gabriel answered for the other vampire, "they won't even notice it's happening."

"That's right. So don't even worry about it," Ricky said calmly and took the piece of paper. "I'll keep you guys posted."

"Thanks, Ricky, I really appreciate it," Gabriel said and shook Ricky's hand while Maya still tried to process the news. It appeared all vampires had some sort of special gift to cope with their lot. Gabriel could see other people's memories, Ricky could dispel doubts. Did Thomas and Yvette have special gifts too? And Zane? Would she develop one too?

A moment later, Ricky was gone. She was alone with Gabriel. She was hot and found it difficult to breathe. She wanted to talk to him about what had happened. To get answers. But she'd felt something creeping up on her earlier. Now she recognized it for what it was.

The fever was coming back.

Maya stood in the middle of the kitchen looking like a deer about to bolt. Gabriel wondered whether he'd scared her so badly with his behavior that she couldn't stand being alone with him. He wanted to make it up to her, but he didn't know where to start. He was afraid that whatever he'd say would be the wrong thing.

"Are you thirsty?" he asked, trying to stamp out the silence between them.

"No. I'm fine. I'm not hungry." Was she truly not hungry yet, or was she denying herself because she didn't want to feed off him in such an intimate way?

"You can feed off my wrist instead of my neck if that makes you more comfortable," he offered. It would be less intimate, but still create the same arousal in him as well as in her.

Maya turned toward the door. "I'm not hungry. I'm not feeling great right now. Maybe I'm coming down with something."

He stopped her when she opened the door. "Coming down with something? Maya, I told you, vampires don't get sick." Did she have to lie so blatantly just to get out of his presence?

"Well, I don't know about other vampires, but I'm feeling lousy, so, if you don't mind, I'd like to lie down." Without another glance at him she walked out of the kitchen.

He took two steps and followed her into the hallway where he watched her walk up the stairs. Shit, he'd truly screwed it up with her. He should explain things to her, tell her that whatever she was thinking of him was probably wrong. Of course, he didn't know what she was thinking. But he could guess. After coming out of her arousal when Yvette had interrupted them, she probably felt disgusted with him.

"Gabriel," Thomas's voice came from the study.

He turned and responded, "Yes? Anything on the phone records?"

"Unfortunately, AT&T is having a problem with their servers—they've taken them down for emergency maintenance. I can't get into them right now. Could take as long as twelve hours they're estimating."

"Damn," Gabriel cursed.

"But we've examined the medical files."

Gabriel walked to the study where Thomas stood in the door frame. He closed the door behind them. "What did you find?"

Thomas shook his head, frustration clearly written on his face. "Nothing. See for yourself. They're both as clean as a whistle. No mention of any genetic defects. Maya can't have inherited it from her parents."

Thomas stepped aside to let Gabriel look at the computer. He scrolled through the file, scanning page after page. Maya's father had had a few broken bones, an appendix operation, but nothing else. Her mother's file was a bit denser, but nothing struck him as odd. Some allergies, the occasional infection, some notes by an OB-GYN, a broken ankle.

Gabriel slammed his fist on the desk in frustration. "How can that be?"

Thomas shrugged. "Not sure. The doc can't explain it either. He was certain it had to be inherited. Maybe a birth defect?"

Gabriel looked back at her mother's file. "Let me see what the OB-GYN says here." He skimmed through the notes, until it hit him. It couldn't be, but it was right there. "Her mother had a hysterectomy."

"Cancer?"

"Yes."

"The chemo could have done something to Maya," Thomas mused.

Gabriel looked at the date of the notes and suddenly stared at Thomas. "She had her uterus removed *before* Maya's birth. Maya isn't her daughter."

A stunned Thomas exhaled sharply. "Adopted?"

Gabriel considered it. Back over thirty years ago, surrogacy wasn't as prevalent as today, which meant her father probably wasn't her biological father either. "Most likely." As he said it, he remembered the photos in Maya's living room. "I should have figured it out earlier. I saw pictures of her parents. They looked nothing like her. Maya's skin is so much darker—her parents are both blond and of a much lighter complexion. There's no way she could be their biological daughter."

He looked straight at Thomas. "We have to find her real parents. Only then can we figure out what's wrong with her."

"I think we might have to ask her whether she knows that she's adopted."

Gabriel shook his head. "Let's wait on that. Check the adoption records first. Start with Social Services and see what you can dig up. I don't want to tell her about her genetic abnormality yet—she's got enough to worry about. Promise me you won't mention anything."

"Your choice, Gabriel, but you'll have to tell her eventually. And between you and me, the sooner the better. Women don't like it when they think they've been lied to."

"What suddenly makes you an expert on women?"

Thomas shrugged. "Common sense." After a brief pause, he added, "And you might also want to tell her how you feel about her instead of moping about."

Gabriel snorted. Was it that obvious what he felt? And if Thomas had noticed, did that mean Maya had noticed too? Was that why she was avoiding him? Did she not want his attention? "I don't remember asking for your advice on my private life."

His colleague grinned. "Prerogative of a gay man."

"And besides, there's nothing between me and her." Who was he kidding?

"Uh-huh," Thomas answered.

14

Gabriel didn't want to sleep. It was midmorning and most vampires would be in their beds. Instead, he sat in the armchair in the living room, staring into the low fire crackling in the fireplace. Maya hadn't called to feed off him. He'd listened for her, figuring she would be thirsty by now, but she hadn't asked for him. He guessed she was mad at him. He had to do something about it, but he didn't know what.

He'd used her vulnerability and exploited it without concern for her wellbeing. As if she didn't have enough to deal with as a new vampire. She shouldn't have to fight off a horny vampire who wanted nothing more than to get into her pants.

Why had he suddenly become so aggressive in his sex life? All these years, he'd never had a problem keeping himself in check. He'd never truly pursued a woman before. It had never mattered. Yes, he'd always wanted a companion, a woman to hold, a woman to have sex with, but he'd been okay with taking what he could get and paying for the rest.

Of course, the loneliness had started getting to him, and that's why he'd contacted Drake, but while there had been a desire to get rid of the ugly deformity, there'd never been this urgency before. Now he couldn't wait to be rid of the darn thing for one reason, and one reason only: so he could go to Maya as a real man and woo her. Of course, there was still the ugly scar on his face.

A woman like Maya could do much better than taking a man like him. Once she had adjusted to her new life, she would have all kinds of offers from eligible vampires in the city. If he didn't make a play for her now, he'd have even less of a chance later when all the competition kicked in.

He had to try now. A small glimmer of hope had sparked when she'd responded so passionately in the study. He hoped it hadn't all been due to the feeding. Maybe there was a tiny sliver of attraction she felt for him. Or why accept his demand for a kiss at all? He couldn't give up his fight for her as long as he could cling to this tiny speck of hope.

Gabriel closed his eyes and imagined what it would be like to feel Maya's love, to know she cared for him. He knew he was torturing himself by daydreaming like this, but he couldn't let go, not when it filled his heart with warmth and pride. It was all a dream: to call a woman like Maya his own, to love her day and night, to live with her, share a home, to laugh together.

It was fate that had brought them together, and while he was reluctant to believe in fate, he wanted to believe that they were meant to meet, because he'd realized one thing: he was falling in love with a woman too beautiful for him, yet perfect for him in every way.

A soft knock at the front door made him snap his head around. Who would be coming to a vampire's home during daylight? It had to be a human. Gabriel stood and walked to the door. He sniffed. Or a witch.

He looked through the spy hole and knew it was Miss LeBlanc, the witch who'd only a short while ago leveled a crossbow at him. It appeared that this time she was unarmed.

"You gonna open the door, vampire, or shall I leave?" she said through the door.

How could she tell he was watching her?

"I'll unlock it. Then count to three and come in. I'll be in the first room to your left."

Gabriel flipped the lock and stepped back into the living room, closing the door behind him, so the light from outside wouldn't penetrate into the darkened room. Not only were the front windows made of a special tinted glass, light drapes covered them and while they didn't shut out all light, it was dark enough to be safe for a vampire.

A moment later, he heard the door open. When she joined him in the living room, he pointed toward the sofa. She looked less imposing today, unarmed as she was. Dressed in a business suit, she could have fooled anybody that she was some ordinary human. If he had to guess, he would have put her age at mid-thirties. She was attractive and to his surprise, a smile curled around her mouth.

"This is definitely a first." She looked around the room. "So, this is how you guys live."

"The house belongs to my boss. And, no, we don't live in caves or sleep in coffins."

"Pleasantries aside, I believe you know why I'm here."

He nodded. "You'll help me with my problem."

"You said you would give me anything I wanted."

Gabriel cringed. He'd said it, and he would keep his word. Now the question was, what did she want? "So I did."

"Drake mentioned your gift."

"Figured he couldn't keep that little piece of information to himself. What happened to patient-doctor confidentiality?"

She gave a little snort. "I'm not here to talk about Drake and his ethics." She paused. "Or lack thereof."

"Fair enough. What can I do for you?" As if he didn't already know.

"The use of your gift. One time only."

He nodded and hoped whatever she would do with the memories he extracted from her victim wouldn't cause pain to anybody.

"Good, then we're in agreement. Now, to your problem. Tell me what's so important that you want to deal with the likes of my kind." She leaned forward on the sofa and looked at him expectantly.

Gabriel swallowed hard. This would be embarrassing.

***

Maya threw the bedcovers off. The place was stifling hot. Her red silk nightgown clung to her damp skin. Tiny rivulets of sweat formed, starting on her neck and running down between her breasts.

She knew it was the fever, but she'd hoped as a vampire she wouldn't be ill anymore. Hadn't Gabriel told her that vampires didn't get sick? Yet the fever was gripping her again, and this time it was worse than it had ever been. Her skin was hot to the touch, her insides were burning already, and it had only started an hour ago. She'd felt it creeping up on her during the conversation with Ricky and Gabriel and had hoped it would stop. But it hadn't.

She had to do something about it, had to cool her body down so she wouldn't burn up. With shaking legs she stumbled out of bed. Every step she took ached and contributed to the heat in her body as if adding fuel to the fire. Her head spun as she tried to focus on the bathroom door. A cold shower—she had to take a cold shower.

Another step and another brought her closer to the bathroom, but her instinct told her it wouldn't work. Deep down she knew what her body needed and craved. She'd always known, but never wanted to admit it.

The fevers made her crave a man's touch. Ever since the fevers had begun when she was thirteen, all she'd been able to think of was having a man touch her, kiss her, fuck her. She'd never given into it, and always made it through her pain. The doctors hadn't been able to explain it, and had written it off to some exotic virus she might have picked up somewhere—like malaria. Yet, she'd never been anywhere, and blood tests had come back negative.

Her own research into her condition had dead-ended. And the fevers continued several times a year. Sometimes mild, sometimes stronger. And they were always accompanied by cravings for sex.

This time it was worse. She knew now that there was only one man who could douse the fire in her body: Gabriel. Her body didn't listen to her brain anymore and changed direction. Instead of continuing to the bathroom where cold water beckoned, her shaking legs carried her toward the door of the bedroom.

Her breathing sped up. She needed more and more oxygen to make her body work. It wasn't enough. She wouldn't make it, not this time.

Maya reached for the door handle, turned it and pulled. Black blotches appeared in front of her eyes, and she lost her balance as the door swung toward her.

***

Gabriel undid his belt to show the witch what he needed help with when a loud thump from upstairs startled him. He rushed toward the door and looked into the hallway, where he saw Thomas running upstairs.

Panic gripped him. Without giving the witch a second thought, he ran after Thomas. He reached the door to the guest room seconds after Thomas. There, just inside the open door lay Maya sprawled on the floor, her skin glistening, her short red nightdress clinging to her.

Before Thomas could touch her, Gabriel was by her side and gathered her in his arms. "Maya, can you hear me?"

As he held her slim body next to his, he could feel the heat emanating from her.

"What's wrong with her?" Thomas asked, his voice full of concern.

"She's burning up."

"You think it's the fever?"

Gabriel wondered for a second how Thomas knew about those, then realized that he would have talked to Drake when reviewing the medical files. "It looks like it. I just don't understand it. Any illness she might have had as a human should have been eradicated by the turning."

Thomas nodded. "We'd better get the doc."

"I can help," the witch said from the door. Gabriel hadn't noticed her follow them.

Instantly, Thomas shot up from his crouching position and leveled a hostile glare at the woman, ready to attack.

"Thomas, it's okay. She's here to help."

"You let a witch into Samson's house?"

Gabriel didn't get a chance to reply. "Would you get out of my way, vampire," she addressed Thomas, "so I can help that woman? Or would you rather we discussed the problems between our two species while she burns up?"

Without another word, Thomas stepped aside and let her inside the room.

"Carry her to the bed. I want to examine her," the witch dictated.

Gabriel stood, pulling Maya closer into his arms. As she shifted, he suddenly felt her move her head into the crook of his neck. A moment later, her tongue licked him, making his skin tingle pleasantly. Then he felt her teeth. He barely made it to the bed before her fangs lodged in his neck and she began to suckle.

He sat on the edge of the bed, holding her in his arms while she fed. Maybe she had collapsed because of the hunger, but Gabriel knew instinctively that it wasn't the answer. Something else was seriously wrong with her.

"She drinks your blood?" the witch asked, her voice full of disbelief.

Gabriel looked at her as she watched them. "She refuses human blood." His eyes searched Thomas. "Thomas, get Drake here."

"It's daytime," the witch commented.

"Doesn't matter," Thomas answered. "I'll send a blackout van with one of our human guards." He let his eyes glance up and down the witch. "You sure you'll be safe with her?"

"Miss LeBlanc doesn't want to harm any of us, trust me."

Thomas shrugged. "If you say so." He left the room.

The witch cleared her throat, prompting Gabriel to look at her. "How long will she feed?"

"As long as she needs to," Gabriel answered. He stroked his hand over Maya's hair and shoulders and suppressed the urge to touch her intimately. Already now he was aroused, and the presence of the witch in the room did nothing to dampen that arousal. Only his sense for dignity and privacy—more for Maya than for himself—kept him from devouring her with his hands.

It seemed like an eternity before Maya released his neck and licked over the incisions to close them. Carefully, he released her from his arms and laid her on the covers. Her eyes were closed. As he removed his hands from her, her body started thrashing. Moans left her lips, indicating she was in pain.

"She seemed calmer in your arms," the witch commented.

It appeared that way to Gabriel too, but he couldn't be certain.

"Do something for me," the witch commanded. "Take her into your arms again."

"What will that serve?" Other than getting him all hot and horny again?

"I need to see how she reacts."

Gabriel did as she asked and gathered Maya in his arms again. Her thrashing stopped, but her body writhed against him. He felt embarrassed when he realized that Maya was rubbing herself against him, her hands immediately going to his groin. He couldn't suppress his own arousal at her action. Hoping the witch hadn't seen Maya's subconscious gestures and trying to protect her modesty, he pulled her hands up to his chest.

"That's interesting." So much for his and Maya's dignity—the witch had seen exactly what the unconscious Maya was trying to do to him. "Are the two of you lovers?"

Gabriel shot her an annoyed look. "No. From the things I told you earlier, I figured you knew that I don't have a lover."

"So she's the reason why you want me to help you with your problem," she hedged.

He didn't like her probing into his personal life. "It's immaterial why I want your help. I'm paying you, aren't I?"

"Wow, touchy. Just proves my point." She shrugged and put her attention back to Maya. "Lay her back down."

Again, Maya tossed and turned. Her skin was flushed. More sweat built on her forehead, her neck and chest. Her nipples were clearly visible through the damp fabric, and he felt the need to protect her modesty. As he pulled on the sheet to cover her, the witch stopped him.

"I know you want to protect her, but she's hot enough. Trust me, vampire, you're the only one in this room who's getting off by looking at her body."

Gabriel snarled at her, but had no reply to her unfortunately accurate assessment. He looked away. "Can you figure out what's wrong with her?"

"I have a suspicion, but I'd like to confer with Drake when he gets here."

***

By the time Drake arrived a half hour later, Maya's condition had worsened. Her body temperature was sizzling, her breathing labored, and she was clearly in pain. But the entire time she hadn't opened her eyes even once. She was delirious.

"What happened?" Drake asked as he entered the bedroom.

Gabriel shook his head. "I don't know. She told me she was coming down with something and went to bed without feeding from me. A few hours later she collapsed."

"Has she fed since?"

"Yes, but her condition isn't improving. It's getting worse by the minute."

Drake bent over the bed and looked at Maya, touched her forehead, and looked into her pupils. Only now he seemed to notice the witch, who'd stood near the fireplace and now approached the bed.

"Ah, Francine, what a surprise to see you here."

"Drake."

"Any ideas?" he asked and gestured to Maya.

"As a matter of fact, yes."

"Care to share?"

She nodded. "Excuse us a minute, vampire," she said to Gabriel and gestured to Drake to follow her into the bathroom.

Gabriel looked at Thomas, who'd entered the bedroom behind Drake. "Odd pair," Thomas commented.

"They can be as odd as they like, as long as they can help Maya." Gabriel stroked his hand over Maya's hot face. Instantly her head turned toward his hand and her mouth sought out his fingers, quickly sucking his thumb into her mouth. Gabriel gulped down a quick breath. Even unconscious, she was killing him. He could barely suppress his desire for her as it was, but when she sucked his thumb like that, all he could think of was her sucking his cock in the same manner.

He listened for the mumbled voices from the bathroom, but couldn't make out what they were saying. They seemed to talk quietly in order not to be overheard.

Gabriel pulled his thumb out of Maya's mouth and stroked her lips with it. Her tongue darted out and licked him. He leaned down to her, bringing his mouth closer to her ear. "Baby, you're driving me insane. I don't have any restraints left. If you don't stop, I don't know what I'll do."

She sighed and pulled his thumb back into her mouth. His cock strained against the zipper of his jeans, the metal teeth cutting into his flesh. He clenched his other hand into a fist, fighting the urge to take her. With a groan, he pulled his thumb from her mouth and stepped away from the bed.

"Have you told her how you feel about her?" Thomas asked.

Gabriel turned his head to look at him. "And then?"

"Don't you want to know whether she feels the same?"

"And what if she doesn't?"

Thomas cast a look back at Maya. "The way she craves your blood, I'd venture a guess that she craves your body just as much."

Gabriel was saved from answering when the bathroom door finally opened and Drake and the witch stepped out, their faces serious. His stomach sank. How bad could the news be?

"We both agree." Drake glanced at Maya.

"What is it?" Gabriel asked and ran his hand through his hair.

"She's in heat."

Gabriel didn't understand. "Heat? What do you mean?"

"Sexual heat," Drake explained. "Like a feline."

"But that's impossible," Gabriel protested. Heat was a sign of fertility. "She's a vampire. Vampire females don't go into heat—they're sterile."

"I know that. Don't you think I know that? But she isn't fully vampire—whatever else she is, it's making her go into heat."

"So, it's going to go away again?" If it really was sexual heat, surely it was only temporary.

"It would, but—"

"But what?"

"She's burning up. It's too much for her body. She could die. And there's only one way to stop the heat."

Gabriel had stopped listening. "Die? No. We can't allow that. We can't let her die. Doc? There must be something we can do."

"Not we," Drake said. "You."

Gabriel snapped his gaze to Drake and the witch. "I?"

The witch took a step toward him. "The only way to stop sexual heat is to satisfy her."

Her words echoed in his head. *Satisfy her.*

"How?"

Drake had the audacity to chuckle. "I'll leave that entirely up to you, Gabriel. I trust you do know how to make a woman come."

Finally it sunk in. They wanted him to make love to Maya. Stepping closer to the doctor, he hissed low under his breath, "But, I can't. You know I can't."

Behind him, Thomas cleared his throat. "If you want me to do it, I will. After all, it'll be like touching my sister. It won't mean anything."

Gabriel swiveled. "No!" Despite the fact that Thomas was gay and had no interest in Maya, he would never allow any man to touch her.

Thomas gave a crooked smile, and Gabriel instantly realized that he'd only made the offer to get a reaction out of him. Well, he'd gotten one, and if he wasn't careful he'd get the taste of his fist in addition to it.

"I'm not saying you should fuck her," Drake added, "God, even I wouldn't suggest doing such a thing to an unconscious woman, but there are other ways. Use your hands and your mouth on her. She needs to orgasm. It's the only way the heat will break."

15

The room was eerily quiet except for Maya's heavy breathing and the rustling of the sheets as she tossed and turned. They had all left: the doctor, the witch, and even Thomas, to give them privacy. Gabriel knew that Thomas was still somewhere in the house, but had retreated far enough so his sensitive hearing wouldn't pick up what Gabriel and Maya were doing. It was embarrassing enough that they all knew what was about to happen. Yet it didn't dampen his arousal.

This certainly wasn't what he'd planned. For starters, when he made love to her, he'd wanted her conscious and fully aware of him—fully accepting him—and not in this feverish state where she drifted in and out of consciousness. But he wanted to touch her and make love to her, even knowing what state she was in, and he cursed himself for it. She was vulnerable, and he was going to exploit her for his own pleasure.

Disgusted, he turned away from the bed. Would she hate him for it when she came to her senses and realized what he'd done, hate him for touching her without her permission? Would he lose her and any chance he might have ever had of obtaining her affections? But he had no choice, because he couldn't let her die.

Even in her delirious state, she'd sought to be close to him. She'd writhed against him just the way she had when she'd fed from him before. And the way she'd sucked his thumb, wasn't that proof enough that she wanted him?

Her heavy thrashing made him turn back to her. She needed him, and no matter what happened later, he couldn't ignore that need. Stripping off his shoes in midstride, he climbed onto the bed and gathered her in his arms.

"I'm here, baby, I'm here."

She seemed to breathe easier as he pressed her heated body to his. She appeared hotter than when he'd held her only minutes earlier. The doctor was right, if he didn't satisfy her, she would burn up.

He wouldn't undress her in order to leave her as much dignity as possible under the circumstances. And he wouldn't take any of his clothes off either so he could maintain a semblance of distance. Only his hand would touch her under cover of her nightgown. He wouldn't look at her naked body, only touch her. That way she would understand that he'd had no choice and that he'd tried everything not to take advantage of her.

Gabriel tipped her chin up with his hand and brought his lips to hers for a feather light kiss. They tasted of salt and woman, fertile and willing. He knew he shouldn't kiss her, but when he inhaled her scent, his body shut down his brain, and all he could do was react to the age-old knowledge of the mating call.

How he knew she was his, he couldn't explain, but his instinct told him that the woman in his arms was perfect for him. He'd never felt the same way for anybody else, not even for Jane, the wife who'd left him after their wedding night. He'd never felt the connection he felt to Maya, as if their lifelines were interlinked, one complete only with the other.

The more he inhaled her scent the deeper he felt the connection to her life force. When her lips parted under his, he invaded her and captured her tongue with his, stroking and licking, dancing and withdrawing. His saliva mingled with hers, and the taste of their combined fluids drugged him. He knew then that something was happening between them that couldn't be explained by mere lust and attraction. He would talk to the doctor about it, but not now. Now, he had to save the woman he loved.

Loved?

The realization jolted him. And then it soothed him.

"I love you," he whispered against her lips, then trailed his mouth along her neck to kiss her heated skin. He smelled the enticing scent of her blood coming from her plump vein and growled. His fangs lengthened and pushed passed his lips.

He jerked away from her. No, he couldn't bite her, couldn't allow himself to perform the highly intimate act of drinking from his woman if she hadn't permitted it. His, yes, he called her his, because for right now that's what she was: his.

His gaze swept over her trembling body and the blood-red nightgown she wore. A nightgown that barely covered her to mid-thigh, the fabric so thin, he could clearly see the outline of her hard nipples sitting on top of her plump breasts. The gown's spaghetti straps moved whenever her body twisted, and eventually they would drop from her shoulders and release the fabric covering her perfectly round globes.

Gabriel's hand slid to those breasts and cupped one of them. It filled his hand, the hard nipple rubbing against the center of his palm. His thumb explored her, caressed her flesh through the silk and grazed her nipple.

Her tossing stopped, and she arched into his touch. Without thinking, he pulled on the fabric, dislodged the strap and freed the beautiful mound he was fondling. Her skin was soft and smooth. Dropping his head, he licked his tongue over the nipple. He realized instantly that despite her semiconscious state she felt what he was doing: her hand slid onto the back of his neck to hold him to her breast.

"Yes," she mumbled, her voice sounding relieved as if she'd waited for a long time for this to happen. Did she want him? Did she know it was he who touched her?

Gabriel sucked the beautiful flesh deeper into his mouth and continued circling his tongue over the captured nipple while at the same time kneading her breast in his palm. He couldn't get enough of the feel of her, the texture of her skin, the scent of it.

He felt his pants constrict as his cock rapidly pumped full with blood and went hard in anticipation. Only, it would be in vain. The message that he wouldn't fuck her had obviously not reached his rampant cock.

He trailed his fingers down over her stomach, the thin silk bunching under her breasts. Going past her thighs he reached underneath her nightgown, reversed his travels and moved back north. When he reached the apex of her thighs, he touched her panties. Instantly, she moaned and arched her back off the bed.

Maya's panties were soaked with her arousal, a scent so intense it nearly robbed him of all reason. Trying to tamp down his lust, he stroked his fingers against the wet fabric and clearly felt her warm female flesh underneath.

"Oh, God, Maya," he despaired, not knowing how to hold himself back, how not to ravish her when every cell in his body screamed for him to take her.

Despite the fact that he'd promised himself not to look at her naked skin—well, he'd already broken that promise by exposing her breasts—he pulled down her panties and laid her bare. Her dark curls were trimmed in a slim bikini line, pointing down toward the core of her body. As if he needed any further directions.

His fingers followed downward and her legs immediately spread wider, inviting him to look at her, touch her, devour her. As he worked his way down her body, following the scent he would never be able to resist, her moans became more pronounced, as if she knew exactly what he was about to do—even if he didn't.

All he'd planned was to look at her, just once, just so he had something he could remember when he was alone in his bed. But when his gaze fell onto her beautiful pussy, those glistening pink lips called to him, beckoned him to taste her.

He'd never done anything like it. He understood the concept, of course. He'd even seen it done, not just recently when he'd watched Zane in the club, but also in plenty of porn movies. But he'd never actually put his mouth to a woman's pussy. Yet at this moment, there was no doubt in his mind that this was exactly what he craved: to eat Maya's delectable pussy, to feast on her, drink her nectar and lick her until she came apart in his mouth.

He'd never seen the fascination other men had with it—until now. She would be at his mercy, vulnerable and spread wide, unable to escape his seeking tongue. Even if she woke while he sucked her, he wouldn't stop. Once he started, he knew there wouldn't be any stopping him.

Gabriel glanced back at her face. Her eyes were still closed, but her lips were parted. When he slid one finger along her wet folds, he watched as she drew her lower lip into her mouth and bit on it. He moved his finger higher and found the little hooded bundle of flesh he was looking for. The moment he circled it with his moist finger, she moaned and twisted in the sheets. Her teeth released her lip, and she panted.

"Baby, I need to do this." He couldn't wait any longer. With a groan he sank down between her legs and opened her pussy up with both his hands. Her flesh was pink and moist and the most beautiful thing he'd ever seen. His tongue darted out and took its first tentative lick against her female flesh, lapping up the juices that oozed from her slit.

As they hit the taste buds on the back of his tongue, his body went rigid. A bolt akin to a lightning strike hit his body and vibrated through him. He shuddered.

Holy hell!

No other taste had ever filled him with such satisfaction and at the same time made him hunger for more. This was what he'd been waiting for all his life without even knowing. Everything about her was perfect.

Gabriel lifted his head and growled. He would kill anybody who dared take her away from him. And he wouldn't stop at the gates of heaven nor hell if the Grim Reaper ripped her from his arms. Because he recognized her now: Maya was his mate. Losing her would mean losing the only chance he had at happiness.

With this knowledge, he sank his mouth back onto her core and gave her what her body so desperately needed. His mind catalogued every groove of her pussy, every fold, every ridge as he enjoyed lapping his tongue against her slit. He noticed every tiny movement she made and every breath she took.

His heart drummed in his chest.

She was a feast, and he'd never had a more sumptuous buffet spread out only for him to indulge in. Without haste he devoured her, nibbled on her soft flesh, licked and sucked her heated skin. He watched for every reaction from her, every moan, every sigh.

His hands slipped underneath her ass to tilt her upwards so he could drive his tongue into her tight channel.

"Oh!" he heard her moan and wondered whether she was conscious. He didn't want to think of it, because he wouldn't be able to stop now, even if she begged him to. Or would she beg him to continue?

Determined to give her the ultimate pleasure, he fucked his tongue in and out of her pussy, then alternated it with licking her clit. The little bundle of flesh was engorged and erect. Every time he flicked his tongue against it, her body trembled. Gabriel sensed that she was close, and even though he didn't want this to end, he knew what he had to do.

He slipped a finger into her wet folds and felt her muscles grip him tightly. He growled. If only it was his cock sheathing itself in her. With his mouth he sucked her clit and pulled it between his lips, pressing them together tightly.

Maya's body shook. He felt the spasms in her pussy clench his finger and the waves lap against his lips as her climax rocked through her. Her scream was the purest sound of release he'd ever heard.

Gabriel kept his mouth surrounding her clit and licked against it gently as she rode out her orgasm.

Maya felt the waves of pleasure course through her body and greeted the release they brought with them. The heat in her body dissipated, and for the first time in hours she could breathe. As she took a long deep breath, her nostrils flared. At the same time, she noticed the heaviness on her groin and someone's hot breath on her pussy.

Her eyes flew open.

There, between her spread legs, Gabriel's mouth was centered over her still-throbbing clit, and his tongue still stroked against it, threatening to ignite her once more.

"Gabriel."

As if stung by a hornet, his head reared up, and his gaze collided with hers. She'd never seen him like this. His eyes were dark with passion and his lips raw and moist from her juices. He'd sucked her while she'd been unconscious. She should feel violated, embarrassed at least, but strangely no such thoughts took hold. Was she turning into a completely wanton creature now that she was a vampire?

"Maya, I can explain." His voice was laced with guilt and regret. She didn't understand it. She watched him shift his position and climb up the bed to sit next to her as his hand quickly pulled on her nightdress to cover her nakedness with the fabric.

She noticed now how nervous he was as if he'd gotten caught doing something he shouldn't be doing. Well, she *had* caught him, but she didn't mind what he'd been doing. Her only regret was that she hadn't been awake for it.

"What were you doing?" she asked.

Gabriel ran his hand through his long hair, which was loose today— no ponytail. She liked it and felt the urge to sink her hands into the rich mane.

"I'm sorry. I had to do it. The doc and the witch, they both said . . . " He broke off and looked away.

Why was he avoiding her now? She gripped his chin with her hand and forced him to look at her. "Tell me what's going on."

He blinked. "You were in heat. The doc said you'd die if nobody satisfied you. So they decided that I should do it." He dropped his lids and looked down.

"They?"

"Drake and the witch."

Maya didn't know who the witch was, but she didn't care. What was important was that Gabriel had been forced to do this. He'd done it to save her, not because he wanted her. "They made you do it?"

He nodded. "Please believe me. I would have never taken advantage of you this way if I hadn't feared for your life."

Maya swallowed the lump in her throat that had risen at his words. He would have never touched her otherwise. Only because she had been in danger. So he still felt he was responsible for her—that was all. "I thank you, and I'm sorry that you were forced to do this against your will." She steeled herself against the pain it caused her to know that he'd touched her without wanting to.

"Maya, that's not what I meant."

She stared at him as he looked up again.

"I wanted to do it. I wanted nothing more than to make you come with my hands and my mouth. I'd promised myself to leave you as much dignity as I could, but Maya, when I looked at you, I couldn't help myself. I . . . " There was anguish in his face. She couldn't fathom why. He'd wanted to touch her, and the knowledge of it warmed her heart. He'd felt something. He was attracted to her, just the way she was attracted to him.

"Gabriel, why are you torturing yourself?" She reached for his face and cupped her palm over his scar. He flinched as if he'd expected her to slap him.

"You're not mad at me? You don't hate me for it?" he asked.

Maya inched toward him. "Mad?" She tilted his face to her and pulled him closer. "No, I'm not mad. I'm only disappointed."

She saw him swallow hard. "God, I'm sorry."

She shook her head and smiled. "I'm only disappointed because I wasn't conscious for it."

Something changed in his eyes. There was a flicker of surprise in his irises and then a sharp intake of breath. "You mean . . . ?"

Gabriel's hand touched her cheek and his thumb stroked over her lips. She parted her lips and licked at the pad of his thumb. "Gabriel, I barely know you, but when you touch me, I feel alive. More alive than I ever was as a human."

"When Drake told me you might die, I almost lost my mind. Maya, I don't know what's happening between us, but I know I need you."

Her heart leapt at his admission. She wanted to be needed. And she wanted this proud vampire to want her. "Are you going to kiss me?"

In one swift move, his lips captured hers. She tasted herself on his tongue when he stroked against her and invaded her mouth, but the taste only added to her excitement. Gabriel wanted her. He'd shown her in one of the most intimate ways how much he wanted her, and she hadn't even been able to consciously feel it. She would change this very quickly. This time she would be experiencing every single second of their lovemaking and not miss a thing.

His kiss was one of possession and passion. No man had ever kissed her like that, with such fervor, such determination. And yet such tenderness and reverence—as if he worshipped her. She gave herself over to the delicious feeling of being desired by a passionate man. Her entire being hummed from his kiss, and she felt herself become aroused once more.

All the pain she'd been through was forgotten. This last episode had been her worst by far. Never had she felt the fever so intensely. What had Gabriel called it? Heat? She didn't know what he'd meant by it, but she'd sensed even in her delirium that her body had been burning. She would have to ask Drake about it later, but now she didn't want to waste the moment.

She was in Gabriel's arms, arms that wrapped around her back and held her to him with such fierceness she could barely breathe. It didn't matter. She didn't need to breathe when she could inhale his scent instead. Just like his blood, the taste of his lips was drugging. Her body responded to him so naturally, she couldn't have pulled away from him even if she'd wanted to.

This was the man she wanted to make love to. She instinctively knew that he would be the one who could fill that gaping void that she'd always felt when having sex with other men. Nobody had ever been able to completely satisfy her cravings, nor had she even been able to truly express to anybody what she needed. She'd never felt safe enough with anybody to admit her darkest desires, but in Gabriel's arms she felt secure and cherished.

When he released her lips, she saw him smile at her.

"We were so worried about you."

"I get these fevers, but this time it was worse than ever before."

He nodded. "I know."

"You know? How?"

He stroked his palm over her cheek. "We looked at your medical file."

She opened her mouth to voice a comment about Drake's lack of ethics, but Gabriel put his finger to her lips.

"I'm sorry, but I forced Drake to tell me. Anything that concerns you concerns me."

"Why?"

He placed a soft kiss on her lips before he answered. "Because I'm only happy when I know you're safe and you're well. I care about you—a lot."

Maya felt her heart swell at his admission. "You do?"

"More than I can tell you."

She took a deep breath and let the knowledge sink in. It felt good. For a moment, she merely smiled at him, then she brought her thoughts back to other things. "Didn't you say that vampires don't get sick?"

"Yes, that's true for all of us. But the doctor doesn't think it's an illness. He thinks it's heat—the way a feline would go into sexual heat during her cycle."

"But I'm not a cat—I'm a vampire now. And Yvette told me that vampire females are infertile. So it doesn't make sense that I would go into heat. What for?"

Gabriel stared at her. "Yvette told you that?"

"You mean it's not true?" Was there hope after all?

"No, it's true." He swallowed. "But *I* should have been the one telling you this. In fact, I should explain things to you. There are so many things nobody's told you yet. I should be doing that. I'm sorry, I haven't so far."

She pushed back the disappointment—so she probably was sterile. Hopefully, she would come to terms with it one day. Would Gabriel? "It's not your fault. I didn't give you much of a chance to explain things to me."

He pulled her closer to his chest. "How about I tell you now? Or are you tired?"

"No, I'm not tired."

"Good. Where shall I start?" he asked.

"How about at the beginning?"

"The beginning?"

16

Maya played with the buttons of Gabriel's shirt, easing one after the other open before she slipped her hand onto his naked chest.

"Are you trying to distract me? Because if you are, you're doing an excellent job," he said in a low voice. Damn, his voice was sexy.

"How did it all start? The vampires. How did vampires come to be?"

Gabriel took her hand and clasped it with his, stopping her from stroking his chest but keeping it pressed against his warm skin. "There are many legends, or course, but much of the lore in popular fiction is false. The belief among our kind is much different. It's said that the first vampire was an evil man who made a pact with the Devil and drew the wrath of God onto him. He was a misguided man destroyed by greed. He wanted to rule the world, but rule it with violence. When God learned of his plan, he cursed him to walk the night, so his own creatures would be safe from him by day."

Maya listened with bated breath. "But why did God give him such powers then, and the lust for human blood? Wouldn't that go against his wish to protect humans from him?"

"God didn't give him those powers. The Devil did. He protects his own. When God condemned our ancestor to the night, the Devil bestowed him with powers to survive the night and frighten humans. He made him strong during the night, but couldn't change anything about his weakness to the light. And so the first vampire was created."

Disgust rose in Maya. "Does this mean we worship the Devil?"

Gabriel laughed and shook his head. "No. We have our free will. We alone decide how we act—never forget that. You can be as good or as evil as you decide. It's in your own heart. Your decisions are still your own, and don't let anybody tell you otherwise."

She relaxed at his words. "How did you become a vampire?"

Gabriel closed his eyes as if wishing the memories away. When he opened them again, he gave her a sad smile. "I wasn't very happy in my human life. I was alone, and with the scar on my face, female companionship was difficult to attract. I had the misguided notion that if I were a powerful man, things would change. So when I got to know a man who seemed to have everything I wanted, I spoke to him, and he took pity on me. My sire was a kind man, but it turned out that even as a vampire, I was still the same man: lonely and with a disfiguring scar."

Maya stroked her hand over his face. She didn't mind the scar, but if it seemed to bother him, maybe something could be done about it. "There are many good plastic surgeons today who would—"

He stilled her hand with his. "My body was set in stone the moment I turned into a vampire. Just like my hair would grow back to this length if I cut it short, anything I change on my body will be restored while I sleep, so that I'll look exactly like I did at my turning. A vampire can't change his physical form."

Maya's hand instantly went to her face. "You mean I will look exactly like this forever?"

He nodded. "Long dark hair, beautiful eyes, no wrinkles, just a few laugh lines."

She grinned. "Just as well that I shaved my legs the night of the attack then."

Gabriel broke out in a hearty laugh. She'd never heard him laugh, and she discovered she liked it, liked the way his deep rumble went through her body. There was a twinkle in his eyes when he looked at her. "Only a woman can distill things down to their most elemental." Then his hand ran down her torso to her thigh. "Even though, I must admit, I do like those smooth legs of yours."

She took hold of his hand. Not that she didn't want what he was offering, but since she had him talking, she wanted to know more. "What else will change in my life? How will people not realize that I don't get older?"

"Ah, that's the difficult part. In general, most of us live quiet lives. We have our own communities and stay away from humans as much as we can. It was easier in the eighteenth and nineteenth centuries when recordkeeping was not as thorough as today. With Social Security numbers and the like, we have unfortunately taken to forging a lot of documents."

"You mean like fake IDs?"

"Something like that. We do a lot of planning these days. Every twenty-five to thirty years we birth a new identity—we report the birth of a child, establish a Social Security number and all kinds of school and graduation records in order to set up a history."

"That sounds complicated."

"Not when you have a few talented IT guys among your kind, who can hack into just about any computer record. In fact, with the advent of computers, it's made our lives easier again. No more breaking into City Halls at night or bribing a few well-placed employees in the county recorder's offices." He winked at her, but her mind was already on how difficult all this sounded.

"I have no idea how I would do any of this. Where do I even start?"

Gabriel shelved her chin on his hand. "Don't worry about it. I'll take care of everything for you." The sincerity in his eyes was real. She knew instinctively that he would give her everything she needed. But could she accept this?

"I can't be dependent on you."

A frown disturbed his features. "But I want to take care of you."

"I've always done everything for myself. I don't know how to rely on anybody else."

"We all rely on other vampires: to help us create identities for us, to keep our secrets, to protect us. It's like a big family. Nobody will think you weak for relying on others of our kind."

"My kind—it feels so strange to say that. I don't want to offend anybody, but they don't feel like my kind. They're all so strong and secure, and I feel anything but. And besides, I'm not even a normal vampire: I get sick, human blood disgusts me—"

"I'm sure there's a perfectly plausible explanation for that. And we're going to find it. In the meantime, you'll feed from me."

"You don't mind?"

He chuckled softly. "Mind?" His arms wrapped tightly around her as he pulled her closer. "When I feel your fangs in my neck, I'm practically in heaven. It's the most arousing thing I've ever felt."

Her breath caught in her throat. She'd found it just as arousing. "Is it always like that for you?"

Gabriel's eyes widened in surprise. "Always? Maya, you're the only one who's ever fed from me. I wouldn't know what it's like with anybody else—and honestly, I don't care to know. I'm perfectly happy to let you drink my blood every day for as long as you want to."

As long as she wanted to? What was he trying to tell her? Did this mean he was interested in a long-term relationship? She remembered what Yvette had told her—that a vampire wanted a human to bond with so he could have children. Did he want that? Was this also what he was ultimately looking for? She couldn't ask him outright. Everything was too new. It was as if she asked a man after the first date whether he wanted children. Vampire or not—no man wanted a woman clinging to him after a few dates. And besides, they hadn't even been on a date.

Going down on her while she was unconscious didn't exactly qualify as a date. Also, there was something else she wanted. "Gabriel?"

He pressed his forehead to hers. "Hmm?"

"Make love to me." She needed to feel him. Her hand went to the front of his jeans where she could feel his hard length strain against it. Before she could even attempt to pry the button open, he clasped her hand with his.

"I'd much rather show you what you missed while you were unconscious."

Was he for real? Gabriel wanted to go down on her when he could take his own pleasure instead? "You mean do it again?"

"May I?"

She met his look. It was full of desire and promise. He wanted her. There was no doubt about it. Maya pulled his head toward hers. "Touch me," she breathed against his lips.

When his mouth claimed hers, she felt an unknown euphoria travel through her body. Everything about him was so familiar, yet so new. His kiss was different from the times when he'd kissed her before. Gone was the hesitation she'd felt from him before, replaced by the confidence of a man who was used to making demands.

His hands explored her with sure strokes. His fingers teased her heated skin, promising pleasure, demanding surrender. Like a conqueror he forged ahead, his tongue dueling with hers, his lips crushing any doubt she'd ever had.

Closer and closer he pressed her to him, his body heat searing her, yet she couldn't pull back, didn't want to. He set her aflame. No other man had ever been able to ignite her like he did with merely a kiss and a caress. Like her body knew him, recognized him, and connected to him on a different level.

His hands on her conjured up images of wild and untamed sex, not simply a joining of bodies, but of minds and souls. A deeper connection. All the things she'd ever wanted from a man—all the forbidden cravings she'd never voiced—tumbled to the forefront. She wanted to be taken by him in every way possible.

As his lips traveled south, and he sucked one nipple into his mouth and greedily devoured it, her body heat spiked. She was feverish, but this wasn't the fever she knew. This was desire for Gabriel. She arched toward him, demanding he give her more. With a low growl, he scraped his teeth against her sensitive nipple.

"Oh, God . . . Gabriel!"

His chuckle was a deep rumble. By the sound of it, he knew exactly what he was doing to her. He was turning her into putty in his hands. No man had ever been able to do that.

He only lifted his head briefly, his dark chocolate eyes now sparkling red, his fangs protruding from his lips. "I haven't even started . . . "

Just the thought of what his words implied made her shiver with delight. A moment later, his mouth moved lower, planting open-mouthed kisses interlaced with playful bites down her stomach. Each one of them felt like a little explosion going off inside her. Had she ever been this sensitive to a man's touch, or was her vampire side doing this to her?

No, this couldn't just be because she was a vampire now. Even if she were still human, she was certain, Gabriel's touch would ignite her the same way. But she couldn't think any further, because the second his mouth reached her pussy and buried itself in her dark thatch of hair, her brain shut down. All she could do now was to feel.

When his tongue lapped at her moist folds, Maya moaned. He answered with a growl. She couldn't imagine a sexier sound. As she steeled herself for the onslaught of sensations his tongue unleashed on her, she slid her hands into his hair and felt him tremble. A smile stole onto her lips. The knowledge that she had the same effect on him as he had on her filled her with satisfaction.

His tongue drove deep into her while his thumb rubbed over her clit. His action stole her breath. Again he speared his tongue and forged deep into her, then he pulled back and let his tongue slide over her clit. Her need spiraled.

"Need you inside," Maya demanded. She wanted to feel his hard shaft inside her, filling her, taking her, making her submit to him.

A finger plunged into her, then a second one, but she wanted more, needed more.

"Your cock. Let me feel you inside."

But Gabriel didn't heed her demand; instead, he drove three fingers into her and sucked greedily on her engorged clit. Before she could repeat her demand, he clamped down on her clit and drove her over the edge. The waves of pleasure crashed over her like a tsunami annihilating the Pacific coast.

By the time her breathing returned to normal and her body's spasms had subsided, Gabriel had pulled her back into his arms and cradled her to his chest.

She lifted her head to look at him. "I want you inside me."

He smiled and put his finger on her lips. "Next time, baby, next time."

How could he not want this when she clearly felt his raging erection press against her stomach? "Now, please."

Gabriel cupped her face with his palm. "You need to rest a little. I want you, baby, don't ever doubt that. And soon, I'll make you mine."

His kiss prevented her next question.

17

Maya took a deep breath before she stepped into the kitchen. She felt invigorated by her shower and by having slept in Gabriel's arms. He had given her more pleasure by touching and kissing her than she had ever felt during regular sex. When she was with him, things felt right again in her life. Almost as if everything was normal again, no, not normal—better.

For the first time since the transformation, she had a true awareness of her new body. She felt how her senses were attuned to her surroundings, how her body processed stimuli differently. It was a strange experience, almost as if this wasn't her body, but somebody else's. Somebody else's, because for the first time in her life, she'd felt true sexual satisfaction in this body. Or maybe it wasn't that she had a vampire body now, maybe it was all because of what Gabriel had done: he'd showered her with tenderness and passion without taking any pleasure for himself.

Maya knew Gabriel was in the kitchen even before she entered it. He'd slipped out of bed an hour before sunset, reassuring her that he would want nothing more than spend the entire night in bed with her. But he had work to do.

Gabriel greeted her with the smile of a satisfied man plastered on his face and drew her into his arms.

"Did you sleep well?" he asked against her lips.

"Only up until you left the bed."

His lips curled upwards before he brushed them against her mouth. Then he straightened, and his face turned serious again. "I had to get in contact with my people. I spoke to Ricky, but he hasn't been able to get in touch with your friends yet. I guess they're harder to pin down than we thought."

"I could page them if you want."

Gabriel shook his head. "And tell them what? Ricky said that a neighbor saw Paulette leave with an overnight bag."

"Oh, I forgot. She has that one-day seminar in Seattle once a month and likes to go there the night before so she won't be too tired."

"Good. Then she'll be back tomorrow. I'll tell Ricky. As for Barbara, he's trying to catch her at the hospital." He looked at his watch. "I have to meet with Zane now. Do you want to feed before I leave?"

The thought of sinking her fangs into his neck made Maya feel flushed again. If she fed from him now, there was no way he would leave this house within the next hour or two, because for certain she would drag him back to bed.

"No, I'm fine right now."

He gave her a look she thought might be disappointment. "If you say so."

Maya stretched her arms out and put her fingers to his lips. "You know what will happen if I feed from you right now, don't you? So why don't you go and meet with Zane. In the meantime, I'll work up an appetite." She licked her lips. "I'm sure I'll be ravenous when you get back."

The wicked glint in his eyes made her heart beat twice as fast as before.

"Good. I look forward to dinner."

She followed him out into the hallway, where Gabriel called out, "Thomas, where are you?"

A moment later, Thomas emerged from Samson's study. "What do you need?"

"Take care of Maya. I have to go see Zane." Before he turned, he added, "Any news on the phone records?"

Thomas shook his head. "AT&T's servers are still down. I'm having Eddie monitor them. He's supposed to call me as soon as they're up again."

Gabriel nodded. "Thanks."

After a quick kiss on her lips, he was gone. Maya turned around to look at Thomas. "What phone records?"

"Yours—we've figured that maybe the rogue called you at some point, especially if you were dating him."

Maya cringed at the thought. She could have never been intimate with somebody so evil, could she? Would she have recognized what he was like early enough—before she'd jumped into bed with him? Why could she not remember anything about him? For a moment, she closed her eyes and concentrated, but no flash of memory came.

"You okay?" Thomas's voice sounded concerned. "It was touch-and-go for a while there. Are you well?"

She was acutely aware that Thomas knew full well what she and Gabriel had been doing during the last few hours, and she felt surprisingly tongue-tied about it. When she lowered her lids to avoid his gaze and only mumbled a quick "yes," he clicked his tongue.

"There's nothing wrong with what you guys did. Gabriel is a good man."

"I barely know him, but for some reason, I *do* know him. Does that make sense?"

"As I said, it's all good."

Maya lifted her head and smiled at him. She liked Thomas and knew she could have an easy friendship with him. "Thanks. About those phone records: I get itemized online bills from my cell phone provider. Would that help?"

Thomas nodded eagerly. "Sure would. I can't hack into AT&T right now, so if we can access the records any other way, it would speed up the search."

"I only have the last three months online. This month's isn't available yet."

"Better than nothing."

But after spending half an hour looking through the cell phone bills, Maya had to admit defeat. "I know all those people: friends, patients, colleagues. There's not a single unfamiliar name among them. Sorry."

Thomas shrugged his shoulders. "It was worth a try."

"Maybe he called me on the landline—unfortunately I don't get itemized bills for that."

"Don't worry. As soon as the servers of the telephone company are back up, I'll access the records and have you look through them. In the meantime, there's not much else we can do about that."

Never one to sit around idle, Maya felt restless. She was sure it would take hours until Gabriel was back. "Do you think you could teach me a few things? Gabriel mentioned that you do mentoring."

"That's right; I have a new vampire under my wings right now. It's a very rewarding role."

"What do you teach him or her?"

"Him," he answered. "I teach Eddie how to control his urges, how to use his special skills."

Maya smiled at him. "Gabriel told me you're the best at teaching mind control."

Thomas raised an eyebrow. "Starting with the hard stuff—you're ambitious."

"I've always been an A-student."

"This is a little different than studying. It's got more to do with emotions than with knowledge. I think we should wait and work on some more elemental skills, like how to control your strength."

Maya squared her chest. "No. I want to learn mind control. And I want to learn it now."

Thomas smirked. "Gabriel is going to have his hands full with you." Then he laughed. "Does he know yet?"

"Know what?"

"That you're headstrong."

"He's a smart man; he'll figure it out soon enough."

"Okay then. But we need somebody to try mind control on." Thomas wrinkled his forehead. "Ever been to a gay bar?"

"Why are we going to a gay bar?"

"Because it's the least likely place somebody will recognize you."

Maya shrugged. "If you keep the lesbians away from me, I'm game."

"Deal. Just don't keep the cute guys away from *me*."

"As if I could." Maya looked Thomas up and down. He was a formidable specimen of the male kind, and the way he filled out his leather pants was distracting to say the least. Thankfully, she had her heart set on Gabriel; otherwise, she would be in serious trouble falling for a gay man.

"Thanks. That's nice of you to say." Thomas seemed surprised at her comment.

Half an hour later, she and Thomas squeezed through a throng of people to get into the Q Bar in the heart of the Castro. He used his body to drag her behind him through the crowd which miraculously parted to let them through. The bouncer barely looked at them before he waved them in.

Maya voiced her suspicion. "Did you use mind control on—"

He cut her off. "Don't use those words. Call it *skill* while we're in public."

She nodded, doubting anybody had heard her in the crowded bar where the music blared and everybody tried to shout over each other. "Did you use your skill?" she asked instead.

She knew she didn't have to shout. Thomas could hear her just fine, as she could him. In fact, she noticed how she was able to tune in and out of conversations at will.

"I didn't have to. The bouncer knows me. I don't waste my skill where it's not needed. It takes energy. If you use it to excess, it exhausts you. Only use it when it's necessary. And never on one of our kind."

Maya nodded. "Yvette told me already."

"Good. Then you're forewarned. Very few of us can avoid a battle and pull their skill back once we're attacked."

Curiosity overtook her. "Can you?"

Thomas gave her a serious look. "Too personal a question. I'll pass."

"Sorry." She turned toward the bar, not wanting to see his reprimanding look.

With a hand on his shoulder he turned her back to him. "There are things each of us keeps close to his heart—you'll understand one day. We all have things we won't talk about. Just like you do."

Maya's breath hitched. What did he know about her? For a few moments, she felt frozen in time.

"Maya, I can't read your mind, so relax. I have no interest in knowing what you don't want anybody to know. Someone else might though." He winked and grinned. "Now let's start with our little lesson; otherwise, I might be accused of just using you as an excuse to go out."

The tenseness in Maya's shoulders eased, and she smiled back at him. "You mean you weren't?"

"If you tell Gabriel that I was, I swear I'll tell him you forced me."

"You're a nice guy, you know that, Thomas?"

He tossed a look to his right, then his left. "Don't say that so loud, woman. If that news spreads, I'll never get another date around here." He frowned in mock anger. "Nice guys don't get laid."

"Okay, then, teach me." Maya was curious now. If she had to embrace her new life, she would make the most of it. And if this meant she got some superpower, then even better.

"Good. Here's what you do. See that man nursing his drink in the corner? He's shy. I want you to make him get up and walk up to that dark-haired hunk at the bar and put his hand on his ass."

Maya looked at the man Thomas was referring to. He sat in the corner, his lids lowered as if he was ashamed to be here. Every so often, he led his beer glass to his lips and sipped. She felt sorry for him. He clearly didn't feel comfortable. Then her eyes drifted to the dark-haired man at the bar. She looked him up and down. "You've got to be kidding me, Thomas. He's got no chance."

"That's precisely the point. That's why you will help him. You'll plant the confidence in his mind so he can walk up to that guy and ask him out. You'll control his mind to think he has a chance."

Maya shook her head. "How?"

Thomas looked straight into her face. "Look inside yourself. Concentrate on your heartbeat. Then concentrate on the man in the corner and tell him what to do. Send your thoughts out to him. Try it."

She took a few deep breaths, then tried to shut out the noise from the bar. She'd done yoga before, so she tried to remember what it felt like to center her body and calm her mind. A pleasant warmth filled her body. "I feel warm."

"That's good," Thomas praised. "Your body is telling you you're collecting your strength. It's the energy that you gather inside you that creates the warm feeling."

She nodded without responding, trying not to break her concentration. She looked at the man and formed words in her mind.

Get up. Go to the bar. Put your hands on the dark-haired man's ass.

Maya repeated her thoughts and directed them toward the man again. But he didn't move.

"Try again," Thomas encouraged her. "Put all your energy into it. Think of nothing else."

Again, she collected her strength and calmed her mind. All she tried to concentrate on was the man in the corner, how he sat there, eyes lowered to his beer, his hand clasping the glass. She closed her eyes and sent her thoughts to him again, telling him to put the beer down and get up. The sound of a shattering glass made her snap her eyes open.

She stared at her victim. Before him on the table were the remnants of the glass, the spilled beer running down the edges of the table. With horror, he stared at his hands, which had crushed the glass.

Maya spun to face Thomas. "Did I do that?"

"Did you tell him to break the beer glass?"

"No, of course not. I told him to set the beer down and get up."

Thomas rubbed his chin. "Hmm. That's odd. Let's try again. But I think that poor sod's suffered enough for one night. I think he needs a bit of a treat right now."

"What do you mean?"

"Watch." Thomas turned away from her and looked into the direction of the hunk at the bar. A moment later, the man turned and looked toward the guy in the corner. Without hesitation, he walked toward him, sat down next to him and took his hand.

Maya tuned into their conversation.

"I'm an EMT. Let me look at your hand. You don't want that to get infected."

The shy man gave him a grateful smile. "Thanks."

"Why don't I bandage that up for you? I live just around the corner and have a first-aid kit at home."

Maya picked up on the suggestive look the EMT gave the shy man. A moment later, the two got up and left the bar.

"You're a genius. How did you know that guy was an EMT?"

Thomas grinned. "I dated him before."

"But he didn't look as if he recognized you," Maya protested. Or was it usual among gays that they pretended they didn't know each other after things were over?

"That's because he doesn't. I wiped his memory after it was over."

Maya opened her mouth to make her displeasure known, but Thomas raised his palm. "Security measure. I'll teach you some other time. One skill at a time. And just so you know, no, I didn't use my skill to get a date with him. I can still get laid without it."

Maya smirked. She'd never doubted that he could attract other men.
"Now back to the task at hand."

"What if I never learn it?" She hated failure.

"You'll learn it. Don't worry, we all did."

But Thomas's optimism faded with every try. First, Maya managed
to pop a button off a man's jeans while trying to get him to walk to the
bathroom. The next time she tried to persuade a man to walk up to the
bar to make a pass at the bartender, a bar stool knocked the man in his
groin and stopped him in his tracks.

"Ouch," Thomas grimaced.

"I'm not doing this on purpose," Maya assured him. She was getting
frustrated by now. As hard as she tried to concentrate, she was unable to
make anybody do anything at all. Instead she kept on moving objects
around.

"This is obviously not working the way we anticipated. Let's try
something else."

"Wiping memories?" she asked, hoping they could erase all those
embarrassing incidents from people's minds.

"No. You're not ready for that."

Maya pouted. She was a failure. And she didn't like that feeling at
all. Already she was a truly odd vampire who craved the blood of her
sire instead of that of a human. Then she went into heat when vampires
shouldn't go into heat because they were sterile. And now she couldn't
even master mind control. How pathetic was that?

"Get me that bowl of nuts from the end of the bar," Thomas ordered.

Maya looked as the small, nearly empty bowl, which nobody
seemed to claim. "But you don't eat."

"Just get it."

She took a step toward it, but Thomas held her back with his arm.
"With your mind."

"And how am I supposed to do that?"

"The same way you broke that glass and moved that bar stool. Just
do it."

Unconvinced that it would work, Maya merely gave the whole thing
half her attention.

Bowl, move and stop in front of Thomas.

She jolted when the bowl indeed moved and slid along the bar until it came to a halt in front of Thomas.

"I thought you didn't want to teach me another skill."

"I didn't. This is you. And only you. It appears," he dropped his voice and moved his head closer to her ear, "that you can't impose your mind on humans, but you have no trouble with inanimate objects, which, if I might add, none of our kind can do. I think you're unique."

Unique. "Don't tell me that's another word for *special*. I don't want to be special. I want to be normal," she snapped. Couldn't she at least be a normal vampire? Or was that too much to ask?

"Now, now," Thomas's calm voice tried to soothe her, "not everybody is lucky enough to have an extraordinary gift like that. There'll be a day when you'll be grateful you have this skill."

Maya huffed. "I doubt it."

"Thomas!" a male voice called out only a few feet away from them.

Thomas spun his head to look at the man. Maya watched the young blond man as he came closer. She sensed his aura and knew immediately that he was a vampire. So this was what Yvette had been talking about.

When he stopped close enough to touch, Maya noticed the glare Thomas leveled at him. "Eddie, what the fuck are you doing in a gay bar?"

Before Maya could figure out why Thomas was so angry with him, Eddie addressed her. "I'm Eddie. I'm one of the guys who found you that night."

Maya stretched out her hand, and he took it. "Thank you. I'm very grateful."

"You're welcome." Then he looked back at Thomas. "And I wouldn't be here if Gabriel hadn't sent me to find you. That man is livid."

"Why's Gabriel upset?" Maya asked before Thomas could reply.

Eddie grinned. "He got back to the house and found it empty. Now he's sent every single v—uh, bodyguard," he corrected himself, "out to search for you."

Maya's hair on her neck stood. "What's his problem? I'm just out with Thomas."

"Apparently he didn't authorize you to leave the house."

"Authorize?" A cold shudder raked her body. Control. Somebody was trying to control her again. Again? Why did this feel so familiar? A strange sense of *déjà vu* filled her. She'd never let anybody control her life. So why did it feel like this had happened before?

A flash of memory came and went just as quickly. Too quickly to register what it was. Control—it was the only word her brain could form. Had there been somebody in her past who'd wanted to control her? Instinctively her hand went to her neck, to the spot where the rogue had bitten her, where he'd lodged his fangs into her and drained her. A blast of cold air washed over her, like the fog this city was famous for.

Suddenly everything felt wrong. She felt fear clamp down on her and realized that she'd never again feel safe. Now that she knew what was out there in this world, the cocoon of safety she'd thought herself in when she was human didn't exist. It never had, and it never would again.

"Maya," Thomas's voice jolted her.

"Yes?"

"I said we'd better get back," Thomas replied. Then he looked at Eddie. "And you're coming with us."

"What if I wanted to hang out here for a while?" Maya could tell that Eddie was merely teasing, but she wasn't sure Thomas picked up on that.

"Out. Now." Thomas's tone was harsh and unyielding. Eddie answered with a grin and a wink toward Maya.

But Maya didn't feel like smiling. She couldn't allow anybody to control her, least of all Gabriel. If she did, she would lose what little of herself was left. She'd already lost her sense of security, her humanity, and her livelihood. She had to hold onto the last thing she had left: control over her decisions. She couldn't allow anybody to make those for her.

18

Gabriel balled his hands into fists. How could Thomas show such poor judgment by taking Maya out of the house without sufficient backup to protect her? Had he already forgotten that the rogue was still out there, ready to attack her a second time? He couldn't risk anything happening to her. He'd only just found her—the only woman he'd ever wanted for himself—and nobody had the right to take her away from him.

The fear in his gut churned to anger. Without Maya in his life, all light would vanish from it. After the hours he'd spent with her in bed where she'd allowed him to touch and kiss her, he'd felt happier than he ever had in his entire life. He'd floated on Cloud Nine until he'd met up with Zane to get a detailed update on his investigation.

The results Zane had presented had been bleak. Of all possible vampire males who could be responsible for the attack on Maya, some of Scanguards' own were on the list. A frown crossed Gabriel's face when he recalled the names on the list: names of vampires whose whereabouts couldn't be confirmed at the time of the attack. Men he'd known for a long time: three excellent guards from Scanguards, and even Ricky and Zane were on the list.

Zane, straightforward as he was, had admitted to him that he too didn't have an alibi, at least not one that could be verified—apparently he'd been at some dive fucking anything in sight. And true to his *modus operandi*, he'd wiped everybody's memory of him. Apparently, Ricky had done the same at a different nightspot. Considering his recent breakup with Holly, that was to be expected and certainly not unusual.

Gabriel swallowed away his doubts. No, nobody that close to them could be responsible for this. If he couldn't trust his own people, who could he trust? But still, could he simply dismiss the possibility because they were part of Scanguards? Zane had been in Maya's room when she'd woken, but he had made no attempts at approaching her since.

Was it deliberate? Was he staying away from her so he wouldn't attract any attention?

The noise of two motorcycles halting in front of the house interrupted his dark thoughts. Gabriel rushed to the door and swung it open to see Maya rise off the back of Thomas's Ducati. Eddie was riding the second bike. Gabriel had known instinctively that if anybody could find Thomas, it would be Eddie. After all, he spent the most time with him.

Still seething with anger over Thomas's irresponsible action, he suppressed his urge to run to Maya and take her into his arms. He had to deal with Thomas first and make it clear to him that any further actions that endangered Maya couldn't be tolerated and would be punished.

As the three marched toward him, Gabriel stepped aside to let them enter. He slammed the door as soon as they were inside the foyer.

"Did you have any idea what you were doing, Thomas?" Gabriel thundered. "Maya could have been attacked out there."

"Gabriel, she was never in any danger."

Gabriel crossed the distance between him and Thomas and went nose-to-nose with him. "You had no right to take her out of the house and put her at risk. I forbid you to—"

"Gabriel, stop!" Maya cut in. He snapped his head toward her and found her standing with her hands at her hips. "That's enough. I asked Thomas to get me out of the house. I've been cooped up here for days. You can't keep me locked up here forever."

"Is that what you thought? That I'm keeping you prisoner?" All he'd done was protect her. Didn't she realize that?

"It sure feels like it," she grumbled under her breath, but Gabriel had no trouble picking up her words. They hurt.

"I was only trying to protect you. The rogue is still out there. He could strike at any time—you're not safe out there."

"I'm not safe anywhere! But you can't protect me from everything."

"I can," Gabriel protested. "And I will. Even if I have to—"

"Lock me up and watch me twenty-four hours a day?" Maya tilted her chin up, defiance clearly written in her beautiful face.

"That's not what I wanted to say."

"But you were thinking it. I've led an independent life up till now. And I won't change that—not for you or anybody else. Nobody will control me."

He took a step toward her, but she raised her hand, making him stop in his tracks.

"I have to be able to defend myself. I can't rely on somebody else to be there for me all the time." She turned.

"Maya, listen."

But she continued up the stairs. "I'm going to sleep. My mind control lesson with Thomas has exhausted me."

Mind control lesson? Gabriel spun around to face Thomas, who still stood in the hallway together with Eddie.

"Why didn't you say you were teaching her mind control?"

"Because you didn't let me get a word in edgewise."

Gabriel ran his fingers through his hair and let out a ragged breath. "It's driving me crazy. When I'm not with her, I worry. Do you understand that?"

Thomas only shook his head. "You've got it bad. But if you don't let go, you're gonna lose her. She's a strong woman."

"Hell, what do I know about relationships? All I know is that I have to protect her. The rogue's still out there." Apart from his short-lived marriage to Jane, he'd never had a relationship with a woman that didn't involve an exchange of money for services. Was he supposed to go to her and apologize, and if yes, when? Or was he supposed to wait until she gave him a sign of when she was ready to talk?

How the hell would he know! He couldn't very well ask anybody.

"Protect her, but don't suffocate her."

Gabriel stared at his colleague. Had he really been too heavy-handed? All he was trying to do was to protect her from danger. He'd protected others all his life in his capacity as a bodyguard, so why would this be any different? "It seems that I don't know the difference."

"Then you'd better learn it fast. Maya is unique—she won't take any crap from anybody. And by the way, she won't learn mind control."

"What?"

Even Eddie gasped at the news. Mind control was an essential tool for any vampire, as important as his fangs were for feeding.

"I tried to teach her, but she can't influence any human. Now, inanimate objects—that's another story," Thomas baited him.

"Explain."

"She can move objects with her mind. Maya tried to plant suggestions in people's minds, but instead she moved things. Glasses. Chairs. She has a unique gift."

"But what will she do without mind control?" Eddie interrupted.

Thomas shrugged. "We'll have to see how things develop. She might be able to compensate somehow."

Gabriel felt worry course through him. Without mind control, she had no protection against the human world. If anything, he had to step up his efforts to protect her, not loosen the reins as Thomas had suggested. "Compensate how?"

Thomas smiled. "She needs somebody she can trust. And not a bull in a china shop who orders her around. This woman—" He pointed to the second floor. "—doesn't like to be told what to do. If you want to remain in her good graces, I suggest you see her for what she is: an independent and strong woman. She doesn't want a babysitter or a bodyguard."

Gabriel nodded. Maya had been through enough. She was faced with too many changes right now. Her whole life had been uprooted and her identity put in question. What was she without her devotion to her profession, her friends, her family? He'd assumed that just because she'd responded to him with such abandon, that he would be enough for her. He'd thought that she would simply accept his help and his judgment and fall in step with him.

He'd forgotten that she was an individual, who needed to make her own decisions. And if he wanted to keep her, he had to give her that freedom. As hard as this was for him.

Gabriel remembered when he'd held her in his arms and pleasured her—not when she'd been delirious, but later, when she'd been awake and fully aware of what he was doing. She'd responded to him, looked at him with such desire in her eyes that he couldn't think even for one second that she hadn't wanted him then.

Maybe once he truly laid claim to her, once he was able to really make love to her, then things would be different. But he hadn't been able to do that so far, and even if he followed her now and apologized for his gruffness, he couldn't take her to bed like a man should. He couldn't allow her to see him naked. She would recoil from him, and then he would lose her forever. No, he had to give her and himself the time to sort out the obstacles between them. She needed time to calm down and see his reaction for what it truly was: a move to protect rather than control her. And he needed time to take care of his problem.

Eddie's cell phone suddenly pinged. Gabriel turned his head and watched him open it and read the alert. "Excellent, AT&T's servers are back up."

Gabriel felt relief wash through him at the news. "Go, both of you, and get me the data. Just fax the phone list over once you have it. Oh, and call Yvette on your way to ask her to take over for you here."

"Will do," Thomas confirmed and opened the door, Eddie on his heels. With a start, Thomas pulled back and looked over his shoulder. "It appears you have a visitor."

***

Maya let herself fall on the covers of the bed. As she turned her face, she could still smell Gabriel's scent lingering in the pillows. How had everything suddenly gotten so complicated? Only hours ago she'd felt happy and satisfied. Now things were in an uproar.

The man who'd stood in the entrance door when they'd come back from the Castro wasn't the same man who'd held her in his arms and touched her with almost worshipful reverence. This wasn't the Gabriel she thought she knew, not the tender, careful lover of the day before. This Gabriel was different: harsh, unyielding, powerful.

And from his exchange with Thomas, she knew he indeed did have the power he wielded so easily now. This wasn't the man who'd kissed her tenderly and had told her he looked forward to dinner, as if he were the one feasting on her instead of the other way around. As if she could feed from him right now. She couldn't face him right now, not after what she'd said to him only a few minutes ago.

She knew why she'd reacted so harshly to his reprimand. It was the flash of memory that had assaulted her in the bar.

Control.

The word spread in her mind again. Something about it filled her with fear. And when she'd seen Gabriel standing in the doorway, she'd seen it in his eyes: he was used to controlling those around him—maybe not because it was his nature, but because he was the boss. And at that moment, he'd scared her.

She had the strangest feeling that she'd had a similar conversation with somebody else. When she'd accused Gabriel of wanting to watch her twenty-four hours, she hadn't really spoken to him. The words had come to her from a memory she didn't have.

Maya shivered when her mind led her to connect the dots. The words had come from the memory the rogue had erased—words she'd spoken to the faceless monster who'd turned her. He'd wanted to control her, possess her. Instinctively, she knew that now, even if she didn't remember it. Her memory of that time was still blank, but her body had retained sense memory. When she'd heard herself say those words to Gabriel, her body had remembered the fear she'd felt when she'd confronted the rogue with them.

She had to explain to Gabriel that she hadn't wanted to snap at him. That this wasn't about him but about her own fears. He would understand.

19

Gabriel set the empty glass of blood on the coffee table, then looked at Francine, who'd made herself comfortable on the couch.

The witch gave him a long look. "I'm concerned."

Gabriel's spine stiffened. "About?"

"I've had a long talk with Drake. I have some suspicions about Maya."

"Suspicions?" He felt himself become defensive.

"Relax, vampire. When I say suspicions, I don't imply that she's deceiving anybody. She truly doesn't know what's wrong with her."

"There's nothing wrong with her." In fact, he'd never met a more perfect woman.

The witch smiled knowingly. "Do you guys ever come off that testosterone rush, or are you always this jumpy?"

When he opened his mouth to retort, she merely cut him off with a move of her hand. "Luckily, I'm not the one who'll have to deal with your ego. I'm much more interested in Maya's condition."

Gabriel exhaled sharply. "Why is that?"

"She's a vampire, yet she drinks your blood and rejects that of humans. She went into heat when vampire females are known to be sterile."

"You know an awful lot about vampires."

She shrugged. "It's important to know your enemies: the better to fight them. But pleasantries aside, have you considered the possibility that you giving Maya your blood has triggered her symptoms?"

Gabriel shot up from his seat. "You're suggesting my blood is not good for her?"

"You sure are one to jump to conclusions. No. All I'm saying is that your blood could have awakened some latent genes in her. You told me yourself when we talked about your problem that your turning was just as difficult as hers. What if you have more than that in common?"

He raised an eyebrow. He'd told the witch an awful lot about his predicament that night just before Maya had collapsed. "We couldn't be more different from each other." She was perfect, and he was anything but. Even the witch had to know that.

"She craves your blood—and yours alone, as I understand it. Not the blood of a human, nor the blood of any other vampire."

"Because I finished the turning."

"No. Because there's something in your blood that she needs. Maybe something her body recognizes."

"You make it sound like I'm a drug to her."

"In a way you are. But we won't know for sure until I've analyzed blood samples of both of you."

Gabriel narrowed his eyes. "If this is a trick for you to get vampire blood so you can—"

Francine let out an exasperated huff. "I don't think I've ever met a vampire, who's more suspicious than you are. Trust me, vampire: if I wanted to harm you, I could have done so long ago."

Trust her? Maybe he had to if he wanted to know what was wrong with Maya and with him. "Maybe if you called me *Gabriel* instead of *vampire*, I'd have an easier time trusting in your good intentions." He paused. "Francine."

She raised an eyebrow. "If that's all it takes, I can do that." She paused for effect. "Gabriel."

Gabriel relaxed and sat back down in the armchair by the fireplace. "How much of my blood do you need?"

"Just a small vial. I'll take it to my lab and analyze it. Won't take more than an hour."

"You have a lab?"

"You didn't think I could live off being a witch, did you? I work at a commercial lab downtown. It pays—" She winked. "—enough to buy crow's feet for my potions."

"Let's go upstairs. I hope you don't mind if we perform the bloodletting in the bedroom. I'd rather not be interrupted. My associates would find it strange to say the least if I gave blood to a witch."

She stood and took her satchel which presumably contained all kinds of witchy things. "Normally I'd say no way, but seeing how infatuated you are with Maya, I daresay you're no danger to me."

For the first time since the witch had arrived, Gabriel let out a small chuckle. "You're an attractive woman, but no offense—I have no interest in you or any other woman besides Maya."

Once in the master bedroom, Gabriel closed the door quietly behind him. "Just one request: let's be quiet. Maya is next door, and I don't want her to hear us."

"Fine."

Francine took out a tourniquet and a syringe. Gabriel merely glanced at it and shook his head.

"That won't be necessary. Just give me the vial."

She handed it to him. He willed his fingers to turn into claws and sliced a small cut into his thumb. Blood instantly oozed from it. Gabriel held the vial underneath it and filled it with the red liquid. A moment later, he licked his thumb with his tongue, closing the incision.

Francine took the vial from him and closed it before putting it into her bag. "Good. I'll leave you one for Maya. Call me when you have it ready for me, and I'll send somebody over to get it. Now, let's check on your problem. I believe we were interrupted last time just as I was about to examine you."

Gabriel swallowed. This was the part he dreaded most. "Can I have your word that whatever you discover, you won't discuss with anybody?"

"Witch–vampire confidentiality, goes without saying," she joked, but Gabriel didn't feel like laughing.

With unsteady hands, he loosened his belt, then opened the button of his jeans. The noise the zipper made as he lowered it seemed to echo in the room. Could everybody in the house hear it? When he shoved his pants down mid-thigh, he heard Francine's breath whoosh out of her lungs.

As he stood before her, she dropped down onto the chaise longue, bringing her head level with his crotch. "Oh, boy," she whispered.

***

Maya's stomach growled, but she tried to tamp down her hunger. She'd paced for a good length of time, deciding what to do. Now, she couldn't stall any longer. She had to face Gabriel and explain to him why she'd reacted so harshly when she'd returned. For the sake of what was growing between them, she had to make the first step and apologize for her harsh words.

And then she needed to feed. By God, she craved him. Not just his blood, but his touch, his lips, his kisses. She felt weak in the knees just thinking about him, remembering how he'd touched her and kissed her, how he'd made her come, using his tongue and his hands. Small beads of perspiration collected on her neck. She felt hot just thinking about being in his arms.

Maya closed the bedroom door behind her and walked down the corridor. At the stairs, she halted. She could clearly sense Gabriel's presence. In fact, she could smell his blood. Was it more intense now because she was famished or had she always been able to smell his blood from such a distance? When she turned her head, she realized that the smell was becoming more intense—it wasn't coming from downstairs, but from the master bedroom.

Maya smiled to herself. If Gabriel was in bed, even better. She could first drink his blood and then devour him. On tiptoes, she walked to his door. As quietly as she could, she turned the doorknob and pushed the door open.

As soon as she took one step into the room, she froze in horror.

Maya stopped breathing.

Gabriel stood near the fireplace, facing her. But he wasn't looking at her. His gaze was focused on the woman who sat in front of him on the chaise longue with her back turned to Maya. His face was contorted as if in pain.

But that wasn't the worst of it. The worst was Gabriel's pants were dropped to his knees, his naked thighs showing, while his crotch was blocked out by the woman's head.

Maya blinked, but she wasn't imagining this. The strange woman was giving Gabriel a blowjob! And the look on Gabriel's face wasn't pain. No, it had to be pleasure.

How could he do this to her?

A sob tore from her throat.

Gabriel's gaze shot to her, and at the same moment the woman turned. They both stared at her, shocked looks on their faces.

Gabriel tugged at his pants, but failed to pull them up. "Maya, please, this isn't what it looks like." The woman turned fully, still blocking her view of Gabriel's crotch. As if Maya needed to see his hard-on to know what they were doing. She needed no proof of it. All the proof was written in their guilty faces.

She spun on her heels and rushed out of the room.

"Maya, listen to me. I can explain."

His words were lame at best. What was there to explain? He'd brought another woman to the house right after she'd told him she didn't want to be controlled. Was that his answer to her anger? That he didn't care what she thought? How cruel.

Maya ran down the stairs, faster than ever before. So this was vampire speed? Just as well. She had to get away, from him and from this place. In the foyer, she saw a set of keys on the sideboard. She knew there was a car in the garage—Gabriel had taken it when he'd met up with Zane earlier.

She snatched the keys and ran down into the garage. With a click, the doors of the Audi R8 unlocked. She'd never driven a sports car before, but it would do. Maya jumped into the car, slammed the door shut and jammed the keys into the lock.

A second later, the engine roared to life. The garage-door opener was where she expected it to be—on the visor. Valuable seconds passed as the garage door rose. When it was halfway up, Maya hit the gas pedal and raced out.

Her new superior vampire senses helped her avoid a crash as she pulled onto the street. From the corner of her eye, she saw Yvette stopping on the sidewalk, looking at her. Maya ignored her, pressed the gas pedal harder and raced down the road.

Her eyes burned, and only now she realized she was crying.

Damn Gabriel!

She'd let him come too close, and all it had gotten her was a hell of a lot of pain. He was just the way Yvette had made him out to be; all he wanted was a human woman, not an infertile vampire. It hadn't escaped her notice that the woman who'd had her head buried in Gabriel's crotch was human. Her scent had definitely been human, if just a little off. But certainly she wasn't a vampire.

Maya sniffed. It hadn't taken him long at all to replace her. After all the things he'd said when he'd been in her bed; the promises that he'd take care of her, that he'd always be there for her. Had he lied when he'd claimed that Maya feeding off him was heaven for him?

With the back of her hand, Maya wiped the tears off her cheek. If it meant that men like Gabriel could treat her with such disrespect, such callousness, then she didn't want to be a vampire.

She hit the brakes at a stoplight, letting the engine idle, and took a deep breath. Were vampires really all that different from humans? When she recalled the situation in Gabriel's bedroom, she realized with disgust that even his "it's not what it looks like" was decidedly human—any man would have said the same to get out of this mess. No, vampires weren't really all that different when it came to that. What it boiled down to was that Gabriel was just another cheating bastard, no worse than any human man.

So she would just have to do what she would do with any other man: forget him. And bitch about him with her girlfriends. Yes, that's exactly what she needed now.

Maya checked her watch. Paulette would be at home and wouldn't mind if she showed up unannounced. She'd break open a bottle of wine and commiserate with her. For a moment, Maya wondered how much to tell her, but then she decided that honesty was the best way to go. If she wanted to keep Paulette as her friend—and she desperately needed a friend on whose shoulder to cry—she had to tell her the truth. Slowly, and very gently.

20

Gabriel almost collided with Yvette when he ran into the foyer. If he hadn't been struggling to pull his pants up and gotten the witch's hair caught in his zipper, he would have caught Maya before she'd managed to flee the house.

"Have you seen Maya?" he asked gruffly.

Yvette raised an eyebrow. "She left in Samson's Audi." Then she walked calmly past him as if it didn't matter.

Anger churned in him. He spun around and grabbed Yvette by the shoulders. "And you didn't stop her?"

She shook off his hold and snarled at him. "I don't make a habit of jumping in front of cars driven by pissed-off females."

He narrowed his eyes. He wouldn't take any disrespect from his subordinates. "It's your job to protect her."

"I was OFF DUTY! Why didn't you protect her? She must have had a reason to run out of here, so maybe you should look at yourself before you blame somebody else." Yvette planted her fists at her hips and glared at him.

It was all too clear to him. "You don't like her."

"And why should I?" She let out a huff. "She gets attacked and turned, and everybody goes gaga over her, as if she's someone special. And where does that leave me?"

Gabriel took a step back as the realization sunk in once more. Yvette had had designs on him. "By *everybody*, you mean me, don't you?"

"Forget it!" she spat and turned.

A viselike grip on her arm held her back. Yvette swallowed back the tears—she wouldn't give Gabriel the satisfaction of admitting that he'd hurt her. All these years they'd worked together and she'd thought they'd gotten closer. Their relationship had evolved from a purely professional one to more of a friendship. She'd hoped that eventually Gabriel would let his guard down and come to her for more than work and friendship. She'd given him enough signals to show her willingness to take things further.

She'd given him time to get used to the idea, and then Maya had shown up. And within days, Gabriel had turned into a horny, lusting man just like all the others. Only, he wasn't lusting after her, he was lusting after Maya. What did Maya have that she didn't?

"Take your hand off my arm or I'll break it," she warned him.

He must have heard the seriousness in her voice, because a moment later he let go. "I think a talk between you and me is long overdue."

She turned to look at him. "There's nothing to be said." If he thought he could get her to confess her feelings, he'd be waiting till the Devil strapped on ice skates and skated in hell.

Was there pity in Gabriel's gaze? No, she didn't want pity.

"Yvette, I've never given you any reason to believe that I had any interest in you other than as a valued colleague and friend. I have no other feelings for you. If I ever gave you the impression that I did, I apologize."

He apologized to her? That was rich! "You men are all the same. Nothing will ever change that, will it? A new woman shows up, and suddenly you start panting. Damn it, you don't even know her!" She knew she was out of line talking to him like that, but at this point she didn't care anymore. Let him fire her. Maybe it would be best for all of them.

"No, I don't know her. But I love her."

His words were like a stab to her chest with a sharp knife. She met his gaze, and there in his eyes she saw it. It was true. He loved her. No pretense, no bravado, just pure and simple honesty. Something in her shut down. If she'd had any hope left that one day there could be something between them, that his infatuation with Maya would fade, the sparkle in his eyes told her it would never happen. He'd found what he was looking for.

"She's your mate?" Her voice cracked.

"If she'll have me. Unfortunately she's misinterpreted something and hates me right now."

Yvette recalled the look she'd caught from Maya. "I don't think hate is the right word. A woman who hates doesn't cry, not like Maya did."

Tears had streamed down her face, pain so clearly etched into her features. "She wants you still."

There was a glint of hope in Gabriel's gaze now, and something inside Yvette shriveled. She wasn't a bad person, just a misguided one. All these years she'd hoped for Gabriel to turn to her for more than just friendship, yet he was right: he'd never given her any reason to believe he was interested in her. She'd been the one imagining it. Because she'd been lonely. How pathetic was that?

She was better than that, stronger. "I'll help you find her."

"You will?" Gabriel took a step toward her and opened his arms in an awkward attempt to embrace her, emotion clearly overwhelming him.

Yvette pulled back. "No hugs."

He dropped his arms and lowered his lids, looking embarrassed by his exuberance and her rejection, but at the same time relieved. "Thank you."

"She's headed south."

Gabriel blinked. "Her apartment in Noe Valley. Let's go." He looked to the door then back at her. "Is that your dog?"

Yvette turned. On the threshold, the dog who'd been following her for the last few blocks sat waiting patiently. Before him, it had been a different dog. And before that, a cat. "I have no idea why every damn cat and dog in this town keeps following me. It's like I've turned into some goddamn dog whisperer or something." She motioned to the dog. "Shoo!" She didn't even like animals.

"I think he likes you."

She sniffed and was about to retort when a whiff of something entirely disagreeable caught in her nostrils. Within a blink of an eye, she swiveled and looked up at the stairs, where a woman she'd never seen before stood. "What the hell is a witch doing in Samson's house?"

***

Maya put the Audi in park and switched off the ignition. As she stepped out of the car and into the night, she took in her surroundings. Never before had she been so aware of her senses. At the end of the residential street, a neighbor walked his little white Westie. When she concentrated, she could hear the clatter of dishes in a kitchen nearby. The news blared from a TV in a house across the street.

She'd never noticed these noises before and had always thought of Paulette's neighborhood as eerily quiet. It wasn't—not anymore anyway. With her enhanced senses, she could hear that life was happening inside the little houses dotted along the hill. From her vantage point, she could see the ocean or could have seen it if it weren't for the fog hanging out at the beach.

Midtown Terrace was a middle-class neighborhood, the houses all built in the late 50s, their floor plans all essentially the same with a few variations. Paulette's house was no different: three bedrooms and one bathroom over a two-car garage. A small yard out the back. Maya had spent many an evening here with Paulette and their friend Barbara, drinking, eating, joking, and ultimately bitching about the horrible dates they'd had. Just like all girlfriends did.

Maya hesitated as she approached the front door, stopping at the foot of the terrazzo steps. Would she look any different to Paulette? When Maya hugged her, would she crush her with her superior strength just like she'd smashed the little night table in Samson's house? Maybe it was best not to hug her. Safer for Paulette.

She lifted her foot and set it on the first step. There was a chill in the night air, but Maya didn't feel cold. Her vampire body seemed to protect itself from the cold despite the fact she'd forgotten to don a jacket. And in June in San Francisco you needed a jacket—a thick one. Clearly, there were some advantages to being a vampire. Maybe one day she'd truly accept that and make the best of it.

Would Paulette freak if she found out what she was now? Would she even believe it? They had always played pranks on each other. It was their way of showing friendship, and so Paulette would think that she was joking. She'd then have to prove what she was. And she'd have to do it without frightening her best friend.

She didn't want to frighten anybody.

Maya took a deep breath to give herself the courage to walk up the steps and face her friend. Something stung her nostrils. Her stomach flipped. She'd only ever had that same feeling of disgust when she'd tried to drink the bottled human blood. A thought raced through her mind, one she didn't want to acknowledge.

Her heart pounded as she ran up the stairs and reached for the doorbell. But she didn't ring it. She didn't have to—the front door was ajar.

Even though the neighborhood was a safe and quiet one, nobody ever left their door open. Nobody. Certainly not Paulette.

She pushed the door fully open. A bout of nausea overwhelmed her as she inhaled.

"Oh God, no," she whispered to herself.

The scent stinging her nostrils and assaulting her sensitive stomach grew more intense as she stepped into the house. The lights were on in the living room, but it was empty.

Maya's vocal cords clamped up. She was unable to call out to her friend, because deep down she already knew it wouldn't make a difference. The house was quiet. There wasn't a single sound except for the dripping faucet in the bathroom.

Her soft-soled shoes made barely a sound as she slid down the corridor to the bedrooms like a thief. The light drifting into the hallway came from underneath a bedroom door. Paulette's bedroom.

Maya steeled herself against what she already knew she would find and turned the knob. She pushed the door open, finding it uncharacteristically heavy. It creaked, but she barely heard the sound because the scene in the bedroom made her heart drum so loud it drowned out any sound.

The bed was a pool of blood—dried, but still fresh enough for her stomach to turn. Had she had any contents in it, she would have lost them now, but it appeared vampires couldn't throw up. Even though she wanted to, needed to, to curb the nausea.

The sheets were tangled as if there'd been a struggle. Paulette hadn't died easily, but Maya knew she was dead, even though there was no body. She raised her eyes to the wall behind the bed and hugged her arms around her torso.

Scrawled in blood was a message, and it was meant for her.

It's your fault, Maya.

A sound finally left her throat, but it amounted to nothing more than a helpless gurgle. Her friend had died because of her. He'd done it. She knew it. The man who'd attacked her: he'd killed her friend to cover his tracks.

All because Maya had told Paulette about him, even though she didn't remember doing so. Paulette had to have known about him for him to attack her. Maybe she'd even known his name and what he looked like. It had cost her her life.

She felt numb all over her body. It was all her fault. She should have taken care of her friend. She should have known he'd come after her. Why hadn't she thought about it? Why?

The door fell shut behind her and made her spin around with vampire speed.

A scream left her throat.

Paulette!

She hung there, on the back of the door, her limp body bloodied, her pajamas shredded by claws. No heartbeat—Maya would have heard it from where she stood. She was gone. Long gone.

21

"I couldn't reach Thomas," Yvette said as she flipped her cell phone shut and looked at Gabriel, who was driving while dialing a number on his own cell phone.

Gabriel listened to the recording on the other line and cursed. "Zane's not answering either."

"We're almost there," Yvette tried to calm him.

He gave her a sideways glance. At least now that the air had been cleared between them, Yvette was a hundred percent behind him. And he needed all the help he could get. Maya was out there on her own—and so was the rogue. The bastard would find her and Gabriel would lose her forever. He couldn't allow it. He needed to protect her.

"Zane. Maya's gone. Search for her. This is first priority." Gabriel left the voicemail and flipped the cell shut.

Moments later, he pulled up in front of Maya's apartment and jumped out of the car. He ran up the stairs, Yvette close behind him.

The door was locked, but Gabriel didn't care. With barely any effort, he kicked against the lock, and the wood splintered. He jerked the door open and ran upstairs.

At Maya's apartment, he did the same thing—if she was there, she wouldn't respond to a polite knock anyway. She was too pissed at him. For now, he didn't care. All he needed was to get her back to the house where she would be safe. Then he'd explain things to her.

How could she have possibly thought he was getting head from the witch? Sure, the situation had looked a little odd, but had she only waited, she would have realized that there was nothing sexual about any of it. The witch had merely examined him like a doctor would a patient and then tried a little herbal concoction on him to test how the damn thing reacted.

Of course, the useless piece of flesh hadn't reacted to anything at all until—Gabriel stopped in his tracks and let the realization sink in. His additional piece of flesh had stirred the moment Maya had entered the room. And when she'd run out on him, it had faltered again and shrunken back to its original state. The witch had given him an odd look, now that he thought of it, but he'd been too panicked about Maya's misinterpretation of the situation to give it much consideration until now. Now he was wondering if—

"Are we going in?" Yvette asked behind him.

Gabriel pushed aside his thoughts about the deformity and stepped inside the apartment. He sniffed, trying to ascertain if Maya had been here. His gaze swept through the place. It still looked the way they'd left it only two nights earlier. Nothing had changed. And there was no fresh scent of Maya. She hadn't been here.

"Where else would she go?" Gabriel asked and ran his hands through his hair.

Yvette opened her mouth, but then her cell phone rang. She picked it up. "Thomas? Did you get my message?"

Gabriel could hear Thomas's reply. *"Yes, the GPS on Samson's Audi shows me she's in my area. Wait . . . She's moving. Heading northwest."*

"Where to?" Gabriel ground out.

Yvette lifted her hand and listened to Thomas. "Where—"

"I heard him. I think she's going to Parnassus."

"Parnassus?" Yvette asked.

"The hospital."

"Meet us there," Yvette ordered and flipped the phone shut.

"Call Amaury. I'm calling Ricky." Gabriel rushed out the door and back down to the car. As he jumped in, the call to Ricky connected.

"Maya's left the house."

"Shit, what happened?" Ricky's concerned voice reached his ear.

"She's on her way to the hospital, probably to see her friends there. We need to find her and bring her back before the rogue gets her. Meet us there."

"Will do." Ricky disconnected the call.

"Amaury's on his way too," Yvette reported as she fell into the passenger seat.

Gabriel hit the gas pedal and sped down the street. The limousine Carl normally drove wasn't as fast as Samson's Audi, but it had GPS and would help him get to Maya, hopefully before the rogue did.

***

Maya's heart raced as she pulled the Audi to a stop right in front of the hospital's no-parking zone. For all she cared, they could tow Samson's car—she didn't have a second to lose. If her stalker had killed Paulette to silence her, Barbara would be next. If she hadn't already been . . . She swallowed hard.

How he could possibly know about Paulette and Barbara, she wasn't sure. Unless, of course, she'd actually introduced her girlfriends to him. But then, wouldn't he have merely wiped their memories too? Something didn't make sense here.

Was the rogue trying to send her a message? Was this revenge for not giving into his advances? Because she was even more convinced now that he had to be a spurned lover. No one else would spit the kind of hatred that had radiated from the bloody message in Paulette's bedroom.

It's your fault, Maya.

The words echoed in her mind like a broken record. Could she have saved Paulette? Had she only thought things through, she would have considered this danger right when Gabriel's colleague Ricky had shown up and offered to help. Maybe he'd already talked to Paulette—she'd given him her contact info after all. Maybe he'd even led the stalker to her. How could she know?

It didn't matter. In the end, it was her responsibility to protect her friends. She should have gone with him and warned Paulette. Urged her to go someplace safe. But that night she'd gone into heat and her mind had been clouded. She'd only thought of herself then. And because of her selfishness her friend was dead. It *was* her fault.

Maya swallowed the lump in her throat and rushed up the stairs to the ward. She knew Barbara was on service all week and would most likely be in the on-call room of her ward. As she reached the double doors that separated the public area of the hospital from the restricted part, she realized to her horror that she didn't have her access card with her.

She cursed and looked around her, but nobody was in sight. The clock in the corridor showed a few minutes past one o'clock—the regular staff would be long gone, and only the night shift would man the stations. Barbara's ward wasn't a critical care area, so staffing was thin and consisted mostly of a couple of nurses and one on-call doctor, Barbara herself. None of them were in sight.

Maya pushed against the doors, but they didn't budge. Through the glass windows she could see the button that allowed people to leave the area without using their access cards, but there was no way in. If she could get somebody to press the button for her, then she would be in luck, but there was no human around on whom she could try out her mind control skill. Not that it would have worked anyway—despite Thomas's coaching. All she'd been able to influence was a chair and some glasses and bowls.

She stopped her thoughts in their tracks. That was it! She just needed to move something and push the button with it. Maya peered through the window again and saw a metal chart in one of the holders on the wall. It would do. She concentrated her mind on the metal item and willed it to lift from its pocket on the wall. She watched with bated breath as the item moved and hung suspended in the air as if held by invisible strings.

Maya didn't dare breathe so she wouldn't lose her concentration. A few seconds later, she managed to set the chart in motion, moving it toward the button. With her last ounce of will, she slammed the metal against the button, before it fell to the ground with a loud clang.

As she looked at the chart on the floor, realization hit her: she could have easily just willed the button to depress without using the metal item. Clearly, she still had lots to learn about her new skill.

The double doors opened, and she slipped through.

Relieved, she ran down the hall to the small room where the on-call physician rested during the night. Barbara should be there unless she'd been called to a hospital bed.

Maya pressed the door handle down and eased the door open, trying not to startle her friend. Soft light from a desk lamp greeted her. The on-call room was sparsely furnished: a desk and chair, a small cabinet, a sink, and a single bed. She let out a relieved breath when she saw Barbara in a peaceful slumber. Maya shut the door behind her, and Barbara stirred.

A moment later, she shot up from her prone position and swung her legs out of bed, her eyes still closed. When she opened them and spotted

Maya standing only a few feet away from her, Barbara jolted upright. "Shit, Maya!"

"Sorry—" But Maya didn't get any further.

"Everybody's looking for you. Where the hell have you been? The chief is pissed and so are the other attendings—they all had to pick up the slack for you."

Maya put her hand on Barbara's arm. "I can't explain right now. I need your help."

Barbara gave her a startled look. "Do you need money? What's going on?"

A strobe light blinked on the wall, and an instant later a voice came over the loudspeaker. *"Code Blue, Code Blue, Room 748 Long, all team members, Code Blue, Code Blue."*

Barbara grabbed Maya's hand and squeezed it. "That's me. I have to go. Wait here. I'll be back shortly. We'll talk when I'm back."

"No, I'm coming with you."

"Just wait. It won't take long."

"No, it's not safe. I'm coming with you."

Barbara gave her a curious look "Not safe?"

"Please, let me come with you."

Her friend grabbed a white coat from the hook. "Here, at least put that on, so you won't look out of place. And then you'd better talk fast."

Maya slipped into the coat and was right behind Barbara when she opened the door. A second later, she shut it again.

"Shit, the chief's right out there. If he sees you, he'll stop you. He must have gotten called in on a consult."

Maya cursed. "Damn it!" This was just her bad luck.

"I'll be right back."

"No, wait!" But before Maya could stop her, she dashed out of the room. Her steps echoed in the corridor. Maya's skin prickled uncomfortably. She didn't want Barbara wandering the corridors on her own. Opening the door a tiny slit, she peered outside. The chief was still standing there. There was no way she would get past him without him seeing her.

Maya shut the door in frustration.

She could only hope that Barbara knew about her stalker. Then this nightmare would be over soon. Once Maya knew his name and what he looked like, they could find him. She could tell Thomas, and he'd make sure the rogue was taken out. She didn't want to think of talking to Gabriel. Not right now.

Once the rogue was captured, she would be safe again and so would Barbara. Then she would tell her friend the truth, and together they'd bury Paulette. Somehow she would get her life back together, as much as she could with the guilt she carried on her shoulders. The guilt of knowing she was responsible for Paulette's violent death.

22

Gabriel turned a corner in the hospital and almost collided with Ricky. "Thank God! You got here really fast," Gabriel said. Next to him, Yvette skidded to a halt as well.

"You were lucky; I was in the neighborhood."

"Have you seen Thomas?"

"No. Is he supposed to be here?" Ricky asked.

Yvette nodded. "He should have arrived before all of us. He was coming straight from Twin Peaks."

"Let's split up," Gabriel suggested. "Use mind control if you need to get access anywhere you need to. We have to find her."

Ricky nodded enthusiastically. "Yes, we do. I'll take the seventh floor."

"Yvette, take the fifth floor; that's where one of her friends works—maybe she went there. I'll take this one. If you don't find her on your respective floors, move three floors higher." Gabriel issued his orders with a calmness he didn't feel. What helped him was his experience—he knew how to track someone in a crisis situation. It was what he'd done for so long, and done well—Maya's life depended on it now. There was only one handicap: the corridors of the hospital reeked of bleach. It stung his nostrils and impeded his ability to filter out Maya's scent. His only consolation was that if the rogue was close, he'd have the same problem—it leveled the playing field.

As Yvette and Ricky left, Gabriel stalked the corridors. He'd checked the directory on the way up for Maya's office. If she was here, she would probably go there—either to hide out for a while or to retrieve whatever personal items she had there, maybe a spare key to her apartment or some money or credit cards. She hadn't taken any of her things with her when she'd fled the house, not even her handbag.

It was telling: no woman ever left the house without her handbag. It proved to him that Maya was in an extremely agitated state and would most likely act irrationally. He had to get to her before she put herself in even more danger than she already was. Besides, she hadn't fed from him since before her outing in the Castro. She had to be famished, which would make her weak and less likely to think clearly.

Gabriel reached Maya's office suite and pressed the door handle down. The door didn't move. No matter—with a forceful push against the lock, the wood splintered. He slid inside unseen. Four office doors presented themselves to him, each of them with the name of a doctor stenciled on it. He opened the door with Maya's name without knocking. If she was there, she would have already heard him, and if she wasn't, there was no point in knocking.

The room was empty. He inhaled deeply and sniffed. There was a low lingering scent of her, but it wasn't new. She hadn't been in her office in days. His heart sank.

With a sigh, he dialed Thomas's number. He answered instantly.

"Where are you?" Gabriel asked.

"Seventh floor."

"Go farther up—Ricky is already covering that floor. I'll do another quick sweep of the sixth and then move higher. Yvette is on the fifth."

"Sure," Thomas answered. A split-second later, Gabriel heard a distant scream come through the line.

Shock coursed through his system. "Was that Maya?"

"Don't know." The line went dead.

"Shit!" Gabriel ran out into the hall. He spotted the sign for the stairs and rushed to them, then took three steps at a time. With vampire speed, he ran up to the next floor before he slowed down again trying to get his bearings. He sniffed again. The scent of blood assaulted him. He ran toward it.

As he turned a corner, he saw a group of people gathering around a person on the floor. Gabriel zeroed in on the site. A pool of blood spread from underneath the person's white doctor's coat.

A grip on his forearm made him spin to his right. "Thomas."

Thomas pulled him into a side corridor. "It's not Maya. Some doctor—looks like cold-blooded murder to me."

"Did you see who it is?"

"Her name is Dr. Barbara Silverstein."

Gabriel's heart stopped as cold fear gripped him. "That's Maya's friend. Thomas, he's here. The rogue is in the hospital."

***

Maya's skin prickled. It had been too long since Code Blue was called. She was getting impatient, and she felt like a sitting duck waiting for Barbara in the on-call room. She needed to check on her.

She listened for any sound from the corridor before she opened the door a fraction, then peered out. The bright hallway was empty now. Maya stepped outside and quietly closed the door behind her. Something compelled her to make no noise. She was grateful that she wore soft-soled shoes; they made no sound on the light-gray linoleum floor.

Somewhere in the distance, a door opened. Maya moved along the corridor and dove into the next alcove that housed a small sink. She flattened herself against the wall when she heard footsteps coming toward her. Her eyes darted around her tiny hiding place, but there was nothing she could use as a weapon. She hoped whoever came her way wasn't an enemy and she wouldn't have to try out her vampire skills.

Other than using her fangs on Gabriel, she'd never truly used her new strength on anybody. She knew she had claws—she'd scratched Gabriel with them by accident that fateful night when she'd fed from him for the first time—and she hoped they would just appear the way her fangs did when she needed them.

The footsteps approached and were almost upon her when a soft ping drifted to her ears. The person stopped in her tracks. "Darn," the female voice grumbled under her breath.

Maya recognized the ping as a call for the nurses' station—one of the patients had pressed their call button. The nurse turned on her heels and walked in the other direction. Maya relaxed when she heard her enter a room and close the door behind her. She counted to three and emerged from her hiding place.

Swiftly, she walked to the empty nurses' station and looked around to make sure nobody saw her. Then she walked behind the counter and crouched down near the desk. She pulled the bottom drawer open and reached in. She knew that all nurses kept a couple of extra access cards hidden in their desks in case a doctor had forgotten theirs and needed to get somewhere before security could issue a new one.

Luckily, this nurses' station wasn't any different. After opening a third drawer, she found a spare access card and shoved it into her jeans pocket. She needed to be able to get around the hospital unimpeded, and now she could.

As she rose from her crouching position, the little hairs on the back of her neck stood. A shiver ran down her spine. She sniffed without making a sound. No human was in her vicinity. The faint scent she picked up could belong to a vampire, but she wasn't sure—there was too much bleach scent in the vicinity.

Maya darted around the desk and out of the nurses' station. Her hands felt clammy, and her heart raced—signs that told her she had to get away. Her instinct for flight or fight was alive and well. Flight won out. She wasn't stupid enough to try to fight a vampire who could be stronger than she, older and more experienced. Her advantage was that she knew the hospital—every corner, every supply room, and every shortcut. Whoever was on her trail didn't know the place as well as she did—she hoped. This was her only chance.

She had to get to Barbara and protect her. She should have never allowed her to respond to the Code Blue, but knowing the oath they'd both sworn as doctors, she realized that she couldn't have stopped her from doing her duty. Maya would have done the same. Nevertheless, she should have insisted on going with her and blown past her boss. Hell, she should have flashed her fangs if she'd needed to.

Maya ran along the corridor to get to the service stairs. They were safer than taking the elevator. In an elevator she would be trapped, but the stairs would get her safely to the seventh floor to find Barbara. She halted just before the corridor when faint footsteps reached her sensitive ears—it was somebody trying hard not to be heard. She couldn't filter out the person's scent—the smell of ammonia and bleach was too overwhelming. The corridor must have only recently been cleaned. Frantically, Maya scanned the doors along the corridor. There was only one choice. She opened a door and slipped inside the dark room. Without a sound, she closed the door behind her and listened.

Her eyes adjusted to the darkness, and she realized she had no problems seeing her surroundings. The janitor's room was a little bigger than a closet and filled with cleaning supplies, brooms, and buckets.

A sound from the corridor made her hold her breath. The person had stopped not far from her hiding spot. Had she been spotted? Had he tracked her by her scent? Maybe he had better senses and wasn't as affected by the cleaning materials in the hospital as her own sense of smell was.

In desperation, Maya grabbed the broom and broke the wooden handle. It splintered, providing her with an effective weapon: a wooden stake. She pressed herself to one side of the wall next to the door and waited.

Her hearing was so sensitive she could hear when someone touched the door handle. Adrenaline shot through her body. Light drifted into the small room as the door swung in. Maya lunged at the attacker, the makeshift stake ready to plunge into the person's heart.

A hand gripped her wrist in a vice and squeezed, making her drop the stake. Oh God, no!

23

"I got your message," the voice behind him announced. Gabriel turned and looked at his second-in-command, Zane. He looked like hell twice warmed over.

"About time," Gabriel chastised. "I need every man I can get. Maya's friend has been killed and she's somewhere in the hospital. We need to find her. The rogue is here."

Gabriel's cell vibrated. He flipped it open. "Yeah?"

"I'm in the hospital. Which floor are you on?" Amaury asked.

"Seventh." He disconnected the call without waiting for Amaury to respond.

"Okay, here's what we're going to do. Thomas, I want you to try and get close to the murdered doctor and see if you can pick up traces of the vampire who did this."

Thomas nodded.

"Use whatever means necessary. And check in with Ricky—he said he'd be on this floor. I don't see him anywhere." Then he turned to Zane. "Zane, take floors one through four and five—"

"I can do those floors," Amaury's voice came from the stairs. He strode into view, his broad six-and-a-half-foot frame filling the door to the stairway fully.

Gabriel nodded to him, grateful that everyone was showing up to help. "Good. Zane take floors twelve and thirteen."

"Consider it done," Zane answered and went to the stairway, greeting Amaury with a slap on his arm in passing.

"Let's do it, Amaury."

Thomas raised his hand in goodbye and walked toward the other end of the corridor to where the sounds from the shocked hospital workers were becoming louder. Gabriel and Amaury went the other way.

"How are you holding up?" Amaury asked.

"It's killing me not knowing where she is. Whether she's safe." Gabriel gave Amaury a serious look. "And with the stench of bleach in this hospital, I can't even latch onto her scent."

"We'll find her."

"I'll take nine, ten and eleven. Nobody's been to eight yet."

"I'll take care of it when I'm done with four and five," Amaury promised and gave him a wry smile before Gabriel rushed past him and ran up the stairs ahead of him.

On the tenth floor, he stepped out into the corridor and stalked along the hallway, his nostrils taking in every scent, but the hospital smells were too prominent. There was no hint of Maya. With every minute, hope faded.

Gabriel ran his hands through his hair. He couldn't lose her. He'd only just found her. This wasn't fair. How could life be so cruel to him? Didn't he deserve a little happiness? Was it too much to ask?

Something vibrated against his groin. Gabriel stopped and pulled his cell out of his pocket. He looked at the text message.

Have Maya, Rm 534C. Be careful. Rogue is near.

He heaved a sigh of relief when he recognized the sender's number: Yvette. With a few clicks on his phone, he forwarded the message to his colleagues as he ran toward the stairway. Once they were together, the rogue would have no chance of defeating them.

***

Maya let herself rest against the wall of the janitor's closet. Yvette had closed the door, but as a precaution they hadn't switched the light on.

"He's out there somewhere. I sensed him, I swear," Maya insisted and stared at Yvette in the dark. She had no difficulty making out the beauty's features in the dim light that filtered through the bottom of the door.

"I didn't sense any strange vampire, but with all the bleach in here, I don't know . . . " Yvette responded. Yet she didn't open the door, and she'd complied with Maya's wishes to send the others a warning by text message. "Gabriel and the others will be here shortly. You'll be safe."

Maya reached for her hand and squeezed it. "Thanks. I mean it. I'm sorry I almost killed you."

Yvette shrugged. "I would have done the same in your situation." She nodded toward the broken broom. "Quick thinking."

"I'm assuming a stake through the heart will kill a vampire?" Maya hoped she hadn't been completely off the mark.

"That, and a few other things. Don't worry, once this is over, Gabriel will give you a crash course in everything you need to know. You couldn't have a better teacher. He's been around for a very long time."

Maya averted her eyes. "I'd rather somebody else taught me. Maybe Thomas." Yes, Thomas would be a much safer bet: no danger to her heart.

"I thought you and Gabriel . . . " Yvette let her voice trail off.

"You thought wrong. He has no interest in me."

Yvette chuckled softly as if she knew otherwise. "Honey, you wanna tell him that or shall I? Because the man is under the impression he's in love with you. And by the looks of it, I'd say he's not alone in his feelings."

Maya snapped her gaze to Yvette.

"Oh, yes; don't look at me like it's such a surprise to you. He was ready to bite my head off when he found out I saw you leave and didn't stop you." Despite the heated discussion, they both kept their voices to a mere whisper to avoid detection by the rogue if he was still roaming the hospital corridors.

"You're wrong. He doesn't love me. He's got somebody else." Maya pushed down her rising tears. It wasn't fair for Yvette to bait her like this—although maybe Gabriel had her fooled as well.

"Gabriel? Are we talking about the same guy? Mr. Lonesome himself? In all the years I've known him, I've never seen him with a woman. He's never dated, and from what I've figured out, he doesn't even go along to any of their fuck fests—"

"Their what?"

"Some of the guys are a little rambunctious and need to let off steam from time to time. They think I don't know, but trust me—I know. The vampires who're not bonded, they can get quite wild when they roam the cities and go out looking for pussy. All I'm saying is that Gabriel never participates."

Maya swallowed back her shock. Yvette's frank language was unexpected, but why should vampires be any different from other men? But that wasn't the point. Even if Gabriel didn't participate, it didn't change anything about the fact that she'd caught him getting a blowjob from some woman.

"I suppose he's just more secretive about it. Doesn't change anything about the facts," Maya insisted.

"Which are?" Yvette prompted.

"There was a woman at the house when I left." That was all she would say. Yvette could draw her own conclusions. By the looks of it, she was a very smart woman. She would put two and two together and make sure it added up.

"The witch? You're talking about the witch?" Then she had the audacity to chuckle. "You honestly think he has something going with a witch?"

"She was in his room," Maya hissed under her breath, careful not to raise her voice in case the rogue was near.

"And I'm sure there's an explanation for that."

Maya crossed her arms over her chest. She'd already heard his explanation: *it's not what it looks like*. As if that explained why he'd had his pants down his thighs with the woman's head in his crotch. He was just the same kind of philanderer as the vampires Yvette was referring to, the only difference being that Gabriel liked to conduct his debauchery in private. And Maya wanted no part of it.

"I—"

Yvette put a finger on her lips. "Shh."

Maya's ears perked up. She stopped breathing and listened for any sound from the corridor outside. In the distance, she heard footsteps. Somebody was coming. She exchanged a look with Yvette, who nodded. She was trying to make out what direction the footsteps were coming from when she realized that there was more than one person approaching.

Maya ignored the chill that settled on her skin and tightened like a noose around her neck. She could sense him—he was near. Her grip tightened on the stake she still held in her hand. She wanted to sink deeper into the closet, but in the next instant the door was ripped open. Light flooded the room, and for a millisecond she felt blinded.

"Thank God it's you," Yvette exclaimed and stepped out into the corridor. Maya caught a glimpse of red hair before Yvette blocked the person out with her body. Then another set of heavy footsteps rushed closer.

"Where is she?" Gabriel's frantic voice echoed in the hallway.

A moment later, he'd pushed Yvette and the other vampire she now recognized as Ricky aside. Gabriel pulled her into his arms.

Maya had no time to protest before he took her mouth and kissed her. This wasn't the tender kiss he'd bestowed on her earlier: it was fierce, demanding, and desperate. She was too stunned to do anything but react to him. Her body melted into his and allowed him to invade her mouth with his seeking tongue.

Vaguely, she heard others arrive behind him, but everything was a blur. Gabriel demanded her full attention. It took her a full minute to gain control over herself and to remember what he'd done to her. Just because she was safe now didn't mean she'd forgive him for betraying her.

She shoved against his chest and swung her hand back to slap him. But her action was cut short—he'd caught her wrist just before her palm connected with his face.

There was a flash of red in his eyes, but when he spoke, his voice was calm. "You might think I deserve that, but I don't. You and I have some talking to do." He released her wrist.

And just then, Maya's stomach growled. Damn, she was starving, and Gabriel's taste on her lips reminded her all too much of what his blood tasted like. She pushed the hunger away. Somebody else was more important than herself. "I need to find Barbara."

The silence that followed her statement was eerie. Maya looked at the assembled vampires: Thomas, Zane, Ricky, Yvette, and another one she hadn't met before. He was as broad and as big as a football player, and his hair was raven black and reached to his shoulders. Her perusal of him was cut short when Gabriel put his hand on her arm. She tossed him an annoyed glare, but he ignored it.

"Barbara is dead. I'm sorry," Gabriel said.

Had he not reached for her and wrapped his strong arms around her instantly, Maya would have fallen when her knees buckled at the horrific news. Dead?

"Oh, God, no!" Her voice broke.

"I'm taking her home," Gabriel informed his colleagues as he lifted Maya into his arms. "Zane, Amaury, you get access to the security tapes and see if the murder was captured on camera." They nodded.

Maya felt far away while Gabriel issued his orders. All she could think about was her two friends: dead. And all because of her.

"Yvette, Ricky, stay together and see what you can find on the seventh floor. Thomas, get Eddie here. I want you to work in pairs only. Nobody stays on their own. Is that understood?"

"Eddie's already on his way," Thomas confirmed. "Don't you want one of us to come to the house with you?"

Gabriel snarled. "Existing evidence to the contrary, I'm more than capable of protecting Maya myself. Now go, all of you. You know what to do. Let's get this bastard."

24

Gabriel parked Samson's Audi in the garage and killed the engine. He glanced toward the passenger seat and cringed. Maya hadn't said a single word since they'd left the hospital. When she opened the door and stepped out of the car, her movements were robotic, as if she was sleepwalking.

Gabriel followed her upstairs. In the hallway, he took her hand and led her into the living room. Carl appeared instantly. "Can I get you anything?" His voice was quiet as if he sensed Maya wasn't well.

Gabriel shook his head. "Thanks, Carl. Just make sure we aren't disturbed."

Carl nodded and closed the door behind him, leaving him alone with Maya, who had turned away from him and stared into the fire.

"It's all my fault."

Gabriel crossed the distance between them and stopped behind her. "No. It's the rogue's fault. Don't ever think it's yours."

"How can I not? Because of me, my two friends are dead." A sob tore from her chest.

"Your *two* friends?" A terrible sense of unease rolled over Gabriel.

Maya turned, her eyes wet with tears. "Paulette is dead. I found her—it was him. He killed her."

He pulled her into his arms and held her. "I'm so sorry, baby. I wish I could undo it."

She pushed against him, freeing herself from his embrace. "He wrote it in her blood. *'It's your fault, Maya.'*"

Gabriel shivered at the thought of Maya seeing her friend's dead body, her blood.

"I should have warned Barbara," she continued blaming herself. "I knew Paulette was dead when I spoke to Barbara."

He took her chin and made her look at him. "You spoke to her. What did she tell you?"

"I didn't get a chance to ask her about him. She was called to a Code Blue. I should have never let her go. I should have insisted."

"It's not your fault. He killed her because she knew who he is. It's my fault. We should have brought your friends in immediately. I should have known it wasn't safe for them." Gabriel cursed himself for his bad planning. Two lives could have been saved if he'd only thought things through. But when it came to Maya, he never thought things through properly. He was too distracted when it came to her.

"She's still in her house. He hung her on a hook on her bedroom door, like she was a slab of beef. And I didn't even have the guts to take her down and give her some dignity. I just ran."

Gabriel stroked softly over her hair and pulled her back into his arms. She buried her head in his chest, her tears soaking his shirt. "I'll send someone to Paulette's house."

Without releasing Maya, he pulled out his cell and speed dialed Yvette's number. She answered immediately.

"Yvette, I need you to take care of something for me. I want you and Ricky to go to Paulette's house. She's Maya's other friend. She's dead too."

"Oh, fuck," was Yvette's response.

"Yeah, I know. Comb the place for any evidence. Ricky has the address—he was supposed to find her and find out what she knew about Maya's stalker. I guess it's too late for that now."

"I'm on it."

He terminated the call. Then he turned back to Maya and gave her a long look. "Maya, I know what happened to your friends is painful for you, and I wish I could give you some time to grieve, but we don't have that time. To keep you safe, I have to be sure that you trust me one hundred percent, and I know you don't right now."

She pushed away from him. "I can't do this, Gabriel. I can't think of myself when I know that my friends are dead because of me."

"You have to stop saying that. It's what he wants you to believe. He wants to break your spirit, and I won't allow that. Do you hear me?" He cupped her shoulders and shook her gently. "We will avenge your friends. He will pay for their deaths. I promise you that."

"I don't want to talk right now. Not to you."

"Then don't. Just listen to me. What you saw in my bedroom wasn't what you thought it was."

Maya tried to pull away from his grip, but he held firm. She would have to listen to him. He needed her trust to keep her safe. And he was prepared to gain that trust even if it meant laying himself bare.

"The woman you saw wasn't giving me a blowjob. There was nothing sexual about it. She's a healer." He paused to give her time to process what he'd said.

Her defiant look finally turned to reluctant curiosity. "What kind of healer?"

"She's a witch, and I have a problem nobody has been able to solve. But she thinks she can."

Maya's gaze dropped to his jeans. "What kind of problem?"

Gabriel cleared his throat. There was really no easy way to say this. How should he phrase it? "It's a physical thing." He knew that didn't explain it, so he tried again. "It has to do with my . . . " He broke off again. This wasn't easy at all. How had he ever thought he could come clean and tell her what ailed him when he was scared shitless that she'd leave him if she found out?

"Gabriel. If it's something physical, you can tell me. I'm a urologist; I deal with men's reproductive organs all the time."

Gabriel cringed, but still couldn't open his mouth.

Maya put her hand on the front of his jeans and jerked at the button. "Well, if you can't tell me about it, then I'll have to examine you."

That jolted him. He imprisoned her hand with his, preventing her from opening his pants. "I don't want you to see it."

She pulled her hand out of his and stepped back. "Okay, Gabriel. Here's the deal: if you can't tell me what the problem is, I'm just going to have to believe my first assumption is right, and that you cheated on me. In any case, I'll remain hopping mad at you, and as soon as this is all over, I'll be out of your life. Is that what you want?"

"No!" The word came out so fast and furious, he surprised himself. He wouldn't allow her to leave him. He needed her. She was his mate. And besides, had she already forgotten that all she drank was his blood? She would starve without him.

"Fine." With shaking hands, he opened the button of his jeans. "It's tormented me. Caused women to recoil from me my whole life. I've had this even before I became a vampire. Nothing I've tried to get rid of it has worked."

Gabriel searched her eyes before he continued, "Maya, I want you to know no matter what happens or what you might think of me when you see this, I love you. I had hoped the witch would be able to do something about this, so you wouldn't have to see it."

So you wouldn't leave me like the others.

Slowly, he lowered the zipper and pushed his pants down. As always when in Maya's presence, his cock was hard, and it tented his boxers. The mass above it felt swollen too. Closing his eyes, he pulled down his underwear and showed himself to her in all his vulnerability.

Maya sucked in a gulp of air. For a moment she felt as if time stood still. Gabriel stood in front of her, his naked groin exposed to her. She knew immediately what it had cost him to do this. Without a doubt, he felt horrified right now. She looked back at his face and noticed that his eyes were still closed.

"I'm going to touch you," she announced calmly. "I won't hurt you."

She dropped down to her knees. When she looked at what lay before her eyes, she knew he'd spoken the truth. The witch had been there to help him with his problem. She now also understood why he hadn't wanted to have sex with her. Even though he could have quite . . . impressively.

Her gaze fell onto his cock. Proud and erect, it curved slightly upwards, eight inches of hard maleness, perfect and flawless. Its head was almost purple; just further evidence that it was pumped full with blood. Maya reached out and slid her hand along the underside, caressing the velvety skin.

A hiss left Gabriel's lips.

"I won't hurt you," she whispered.

"That's not what I'm worried about right now. Haven't you seen enough? Can't I get dressed now?"

Maya let a smile curve her lips. "Shh. I'm just examining you, and if you stop me, I will have to shut you up. And I'll let you imagine how I'm going to accomplish that." She gave his cock a firm squeeze, making a fist around his hard length. She was sure he could figure out her meaning.

Now that she knew how to control him, she moved her gaze to the area about one inch above the root of his cock. "Don't move." She let go of his cock.

The mass of flesh attached to his pelvis just at the edge of his thick thatch of black pubic hair looked red and angry. At first sight, it looked like an oversized mole – a five-inch-long one. Maya estimated the diameter of it to be about one-and-a-half inches. Those-one-and-a-half inches were attached to Gabriel's lower belly, just the way his cock was.

No wonder he was afraid of rejection: she'd had patients who'd worried about a lot less than what he was dealing with. She'd treated a man who'd had a peanut-size wart on his penis—and the thought of a woman looking at him naked had shaken him so much, he'd started suffering from erectile dysfunction. It had taken him months and the professional help of a psychiatrist to find his confidence again. She could only imagine how this deformity affected Gabriel. Her heart was aching for him.

"I'm going to touch it."

"Maya, please. You don't have to do that. It's—"

But Maya's fingers were already connecting with the fleshy mass. Then she flinched. Had it moved on its own? "I said don't move."

"I didn't."

She stared back at the protrusion and ran her fingers along it. The skin appeared wrinkled with folds upon folds, but it also felt smooth and soft. In fact, the texture was similar to that of his cock, except his cock was still fully erect and therefore not wrinkled.

"Does it ever change shape?" she asked him and looked up.

Gabriel's eyes were open, watching her during her examination. "No. Only, it's . . . "

She waited, but he looked away. "It's what?"

"It's grown in the last week. It's getting bigger. Even now it looks bigger than two nights ago." Their gazes collided.

"Are you sure?"

He nodded.

"Do you know what's causing it to grow? Have you done anything different in the last week? Anything?"

He shook his head. "No. There's nothing different in my life. I wake up, I feed, I work, I sleep. That's all."

"Are you sure?"

"Yes, everything is as always, except that you're here, and you're feeding from me."

Maya swallowed. Now that he reminded her, she felt her hunger push to the forefront again. "Do you think the change could have something to do with me drinking your blood?"

She sensed him shrug, but didn't take her eyes off his groin. Something about the growth felt odd. But she couldn't put her finger on it.

"I'm not sure, but the first time I noticed that it had grown was after you fed from me the first time. You remember, in the study?"

Of course she remembered. How could she forget the way he'd kissed her and pressed himself against her? "Did you also have an erection at the same time?" She didn't know why she asked him when she knew what the answer was.

She looked up at him and saw a shy smile play around his mouth. "Maya, I have a hard-on whenever I'm around you."

She tried not to feel too happy about his statement, but couldn't avoid it. What woman didn't want to have that kind of effect on the man she wanted? "Maybe it has something to do with you being aroused."

"No. When I was with other women, it never happened." He stared at her as if he'd said something wrong. "Long before I met you. I haven't been with anybody in a long time. And I wouldn't look at anybody else but you," he scrambled to add.

She pressed her palm onto his chest and stopped him. "Gabriel, we all have a past. You haven't been with anyone since you and I. . . since we . . . " Now she was the one who couldn't say the words.

"Made love?" he helped and placed his palm over her hand.

Maya locked eyes with him. "Yes. I know that now. That there was nothing going on with the witch. I'm sorry I couldn't trust you before." She rose. "Now you can get dressed. Unless . . . " She paused. " . . . you don't want to."

She needed to affirm life, to forget the things she'd seen tonight. Life was so short, and sometimes the only thing one could do was grab onto what was right in front of her. Take what was there while it was there. What would happen in a few hours, a few days? She realized that nothing should ever be postponed, because there might never be another chance.

Gabriel looked at her and touched her cheek with his palm. "As much as I would love for both of us to get naked right now, it wouldn't be right. You're kind not to have run away screaming, but no woman wants to be fucked by me, not while I have this."

Maya clamped her hand onto the back of his neck and pulled him closer until their lips were only a fraction of an inch from each other. "You listen to me now, Gabriel. I will decide who fucks me, and I won't let your misplaced sense of shame get in the way of that. Whatever this is, we'll deal with it."

"You don't understand. It can't be removed. I've tried surgery. It grows back."

She brushed her lips against his and felt his erection poke her stomach. "Do you want me?"

"Of course I want you."

"Then we'll figure it out. If you want to wait, that's fine, but watch your back, because one day you'll find yourself flat on it and I'll be right there taking what I want. I figure as a vampire I'm strong enough to rip your clothes off and ride you until you come. And frankly, I won't care if you sprouted a tail as long as you have a hard-on to impale me with."

Her last words were just a whisper against his lips. She felt his breath rush out of him before he took her mouth and kissed her. A moment later, she found herself without ground under her feet, suspended in Gabriel's strong arms, pressed flush against his still half-naked body. She could only hope that nobody would enter the living room or they would get an eyeful of Gabriel's naked backside.

Maya slid her hands down toward said backside. When she dug her fingers into his firm flesh, he moaned into her mouth and intensified his kiss. She'd never seen him this passionate, not even when he'd satisfied her after she'd been in heat. It was almost as if some restraint in him had burst and he was finally allowing himself to do what he wanted.

She tore her mouth away from his to breathe. "I want you now. I don't want to wait."

His eyes were dark, staring back at her with disbelief. "Maya, please don't toy with me."

She freed herself, but only to open her own pants and pull them down. "I'm not toying with you." As soon as she'd stepped out of her jeans—and it was fast, given her vampire speed—she pulled him close again. "Fuck me, now." She knew if she waited any longer she'd burn up. She needed him inside her now, and she didn't care about anything else.

"Baby," Gabriel whispered against her lips and shifted them. A moment later, he pressed her against the wall. "Next time, we'll do it like civilized people. But right now—" His hand went to her panties and with one swift move, he ripped them off her. "—right now, I want you fast and hard."

Gabriel gave her no time to let his words sink in, but pinned her with his body and spread her legs apart. For a second, he held himself completely still and looked at Maya's expressive eyes where he saw desire glow back at him. Even after what she'd seen, she still wanted him. She hadn't rejected him, she hadn't run, and most of all, she trusted him.

How this was possible, he didn't know. He recognized her need to forget the pain she felt, but that couldn't be everything. It couldn't be the reason she allowed him to take her. No, when he looked into her eyes he saw more than just desire and passion. He saw affection.

"I love you," he confessed, laying his heart bare just like he'd bared his body. Then the beast in him took over, and he thrust into her with a ferocity he'd never known. And at that moment he was thankful for the fact that she was a vampire, for the passion he unleashed on her would have torn a human apart. Maya met his thrusts with as much power and determination as he dealt them with.

Her tight channel was slick, and the scent of it whipped his desire into overdrive. This woman was all he'd ever wanted and all he would ever want for the rest of his long life. As her legs wrapped around his hips, he threw his head back and roared. This was the woman he wanted to claim as his mate at any cost.

He felt Maya's claws dig into his back and realized that her vampire side was emerging. His own body hardened. When he looked at her face, he saw her fangs push out between her lips, evidence that she was losing control. He greeted the knowledge with a growl. "Mine."

At the possessive word, her gaze collided with his. He saw his sentiment echoed in the depth of her eyes. She panted heavily, her chest rising and falling in quick succession. Her parted lips showed her fangs clearly now. They reminded him of the pleasure he'd felt when she'd fed from him.

"I want you, Gabriel."

"Then take me. Feed from me," he commanded.

"Now?" Her eyes widened.

"Now." He pulled back and plunged deep back into her, punctuating his point. Her muscles contracted around him, squeezing him like a tight fist. Gabriel tried to ignore the flesh that slapped against her mound with every thrust, but it became more difficult with every stroke. It felt as if the darn thing was lengthening. But before he could look down to investigate, he felt Maya's fangs in his neck.

Everything was forgotten with the first pull on his vein. His heart pumped vigorously to bring the blood to the vein she was suckling from. He could sense her hunger now, physically sense it. Her heart beat against his in a tantalizing staccato, and his own heartbeat matched hers beat for beat.

Gabriel slowed his thrusts as a sense of utter bliss built in his chest. In his many decades as a vampire, he'd never felt the kind of high he felt now as the woman he loved took his blood inside her at the same time as he impaled her over and over again with his hard shaft. It didn't matter that this was not the way he'd imagined making love to her.

He'd dreamed of laying her on a soft bed, with candles illuminating the room, soft music playing in the background. Worshipping her, loving her. This was different. The intensity of their lovemaking shocked him to the core. He'd never expected her to be this wild and primal.

But here she was, allowing him to fuck her in the living room of his boss's house where at any time somebody could interrupt them. Yet, he couldn't stop. All he wanted was for her to come apart in his arms, to feel the love he held in his heart, to understand that he would do anything for her.

His pistoning cock knew no end—relentlessly it drove into her to feel the tightness of her sheath, the slickness of her quivering pussy. It had found its home. He felt the pressure in his balls build.

"Baby, I can't hold back any longer." But he wanted her to come with him. He didn't want to be selfish.

Maya let go of his neck and licked over the incisions. Then she looked at him, her lips glistening with his blood. "Then come."

Gabriel clenched his jaw, trying to hold back. "Not before you do."

A little smile curved around her lips. "Please, come."

He could feel her muscles clench around his cock, and he knew she'd deliberately done it. His release was inevitable. He felt the onslaught of sensations as his seed shot through his cock and filled her. "*Fuck!*"

He pulled back and plunged deep once more, letting his orgasm engulf him. As he collapsed against her, regret followed bliss. She hadn't come. He'd failed.

"I'm sorry," he whispered.

Her hands in his hair, she pulled his head back from where he'd buried it against the crook of her neck. She smiled at him. "Sorry for what?"

"You didn't come."

"My body doesn't quite work that way."

Gabriel cringed. "I was too rough with you. I didn't do it right. Baby, I'm so sorry." He'd let his baser instincts take over.

She put her finger on his lips. "No. That's not it. I loved it, every single second of it. But I don't come from penetration. No man has ever made me come like that."

"You came when I licked you."

"Because the only way I can come is if my clitoris is stimulated."

He wished he knew more about a woman's body than the limited experience he had. He'd have to learn—fast. "We'll try again. I'll promise you, you'll come when I'm inside you."

He'd just been handed a challenge, and by God, he'd meet that challenge even if it cost him his last breath. He needed her to come with him so they could share that ultimate ecstasy and experience the closeness that would only come when they were both soaring, letting their bodies fall and catch each other.

25

Gabriel laid Maya in front of him on the couch, her body completely naked now. He'd ravished her like an animal, yet she smiled at him. His body still hummed from the amazing experience of being inside her and pounding his cock into her. But he felt regret, regret at not having given her the same pleasure she'd given him.

He promised himself that he wouldn't lose control again until she was sated. A man who couldn't satisfy his woman had everything to lose. If he couldn't give her what she needed, she'd find it somewhere else—and there was no way in hell he'd allow that to happen.

He still couldn't believe that she hadn't recoiled from him at the sight of the flesh above his cock. Why was she so different from other women?

When all this was over, he would make certain she understood what he wanted from her: a blood-bond, an irrevocable bond stronger than any marriage in the human world. While he would have to continue drinking human blood, he would partake of hers mostly during sex, first to establish the bond, then later to renew and sustain it.

And Maya would only ever feed from him. The bond would allow them to know each other's thoughts and be aware of each other even if they were apart. Everything that belonged to him would also belong to her. And he'd always be true to her. Already now, no other woman interested him, and the blood-bond would make their love for each other even stronger.

She hadn't told him that she loved him, but he was almost sure she did—only a woman in love would be able to see past his deformity and allow him to touch her. And the way she'd caressed the ugly piece of flesh . . . it had been with such tenderness that he was certain she wasn't disgusted. She cared for him, he knew that much. And even if she didn't love him yet, he would do anything in his power to make her fall in love with him.

"Teach me," he whispered to her.

There was a curious look on Maya's face. "Teach you what?"

"How to satisfy you. I want to know how your body works."

She chuckled. "Gabriel, I think you know very well how my body works. Have you already forgotten what you did yesterday?"

He hadn't forgotten—not a single second of it. But this was different. "I'll never forget that, trust me." He let his fingers trail to the juncture of her thighs. She opened for him without coaxing. "But I want you to feel the same way when I'm inside you."

She was wet when he slipped a finger inside her. Her lids closed halfway at his action. "Mmm," she hummed.

Gabriel's cell phone rang. "Damn!" Letting his finger slip from her tight sheath, he reached for it and looked at the number. It was a number he'd memorized over the last few days. "Sorry, baby, I've got to take that." He noticed Maya's disappointed look.

He flipped the phone open. "Francine."

"Hey vamp—Gabriel," she corrected herself. "We need to meet."

"Now?" He swept a long look over Maya's naked body.

"Now. I've found it. So if you want to know what ails you, you'd better come now before I change my mind."

Excitement coursed through him. She knew what was wrong with him? "Where are you?"

"At the lab." She gave him an address in Laurel Heights, only minutes from Samson's house.

"I'll be there shortly."

As he flipped the phone shut, he looked at Maya. She didn't look at him, and he sensed her frustration. In fact, now that he thought of it, he could sense a lot of things about her, not quite as strong as what he knew a blood-bond would do, but a strong connection nevertheless. He wondered whether the fact that she'd only recently fed from him did that and his own blood created that connection, or whether it was the fact that they'd had sex.

"The witch knows what's wrong with me and wants to see me."

A quiet sigh came from Maya. "Maybe there's nothing wrong with you, Gabriel. I really don't mind it."

"But I do. I don't want to be a monster anymore."

"You don't look like a monster to me." She wanted to keep him, deformity or not. She knew not every woman would be this welcoming, especially not a human. But if he had his deformity removed, what would stop him from going out there and looking for a human woman? Maya closed her eyes, hating herself for her selfish thoughts. How could she even contemplate stopping him from finding a cure? Had she lost all good in her? Was she prepared to do anything just so he'd stay with her and wouldn't find another lover?

"What's wrong?"

She opened her eyes and looked into his confused face. Sure, he'd told her he loved her, but that was in the heat of passion. It didn't count. Men said a lot of things when their dick took over. Vampire surely weren't any different from other men.

"Listen, Gabriel, I want you to know that it's okay. You don't have to get it removed on my account. I'm okay with it, really. It doesn't bother me. In fact, I'd rather you didn't do anything about it."

A stunned look traveled over his features. "Maya," he urged her. "Why would you not want this for me? I thought you and I had something here."

She swallowed hard, but couldn't stop her next words from passing over her lips. "Once you're normal, you can have any woman you want. You could have a human woman, not an infertile vampire. So you can have children."

Gabriel cursed. "God damn it! Who's been planting those ideas in your head?"

Maya averted her eyes. She'd made him angry. "Yvette."

"I wish Yvette would keep her big trap shut and not talk of things she knows nothing about." He ran his hand through his long hair and sighed. "God, Maya, Yvette doesn't know what I want. Do I want a child? Of course, but . . . I mean, you . . . " He shook his head. "This is a talk that'll take a lot longer than one minute. There's so much I have to explain to you. But I have to go now. I promise you, as soon as I'm back, we'll talk about this. About you and me. About us. Will you give me the time I need to see the witch before we talk?"

"Okay," she said quickly. "Go." She wanted to believe that he loved and wanted her, but he'd said he wanted a child. A child she could never give him.

He pressed a hard kiss on her lips before he pulled away. "I'll have Yvette come to protect you while I'm gone. Carl is here. He'll take care of you while you're waiting for Yvette. You can trust her, despite the things she says." Then he dressed faster than she'd ever seen any man dress and was gone just as quickly.

***

Thomas's fingers flew over the keyboard as he entered commands into the computer. Hacking into any company's systems was second nature to him. He and Eddie had gotten interrupted earlier by the search for Maya, but now he was back at the computer, finally hacking into the telephone company's systems. The delay had cost them.

"Can you teach me that?" Eddie asked from behind him, standing entirely too close. Over the last few weeks, Eddie's habit of sticking close to him had started to rattle his nerves.

Thomas was sure Eddie wasn't even aware of it, for all Eddie seemed to do was look up to him. After Eddie had been turned only a short few months ago, Thomas had been assigned to become his mentor. Out of practicality, he'd allowed the kid to move in with him.

"I'll give you a crash course later, but I think Gabriel wants this data quickly."

A list popped up on the screen. "That's Maya's phone records. Gabriel thinks that the rogue might have called her, or that she called him."

Eddie's arm reached over his shoulder and pointed at the screen. His scent drifted into Thomas's nose. "But that's just phone numbers. How are we going to find out who these people are?"

"I'm cross-referencing the list with phone books and listings by the cell phone companies." Thomas typed in a command and hit the enter button. The screen flashed in response and split into two halves. Names started running along on the right side of the screen, too fast to read. "Whenever it finds a match, it'll slot the name into the list."

"Wow, that's cool. But how are we gonna find who's the guy? Looks like she got a hell of a lot of calls."

Thomas turned back toward Eddie. "We're not. Maya is. As soon as the search is done in about half an hour, we'll fax it over to her. She'll flag any name that's not familiar. Since he wiped her memory she won't have any recollection of his name. He'll be among the people Maya doesn't recognize. Then, we'll do our work and check them out."

Eddie smiled and patted Thomas's shoulder. "Excellent plan."

Thomas gave a weary smile back. His other friends often did the same: pat him on the back, squeeze his shoulder in a show of friendship, but when Eddie did it, Thomas felt something he shouldn't allow himself to feel. Because Eddie was straight, and nothing would come of it.

26

Yvette looked at the gruesome scene in Paulette's bedroom. The bloody message on the wall gave her the creeps and the scent of dried human blood stung her nostrils. She glanced at Ricky, who rummaged through the nightstand.

"That guy's a psychopath," she declared.

Ricky didn't look up when he responded, "Who the hell knows what he is?"

"Definitely infatuated with her. Just like everybody else," she grumbled. She still felt a twinge of pain when she recalled how Gabriel had kissed Maya at the hospital. There was no doubt in her mind now that he loved her. Well, she'd get over it—at least Gabriel would finally be happy. One day, she'd find the right man too.

"Particularly Gabriel. What's going on between those two?"

The snide tone in Ricky's voice made her look up, but before she could reply, her cell phone rang. She looked at the number. "That's him now."

She punched the talk button and pressed the phone to her ear. "Gabriel?"

"I need you to come to Samson's immediately."

"But I'm at Paulette's house with Ricky." And he'd been the one who'd ordered her there not even an hour ago.

"This takes precedence. Ricky can continue the work at the house by himself. I need you here to protect Maya. I have to leave the house for an hour. And I don't want Carl to be the one to protect her. He's not trained for that."

At least the order meant that Gabriel still trusted her and that their little talk earlier had cleared the air. "Sure, I'll drive right over."

She was about to disconnect, when Gabriel added, "And Yvette, do me a favor, and don't fill Maya's head with snippets of information about what vampire males may or may not want—I'm not like any other vampire, and I don't want Maya to get the wrong impression."

"I haven't said anything to—"

"You told her vampire males only want to bond with human women so they can have children."

"Oh, *that*," she admitted grudgingly. She'd already forgotten about it. And besides, that was before—when she was jealous of Maya. It was different now.

"Yes, *that*. Please?"

Yvette was surprised at the soft tone of his voice. Something was different about him. He seemed less edgy than usual. "I promise. I'll keep my mouth shut."

"Thanks." A click in the line told her he'd disconnected the call.

Yvette turned on her heels and almost bumped into Ricky.

"What's going on?" he asked.

"Gabriel has ordered me to the house to protect Maya. So, you're on your own here."

"I thought *he* was protecting her."

"He has to leave the house."

"Isn't Carl there?"

"You know as well as I do that he's not a trained bodyguard. I bet the rogue could easily overpower him."

"I bet he could even take you," Ricky agreed. "Why don't I go to the house and you finish up here?"

Yvette continued into the hallway without even casting a look back at him. "Because Gabriel ordered me, not you. See you later."

His footsteps followed her. "Come on, don't be such a pest."

The little hairs on the back of her neck rose as suspicion crept up her spine. Ricky had never cared to swap assignments before. Gabriel had warned them days ago that Ricky was a little volatile at present, but this was downright annoying. "I said no. What part of no don't you get?"

The attack hit her without warning. His claws dug into her back and flung her against the wall. As she crashed into it, she heard one of her ribs snap and felt the pain radiate through her body. She landed on her feet, her body leaving a dent in the drywall behind her.

Returning Ricky's aggression, her body hardened at the same time as her fangs descended and her fingers turned into claws. Before she could fight back, he slashed his claws against her stomach, slicing through her tight T-shirt. The metallic scent of her own blood assaulted her instantly.

"Fucking bastard," she cursed and kicked out with her right leg, knocking the wind out of him. He stumbled against a door behind him. "What the fuck is this about?" she yelled as she went after him.

But she hadn't counted on him being armed.

When Ricky pulled a chain with a ball at each end out of his jacket pocket, she was unprepared. He swung it with precision and cunning, his wrist releasing it an instant later. The chain wrapped around her knees and made her lose her balance.

Yvette crashed against the wall once more, her hand already reaching for the chain and balls. She hissed in pain when she touched the metal. Silver!

How in hell had he swung it without burning himself? She cut him a quick glance and saw him grin, then wave his right hand at her. She zeroed in on it, and only now noticed the flesh colored glove he wore on that hand. He must have put in on when he'd followed her out of the bedroom.

When he bent over her, she swiped at him with her claws, but he jumped out of her way with preternatural ease, and landed on her chest, his knees pinning down her shoulders, disabling her from moving her arms. He was heavier than she and stronger. Yvette flashed her fangs at him.

But he only laughed. "Should have let me go to the house like I told you. But no, you're a controlling bitch who has to have the last word on everything. I'll show you women who's boss."

The words sank deep into her. *Women* he'd said. Instantly she knew what this was about. "Maya."

"Yes, Maya. I'll get her now. She's been mine all along. And neither you nor Gabriel can keep me away from her any longer."

Yvette shivered. Ricky was the rogue. All along he'd hidden in their midst, and nobody had suspected him.

"How did you do it? How did you evade us for so long?"

He chuckled to himself, then he gave her a cold stare. "Zane had his doubts about me when he checked my alibi, but even he isn't strong enough to get past my gift."

Yvette cursed.

"Yes, finally my gift has turned out to be quite useful. You guys always used me to smooth things over when there was a problem. I let you. But finally, I figured I'd use it for myself. Zane firmly believes I had nothing to do with Maya's attack. Nobody suspects me, because the minute I sense their doubts, I invade their mind and control those doubts. Poof!" He made a theatrical hand movement.

He'd played them all, and now that he knew Maya was alone at the house with only Carl as protection, he'd get her. "Gabriel will get you," she spat.

"By the time Gabriel gets back to the house, I'll be long gone, and Maya will be with me. Nobody will ever see us again."

"You traitor."

"Call me what you want, I don't care." He stuck his hand into his jacket pocket.

Yvette froze. He'd stake her, she knew it. Her eyes widened. When he locked eyes with her, he laughed again, a cold emotionless laugh.

"A stake's too good for you. You don't deserve to die like a man. Women like you, who play with men's feelings, who lead us around by our noses, make us think you love us, and then just drop us like a hot potato when you've had enough. Not anymore." He slapped his hand across her face, whipping her head to the side. Pain seared through her neck and jaw, but she knew his speech wasn't meant for her—it was meant for Maya. He was angry at her.

"No, you, fucking bitch, will fry in the sun."

He pulled out another chain from his pocket and wrapped one end around her left wrist. The metal stung and her skin sizzled as if somebody had dropped acid onto it. The bastard was binding her with silver—a metal she couldn't break.

Quickly, he removed his leg from one shoulder and brought her arms together, tying her up over her head. Then he jumped up, took her by her hands and dragged her along the floor into the living area.

"You're gonna pay for this!" she promised.

"I doubt that very much, especially given that you'll be dust in a few hours."

Ricky lifted her up onto her feet. When she was eyelevel with him, she spat into his face. All it earned her was another swipe with his claws. She barely felt the pain now.

Without much ado, he secured her bound hands onto a hook over the fireplace, effectively suspending her a few inches in the air. Then he secured her legs against the grid in front of the fireplace, immobilizing her.

With a few long strides, he went to the window and pulled back the curtains. Once the sun came up, it would shine straight onto her, and within minutes she would fry. It would be a painful death, not the quick relief a stake would bring.

Trying to stall him, she said, "What happened with Holly? Did you go after Maya because Holly dumped you?"

He snarled. "Nobody dumped me. I broke it off with the stupid bitch when I met Maya. I wined and dined her, I promised her the world, anything she could possibly want. And what did Maya do? Throw it all back at me like I was some beggar. Now I'll make her beg."

The thought of what might happen to Maya frightened her. If Ricky took her, Gabriel would be devastated. "I'll get you for this."

He cast her another quick glance and shrugged. "If it makes you feel better to say that, go ahead, but the reality is, you won't. Enjoy the sunrise. The weather report said there won't be any fog tomorrow."

His evil laugh echoed through the house as he strode out, slamming the door with such force that the lock broke and the door swung inside again, remaining ajar.

27

The door mechanism buzzed loudly, and Gabriel pressed the door open. Inside the modern commercial building, he turned to his left, following the witch's instructions. As he walked along the sterile corridor with its white walls and light green linoleum floor, his heart beat heavy in his chest. He wanted to claim Maya as his own, but he wanted to do it without this deformity. Despite the fact that she'd let him fuck her, he wasn't convinced that she could truly look past this ugly thing. Fucking a guy who was a freak was one thing. Marrying— blood-bonding with such a freak—was another.

He pushed the door that said "Lab 87" open and stepped into the brightly lit room.

"I'm in the back," Francine's voice immediately greeted him. He followed the sound and walked past the work benches, the sinks and centrifuges and the large refrigerators and freezers that lined the path to a small office. In it, he found the witch sitting behind a messy desk.

She looked up when he entered and pointed to the chair opposite her. "Take a seat."

Despite feeling antsy, he dropped into the chair and leaned back. "You have an answer for me?"

She *tsk*ed. "No *good evening, how are you?*"

He frowned. "Are we still playing games?"

"Cheer up; I've got good news for you."

Gabriel straightened in his chair and leaned forward. "Don't keep me on tenterhooks. I know it gives you pleasure to see me suffer, but for once just give it to me straight."

"You should really grow a sense of humor, Gabriel. Life is not all dark and without fun."

He merely lifted an eyebrow, indicating he was out of patience.

"Fine, fine. To the news then. You're not a full-blooded vampire. I tested your blood and it came back with—"

"What do you mean, *not a full-blooded vampire*? Of course I'm a vampire."

"On the surface, yes. But you have other genes in you too."

"And what's that got to do with my deformity?"

She smiled. "Everything."

"And how would that be considered good news?"

"You're a satyr, Gabriel, and that thing you've got is not a deformity. It's a second penis."

Gabriel jumped up from his chair. "*What?*"

"Just what I'm telling you."

"You mean I'm some sort of beast—half man, half bull?" He tried to wrap his brain around the news.

"No. You're talking about a minotaur. A satyr is a little different. A satyr is a mythical creature, fully man, but a highly sexual creature whose need for carnal pleasure has endowed him with a second appendage for double the pleasure so to speak," the witch explained. There was a soft chuckle in her voice.

Gabriel shook his head. "If you're right in what you're saying, then how the fuck do you explain that deformed thing? It looks nothing like a penis. Double the pleasure, my ass!" He turned away from her and heard how her chair scraped against the floor as she pushed it back and rose.

"Gabriel, listen. There's a reason it doesn't look like a penis." She paused. "Yet."

At her last word he turned. "Yet?"

She nodded. "A satyr's second penis doesn't develop immediately."

Gabriel gave a mirthless laugh. Wasn't it shock enough that he was some kind of beast? "Francine. Do you have any idea how old I am? I'll tell you. I was thirty-three when I was turned, and I've been a vampire for over a hundred and fifty years. Do you know how old that makes my so-called second penis? I'd say that thing is a late bloomer. Are you telling me I have to wait another hundred and fifty years for it to turn into what it's supposed to be?"

So he was still a freak. Well, at least now he had a name for it: satyr. Now he was a half-vampire, half-satyr with a deformity. And she called that good news?

"No. I'd say your transformation is already starting. According to the legend, once a satyr meets his life mate, his genes go to work and change the growth. Haven't you told me that you've already seen a change, as if it appears to be growing?"

He stared at her. "But it doesn't look like a penis."

"Because its final transformation only comes once you've had intercourse with your life mate for the first time. Within hours after that, it'll turn into a fully functioning penis—hard-on and all."

Gabriel took a step back. He'd had sex with Maya only a little over an hour ago. Could it be that something was already happening to him?

"What?" the witch asked.

"Maya and I, we—" Gabriel stopped himself. He couldn't tell her. This was too personal to reveal. But it appeared he didn't have to say another word.

"Ah, I see. Well, then it's just a matter of time."

"Excuse me for a second," Gabriel told her and turned around. He unbuttoned his jeans and eased his zipper open, then pulled his boxers away from his body and stared at his groin. He couldn't believe his own eyes. "Fuck!"

Francine shuffled behind him. "Can I see?"

He held out his arm to the side to prevent her from coming around him. "No!" His eyes glanced back at the place where his deformity had lived for the last nearly two centuries.

It was gone. In its stead was a beautifully formed and perfect cock, slightly shorter and slimmer than his other one, but nevertheless as perfect. He pulled back the skin and revealed the purple head, the tiny hole in its tip indicating that it would be a fully functioning organ.

He quickly arranged the boxer shorts and closed his zipper before he turned to the witch and smiled for the first time since he'd entered her office. "Just like you said."

She frowned a little. "You could have let me look at it. I've never seen a real satyr before."

"As much as I appreciate your help, the answer is no." The only person who would get to see him like that from now on would be Maya. And he sure as hell hoped she liked what she saw.

"There's something else you should know."

"What is it?"

"Satyrs only take other satyrs as life mates. Maya must be a satyr too, given that you and she had sex and it resulted in your second penis developing. I think it's proof enough. It would explain an awful lot."

Gabriel remembered Maya's medical file. "She has two extra pairs of chromosomes."

"Just like you. And her going into heat could have been a reaction to you. While a satyr female goes into heat several times a year, she does so more intensely and more often when she's around a satyr male. And then of course there's the fact that she drinks your blood."

He felt overwhelmed with the knowledge that Francine imparted on him. "What of it?"

"Well, normally satyrs don't drink blood, but since you and Maya are also part vampire, that's natural. But what I'm thinking is that because you gave her your blood to complete the turning, her latent satyr genes awoke and they instantly honed in on you as a source to sustain her."

"Does that mean she's dependent on me and that's why she won't drink human blood?"

Francine shook her head. "She could easily drink human blood and be sustained on it, but her satyr genes are influencing her taste buds. That's why she rejects it. Her satyr genes like your blood because you're similar to her. Does that bother you?"

"What bothers me is thinking that the only reason Maya wants me is because we're both satyrs and I fed her my blood." He still wanted her more than any other woman in the world, but did *she* have any choice?

"Even satyrs have free will. Yes, they're more sexual than other creatures, and are driven more by their carnal needs, but their hearts still tell them who's right for them. Don't worry about it. If you love her, it's not because you're drawn to her because of her satyr genes, but because of who she is in her heart. And the same goes for her."

Gabriel released the breath he didn't know he'd been holding. Now all he had to do was talk to Maya and tell her everything and hope she loved him the way he loved her.

He took Francine's hand into his big palms and squeezed it. "Thank you so much."

When he stepped back to turn, she stopped him. "Aren't you forgetting something?"

He stared at her. What was she talking about? She couldn't possibly want a hug? When he stepped closer and moved in for a friendly embrace, she shook her head. "Your gift. You were going to let me use it."

Gabriel jolted back and let out a nervous laugh. He'd completely forgotten about it. "Of course. Sure." He paused and looked around. "Where do we find the person you want me to do this on?" He glanced at his watch. "I have less than three hours till sunrise."

"*I* am that person."

"You?"

"I misplaced something very valuable. I need you to go into my memory and find it for me."

Gabriel relaxed, relieved that he didn't have to breach some poor soul's privacy without consent. "Not a problem. What are you looking for and how long ago did you lose it?" It was all the information he needed to scan her memories quickly.

"It's a charm to ward off evil. I need to retrieve it."

"As long as you're not going to use it against me . . . " Gabriel mumbled to himself.

"I heard that—and no, you're not the evil I feel."

***

The knock at the door tore Maya away from her thoughts. She'd gotten dressed after her shower and was still wondering how to make Gabriel accept her the way she was, even if that meant he couldn't have what, according to Yvette, all vampire males wanted.

"Come in."

The door opened, and Carl appeared, a stack of papers in his hand. She'd already sensed him. There was a homey scent to him despite the formal outer shell he portrayed.

"A fax arrived. It's from Thomas—the phone records." Carl handed her the papers.

"Thanks, Carl, that's very nice of you to bring it."

"If you need anything else, just call for me."

Maya smiled as he left the room. She fanned through the pages. There were at least thirty or forty of them. Had she really made and received that many calls in six weeks? In the last few days she hadn't made a single one. Which reminded her—she hadn't even called her parents yet.

But she couldn't do that now either. For starters, it was just past four in the morning, and besides, she still didn't know what to tell them.

With a sigh she bent over her phone records. Each row had a telephone number and name together with a date of when the call took place. She started scanning the names and recognized many of her patients' names, her colleagues', and the clinic's. Her parents' number came up many times, as well as Paulette's and Barbara's cells. Then a few other assorted friends, the pizza place down the road when she'd called for takeout and the Indian around the corner. Her bank was on the list, and so was her dentist's office.

She scanned page after page. By the time she was halfway through the stack and still hadn't seen any unfamiliar names, she heard the entrance door being opened. Maya glanced at the clock over the mantle. Finally. Gabriel would probably be upset if he found out how long it had taken Yvette to get here. Well, she wasn't going to tell on her.

As she continued reading down the list of names she heard Carl's voice. "I wasn't expecting you, Ricky."

Ricky? She was sure Gabriel had ordered Yvette to the house. Maya strained her ears to hear the conversation, her sensitive hearing picking up most of the sounds.

"You know how it is with women. Yvette isn't getting on with Maya, so she asked me to take over for her," came Ricky's reply.

Maya sat up, uneasiness spreading inside her. She and Yvette were getting on just fine, particularly since Yvette had protected her at the hospital. Why would she suddenly claim that they weren't getting on?

She shook her head in disbelief and looked back at the fax. Clearly, she'd misjudged the other vampire female, just when she'd thought she'd found a friend she could trust.

Her eyes moved down the rows of names. As if on autopilot she read them: Bill Shaw—a patient; Martha Myers—another patient, Richard O'Leary—

Ricky—

With a small gasp, the papers slid off her lap and onto the floor.

28

Ricky gave Carl an easy grin as the lie rolled off his lips like fresh blood. The butler nodded slowly. "I understand. I'll call Gabriel to let him know about the change of plans."

"I wouldn't bother him. I'm sure he's got enough on his plate right now." Ricky tried to sound casual so he wouldn't make Carl suspicious. He didn't need Gabriel showing up here when he was so close to his goal.

"He gave strict instructions." Carl reached into his jacket pocket and retrieved his cell phone. "It'll just be a minute."

Ricky never let his easy smile waver, not even when he slid his hand into his jacket pocket and reached for the wooden stake he kept there for emergencies. And this was an emergency. "Oh, before I forget," he interrupted Carl before he could punch in Gabriel's number.

The butler gave him an expectant look. "Yes?"

With one swift movement, Ricky pulled out the stake and plunged it into Carl's heart. "Did I mention that I hate it when people don't listen to me?" He was beyond caring about covering his tracks and treating everybody with kid gloves, because after tonight it wouldn't matter anymore.

Before his eyes, Carl's body disintegrated into dust. The cell phone and a few coins of change fell onto the wooden floor making a clanging sound. As the fine ash-like substance settled onto the wood floor, Ricky placed the stake back in his pocket and stepped back, not wanting the dust to dirty his clothes.

Getting rid of Carl had been even easier than anticipated. Gabriel had done the right thing by calling for somebody to protect Maya—that somebody was here right now. He would take care of Maya from now on, like it was always supposed to be.

Ricky inhaled deeply. Her intoxicating scent drifted into his nostrils. He looked up toward the stairs. She was up there on the second floor, most likely in the guestroom. How long he'd waited for this moment. Finally, he'd get his reward.

***

The video surveillance room was a windowless room in the basement of the hospital. Amaury glanced at the security officer who sat propped up against the wall, staring into the void. Zane had used mind control on him to put him into this catatonic state, in which he neither saw nor heard anything.

He and Zane had already gone through several tapes to see who had attacked and killed the doctor. So far, nothing had shown up on the tapes. It was almost as if the rogue knew what camera angles to avoid. Amaury sighed. "This is frustrating."

"Frustrating, yet revealing," Zane answered.

"How so?"

"That was quite a display of emotion on Gabriel's part."

Amaury gave his old friend a sideways grin. "Looks like it's hit him pretty hard."

"She's got quite some fire in her."

"Seems so, even though I'm sure Nina's got more." His own mate was hell on wheels, and he wouldn't have it any other way.

"With how you put up with her, I'd say you're a saint. Only I know better."

"She's just what I need."

"Still in the honeymoon phase, huh?"

"I'm planning for it never to end. Now, let's make sure Gabriel gets his own honeymoon." Amaury pointed back at the screen and sped up the tape.

The monitor showed the main entrance to the hospital. "There's Ricky entering." Zane nodded. Several minutes passed, but the tape showed no one exiting or entering. Then a woman walked in with a small child. She stopped at the information desk. Another few minutes passed.

"There, Samson's R8 is just pulling up," Zane noted. A moment later Maya ran into the hospital and down one corridor, out of the reach of the camera.

Amaury sped through the tape again, until finally Gabriel and Yvette entered. Shortly after, Zane entered on his own. Nothing else happened. Amaury stopped the tape.

"I didn't see you or Thomas go in," Zane noted.

"I took the side entrance where I parked the car. Thomas probably did the same. He knows the area well and probably went in from the back—it's a shortcut from his house."

"So everybody is there, first Ricky, then Maya, then—"

Amaury put his hand on Zane's arm. "Wait a minute. Fuck! First Ricky? Why would Ricky be there before Maya?"

His friend stared back at him. "Let's roll back the tape."

They found the exact spot when Ricky entered the hospital and paused it. At the bottom of the screen, it showed the time: 12:49 a.m.

"This had better not mean what I think it means," Zane cursed. "I had my suspicions about Ricky but then thought I was just being my usual asshole self, considering I don't particularly like Ricky's cheerful attitude. His talent. He must have used it against us. I think he fooled us all."

"One way to find out." Amaury picked up the phone on the desk and punched in a few numbers.

***

Gabriel pulled his focus back from the witch and opened his eyes. "I've restored your memory of where you put the charm. Do you recall now?"

She nodded. "Thank you. Do I have your word that you won't go there yourself to obtain it?"

"I have no interest in charms, no matter how powerful. All I want is—" The ringing of his cell phone interrupted him. "Excuse me."

He looked at the San Francisco number, but didn't recognize it. "Yes?"

"It's Amaury."

Finally, he was returning his call. Tension immediately crept into his bones. "Any news?"

"I'm afraid so. Tell me, when did you call Ricky to meet you at the hospital?"

"When I realized that Maya wasn't at her apartment."

"No, I mean at what time? Check your cell phone log." Something in Amaury's voice compelled him to comply with the request without questioning.

"Hold on," he told his friend and pulled the phone from his ear, pressed the menu button and navigated to the call-log screen. Next to Ricky's name was the time. "I called him at 1:03 a.m., why?"

"What did he tell you when you called? About where he was?"

"He didn't say. He only said he'd get there. What is this about?"

He heard Amaury exhale sharply. "Ricky was already at the hospital when you called him. He arrived before Maya."

Gabriel's heartbeat kicked up. "Shit. Ricky's still on the list of vampires who don't have an alibi for the night Maya was attacked."

"I know. Zane just told me—and he also told me he now remembers that he had doubts about Ricky, but they somehow vanished."

"Ricky's gift!"

Amaury grunted. "He's tricked us. You'd better not let Maya out of your sight right now."

Gabriel's body coiled with fear for his woman. "Amaury, I'm not with Maya. She's at the house with Carl. I sent Yvette to protect her. We need to warn them about Ricky. I'll call Maya and Carl, you call Yvette, then send every available bodyguard to the house. Send out a search party for Ricky. Start at Paulette's house in Midtown Terrace—if we're lucky, he's still there."

He raced out of the lab without even glancing back at the witch and dialed Samson's home phone. A recording answered. *"You have reached a number that is out of service . . . "*

29

Maya reached for the cordless phone next to the bed and punched the call button to get a line. Silence greeted her. She pulled the phone to her ear to verify, but her suspicion was correct: the phone was dead. Ricky had disabled the line to the house.

She threw the useless receiver onto the bed and swiveled. Her eyes scanned the room in record speed—the vampire speed she was grateful for now. Her gaze zeroed in on her handbag. Two large strides and she was there, pulling her cell phone out of it with the next move. She held down the *on* button for a few seconds, her heart beating into her throat as she heard steps on the stairs.

He was coming for her.

Maya silently begged that her battery hadn't run too low in the days she hadn't used the phone and was relieved to see the screen coming on. Good. A few more seconds and the phone was fully booted. But she could only stare at it. This couldn't be happening, not now, not when she needed to call for help! *No Service*, it read.

The sound of the door opening made her lift her head, and then she saw him. Ricky stood just inside the room, the door behind him sliding shut a moment later.

"I had your service disconnected," he said calmly, his Irish lilt a little more pronounced now. "No use wasting money when you won't need to make any more phone calls where we're going."

Maya froze. Her mind worked frantically to assess her chances of getting past him and out of the house, but he was blocking the door effectively and short of her knocking him over, she wouldn't succeed. Her skin prickled uncomfortably now, and she realized it was the same feeling she'd had in the hospital, and also that time when she'd met Ricky in the kitchen. At the time she'd written the feeling off to her illness, the approaching fever, but had she been well, she would have been able to connect the sense of danger in the air with Ricky.

It was too late now.

"I want you to leave," she said as calmly as she could. "Yvette will be coming soon." Despite the suspicion she had, she needed to stall him from whatever he was planning. Her suspicion was confirmed with his next words.

"I'm afraid Yvette's a little tied up right now." He chuckled.

"Is she dead?"

"She will be, soon. But let's not talk about other people. Let's talk about us."

Gabriel would be back soon. Despite the fact that she didn't want to talk to Ricky, she knew she had to keep him talking, but not about herself. "What did you do to her?"

He ignored her question. "You liked me at first. I know you did. Did you know that I dumped my girlfriend for you? And what thanks did I get?"

"I'm sure I didn't ask you to do that for me. I never go after men who're in relationships." And for sure she wouldn't have gone after him—just looking at him made her skin prickle with revulsion.

"We met the night your car stalled. I helped you fix it. You were grateful, very grateful," he insinuated.

She didn't believe it. No, she would have never allowed him to touch her. "No."

"Oh, yes. Shall I tell you more about how it was between us?"

Disgust rose in her stomach and settled uncomfortably at her solar plexus. "There's no *us*. There's never been an *us,* and there'll never be an *us*." Even though she still remembered nothing about him, she knew instinctively that she'd never had sex with Ricky. Her body told her as much. It recoiled from his presence.

"See, that's where you're wrong." He took several steps into the room, closing in on her.

"Gabriel will kill you if you lay a hand on me," she warned and took a step back.

"We'll be long gone by the time Gabriel figures things out and gets back here." He pulled a small, flat device out of his pocket and turned it to her. Maya looked at what appeared to be an iPhone with a map. In the middle of it, a red dot blinked. "I know exactly where he is right now, so don't you worry about Gabriel."

Maya cursed. "You prick!"

"Now, now, are those words for a lover?" The sick grin around his mouth made her physically nauseous. She would never be his lover. She'd rather kill herself before she let him touch her.

"You can't possibly think I'd ever become your lover."

"The way I see it you don't have much of a choice, seeing that you'll be all tied up soon. And then I'll take what I want, whenever I want and how often I want. It's your own fault. It could have been different between us. But no, you had to lead me on, make me want you, and then just turn away as if I was a nobody. And generous as I am, I even gave you a second chance. We started all new, and, you little bitch, you did the same thing again. There are days when I really love my gifts." Then he growled.

"And there are days when I recognize their limitations. Unfortunately now that your doubts about me are confirmed, there's no more dispelling them, nor erasing your memories. It was easier when you were human, at least I could wipe the slate clean. But you left me no choice."

The snarl around his mouth made his average face look ugly. She could practically see the ugliness inside him, the evil that lived within him. Her skin crawled with awareness of the bad vibes his body was projecting. She felt it more intensely now that he was only a few feet away from her. The little hairs on her arms rose as if preparing for an attack. And she knew he'd attack. All she could do was distract him until help arrived.

The silence from downstairs told her that Carl wasn't coming to her defense. Maya feared the worst for the sweet butler, who'd only ever treated her with the greatest respect. "What did you do with Carl?"

His facetious grin confirmed her worst suspicion. "Dust to dust, ashes to ashes."

Maya swallowed hard. She was alone in the house with him. Yvette, the only other person who knew she was alone, was tied up somewhere, Carl was dead, and Gabriel was with the witch. Ricky would instantly know when Gabriel was approaching the house, so she couldn't expect any help from him either.

She was on her own. On her own with a madman—no, make that a mad vampire. Maya let her eyes travel around the room, trying to find anything she could use to her advantage.

"What were you trying to gain by turning me into a vampire?" She had to make sure he continued to talk while she tried to figure out a way of how to get away from him.

"Your undying love and devotion, of course," he teased lightheartedly, "but I'll be happy with just your body, your legs permanently spread for me."

"You sick bastard. You really think I'd spread my legs for you?"

"You did it for Gabriel," he shot back, hatred suddenly flooding his voice. "What has he got that I don't, huh? He sure hasn't got it in the looks department. And he's no charmer either. I'm just as rich as he is, and I'm far better looking. Is it because he lets you drink his blood?"

Maya gasped. She hadn't realized he knew.

"Oh yeah, don't look so surprised. You really think I don't know what's going on here? I can smell him on you. You're positively reeking of him. But don't you worry, a few days with me and his smell will be gone. I'll make sure of it, even if I have to drain you of the last drop of blood and replace it with mine."

"You wouldn't dare!"

He jumped and stood only inches from her now. His breath ghosted over her face, and she felt bile rise. "Wouldn't I?"

"He'll kill you." She knew Gabriel would—whether she was still alive by then, she wasn't sure, but she knew Gabriel would not stop until Ricky was dead.

"He'll never find us. We'll be long out of the country by the time he even knows you're gone. And then we start our lives together, just like we would have if these idiots hadn't interrupted us when I turned you. You would have woken up in my arms and looked up to me as your protector. But I'll rectify that. You'll be mine, and nothing in this world will stop me from making you mine. Don't you ever forget that."

The threat hung heavy in the room, poisoning the atmosphere around her. She understood only too well how serious he was. Not even rape was beyond him. She could see the madness in his eyes. No, he wouldn't stop at anything.

That's why *she* had to stop *him*.

Determination spread within her, and her mind cleared itself of everything else but the thought of getting away from him. Just the way she approached any research problem, she assessed her options one by one and determined the probabilities of succeeding. Her mind raced from one scenario to the next, her heart pumping rapidly to provide her brain with the needed oxygen.

Sweat built on her brow, but she ignored it. Let him think she was scared: it would only serve her purpose. She was beyond fear now—she was in survival mode, and instinct and logic were her best friends. The knowledge that Ricky had killed her two best friends fired her resolve.

"You killed my friends."

"Useless humans. They knew too much. You gossiped about me to them. Their blood is on your hands."

Maya pushed the guilt away. Ricky was the culprit, and she wouldn't allow herself to fall into his trap. He was the evil one, and she would make sure he paid for his deeds. "I'll make you pay."

He only laughed at her threat. Then he turned serious again and gripped her arms. "I should like to see you try, but later. We're leaving. Now."

She heard the faint beeping sound coming from the iPhone in Ricky's pocket and knew Gabriel was on the move. And he knew it too. The time for stalling was over. Maya tried to push against him and wiggle out of his hold, but he only tightened his grip on her wrists. He would break them if she gave him any more resistance.

"I'm stronger than you," he gloated.

She knew that already. But she was smarter. Her gaze drifted to the fireplace where a poker leaned against the mantle. She concentrated on the long metal stick with its sharp two-pronged tip.

Then she funneled all her pain and the hatred for Ricky into her thoughts and directed them toward the poker, willing it to move. But it didn't budge. Her forehead furrowed as she concentrated more. She had to succeed. It had worked in the bar when she was with Thomas. She knew she could do it, if only she could concentrate hard enough.

Ricky pulled at her arms. "Move!"

Maya didn't obey the command and went rigid. A flash of anger washed over his face, before a wicked grin stole onto his face. "Fine, then how about this?"

Before she knew what he was about to do, he pressed his lips onto hers. Bile rose and anger churned in her belly. She clenched her jaw, keeping her lips firmly pressed together as she tried to push him away. But even her vampire strength was no match for his.

Despair and hatred mingled in her head as disgust for him made her feel nauseous. When he pulled her flush against his body and pressed his hips into hers, it was as if he'd flipped a switch inside her brain. She suddenly remembered him.

For weeks he'd chased her, pursued her first with gifts and fancy dinners, then with threats. She'd immediately seen in him the fact that he was obsessed. And it had scared her then. She remembered the one night when he'd come to the hospital, the night when he'd almost raped her. Had her unconscious patient not suddenly flatlined, and the monitor he was hooked up to not alerted the Code Blue team, which had shown up within seconds, he would have succeeded.

Instead he'd wiped her memory right there. But her memories were back now, and she wouldn't let him succeed. He would never touch her again.

She concentrated harder, remembering the poker near the fireplace. All her energy went into this one item. Her body tensed from the effort.

With a surprised grunt, Ricky suddenly let go of her and pulled back. His face distorted in pain and disbelief as he turned his head and looked at his flank. Maya followed his gaze and saw the poker lodged in his side, blood pouring from the opening.

"You bitch!"

She knew it wouldn't kill him, but it gave her some time.

Maya raced from the room and down the stairs. She jerked the front door open and ran into the night. Her eyes darted frantically up and down the street, not sure which way to run. She let instinct take over and turned west toward the part of the city she knew best.

At the next stoplight, she saw a flatbed truck which carried flattened cardboard boxes. She eased onto the back of it taking shelter behind the cargo, making sure the driver didn't see her. When the lights turned green, the truck jerked into motion.

30

Gabriel jumped out of the car, his long legs eating up the distance to the front door of Samson's house. It stood wide open, and light spilled onto the steps. Not a good sign.

The panic that had already gripped him earlier only intensified at the sight of the empty foyer and the silence in the house. He instantly saw the dust on the floor, together with a cell phone, some loose change, and a ring—Carl's ring. Oh, God, no! Ricky had already been here.

The grief for Samson's friend and loyal servant almost made his knees buckle. But he couldn't—wouldn't—be weak now. Not when Maya . . . "Maya! Maya!" he yelled, not expecting any answer. He knew what he would find.

Taking three steps at a time, he ran up the stairs and stormed into the guestroom that Maya had been occupying. The stench of blood instantly assailed him. His eyes zeroed in on a metal fire poker, which lay on the rug, its tip covered in blood.

Gabriel inhaled and for an instant, he felt relieved. The blood wasn't Maya's. She had fought him. A sense of pride spread within him, only to be instantly replaced by more fear. He recognized the blood as Ricky's. Was he dead or had she merely injured him before he was able to take her away with him? There was no telltale dust on the rug so he had to assume both of them were alive.

He stared at the blood-covered metal stick and closed his eyes for a moment, trying to gather his strength. He couldn't lose her, not now, not when he'd just paved the way for them to be together.

Before he could turn to leave the room in order to search for them, he felt a stab in his head. A split second later, his eyes looked at the scene in front of him, a scene that had played out in this very room only minutes earlier. He'd tapped into Maya's memories. How, he didn't know. This had never happened to him before. He'd never been able to access somebody else's memories unless he was physically close.

Maybe his connection to Maya was so strong he didn't need to be close to her to tap into what she'd seen.

Gabriel concentrated and watched as Ricky kissed her brutally. He saw how she used her new skill to disable him so she could get away from him. As she ran out the door, he saw everything through her eyes, including the streets she looked at, the truck she jumped onto.

His feet carried him downstairs and out the door. He slammed it shut and headed for the Audi. While concentrating on traffic with one eye, his inner eye kept the connection with Maya's memories. He recognized the streets and houses she'd passed as the truck she sat on drove farther and farther west.

She'd gotten away from him, but Gabriel didn't delude himself for even a second that Ricky wasn't on her heels already. He had to get to her first and make sure she would be safe.

***

The truck stopped at a red light, and Maya jumped off. They'd reached the east end of Golden Gate Park. She realized the sun would come up soon, and she needed to find shelter before it was too late. While it was tempting to run to the hospital which was only blocks away from the park, Maya knew Ricky would expect her to hide out there and find her. No, she had to go somewhere where he wouldn't suspect her and hide until she could summon help.

She crossed the meadow and passed the children's playground with its carousel. The tennis courts lay to her right. While there was a club house where she could find shelter from the sun, it would be swarming with people as soon as the sun came up and the first tennis players arrived for an early morning game. She wouldn't be safe there for long.

Maya headed deeper into the woods. There was a place she knew of, had heard one of the paramedics talk about when they'd picked up a homeless man. She'd listened to the story of exactly where they'd found him, and knew she would be able to remember the way. She'd been there before. Curiosity had led her there on one of her Sunday walks, partly to check out whether the paramedic had told the truth, and partly because she'd had nothing better to do that afternoon.

She found the path she was looking for and jogged at a fast pace. At every sound, she jerked, ready to speed up if Ricky was coming for her. He'd never give up until he had her; she'd seen it in his eyes. The evil that had rolled off him had been strong, and now that she knew what he was capable of, she was surprised at herself that she hadn't sensed it the moment Gabriel had introduced him in the kitchen.

How had Ricky been able to mask his true intentions from his friends and colleagues for so long? Did it have something to do with Ricky's special gift that Gabriel had mentioned? That he could dispel people's doubts. He'd confessed that he'd done it with hers. She remembered now that her skin had prickled uncomfortably that night she'd met him in the kitchen, but she'd written it off to the approaching fever. Now she knew he'd used his skill on her then.

Even Gabriel had trusted him, enough to send him to talk to Barbara and Paulette. And she'd unwittingly handed her two friends to him on a platter. All he'd had to do was kill them. Maya's stomach lurched at the thought. No, she couldn't allow herself to think this way now. She had to remain strong. Ricky was evil, and he would have found them either way, even without her help. And he would have made sure nobody would be able to find a trace of what he'd done.

Maya stopped at the sound behind her. She held her breath and kept still, afraid of making a move and giving her position away. There, another twig snapped. Somebody was walking in her direction. Her heart beat in her throat and perspiration built on her palms and her neck. She felt the moisture run in tiny rivulets down her back and chest. Had he found her already?

The large tree she had hidden behind blocked her view. But she knew he was there. She heard the rustle of the leaves and the sound of his boots on the ground. Searching the ground beneath her feet for anything she could use as a weapon, she discovered a short wooden stick. Without making a sound, she bent down and palmed it. She hoped it would make a good stake.

Maya took in a much needed breath—and froze as the scent filled her lungs.

She stepped around the tree and leapt at the man who stood in front of her. "Gabriel."

His arms came around her as he pressed her to him and buried his head in her hair. "Oh, Maya . . . I thought I'd lost you."

Before she could answer him, his mouth took hers in a fierce kiss, wiping away the memories of Ricky's touch. When they came up for air, Gabriel stroked his hand over her face.

"Ricky, he's after me. It's him. He's the rogue." The words came spilling from her lips.

"We know. Amaury and Zane figured it out. They alerted me, but I got to the house too late."

"I injured him, but I don't think he'll give up."

Gabriel nodded. "I'll alert the others to where we are. You'll be safe in a few minutes."

He pulled out his cell phone and started to dial.

Maya stared at it, instantly recalling Ricky's own phone. "Shit!" She snatched the cell from his hands before he could react and smashed it against the tree with such force that it splintered into hundreds of tiny pieces.

"What the—"

Gabriel stared at her as she destroyed his only means of communicating with his colleagues. What on earth had gotten into her?

"You led him right to us." There was no accusation in her eyes, only grim horror.

"How?"

"He has a tracker on you. I saw it on his iPhone. He knows where you are. We have to run."

Gabriel cursed himself. Instead of saving her, he'd put her in more danger. He'd found her because of his unique connection to her and the fact that he could tap into her memories. Ricky didn't have those skills and had probably followed him all along. And he, idiot that he was, had led him right to her. He couldn't be far behind them.

"God, I'm sorry."

"This way. I know a place where we can hide."

Without hesitation, he followed her as she ran farther into the woods. He only hoped that Ricky was far enough behind them that they'd have a chance to get away.

They zigzagged through the forested area before they reached the edge of a small meadow. Instead of crossing it, Maya continued hugging the tree line, staying hidden in their shadows. Gabriel was only steps behind her. But he didn't speak, despite the many questions he had. If Ricky was close, any sound could lead him their way. While he was certain he could defeat him if confronted, it was too close to sunrise to fight. Even though he hated the idea of hiding, for Maya's safety's sake, he knew he had to.

When she turned and locked eyes with him, he knew she wasn't angry at him, merely scared. And he wished he could wipe that fear off her face, but there was no time for it now. He gave her a reassuring nod and followed her around a bend on the barely recognizable footpath she appeared to know.

As they came to an earthen mound, she stopped.

Gabriel drew up next to her and saw what she was looking at. Notched into the small hill that looked like an oversized mole hill, was a metal door. It was locked with a padlock.

"Can you open this?" she asked him.

"What is this?"

"An old bomb shelter."

"In San Francisco?"

"Built back during the Cuban Missile Crisis. Can you break the lock?"

He nodded and pulled his knife out of his boot. Luckily, he never left home without it. He held the padlock with one hand, then stuck the knife into it and twisted.

"Quickly. I can feel my skin prickle. He's close," she whispered.

Gabriel didn't question what she sensed. If she felt him close, he wasn't going to doubt her. He doubled his efforts and twisted harder. A moment later, he heard a click, and the lock sprung open. He unhinged it from the door, and pressed down the handle. The door opened to the inside.

Darkness greeted him. "Are you sure?"

Maya was already behind him and pressed inside. "The sun is coming. Quick!"

He stepped inside, pulling Maya with him before he let the door snap shut. All he could hear was her heavy breathing.

31

Yvette heard the dog's hesitant woof just outside the entrance door. She could sense his confusion as he sniffed, wondering whether it was safe to enter. How she was able to connect with an animal, she had no idea, but she'd had the same strange feelings when she'd wandered through the streets of San Francisco a few nights earlier and had noticed how dogs had suddenly started to follow her. One had even gone so far as to follow her all the way to Samson's house. Maybe she'd tapped into a gift she didn't know she had.

"Here, doggie, doggie," she coaxed from her position at the fireplace, still strung up by her wrists, the silver painfully burning her skin. If she ever got out of this one, she'd string Ricky up by his balls and let him suffer until he fried in the rays of the rising sun.

A look out the window told her she didn't have more than fifteen minutes until sunrise. This was cutting it close.

The dog's claws scratched against the wood floor as he entered the house. "Good dog," she praised. As he rounded the corner, she saw him, a light colored lab with big, brown eyes. His head tilted to the side as if he was trying to figure out what was wrong with her.

"Yes, my boy, come here."

The good-natured beast approached and wagged its tail. She spotted a collar around its neck. Good. He had an owner, and hopefully that owner wasn't too far away. "Where's your daddy?" she asked him in the same crooning voice she'd used before. She only hoped that none of her vampire colleagues would ever see her like this. They would all make fun of her, for sure.

"Hey boy, how about you play Lassie for me?" If a TV dog could summon its owner, surely this Labrador could do it too. His eyes looked intelligent, his ears perking up as if listening intently.

"Good doggie, go get you owner," she ordered. "Go get Daddy."

The dog wagged its tail again. Did he understand her? Yvette felt sweat build on her forehead. "Come on, doggie, do this for me, and I'll give you a big meaty bone." Yes, cutting off a piece of Ricky would be just up her alley.

The dog took a few more steps toward her and nudged at her legs.

"Do it, doggie, go on."

"What are you going to have him do? Lick the chains off you?"

At the voice from the door, Yvette snapped her head toward it. "Stop joking and untie me, Zane!" She'd never been so happy to see her nasty colleague than at that moment.

Zane stepped into the living area, his gait relaxed, almost bored. "Never thought I'd see you like that. Looks like you'll finally have to beg me for something."

Yvette clenched her jaw. "You little shit, untie me now."

He laughed, and she froze. She'd never heard him laugh. In fact, she had always assumed he was incapable of laughing. But the rumble that tore from his chest was definitely a laugh.

"I guess that's as close as you'll ever come to begging me for anything, huh?" he ventured as he approached. He pulled leather gloves out of his pockets and put them on. For a moment, she was reminded of the gloves Ricky had worn and instantly tensed when he reached her.

"Now *that*," he commented at her indrawn breath, which she knew he recognized as fear, "*that* just made my day." His grin widened. "Who would have thought that you'd ever be scared of me?"

Yes, and for an instant she had been scared of him, but the moment he loosened the silver chains and freed her, the fear vanished. "You're such a sick bastard."

"Ain't it grand?"

Yvette decided not to comment. Whichever way Zane got his kicks, she didn't really care. All she cared about was that he'd saved her life. And for that, she owed him. On impulse, she pulled his head to her and kissed him on the cheek.

"Thanks, buddy."

She laughed when he pulled away, his lips pulled into a snarl. Zane hated any show of affection and even more so when it was directed at him—and Yvette knew it. She smiled.

"Bitch! Let's go. I have a blackout van outside."

"First, we'll have to warn Gabriel. Ricky's the rogue."

"We already know. I'll fill you in on the way. We're setting up a command post at Thomas's house."

By the time they pulled the van into Thomas's garage, which was located underneath his house, Zane had filled her in on most of the details. Behind them, Yvette heard the garage door roll shut. She gave it another couple of seconds before she opened the door of the van and jumped out. Zane killed the engine and followed her.

Yvette rubbed her chafed wrists. In the blackout van she'd already helped herself to the supplies of bottled blood, but it would take several hours for the wounds to heal. The silver had painfully eaten away the outer layers of her skin, exposing the raw, pink flesh underneath. But she could deal with that. The pain inside her however, was harder to push away. One of their own had tried to kill her. Betrayal like that always cut deep.

She glanced behind her as she ascended to the upper level of Thomas's house. Zane had a grim expression on his face, his lips drawn into a thin line. When he caught her look, he growled. Kissing him on the cheek to thank him for her rescue had clearly rattled him. It made her chuckle.

Hardass.

"One word about what happened back there and I'll string you up myself."

She shook her head and turned the door knob as she reached the top of the stairs, not bothering to reply. As she pushed the door open and took a step into the foyer, she recoiled.

"Fuck!"

Yvette slammed the door shut and bumped into Zane behind her.

"What's wrong?"

"Daylight," she hissed. "He's got the shutters open."

A moment later the door opened, and Thomas's frame silhouetted against the light from behind him. "It's all right, come in."

"You're fucking kidding me." Yvette tried to move farther back into the shadows.

Thomas reached out his hand. "It's not natural light. Come, let me show you."

Hesitantly, she followed him into the open-plan living area. The large room was flooded with light. As her eyes adjusted, she took in the

room. Instinctively she hid behind Thomas—the room had floor-to-
ceiling windows on two sides, and through them she saw the world
outside.

"What the . . . ?"

Thomas beckoned her closer to the windows. He seemed
unconcerned. Outside, it was clearly daytime, and the light flooding
through the windows should have turned him into toast within seconds,
but there he stood, right in front of one of the large windows, admiring
the view over the city below.

"It's not real," he claimed as he turned back to her.

Zane stepped closer, his mouth dropping open at the sight. "It's not
a picture," Zane said. "There are cars moving. Live feed?"

Thomas nodded. "The house is equipped with cameras all around,
filming what's going on outside right at this moment. It projects the
images onto the special shutters I've designed. They block out the
sunlight like regular shutters, but I can project film onto them. What you
see on them is what you would see if the windows were clear. The
projections are accurate depictions of what's going on right outside."

"Ingenious." Zane nodded his approval.

"And the light?"

"A new kind of light bulb that mimics daylight. Pretty realistic by
the looks of your reaction." Thomas smiled at her, and she finally
exhaled.

"I'd say." Only now she realized they weren't alone. In one corner
Eddie stood talking on his cell phone. And to the left where Thomas had
several computer screens hooked up, Amaury sat, the phone pressed to
his ear.

"Ricky tried to kill me."

Thomas nodded, his mood solemn. He seemed to notice her
damaged wrists now. "We figured as much. Do you want some blood?"

"I'm good. I had some in the car. What I want is Ricky's head on a
stick."

Amaury turned to them. "Good to see you, Yvette." The sound in his
voice told her he meant it. They hadn't always been on the best of
terms, but at least now she knew who she could trust.

"What's the latest?" Zane asked.

"Gabriel and Maya have disappeared. We can't trace their cell signals either." Amaury looked at Thomas and pointed at the phone. "That was the human crew you sent to Samson's house. Nobody's there." For a moment, he closed his eyes. When he opened them again, pain was evident in the brilliant blue of his irises. "We have reason to believe that Carl is dead."

"Oh shit," Thomas mumbled.

"What about Ricky?" Yvette asked.

"We have our human bodyguards out looking for him." Amaury stood.

"He's dangerous."

"We know that now."

"Damn, we could have known earlier," Eddie's voice came from the corner as he flipped his phone shut. "That was Holly, Ricky's ex-girlfriend."

"Has she seen him?" came Amaury's question.

"No. But she just told me that she followed him one night. Guess she was jealous and wanted to know who Ricky was so infatuated with. She followed him to an apartment in Noe Valley."

"Maya's place," Yvette uttered under her breath. "What else did she say?"

"She gave me a few of his favorite hangouts."

"Have the daytime guards check them out, see if we can flush him out," Amaury ordered. "His movements are limited right now so this is our best time to find him. Tonight, once he's able to move around again, he can slip through our fingers."

Eddie nodded. "I'm on it."

Yvette stared out the window at the city below. Somewhere down there, Ricky was hiding, and so were Gabriel and Maya—she could only hope that Gabriel had gotten to Maya before Ricky could lay his dirty paws on her. As much as she'd wanted Gabriel for herself, she would never forgive herself for not stopping Ricky if he'd harmed Maya. Gabriel deserved to keep the woman he loved. And she would do anything to make sure he did.

"Ricky has to be hiding somewhere." She clenched her jaw and looked into the round of the four big vampires in her company. "And when we find him, he's mine." Nobody contradicted her.

32

Gabriel ran his hands alongside the door and found a switch. He flipped it. A second later, a neon light flickered and hummed before it steadied itself and illuminated the entire room. He bolted the door from the inside before he turned to take in his surroundings.

The approximately five-hundred-square-foot room was fairly bare. There were several cots stacked on one side, a supply cabinet next to them. In the back was a rudimentary toilet and a small sink. A small desk and chair completed the furnishings. While it wasn't much, the place was surprisingly clean, and most of all, it had no windows through which sunlight could penetrate. For now, they were safe.

Next to him, Maya seemed to have come to the same conclusion. She nodded to herself.

"How did you know about this place?" he asked, turning to her and reaching for her hands.

"A paramedic told me about it a long time ago—they found a sick homeless guy who'd broken in." She looked back at the heavy bolt on the inside of the door. "Ricky won't be able to get in, will he?"

Gabriel pulled her close, seeking contact with her body to appease the worry he'd felt for her. "No. We're safe. At least until sunset." He tipped her chin up to look into her eyes. "I was scared. I thought he'd gotten you."

"How did you even find me?"

"I'm not entirely sure, but for some reason I could see into your memories as you were fleeing Ricky. I followed the streets you saw when you were on the back of the truck."

She shook her head. "How's that possible? I thought you can only go into someone's memories when you're close to them."

He shrugged. "That's like it's always been, but maybe my connection to you is so strong that I don't need to be physically close."

"You mean you saw everything?"

He'd virtually felt Maya's disgust when Ricky had kissed her. It wasn't a memory he'd particularly wanted to see, but nevertheless it only cemented what he planned on doing to him when he caught him. "I'll never let another man touch you ever again, I promise you that. We'll get Ricky and I'll kill him."

"Not if I kill him first," she responded.

There was so much contempt in her voice that Gabriel pulled back a fraction to look into her eyes. That's when it hit him. "You remember."

She nodded. "It all came back when he touched me. Gabriel, he'll never give up. He's obsessed. And he'll stop at nothing. If you knew the things he's done."

Rage boiled up in Gabriel. "Tell me what he did," he bit out through clenched teeth. If that bastard had harmed a single hair on her head, he would draw and quarter him. He'd torture his sorry ass until he begged to be killed.

Maya blinked her eyes shut, then opened them again. "He was about to rape me when he got interrupted. That's when he wiped my memory for the first time."

Gabriel gasped, disgust rolling off him. As gently as he could manage, he stroked over Maya's back. "Oh, baby, I'm so sorry. I wish your memory hadn't come back."

"To be honest, I'm glad it did. At least now I know one thing for sure." She pulled back and locked eyes with him. "Despite what he claims, I never let him touch me. I was never intimate with him."

He felt himself rejoice at the knowledge that Ricky had never laid claim to her. "Baby, I'm so glad for your own sake. But I'm still going to kill him."

"I'm not sure how he managed to keep all this from you and your friends. Did nobody have any suspicions?"

Gabriel had wondered the same, but he now knew with certainty what Ricky must have done. "He used his gift, his gift to dispel doubts. When I went over the list of vampire males, who had no alibi for the time of the attack, Zane was adamant that Ricky was in the clear even though he had no conclusive alibi. I was suspicious of it, but somehow my doubts disappeared just as soon as I wanted to raise them. Ricky must have been near. He must have been watching me and Zane and interfered using his mental gift."

Maya nodded. "I think he did the same to me. I had an uneasy feeling when you introduced me to him in the kitchen, but the feeling went away. And then I was so distracted by the fever that I couldn't think clearly anyway."

"He played us all. But that's over now. I can guarantee you that Amaury has already mobilized the troops. They'll be out looking for him."

"During daytime?" Maya gave him a doubting look.

"Yes. We have plenty of human bodyguards who are loyal to us. They'll be out looking for him now. He won't be able to move."

"Let's hope so." She circled her arms around him and snuggled into his chest.

Gabriel shelved her chin on his palm and dropped his head. Maya met him halfway. The moment their lips met, warmth flooded through him. For the first time in the last hour he felt at ease. He captured her lips and slid his tongue into her mouth, stroking against hers in one smooth sweep. When her body pressed against him in the most trusting way he'd ever felt a woman, he felt himself harden—and this time he could distinctly feel both his cocks. The awareness reminded him of what he needed to tell her.

He severed the kiss and looked at her surprised face. "I have to tell you something."

A small frown line built between her brows, almost as if she was afraid of what he wanted to tell her. "Yes?"

"About what the witch found out." He hesitated. Would she welcome the news? He hoped she would, because if she didn't, there was nothing he could change about it. His body was what it was: that of a satyr, and as such, he was endowed with two penises. He could only hope that if she truly was a satyr too, her instincts would tell her to accept him.

Maya pulled away and turned slightly, avoiding looking at him. Curiosity rose in him. "I told you it doesn't matter if it can't be removed. I'm okay with it."

Gabriel put his hand on her arm and turned her back to look at him. It was time for that talk he'd postponed, because he'd been at a loss of how to explain everything to her in two sentences. Now they had all the time in the world. "I know you told me that. And we've already established you actually want the thing to stay because you're scared. Let's talk about that."

Maya felt his warm hand and looked up to meet his gaze. "Once you're normal again, you'll want somebody else, not me."

"Didn't you hear what I said to you earlier? That I love you."

The words felt good, but still she couldn't believe them. "Yes, you said that, but you also said you want a child. Once you realize that you could have anybody when your deformity is gone, then why wouldn't you want to be with somebody who can give you children?"

Before she knew what was happening, Gabriel pulled her into his arms. "I don't care about that," he said gruffly. "All I ever wanted out of life is a wife who loves me and accepts me for what I am. Becoming a father would have been a bonus, but I don't care about that, not enough. Do you really think I would give up this chance at happiness merely because we won't be able to have children?"

"You mean that?" Her heart beat into her throat.

"I mean it. But—"

So there was a *but*. She shouldn't have rejoiced too early. Her shoulders dropped in defeat.

"You have to accept me, and once I tell you what the witch found out, it's up to you to make a decision. I love you. I want you to know that, but I can't ask you to be mine until you know what I am. It wouldn't be fair."

Now confusion set in. There was a hesitation in his voice she hadn't heard before, almost as if he was uncertain of how to broach the subject. "What you are? What do you mean?"

"I'm not a full-blooded vampire."

The news didn't mean anything to her. How could he not be a full-blooded vampire? By everything she'd seen so far, he was definitely a vampire, and a very potent one at that. She'd seen his fangs, felt his strength. She'd seen him drink blood. "How can you not be a vampire?"

"I am, but I'm not, at least not fully. I wasn't human when I was turned. I just never realized that until now. My turning was much like yours, and now I understand why. Like you I almost died a second time, as if my body was rejecting becoming a vampire. But I pulled through, just like you did."

She remembered all too well how painful it had been. "I live because of you."

He pressed his forehead against hers. "But I don't ever want you to think you owe me for that. I did it for a very selfish reason: I wanted you to live, because I wanted you to be mine. Right there, that moment when I first saw you lying on that bed in Samson's house, I knew I would love you."

"How could you know that? You didn't know anything about me." Yet, there was such certainty in his words.

"My body recognized you. We're alike, Maya, much more than I could have ever guessed. I'm part satyr, and so are you."

The news hit her like a freight train slamming into a brick wall. Satyr? "A beast with hooves?"

Gabriel shook his head. "You mean a Minotaur. Satyrs are different. They are mythical creatures, part man, part animal, but the animal part only manifests itself in their strength and thirst for carnal pleasures and in the male of the species in one other piece of anatomy. Otherwise our bodies look entirely human. All that about hooves and horns came later in mythology. Anyway, that's why I never knew. I didn't know my father, so there was nobody to explain to me what I was."

"And you say I'm a satyr too. But how?" It didn't make any sense. She'd always felt human.

"You're aware that you were adopted?"

She was surprised he knew. "Of course. My parents never made a secret of it. Besides, they're blond and fair skinned, and I'm anything but."

"Your biological parents, or at least your father, must have been a satyr."

"How can the witch be so certain? She hasn't done any tests on me." The witch's claim was too outlandish to believe.

"She doesn't have to because of what's happened to me. I've gone through a change." He swallowed hard. Maya could see his Adam's Apple undulate.

"What kind of change?"

"After we had sex."

"Damn it, Gabriel, would you just come out with it." She planted her hands at her waist, but instead of releasing her, he only pulled her closer.

"This change." He pressed his hips into hers. "The mass of flesh you saw. It's changed. It only does that after a satyr has sex with his satyr mate for the first time. Maya, it's turned into a second penis because you and I had sex."

She gasped, sucking the air into her lungs quickly to supply her brain with oxygen. He had two penises? She pulled away from him and instantly noticed his disappointed frown. But she couldn't concern herself with that right now. Her hand went to the place where his jeans bulged. When her palm connected with the hardness beneath, he jerked for a moment before he pressed against it.

Then she felt it. There wasn't just the outline of one erect cock pulsing under her palm, but she could clearly feel a second one, just as hard but a fraction smaller. It strained against the confinement of his pants.

"I want to see." She licked her lips and went for the zipper.

His hand stopped her, locking her in place. "Maya." His voice was strained, and when she looked at him, she saw the barely contained desire in his eyes. He looked like he wanted to devour her, and considering what she felt under her hand, she had a pretty good idea what he wanted to devour her with.

Her heartbeat kicked up as her body responded in kind. There was nothing that she wanted more than to get her hands on his twin cocks and touch them, take them into her mouth one by one and suck them until he begged her to stop.

"This is not a science lesson."

Was that what he thought she wanted to do, merely examine him? "If you don't get those pants off right now and make love to me, I swear, the moment the sun sets, I'll walk out of here and you'll never see me again."

His droll look was priceless. "You want me to make love to you, and you actually think I would turn you down? Maya, I'm a vampire, I'm a satyr, but above all—I'm a man."

33

Gabriel's brain did a somersault. Maya accepted him for what he was. A small confident smile curled around her red lips, and the glint in her eyes was the same as he'd seen in her before, back in the living room where they'd made love like crazy. "You want me?"

"Yes, and given that we can't get out of here—until sunset anyway—I can't think of anything better than having sex, can you?" she asked and gave him a coquettish wink.

Neither could he. Gabriel folded her into his embrace, his mouth hovering over hers. She lifted her head and offered her lips to him. "Kiss me."

He gave a little smile. "I love kissing you." Then he fitted his lips to hers and pressed a soft kiss to her mouth. A low sigh was Maya's response. Her breath bounced against his, and he parted his lips to drink her in. His senses flooded with her scent and taste.

Gabriel let his hands roam over her back. One drifted down to her ass, cupping her with his large palm and pressing her closer into his hips. He felt his twin erections press into the soft flesh of her stomach, while her full breasts flattened against the hard planes of his chest. Everything felt so right. She was the perfect woman, the yin to his yang.

He speared his tongue and dove into her, dueled with her, stroked, nibbled, and sucked. Her soft moans were music to his ears, her hands on him encouragement to continue with what he was doing. Already Maya had pulled his shirt from his pants and was now sliding her hands onto his naked chest, making him hiss in a much needed breath.

"Now show me what you've got," she whispered against his lips, breathing as heavily as he did.

"Impatient?" He kissed the side of her mouth.

"Curious."

"Scared?" His lips trailed to her neck where he felt her vein throb under his lips.

"Eager," she pressed out between soft moans.

"I hoped that this time I could have offered you a soft bed." The first time he'd taken her against the wall in the living room, and now? He would have liked to make this more special for her.

"I don't care."

"It won't be very comfortable for you."

She pulled his head to hers and looked at him. "I don't want comfortable. I want you."

He lost himself in her dark eyes. "And I want you. But this time, you will come with me if it's the last thing I do."

"Male pride?"

It had nothing to do with pride. "Survival instinct."

She raised an eyebrow, not understanding, so he explained, "I won't have you leave me because I can't satisfy you."

Her lips curled up, and she pressed her hips provocatively against his groin. "You might just have what I need."

"Hold that thought." He pulled himself out of her embrace and walked to the supply cupboard.

"What are you doing?"

Gabriel opened the cupboard and examined the contents. "Making us more comfortable. I can't get you a proper bed, but at least I can provide some of this." He pulled out a couple of thick blankets, which had been shrink-wrapped to protect them from dust and moisture. He ripped the plastic open and pulled them out of their protective covers.

With a few steps he was at the corner where several cots were stacked up. He pulled one aside and spread the blankets onto it to provide more cushioning.

"You're a very practical man," Maya commented.

Gabriel turned to her and smiled. "You'll find out over time that I have many other useful qualities."

She hummed. "Mmm, hmm. Two in particular." Her eyes dropped to his crotch. Heat instantly shot through his body. She was direct, and he appreciated that in her. There was no beating around the bush about what she wanted. And what Maya clearly wanted right now, was him— or rather his two very erect and eager cocks. And he wasn't going to deprive her of that pleasure, or him for that matter. Even if he was a little apprehensive about his own desires right now—his own very dark and very forbidden desires. Because surely a woman like her would never agree to—

"Have you changed your mind?" she asked and stepped closer, her enticing scent instantly drugging him.

"Not a chance." Gabriel reached for her hand and pulled her toward him. "May I undress you?" For some reason, he felt nervous. This was a big step. If she didn't like what he was about to do, she could still leave him. And he wouldn't let that happen. No, he'd keep his own dark desire hidden so he wouldn't frighten her away. Even though he knew exactly what he wanted. The thought of taking Maya from behind with both cocks thrusting into her, one in her sweet pussy, the other in the dark and forbidden passage he suddenly craved, made his erections throb uncontrollably.

"If I can undress you at the same time," she answered then, interrupting his debauched thoughts.

His hands went to her T-shirt, and slowly he pulled it out of her jeans. When he tugged on it, she lifted her hands over her head and allowed him to free her from it. She wore no bra.

Maya felt a whoosh of cold air against her naked breasts and sensed her nipples tighten. Yet she knew it wasn't the cold air that excited her, it was the way Gabriel looked at her: with barely leashed desire. He was hungry for her, just as hungry as she was for him. The things he'd told her about him and about herself suddenly all made sense.

Her unexplainable fevers, her insatiable need for sex, and her inability to feel satisfied with the men she'd been with. Would that all be different now? Would Gabriel satisfy her?

Maya reached for the buttons of his shirt and eased them open one-by-one, exposing his muscular chest. As soon as she stripped him of it, she went for his jeans. Beneath the denim, the bulge had grown to massive proportions.

Two cocks. She knew instinctively what that meant. What was supposed to happen. He would take her with both of them. The desires she'd never been able to put into words and express finally lay within her grasp. She knew what her body had always craved, yet at the same time her brain had tried to push away. To feel two cocks in her at the same time. Here was Gabriel, part vampire, part satyr, who could give her what she'd never dared to dream about: the sexual satisfaction she'd always craved, the dark desires she'd never allowed herself to voice.

When she eased the top button of his jeans open and slid the zipper down, Gabriel exhaled sharply. With both hands she pushed his pants over his hips, then down his legs where he quickly chucked his boots and stepped out of his jeans.

Maya's gaze went back to his boxers, which tented in the front. She slid her hands between skin and waistband and pushed the fabric down, finally exposing what she'd wanted for so long. She barely noticed as he freed himself of the boxer shorts and his socks, so fascinated was she by the sight in front of her.

Even when he helped her get out of her own pants and shoes, she could not take her eyes off the sight.

"Gabriel, you're beautiful," she whispered, her hands reaching for his cocks. Each of her hands grasped one erect shaft, feeling the smooth skin and the hardness beneath. Their purple heads pumped full with blood, primed to explode, pointed at her, fairly asking for attention.

"Fuck!" he gasped breathlessly. "Baby, you're robbing me of my control."

She let a wicked smile curve around her lips as she looked up in his face. "Isn't that the point?"

"No, the point is for me to satisfy you first."

Before she could react, he picked her up in his arms and carried her to the makeshift bed. He gently lowered her onto it. She stretched her naked body out, appreciating the softness the two blankets underneath her provided.

With one leg braced on the floor, Gabriel lowered his body, one knee wedged between her legs. He began kissing her neck. His lips trailed along the sensitive skin just below her earlobe, then farther down, hovering over her pulse where her neck met her shoulder. He suckled at the spot.

Then his lips traveled south, reaching her breasts and the hard nipples that topped them. He palmed one globe and sucked the tip into his mouth, his moan telling her how much he enjoyed the action. Her body heated under his caress, her core turning to liquid and pooling at the apex of her thighs.

Maya shifted, opening her legs wider to allow his hard shafts to rub against her as she wiggled.

"Getting impatient?" he whispered as he licked leisurely over her breast.

"I want you inside me."

"I'm not done here," he claimed and continued torturing her breasts in the most delicious way she'd ever been tortured by a man. His hands kneaded one peak while his mouth suckled on the other almost greedily as if he couldn't get enough of her.

"You can have more of that later," she coaxed him, "but right now, just give me what I want."

He glanced up at her, and his eyes blinked in agreement. "Only because you're asking so nicely," he joked.

Gabriel shifted his body, and suddenly his lower cock nudged at the entrance to her moist channel, while his upper cock was poised at her curly triangle. With his finger he touched her folds. "So wet, baby." Then he dipped into her wetness and spread the moisture over her clit, eliciting a strangled moan from her throat.

But before she could press against his finger, he'd withdrawn his hand. Instead, he guided his upper cock to her clit and rubbed over the now moist button. "Now I'm ready." His voice was a rough rumble coming deep from within his chest.

The moment he thrust forward, his cock drove deep into her, while the second one slid over her clit, stroking her with perfect pressure. He filled her, stretching her so she could accommodate his size. He felt larger than he'd felt that time in the living room, but maybe it was just the position she found herself in: imprisoned underneath his large body, his thighs rubbing against her, his cocks thrusting in concert with each other.

She'd never felt anything this perfect. With wonder, she felt her body join his in perfect synchrony. Her breathless moans mingled with his, their bodies writhing against each other, dancing on a cloud of weightlessness. She felt like falling, yet knew she was safe in his arms, safe underneath his strong body as his thrusts intensified and his rhythm became faster.

With every stroke and every slide, her core heated, her heartbeat raced in a frantic beat toward the inevitable. Gabriel never once broke eye contact, but kept his gaze locked with hers as if to assure her that he could read what she wanted, what she needed from him. His skin glistened with sweat, and his hand came up to stroke her face. "Maya, baby." It looked as if he wanted so say more, but didn't.

Maya felt her clit swell farther with every slide of his cock over it. She sensed the start of her climax in the soles of her feet. And as the ripples traveled upwards, her breath came in shallow pants. She caught Gabriel's smile a moment before the waves of her orgasm hit her. Of its own volition, a scream left her throat. She'd never before screamed during sex. And she'd never come with a man's cock inside her. "Oh, God."

On the last wave of her climax, she felt him stiffen, and a moment later his cock pulsed violently inside her, shooting his seed into her. At the same time, she felt a wetness on her stomach and registered that his second cock had exploded at the same time.

"Oh, God, baby!" he ground out, his eyes mirroring the disbelief in his voice. Even as he collapsed on top of her, he braced himself so she wouldn't carry his entire weight.

He leaned his forehead to hers and breathed heavily. "I had no idea. Maya, I've never come like that. Never so intensely."

She smiled and pressed a soft kiss on his lips. "Neither have I."

Gabriel kissed her deeply, his tongue sweeping against hers in long and commanding strokes. When he released her lips, his mouth trailed down to her neck again, suckling at the same spot where he'd suckled before. But this time, his teeth gently grazed against her skin. Out of nowhere a vision entered her mind: of him sinking his fangs into her and drinking her blood.

She gasped and felt him pull back. "Did I hurt you?"

Maya looked into his passion-clouded eyes and swallowed hard. And before she could stop herself, she expressed her deepest wish. "Bite me."

Gabriel groaned. She wanted him to bite her? She was dangling his greatest temptation in front of him when he had no right to take this much from her. Not with what was going on inside him right now, not with the urge that had started boiling up in him, the urge to do unspeakable things to her. Things no decent woman would allow a man to do, things even most whores would refuse.

"Oh Maya, you have no idea what you're offering me." Conflicting emotions warred in his mind: desire on one hand, caution on the other. He couldn't bind her to him when she might be running from him, recoiling from him when she found out what he wanted from her. To fuck her in the most bestial way. She couldn't possibly want that.

"What's wrong?"

"If I bite you while we have sex and you take my blood at the same time, we would create a blood-bond—Maya, a blood-bond is forever. There's no way out."

Her response came faster than he'd expected. "You don't want forever?"

He recognized the disappointment in her eyes, the hurt. He couldn't let her believe that, not even for a second. "I want forever, but there's something you have to know about me first." He paused and closed his eyes before he spoke again. Laying himself bare was the hardest thing he'd ever done, but she deserved it, deserved honesty about the darkness inside him.

"I want to take you in the most bestial way you can imagine, and I don't think I could suppress that kind of lust for long. Now that I know what I am, now that I realize what my body wants, I can't hold it back much longer." He opened his eyes. "Maya, I want to claim you with both my cocks at the same time, take your pussy with one and your—" He broke off and looked away, not wanting to see the disgust that would soon flood her eyes. "And your ass with the other. Don't you see? It's depraved. I shouldn't want something like that, but I do. If you bond with me, you won't escape that, you'd have to endure it."

His heart beat frantically in his chest. What if she walked away from him now?

"Endure?" With her hand to his chin, she forced him to look at her. "Gabriel, I want everything you have to offer. We're both satyrs. What makes you think that I don't have the exact same wish? What makes you think that I don't crave being taken like that?"

His eyes widened in surprise. "You want this?" He searched her eyes and couldn't see anything that looked even remotely like disgust.

"Why else would a satyr have two cocks but to use them to satisfy his mate?"

First, she'd called him perfect, and now Maya offered to fulfill his darkest desire. In that moment, Gabriel knew he was the luckiest man alive. She was the personification of everything he'd ever wished for: a home, a loving wife, a fulfilled sex life. And while life would be even more perfect if they could have children, it wasn't important enough for him to give her up. His mind was made up—in fact it always had been.

"I pledge my heart and my life to you." His voice almost cracked as he continued, "I want a blood-bond with you, but not here. I want you to have a memory you'll always look back on as special." He looked around the room to indicate that this wasn't it. "When we bond, it will be in a room full of red candles. We'll lie on crisp white sheets as we make love, and everything will be perfect. I promise you."

She smiled at him. "Could it be that you're a hopeless romantic?"

"Not hopeless—hope*ful*." He brushed his lips to hers. "Just promise me you won't tell anybody. Otherwise it might undermine my position."

She rolled her eyes. "Men!" And then she laughed. The sound went right through him and warmed his heart. Maya looked happy, and he promised himself that he'd do everything in his power to make sure she was always this happy.

She seemed to realize that he was staring at her, and her laugh subsided. Her eyes locked with his, and he felt as if she looked into his soul. "I love you."

He choked back the tears that threatened to unman him at her unexpected declaration. "My heart is yours."

The kiss that followed turned from sweet and gentle to heated and demanding in the blink of an eye. He was still inside her and growing hard again, having remained semi-hard the entire time they had talked.

He eased himself out of her hot sheath and broke the kiss.

"Something wrong?" she asked, her voice soft, almost sleepy. He recognized it as that of a very satisfied woman. And it satisfied him to know that he'd been able to make her come.

"Nothing's wrong, baby. I want to make love to you the satyr way, but I don't want to hurt you."

He lifted himself off the cot and marched to the supply cabinet. Earlier, he'd seen medical supplies in there, and if he wasn't mistaken there was a jar of Vaseline among them. It would have to do. When he turned back to her, the lubricant in his hands, Maya had turned onto her stomach. Gabriel sucked in a breath. She would be his undoing, for how would he ever make it out of bed in the next few hundred years with her by his side as his mate?

He let his gaze travel over the curve of her back, then over the soft swells of her round ass, before he followed her shapely legs. She had parted them slightly, allowing him to see the dark curls at their apex, curls that glistened with moisture. Her pink nether lips oozed with the seed he'd planted in her, and he felt the urge to slide his cock back into her enticing channel so it would remain inside her. It was a silly thought because he knew his seed wouldn't take hold in her. Even though— hadn't the witch said something about satyr females being fertile? But there had been so much to take in that he wasn't sure he'd heard right.

Without haste, he approached the cot and sat down at its edge. He wasn't done admiring her beauty and counting his blessings. Despite the scar on his face, despite his two cocks and the dark desires they represented, he'd been graced with the most amazing gift of his life: a woman who wanted him despite everything.

"You're beautiful," he whispered and stroked his palm down the length of her naked back. "I wish I were a painter. I would paint you just like this."

She turned her head to him and smiled. "I'd much rather you made love to me than paint me." Then her eyes zeroed in on the jar in his hands. "Touch me."

Gabriel inhaled deeply and dipped his finger into the lubricant. "I promise I'll be as gentle as possible."

Maya closed her eyes and sighed. When he slid his hand along her crack, her ass arched toward him, opening herself up to him. Helped by the lubrication, his finger ran smoothly down the incline until he reached the tight ring of muscle that guarded the entrance to her dark portal. He heard her suck in a breath when his finger lingered there. Slowly he circled the bud, spreading the lubricant.

The thought of breaching the gate to this dark cave made his body pump more blood into his cocks. He looked down at himself, where his twin shafts stood erect, eager to impale her. Ahead were previously unknown pleasures, and he felt nervousness creep into his skin. He didn't want to hurt her. "I've never done this before."

"Neither have I," she confessed.

With barely noticeable pressure, he probed her dark hole and felt her ease toward him. The tip of his finger slipped past the tight muscle, gripping his digit tightly.

A low moan came from Maya, and he could only echo it. Never in his life had he felt anything this tight. Maya's pussy had gripped him like a snug glove, but the knowledge that she would soon squeeze him even tighter left him breathless. He wouldn't last. His cock wouldn't survive this delight for longer than ten seconds. And maybe it was good that way—he wouldn't subject her to this ordeal for too long. He still didn't believe that she really wanted this as much as he did. More likely she allowed him this dark treat because she wanted him and wouldn't deny him.

He drove his finger deeper into her, giving her time to adjust to the invasion.

"More," she whispered, her voice clouded with passion, hoarse. Her encouragement eradicated his worry that she was hurting, and he slid deeper until his finger was lodged inside her as far as it would go. Then slowly he eased back out, took another dollop of lubrication and pressed back in.

Now Maya was panting heavily, her hips flexing, forcing him inside her faster than before. "Yes!"

Her enthusiasm wasn't lost on him. Did she actually like this? His heart swelled as she fell into a rhythm, alternately pushing her ass back, then pulling forward, so his finger would thrust back and forth inside her. When he recognized that she wanted more, he took charge and finger-fucked her pretty ass the way she demanded it: with long, deep strokes that increased in speed as her breathing became short and shallow.

When she demanded more, he eased a second finger into her, stretching her wider. He couldn't tear himself away from the erotic sight. As his fingers disappeared inside her dark portal, his own heart reached a fever pitch, his cocks oozed pre-cum in anticipation, and his entire body tingled pleasantly.

But he couldn't wait any longer. He shifted and knelt behind her, between her spread thighs. "Get on your hands and knees," he coaxed her and slipped his fingers out of her before he pulled her ass into his groin.

Gabriel once again helped himself to the lubricant and spread it over his upper cock, before he placed it at her entrance. His lower cock was already poised at her pussy, ready to enter her. Her honey teased the head of his hard shaft, promising him pleasure beyond his wildest imagination.

With one hand he held onto her hip, he used the other to guide his second cock as he pressed forward. Almost without effort his tip disappeared inside her, pushing past the tight ring.

"Oh God," she panted.

"Too much?" He was ready to pull out if he caused her pain.

She merely shook her head and eased back toward him, taking him deeper. His lower cock slipped inside her pussy without resistance while his upper one pressed forward. Inside her, he could feel both his cocks rub against the thin membrane between her two channels.

"Oh, fuck!" He couldn't stop himself from cursing at the intense pleasure that spread in his body. Before he knew what he was doing, he thrust forward, seating himself in her to the hilts. The way her body gripped him, squeezed him, he almost lost control right there. "Ohfuckohfuckohfuck . . . " Nothing had ever felt this perfect in his long life. No other pleasure had ever been this intense. If he died right now, he'd die a happy man.

When Maya wiggled beneath him, obviously to entice him to move, he held onto her hips. "Baby, give me a second, or I'll lose it."

She chuckled.

"Go ahead, make fun of me," he teased. "Just wait until you're at the receiving end."

"I *am* at the receiving end," she pointed out.

The distraction her little joke provided helped him gain his composure. "Let's see to it then." Gabriel pulled back, dislodging his cocks but for their heads, before he plunged back in. As he found his rhythm and rode her hard, he marveled at the perfect fit of their bodies. She was truly made for him, her pussy accommodating him in the most perfect way, and her tight ass squeezing him in a way that kept him right at the edge.

The sounds of pleasure coming over her lips warmed his heart and filled him with pride. He was doing this. *He* was giving her pleasure. It was all he could think of. Never had he ridden any woman this hard, this fast, this ferociously. But he was no longer afraid of hurting her. Maya was both a satyr and a vampire, with a body nearly as strong as his, a body built to accommodate him and please him to no end.

For the first time, he silently thanked the circumstances that had brought them together. Even though what had happened to her was horrible, Gabriel knew it was fate. And he would do anything in his power to make her happy so she would never have to regret her new life. He would give her everything she could ever want.

"I love you," he whispered and plunged deeper. "My wife, my mate, my love."

In his eyes she was already his. The bonding ritual would be only a formality—though a very pleasant and arousing formality.

"Gabriel," she called out before her body suddenly spasmed, her muscles tightening around him. He sensed her orgasm as if he was already bonded to her, felt the waves travel through every cell of her body until they hit him and took him with her. His cocks jerked in unison, pumping hot spurts of seed into her as he came like an exploding volcano, his climax taking over his entire body, sending shockwaves through him that no atomic bomb could produce. His vision blurred, and his mind went blank as he felt his body turn weightless like floating in space.

When he collapsed onto her, he barely had enough strength left in him to roll himself to the side and take her with him so she wouldn't suffer under his weight. For several moments he couldn't speak, could only catch his breath.

He slipped his hand onto her breast and felt her heart beat as frantically as his. Maya's hand came up, and her fingers intertwined with his. She turned her head, and he looked into the eyes of a truly sated woman. It was a look he wanted her to wear every day of their lives together.

A soft brush of his lips against hers was all he could manage. He had no words to describe what he felt, but when he locked eyes with her, he knew she understood. They were one.

34

Maya woke to find Gabriel looking at her, his head propped up on his hand. "Why didn't you wake me?"

"You needed to rest."

"What I need is a kiss," she teased and pulled his head toward her. He gave into her willingly, and she captured his lips with hers. She slid her tongue over the seam of his lips, and he parted them with a sigh. His tongue met hers, and they danced.

"Hmm, if you kiss me like that every day, I'll be a very happy man indeed."

She smiled and ran her fingers along his scar. "And if you make love to me every day like you did, I'll be a very happy woman."

"So you're okay with making love the satyr way?"

"Are you fishing for compliments?"

He chuckled, and she'd never seen him so carefree. "What if I am?"

"I guess then I'll have to tell you the truth." Maya felt him stiffen as if he was expecting bad news. "I understand now why there was always something missing in my sex life. I was never truly satisfied. Something was always lacking. As a satyr, I need what you're giving me. No other man but you could ever make me feel whole."

She loved the smile that spread over his face as he took in her words.

His lips were firm and warm when he pressed them against her mouth. But before she could lean into him, he pulled back. "And speaking of what I can give you, you need to feed."

Maya sat up. She was hungry, but she couldn't feed from him, not now. "No, Gabriel. We have no human blood here, and if I feed from you, it'll weaken you."

"It's all right," he insisted and pulled her toward him.

"No. It's not. When we walk out of here, you need to be strong. We don't know what to expect. If I weaken you now, I might put both of us in danger."

He nodded and sat up next to her. She could tell he didn't like it, but she also recognized that he understood her reasoning.

She touched his cheek. "I love feeding from you. You have no idea how much. It's as if I become one with you."

The warmth in his eyes told her he felt the same way. "Soon, then, because I miss it."

At his words her heart made a somersault.

Gabriel's eyes drifted away from her and toward the clock above the desk. She followed his gaze. "It'll be sunset soon. We have to prepare."

The fog blanketed the wooded area as they left the safety of their shelter behind. Maya shivered when the crisp night air touched her warm skin. She hadn't even noticed how much her body had warmed in Gabriel's arms, but the contrast was palpable now.

They didn't speak in order not to attract any attention should Ricky be near. With her hand resting in Gabriel's large palm, they walked away from the bomb shelter in measured steps, careful not to step on any twigs that might snap and give their location away.

Had she not been so tense and worried about the situation, Maya would have marveled at her night vision. She could see everything as clear as by day—except that not even her night vision could penetrate the dense San Francisco fog. She hoped this meant that no other vampire could detect them through the thick mist either. For once she was glad for the fog that descended onto San Francisco every summer. At least it provided cover if the night didn't.

She breathed evenly, telling herself that the place where she had smashed Gabriel's phone was far enough away for Ricky to have lost their trail some fourteen hours earlier. And besides, he would have had to find shelter during the day himself and had hopefully had to leave the area in a hurry.

Maya listened to the sounds of the night, but all she could hear was her own heartbeat and Gabriel's breathing. She glanced at him from the side and noticed the hard lines around his mouth, his eyes scanning the area around them constantly. She remembered that he'd told her once that he'd started out as a bodyguard, and she was glad for this knowledge now. It gave her confidence. Not that she thought Gabriel wouldn't do everything to keep her safe, but knowing he had the right skills to do so put her mind at relative ease.

A squeeze from his hand and a nod of his head indicated that he wanted to change direction. She followed without hesitation; in fact, she would follow him anywhere, even to New York, a city she couldn't imagine living in. But if he needed to return there, she would go with him.

Maya tried to keep her eyes focused on the path ahead, but her mind wandered. Too many things had happened to her in the last few hours. Gabriel's revelation that they were both satyr had stunned her, but she didn't question it. In the last week she'd learned that no matter how outrageous a claim, if it came from Gabriel she could trust in it being true. And it all made sense now. The emptiness she'd always felt during sex had been taken away by complete and utter satisfaction when Gabriel had taken her the satyr way. She'd never felt more complete in her life. If she'd ever had any doubts as to whether she was a satyr, that single act had wiped them from her mind.

The woods seemed to grow denser as their march progressed. She knew they were going east toward the botanical gardens and the tennis courts, but her sense of distance was lacking. She realized Gabriel was avoiding the well-used footpaths and had instead opted to continue through the forested areas where the trees would provide some cover.

In the distance, Maya saw a white structure, and as they neared it, she recognized it as the Victorian era Conservatory of Flowers that housed a vast number of exotic plants. A small gift shop and cashiers hut stood several yards separated from the main structure. Everything was quiet.

Gabriel pointed toward the cashiers hut, indicating it was their destination. She nodded. They crossed the open space, and she felt herself tensing. Despite the thick fog, they would be on display, and their dark shadows would be visible. Maya couldn't help but look over her shoulder, and she noticed Gabriel do the same. Her hands felt clammy, and her heart beat faster than before.

At the hut, Gabriel pressed his face to the glass and peered inside. "There's a phone," he said *sotto voce*. "Can you open the door from the inside?"

She understood. They could have smashed the glass, but the noise would attract Ricky if he was in the vicinity, or any human who was out walking their dog. Maya concentrated, closing her eyes and imagining the deadbolt turning. She heard a click. She was getting good at this.

A moment later, Gabriel tried the door, and it swung open. He eased inside the small structure and pulled her with him, closing the door silently behind them.

When he lifted the receiver and dialed, each key seemed to echo loudly in the small space. She hoped it was only her own senses that amplified the sound. She heard one ring, then a faint voice on the other end.

"Yes?"

"Amaury, it's Gabriel." Gabriel's voice was barely audible.

"Thank God."

"We're at the Conservatory of Flowers in Golden Gate Park. Maya is with me. Come and get us. Be careful; Ricky tracked us to the park."

"Five minutes."

The call disconnected and Gabriel turned to her, pulling her into his arms before lowering his lips to her ear. "Can you get us into the Conservatory? We'll have more places to hide in there."

She nodded.

The Conservatory was a large structure made entirely of glass and steel. The steel had been painted white and was curved to create a dome the length of a football field. A cupola graced the center of the building, reminding her of the cupola of City Hall that was of a similar form.

Gaining entry to it was as easy as unlocking the door to the hut had been. Maya was grateful for the skill she'd been bestowed, and while mind control would have been a neat skill to have, this one proved to be more practical and useful at present.

She inhaled the scent of the plants in the tropically warm hothouse. The smells overpowered her senses, the pollen so strong and fragrant she could barely scent Gabriel next to her. It was as if the flowers blocked out everything else.

The windowpanes had let in the sun during the day and the large halls had heated up. Even now at night, the structure retained most of its warmth. Maya looked around, noticing the walking paths that had been constructed between the large plant beds. Little boards were erected next to each plant species, explaining their name and origin.

Gabriel's arms snaked around her from behind, and for a second it startled her. But he pulled her against his chest and simply kissed her neck. "I can hardly wait to make you my wife," he murmured against her skin. He nibbled on her earlobe and Maya let herself melt into him.

She moaned at the pleasure he gave her with a simple touch. "Don't make me wait too long. I've never liked the idea of a long engagement."

"Two, three days tops," he agreed. "Once this is all over and Ricky is dealt with."

"You shouldn't make her promises you can't keep."

The voice sliced through her like a knife. Gabriel released her and pushed her halfway behind his large frame. She'd never seen him move this fast. Ricky emerged from the shadow of a large fern. She hadn't heard any sound of him entering the glasshouse. Nor smelled him. Even now that she focused on him, all she could smell were the exotic flowers around her.

Gabriel's stance instantly changed, and she could see how he readied himself for a fight. His hand suddenly held a stake. She hadn't even seen when he'd pulled it from his coat where he must have hidden it.

"I always keep my promises," Gabriel replied, his voice tight. "The one I made last night was to kill you."

Before she could stop Gabriel, he pounced. His large frame crashed into the slightly shorter vampire, knocking Ricky off balance. But before Gabriel could land his stake, Ricky had rolled to the side and jumped up. She hadn't figured him to be this agile.

Gabriel swiveled in the blink of an eye and growled low and dark. In his fury, his fangs had erupted through his gums, and Maya could clearly see them almost as if glowing in the dark. His scar seemed to throb.

With one step, Gabriel was again lunging for his opponent, his powerful arms landing a blow against his side. But it wasn't enough. Ricky's leg kicked out a second later, powering into Gabriel's left thigh, unbalancing him. For an instant, Gabriel tumbled sideways, but the branch of a bush next to him provided him with enough support to right himself again.

But the strike had cost him. Ricky's next kick landed in Gabriel's stomach, knocking him into the dirt behind him. Gabriel rolled and jumped up the second he hit the earthen flowerbed. For a large man, he was surprisingly agile.

"Shit!" Gabriel cursed, and a second later she realized that he'd lost his stake. Maya gasped when she saw Ricky lunge for him.

Ricky's head snapped in her direction, and within a split-second he changed tracks and jumped onto a railing surrounding the flowerbed.

That's when she saw the rope. It hung from one of the beams above the plant bed. Ricky had seen it too and now grabbed it. As he held onto the rope, Ricky kicked against the stem of a small palm behind him and catapulted himself in her direction. Maya tried to sidestep him, but she wasn't fast enough. Ricky's arm swung out as he closed in on her. He knocked her off her feet in one clean swoop.

She fell face-forward into the soil. Knowing he was right behind her, she rolled to the side, avoiding him by a hairsbreadth. From the corner of her eye, she saw Gabriel run toward them. Maya pulled herself up, trying to steady her feet, but slipped in the muddy soil.

A hand grabbed for her, and the shiver running over her skin alerted her that it was Ricky. He twisted her arm back and pulled her toward him.

An instant later, she saw Gabriel stop short, his face horrified. She didn't understand why he wasn't approaching. Only when she took a deep breath and expanded her lungs did she realize why: Ricky was pressing a wooden stake against her chest.

"One step farther, and she's dust."

Maya swallowed. Gabriel's eyes flooded with agony. She could see his mind clicking, going through every possible scenario of how to get her out of this situation, but she realized that Ricky held all the cards, and Gabriel would never risk her life.

"You're so predictable, Gabriel. I guess that comes from thinking with your dick," Ricky spat.

"Let her go."

"She should have been mine. I saw her first. If you hadn't interfered, she would have been mine."

Maya felt bile rise in her stomach. "Never."

Ricky pulled her tighter, twisting her arm higher. She ignored the pain and concentrated on her disgust for him instead. "Don't kid yourself, my sweet. You'll still be mine. Once we're gone from here and it's just you and me, you'll have no choice."

"I'll hunt you down," Gabriel warned.

Ricky laughed as he walked backwards, taking her with him. Like a shield, she was plastered against him, and there was no way Gabriel would be able to attack him without risking hurting her. She knew instinctively that it would be up to her to free herself. But Ricky was strong. She knew exactly how strong from their encounter at Samson's house. At least there she had been able to use her skill to defeat him. She could do so again.

Maya's eyes darted around the dark hall, trying to find something she could use to free herself. She came up empty. Except for some water buckets, nothing was in her vicinity that would make an adequate weapon.

They reached the back of the hall, and she felt Ricky open the door behind him to advance into the next part of the structure. She gave Gabriel a last look, locking eyes with him, telling him she loved him, before the door shut and she was alone with Ricky.

He didn't remove the stake from her heart. Clearly, he'd learned from their earlier encounter. "What are you trying to gain by this? You know he'll kill you when he catches up with you."

"Yes, but by that time, I will have had you, and you'll be damaged goods. I'll have used your body so often and so violently that even *he* won't want you back."

Maya's blood froze at the venom in his voice. She tried to shake off the feeling of despair that hit her. No, even if Ricky managed to do to her what he threatened, Gabriel would still love her.

Her ears perked up. In the distance, glass shattered. Was it Gabriel?

Ricky had heard it too. "Time to go."

He pushed her ahead of him, the wooden stake now resting its point on her back. It could be driven into her heart as easily from the back as from the front.

Maya took in her surroundings and noticed a shovel lying on the ground near one of the plant beds. Somebody had forgotten to put away their tools after their work was done. She honed in on the item as they passed the spot. She concentrated and visualized the shovel rising from the ground, hovering in the air.

A clang against a metal surface broke her concentration. She felt Ricky swivel, then pull hard on her arms. "Bitch!"

She twisted her head and saw that the shovel had hit a railing she hadn't seen.

"You try that again, I'll stake you right here."

She somehow doubted his claim. He'd wanted her for so long, that she didn't believe that he would kill her now when he hadn't even forced himself on her yet. She figured he'd at least try to rape her. The sick bastard would surely not forgo that perverted pleasure.

Ricky shoved her through the next door. A movement to her left caught her eye and stopped her in her tracks. Ricky bumped into her, and the wooden stake bounced against her back. Instantly she pulled forward, the contact with the wooden implement having sent her heart rate spiking.

She used the momentum to pull against Ricky's restraining arms. One of her wrists came free, and she twisted herself in a half circle.

Another silent shadow entered her peripheral vision, the figure too small to be Gabriel. Maybe it was just a hallucination.

Her feet suddenly lost traction, and she fell to her side. A shadow leaped over her in the same instant. Somebody had grabbed her feet and made her lose her balance. And it hadn't been Ricky.

As she found herself once again face down, she rolled quickly. Grunts behind her alerted her to a fight. She focused her eyes on the two figures. Yvette's lithe body stood out against Ricky's muscled one, but what she didn't have in body mass, she made up for in agility. She dodged every one of his blows and twisted like a snake, her movements nearly faster than even Maya's enhanced eyesight could follow.

"Gabriel!" she shouted, trying to alert him to her location.

Hasty footsteps came her way. First, she recognized Zane. She'd never been so relieved in her life to see the bald vampire run toward her. Behind him another figure emerged: Amaury, and finally Gabriel ran toward her from a path to her left.

As Zane and Amaury launched themselves into the fight with Ricky, Maya jumped up and threw herself into Gabriel's arms.

"Oh, God, baby, I'm so sorry I couldn't protect you." His arms tightened around her.

"You're here now."

Turning her head, she saw Amaury and Zane restraining Ricky. In front of him stood Yvette, her feet planted wide, her arms by her side. In one hand she held a stake.

"I should make you suffer as you tried to do to me." Yvette spat into his face, and Ricky tried to shake her spit off him, to no avail. Unimpeded, it ran down his chin.

Then Yvette turned her head toward Maya and Gabriel. "He tied me to the fireplace at that dead nurse's house and left me to wait for the sun."

Maya felt a shudder go through her at the thought of Ricky's cruelty.

"Do I have your permission?" Yvette lifted her hand that held the stake so Gabriel could see it.

"Make it quick," Gabriel answered and turned away, taking Maya with him so she couldn't see what was happening.

"You'll be safe now," he whispered and kissed her.

35

The cemetery lay in the dark. Only torches illuminated the area around the newly dug grave. The coffin that held no body was suspended over it, covered with white calla lilies.

Maya looked at the small assembly. The night before, Samson and Delilah had returned, and she had met them for the first time. She'd taken an instant liking to Delilah, the sweet wife of the most powerful vampire in San Francisco. She and Samson had extended their hospitality and asked her and Gabriel to stay until they had decided where to live. She couldn't have imagined a warmer welcome.

Oliver, Samson's daytime assistant, a human, stood next to them, his eyes on the ground. He'd lost a good friend in Carl.

Maya glanced at Amaury and the beautiful blond woman by his side. They made a striking couple, and it seemed in Nina's presence, Amaury was more relaxed and docile than when alone. Despite the fact that Nina was a tall woman, her blood-bonded mate dwarfed her, and she appeared fragile, even though Nina was anything but. The stories the other vampires had told her suggested that she was quite a handful to deal with—and that Amaury enjoyed every second of it.

Maya now also understood the connection between Nina and Eddie. She was surprised to find out that Eddie was her brother. The family resemblance was certainly evident, but she hadn't expected one sibling to be a vampire and the other to be human. But when Thomas told her the story of Eddie's turning, she understood.

Even Dr. Drake and the witch, Francine, were among the mourners. There had been a commotion at first when word had reached them that Francine wanted to attend Carl's funeral, but after Gabriel had explained how instrumental she'd been in Maya's own survival, the vampires had voted to allow a witch in their midst. It was a first, to be sure.

Zane and Yvette stood with a group of vampires Maya didn't recognize. Colleagues from Scanguards, she assumed. When she caught Yvette's eye, she was surprised to see her smile at her and Gabriel, who held Maya's hand. Maya smiled back and felt her heart swell. These people were her family now. They had all accepted her and fought for her so she could live. Carl had given his life protecting her.

The night before, she'd also called her own family and told her parents that she would visit them very soon. Gabriel had promised to help her explain to them what had happened to her, and she hoped that they would continue to love her.

Maya turned her attention back to Samson, whose speech came to an end.

"My friend, wherever you are now, I'll never forget the years we had together."

Two vampires lowered the coffin into the hole. Nobody moved until it had disappeared completely, then Samson took the shovel and tossed the earth after it. But he didn't stop at the customary shovel-full of earth. He continued.

Maya looked to her side, and Gabriel bent down to her. "He sired Carl. It is his duty to see he rests in peace. He dug the grave; he'll fill it," he whispered.

A single tear rolled down Maya's cheek as she understood the meaning of Samson's actions.

When the last grain of dirt had filled the grave, Samson put the shovel aside and spoke. "Good night, my friend."

Then he walked away from the group. Delilah stayed back, making no attempt to follow him. When she approached Maya, she simply said, "He needs to be alone now. He'll meet us at home."

"You seem to understand him without many words," Maya answered.

Delilah smiled and hooked her arm under Maya's. "Gabriel, you don't mind if I steal Maya for a few minutes, do you?" But she didn't wait for his reply and pulled her away.

"Do you mind if we walk through the cemetery for a bit?" Delilah asked.

"Not at all." Maya fell into step with her new friend.

For a moment, Delilah was silent. But then she came out with what she wanted to say. "I know it's not your specialty, but I was hoping you'd consider continuing with medicine in a different field."

Maya raised a surprised eyebrow. "What did you have in mind?"

"OB-GYN," Delilah confessed. "It's not like I can go to a human doctor anymore. Once they do tests on the fetus, they'll realize that it's not entirely human. And this won't be our only child. We plan on having many. And then there's Nina, of course."

"Is she pregnant, too?" Maya asked.

"Amaury wishes." She rolled her eyes and laughed. "They haven't quite fought this one out yet."

"Nina and Amaury fight?"

"All the time."

"I'm sorry to hear that. I thought they looked good together."

Delilah laughed again. "They wouldn't have it any other way. It's what Amaury needs, a woman who doesn't let him get away with anything. Besides, their make-up sex must be spectacular."

Now Maya had to chuckle. "So you think she'll finally give in and have children with him?"

"I don't know. Only those two know. Either way, whatever they decide, it'll work for them."

"I hear talk about children," a voice came from behind them.

They both turned to Francine, who had followed them. "I'm sorry to interrupt, but I hoped to catch you without Gabriel listening in."

"I'll leave you two then," Delilah offered.

Francine held up her hand. "No, please don't. It's only Gabriel I don't want to know yet; otherwise, he might get his hopes up, to be dashed later."

Curiosity rose in Maya. "What is this about?"

"I analyzed your blood, and it's confirmed. You are satyr, not that we didn't already know that. But it led me to something else. Satyr females are fertile. They go into heat, just like you did."

Maya held her breath. Was it possible?

"I'm not one hundred percent certain, but I believe that because you continued to go into heat even after you'd turned vampire, you might still be fertile."

"Do you think it's possible?" Maya asked the witch, trying to wrap her brain around it.

Delilah nudged her gently in the side. "Only one way to find out." A soft smile curled around her lips as she winked.

Francine's mouth widened into a grin. "I agree."

Maya grabbed the woman's hand and squeezed it. Her heart was too full to say anything, but Francine's eyes told her she understood. And Maya knew exactly what she wanted to do right now.

***

Gabriel looked around the crowd still assembled around the grave. Small groups had formed as everybody was talking about Carl and the things that had happened over the last few days. Maya was nowhere to be seen.

He stopped Zane as he walked past him. "Have you seen Maya?"

"She was talking to Thomas earlier."

Gabriel nodded and looked for Thomas. He saw him standing with Eddie. Gabriel strode to him. "Do you know where Maya went? I haven't seen her the last half hour."

Could Thomas hear the desperate tone in his voice? God, he was pathetic. Being separated from her for even a few minutes filled him with worry and longing. Only when she was near him, did he feel at peace.

Thomas gave him a knowing look. "If that isn't the look of a man in love."

"Well, do you know where she went?" he repeated his question.

"You can find her at my house."

Surprise flooded him. "What is she doing at your house?"

"I've offered it to her for the next three days. Eddie and I are supposed to go to Seattle for a training exercise, so the house will be empty. Samson's place is too crowded right now. I figured the two of you would want some privacy, but if you don't—"

"No, of course," Gabriel replied hastily. "We want privacy." He'd already wondered where they would find a place to be alone for the bonding ceremony. Unlike a human wedding, a blood-bond was performed in private, with only the two partners bonding present.

Thomas produced a key and handed it to him. "Here. Enjoy."

Gabriel smiled. He would tell Maya that he wanted to bond tonight. There was no reason to wait any longer.

***

Gabriel closed the door behind him. Thomas's house was quiet and for a moment he wondered if Maya was truly here, but then he inhaled and took in her scent. He followed the delectable scent to the private area of the house. When he pushed the door to the master bedroom open, the sight that greeting him was a dream come true.

The room glowed in the light of dozens of candles. The bed was covered with crisp white sheets, and on it lay Maya, dressed in a flowing blood-red negligee with a neckline plunging to her navel. Gabriel soaked in the image and could feel he was already hard beneath his black pants.

Maya had anticipated his thoughts. He knew instinctively what her display meant: she was ready to blood-bond with him.

"I was waiting for you."

He let the door behind him snap in, before he crossed the distance to the bed.

"I was worried when you disappeared from the funeral."

"I wanted to surprise you," she answered and gave him a longing look from underneath her lashes.

Slowly, he opened the first button of his shirt. "You did."

Maya sat up and moved toward him. "Let me help you with that."

Gabriel tried to swallow back his eagerness. He didn't want to rush this and end up fucking her as frantically as he had in Samson's living room. But when Maya's hand came up to ease the buttons of his shirt open and scraped his skin in the process, he let out a frustrated huff.

"Ah, fuck it!" He ripped his shirt off his body with one swipe of his claws and dropped it to the ground.

"Somebody's impatient," she cooed and licked her lips.

"Is that a problem?"

Her eyes followed his hands as he tugged at his pants, jerking them off his body just as quickly at his shirt, taking his boxers with it in the same move. The widening of her pupils told him that she was looking at his twin erections now. The scent of Maya's arousal drifted into his nostrils.

"No, no problem," she answered slowly, her breath catching in her throat. He liked the way she looked at him as he stood in front of her completely naked. He couldn't remember ever having shed his clothes this quickly.

Gabriel filled his lungs with her scent. "Yeah, I didn't think it would be." He deliberately dropped his gaze to the triangle of dark curls he could see through the gauzy fabric.

When he reached for her, she met him half way. "It's time," was all he said as he looked into her eyes.

"Yes," she replied before she offered her lips for a kiss. He took them, sinking his mouth onto hers, driving his tongue between her parted lips to taste her.

He lowered them onto the bed, covering her body with his. His hands pushed aside the fabric that barely covered her breasts, and he caressed her naked skin. He loved the way the red color contrasted against her dark skin and hair. With the white sheets underneath her, she looked like a beautiful tableau.

"I like what you're wearing," he whispered against her lips. His hand slipped down along her torso to her hip, where he gathered the fabric in his hand and pulled it up. "I won't undress you." In fact, he wanted to bond with her wearing it.

Maya opened her thighs and allowed him to settle at her core. The hot little smile she gave him signaled her approval. "I want you now, Gabriel."

He positioned his lower cock at her wet core and pushed forward. His upper cock slid over her clit in the same instant as he submerged himself in her heat.

A moan dislodged from her lips. "I love the way you do that."

Gabriel locked eyes with her. "That's good then, because I love doing it." To prove his point, he pulled back and repeated the move. And for good measure, he did it again. Then he fell into an easy rhythm. Her body moved in synch with his, or maybe it was the other way around. But did it really matter? All that mattered was that they were together.

He found her lips again and took them, claiming her mouth with his tongue the way his cock claimed her pussy. He would never get enough of her, but he knew that he would enjoy the constant hunger he felt for her. A hunger he could no longer deny.

When he released her lips, he felt his fangs itch. "Bond with me."

A sparkle in her eyes told him she had waited for his demand. When her fangs pushed past her lips, he could barely contain his excitement.

"You're beautiful," he mumbled before he sank his fangs into her neck. Then he felt hers pierce the skin on his shoulder. Her blood was everything he'd dreamed of and more. Thick and rich, it coated his tongue. It nourished his heart and his soul. Maya was his, and he was hers.

Before he lost himself in the euphoric feelings her blood and her wet and warm channel gave him, he reached out with his mind and connected with her.

Mine for eternity.

Mine always, her mind answered back and warmed his heart.

EPILOGUE

Maya arranged the calendar on her new desk and looked around the room. Her own little clinic. Sure, her office hours were unorthodox, but so were her patients. She was now officially the first vampire physician in San Francisco.

Gabriel had bought a beautiful Victorian house close to Samson's, and the basement now housed her medical clinic. He'd encouraged her to continue with her medical career even though it meant she had to start all over again and learn everything she could about a vampire's physical form. Not that she minded. Gabriel was always willing to let her experiment on him. She felt herself smile at the thought.

"You look happy," a voice came from the door.

Maya looked up.

"I knocked," Yvette said and entered. "But you didn't hear me."

"Daydreaming, I guess."

Yvette let appreciative glances travel around the room. "I wish you lots of success with your clinic."

"Thank you. I'm surprised to see you here. I thought you wanted to return to New York."

She could see Yvette hesitate. "That's why I wanted to talk to you. With Ricky dead and Gabriel having taken over the running of the San Francisco office, there've been some changes."

Maya raised an eyebrow. Gabriel had not said much about the future of the company and what he and Samson planned on doing after Ricky's death other than the fact that Gabriel would take Ricky's place and relinquish his position in New York.

"Gabriel has asked me if I wanted to stay in San Francisco. I think he feels he has to offer me something in exchange for saving you from Ricky, when clearly it was a team effort."

Maya took two steps toward Yvette and put her hand on the woman's arm. "You were there first. You took him down. I'm grateful for that. I never thought you'd risk your own life for me; I didn't think you liked me much."

Yvette smiled. "I liked Ricky even less."

"Thank you."

"To get back to Gabriel's offer—I didn't want to accept it unless you were okay with it."

"Why wouldn't I be?"

"It can't have escaped you that I wanted Gabriel for myself."

"I can't blame you for that. He's an amazing man. But you've accepted that he's mine. I have no quarrels with you. If Gabriel wants you to work with him in San Francisco, you shouldn't let him wait for an answer much longer."

Yvette put her hand over Maya's and squeezed it. "I'm glad you feel that way. It makes it easier for me to ask you for something else."

What else could there be? She and Yvette weren't exactly friends, even though she hoped that over the years that would change. "Yes?"

"Drake told me you're a good researcher."

"I was," Maya admitted, feeling a twinge of regret.

"You could be again. There's something—" Yvette broke off.

"What is it?" Concern rose in Maya.

"I want a child. But as you know yourself, vampire females are infertile." Maya heard the desperation in Yvette's voice. If Yvette knew of Maya's hopes for her own ability to conceive, Yvette would only feel more devastated. She couldn't tell her, but she felt for her. She understood her desperation, her longing.

"Yvette."

Yvette looked up.

"I'll do all I can—it'll give me a purpose. I can't promise I'll find a cure, but I'll do my best."

"Baby, are you coming up so we can—" Gabriel said from the door. "Oh, hi, Yvette."

Maya looked at her man. He seemed more handsome as each day passed. "Gabriel, Yvette's come to give you her answer."

"Excellent; let's talk."

Yvette walked toward him, but then looked back. "Thank you, I mean it."

Gabriel was almost out the door when Maya called after him. "Baby, what was it that you wanted?"

He turned and raked a hungry look over her body, making her shiver with pleasure. He could do that to her with just a look. Her voice was hoarse when she said, "Don't answer that. I think I get the idea. I'll be waiting upstairs for you."

ABOUT THE AUTHOR

Tina Folsom was born in Germany and has been living in English speaking countries for over 25 years, the last 14 of them in San Francisco, where she's married to an American.

Tina has always been a bit of a globe trotter: after living in Lausanne, Switzerland, she briefly worked on a cruise ship in the Mediterranean, then lived a year in Munich, before moving to London. There, she became an accountant. But after 8 years she decided to move overseas.

In New York she studied drama at the American Academy of Dramatic Arts, then moved to Los Angeles a year later to pursue studies in screenwriting. This is also where she met her husband, who she followed to San Francisco three months after first meeting him.

In San Francisco, Tina worked as a tax accountant and even opened her own firm, then went into real estate, however, she missed writing. In 2008 she wrote her first romance and never looked back.

She's always loved vampires and decided that vampire and paranormal romance was her calling. She now has 32 novels in English and several dozens in other languages (Spanish, German, and French) and continues to write, as well as have her existing novels translated.

For more about Tina Folsom:
http://www.tinawritesromance.com
http://www.facebook.com/TinaFolsomFans
http://www.twitter.com/Tina_Folsom
You can also email her at tina@tinawritesromance.com

CPSIA information can be obtained
at www.ICGtesting.com
Printed in the USA
LVOW08s1805210318
570659LV00005B/989/P